MW00945066

VITAORTUS

BOOK ONE

by

DEA SCHOFIELD

COPYRIGHT © 2013 DEA SCHOFIELD
ALL RIGHTS RESERVED

For My Daughter,
Roxanne Alexis Schofield and
My Mother, Jan J Lindeman

And for all beings, supernatural or not,
who have a lust for life and desperately want
to see it stick around!

My gratitude to these
first readers, editors and cheerleaders:
Rebecca Helgesen, Angela Johnson, Roxy Schofield,
Jan Lindeman, Nicola Smithers, Karen Thomas,
Maggie Kutac-Lynch, (and L.L for his kind encouragement).

More love and thanks to:
Sean Illemsky, Claire Burns, Debbie Hollander, Nancy Miller,
Katja Yount, Ruth Yount, Gabi Yount, Michele Arkwright.

Sincere appreciation to my writers group:
Phil Budahn, Rebecca Moon Ruark,
Barbara Weitbrecht, Carol Rutherford.

And special love and gratitude
to my brother, Burton A. Yount, whose contribution—
especially the beautiful cover—was invaluable.

TABLE OF CONTENTS

ONE

A Hunting Guise Interrupted

†

He smelled the musk of the red stag long before he saw the animal. It was early summer, so the beast's antlers would be no more than half grown, blood filled and covered in soft velvet. He'd carefully chosen this particular creature, which was past its prime at twelve years of age and had lost last autumn's rutting contests. Though still magnificent, its days as the dominant stag were over. But the sustenance this parcel of land had to offer was finite, which meant it was time to cull. And just as importantly, its sacrifice would temporarily slake his unending need.

So, nose to the ground, the wolf trotted gracefully on his long legs in a zigzag pattern, trying to get a fix on the elusive deer's location. Soon he raised his reddish-grey head and sniffed the air for the highest concentration of scented molecules. *Got him*, he thought, and his green eyes fixated on the direction. But the night was midway between dusk and dawn, and he knew the stag had likely recently bedded down—best to wake it and give a running start if this was to be a proper hunt.

He pointed his snout up towards the nearly full moon and gave a long, strong howl. Such a sound hadn't been heard in these woods for well over a century. For a moment, he wondered if his cry had any effect, but soon his ears twitched at the sounds of scurrying creatures and then a denser, distant snapping of branches told him even more precisely in which direction to run.

Loping silently past trees that had grown familiar to him over several decades, he slowly picked up speed. Eventually coming upon the site of the stag's still warm bed, his wolfish nose forced him to stop and snuffle the flattened vegetation of the forest floor. The moonlight shone down, filtered through the leaves of mature tulip poplars, sassafras, sycamores and oaks. More sounds of fleeing prompted him to spin in a half turn and leap back into the chase. Magic coursed through his limbs and body, which seemed eager to run full-out as he skillfully dodged tree trunks, sparse shrubs and the occasional boulder. Normally he moved with economy in order to save his vital energies.

Soon, the pungent scent was strong and he knew he was getting close. A white-tailed doe suddenly leapt across his path just ahead in a series of panicky bounds. But she was not a target tonight. Nor was she a preferred target; only if he was desperate, which had so far been never in this new home. The native deer rarely ventured into these woods, not liking to compete with their larger cousins and finding the tall, stone boundary wall a deterrent. Her presence, crossing perpendicular the path taken by the stag, surprised him, but he didn't slow.

After a half mile, the compelling musk odor was full-on and he could hear the animal ahead of him as it crashed through the under-growth. The wolf could tell the stag had realized it was the target by the change in the sound of its moves. The beast had switched from a gallop to bounding. And when he was upon it, the big deer panicked and hit a tree with its shoulder. It was knocked off balance and slowed it's leaping. With him now at its fetlocks, it suddenly stopped and spun around, sides heaving with each rapid breath.

They stood and stared at each other for a moment, then the stag lowered its head and made as if to rush him. Instead, it reared up and kicked out with dangerous front hooves. It was an impressive display and might have intimidated a regular wolf. But he was not regular. In fact, a normal wolf simply wouldn't be doing this—not alone anyway.

The moment the stag landed back on its front hooves, the wolf rushed to its side and sank unnaturally sharp and long teeth into the red-haired shoulder. A bellow, like a foghorn blended with a sheep's bleat, erupted from the shocked creature. But before it could make a move, he jerked hard, which forced the head and neck forward and down. And in an instant, the wolf let go of the shoulder and grabbed the large deer just where its carotid artery came close enough to the skin. As the deer's eyes widened and rolled in terror, the wolf searched with his teeth, using his tongue to lever them into position once they found the tube carrying blood to the brain.

Marshaling its waning reserves of strength to engage in a tug of war with the wolf's strong teeth, the deer then inadvertently helped the canid, for he'd found his target and clamped down. When it wrenched against his pulling bite, the artery was suddenly severed as a chunk of flesh, skin and hair came away in the huge canines. The deer bellowed again loudly, but the wolf was silent, working to spit out the flesh stuck on his teeth.

As thick, warm blood spewed and the groaning deer foundered, he lunged back and latched onto the spurting wound. With him attached, the stag slowly, almost acceptingly, sank to the soft, mossy forest floor, still groaning as its breath slowed over the next minute. The canid put his left paw over the dying animal's neck and, with teeth sunk in and tongue slowly lapping, he moved as close to the beast as he could. And then, unintentionally, he began to change.

His thick, shaggy fur slowly diminished, eventually becoming a light covering of reddish-gold hair here and there. His legs elongated and, like his arms and chest, grew thicker by small measures. His face slowly flattened and his closed eyes grew larger and hooded. Still he drank, as a babe suckling at a teat. He had the heart end of the artery flowing straight into his mouth as he gripped it tight with his front teeth and gulped with gusto. He still had the elongated sharp canines, but they were now only an inch long, rather than two.

Soon he was full and there was still blood flowing. He let go of the large tube and moved his face, putting it to the wound so that the last few pumps of the majestic beast's heart spewed red warmth onto his forehead. With his arm over the withers and around the deer's neck, he felt it trickle down his cheeks and into his trim boxed beard and adjoining moustache.

The stag gave a last shuddering breath, its head finally dropping gently to the ground. So did the man, who was a wolf moments ago, breathe; although *his* breath was merely because it felt good to move the muscles of his chest and belly so that the blood moved deeper inside him more easily.

The moon's rays filtering down made his freckled white skin almost glow against the red hair of the deer and the slightest rosy tinge from the newly consumed blood began to show. The animal's coloring was not too dissimilar to his own hair, but without the brilliant metallic highlights. He laid his forehead upon the creature's warm neck and whispered hoarsely, spitting a little through bloody teeth, "*Thank you.*" He'd known the animal from its birth and had even administered inoculations to it when a calf so it wouldn't succumb to New World diseases.

The silent wood was gathered around him, seemingly holding its own breath, watching as the tall and now fully-formed man lay almost lovingly against the carcass of the stag. He knew a fox was watching from beneath a not too distant holly. It would come to lap up the spilled blood and eat the spit-out chunk of flesh when he'd gone. He sensed it jerk to a deeper, fearful crouch as he moved to splay the fingers of his right hand on the ground so that he might rise. He did so with extreme languid grace, his movements matching his strongly muscled, sinewy frame.

He had no fear of that which lived in this habitat — he was neither food nor host for anything living. Gazing down at the animal at his feet, he noticed the earth and twigs stuck to his own knees and hip. Carelessly brushing it all off with his right hand, he then reached for the deer's short, fuzzy antler with his left, gripped tight, and then set off easily.

Having effortlessly dragged the large animal a mile to the top of a treeless hill, he carefully laid it on a rock outcrop. Kneeling, he said another soft word of thanks and then took the beast's chin and stroked it before using it to position the body so that any remaining blood would flow out freely. He closed its eyes, then looked for the knife that had been left there earlier. With an inhuman swiftness and dexterity, he had the animal expertly gutted in moments, so as not to poison the flesh. It would be stripped of its best meat at dawn, before the turkey vultures came.

He then had a leisurely jog home, still naked, his upper parts covered with blood. If anyone had seen him, and not been instantly horrified, they'd have thought he was as much a part of the environment as anything in it. Except that, like the red stag, he was a transplant.

The moon was low on the horizon now, with only an hour or so before dawn. Hidden inside the tree line that surrounded the grounds of the manse, he'd had an underground bathhouse built. It was well camouflaged and it amused him to think there was a 'Bondian' feel to it. But it was necessary too. He occasionally had guests unlike himself staying. It would be, perhaps, a little shocking to be seen naked and covered with blood whilst walking across the lawn or inside the house.

The steps were inside a planting of shrubbery and he quickly descended them and tapped a code onto the keypad. The blood on his fingers had dried, therefore leaving no residue. Once inside, he padded on high-arched, wide-balled feet across a floor of white Carrara marble.

In the shower, he washed his body and hair thoroughly and made sure no trace of blood remained. It showed darkly against the marble as it streaked through the water and froth spiraling down the drain. In the long-ago nights, he'd often had to bathe in lakes and rivers or streams, using soapwort, if he could find it, rather than the specially-made artisanal soap he used today. He appreciated many modern advancements, in spite of the drawbacks that often came with them, but it was critically necessary that his toiletries were all-natural, organic products.

Once dry, he donned a pair of creamy, raw silk and linen pajama bottoms, a matching tank-style cotton undershirt, and slippers. His narrow beard and rich, short, combed-back hair were still damp. And he'd have preferred to go to bed naked, but experience had taught him it was best to be clothed for the potential, though unlikely, interruption. He amused himself with those memories as he made his way down the underground corridor to the main house, having not bothered with the lights because he could see quite well in the dark.

After moving through the cellars of the house, he lithely took the steps two at a time and soon reached the main level. Suddenly he stood stock-still when he heard his name whispered. Then he realized it was his progeny, Georges.

"*Alec!*" Georges half-whispered again.

"Monsieur Picault. What brings you here so nigh on dawn? You know you'll have to stay the day. There is too little night left for you to return home."

Georges stepped from the darkness of the wide, marble corridor. His thick Parisian accent hadn't softened in all the years Alec had known him. "My news is my reason. You must hear. I've been waiting hours for you."

"Ah. Well. I felt able and compelled to hunt. If I'd known you were coming, I'd not have tarried. You should have sought me."

Georges grinned lopsidedly at Alec's archaic expressions, shaking his head beneath the fall of his long dark-brown bangs. His eyes glinted and he said, "Alec, darling, you *must* listen." Then he reached into his pants pocket, producing his phone. Alec snorted gently at the diamond-studded, leopard-skin motif of the casing, which had been a gift to Georges from an admirer. After manipulating the screen a couple of times with his large, delicate fingers, Georges then activated the speaker. A woman's voicemail message played.

After it was over, Alec's green eyes locked onto Georges' blue ones. Both men stood motionless, but Alec's energy frequency spiked. He still had a slippered foot on the first marble stair leading up to the bedrooms and now turned fully and placed it back on the main level. The two men were nearly the same height. They had once been considered practically giants; Georges a little less so because he was much younger. But still, six-foot-four is tall in any century. Alec stood one inch shorter.

He asked quietly, "When did she leave that? Did you speak with her?"

Georges became a little more animated. "*Oui!* Yes! This evening. She asked about *soil!* I told her to take video. She said one had begun germinating and felt sure the rest had started as well."

7

There was no way Alec would allow himself to indulge in high hopes until they were sure. Raising his brows, he asked, "When will you speak again?"

"As soon as I rise, I'll ring."

Again, they stood silently for a moment, just absorbing the information. And then all at once, Alec gathered himself elegantly and said, as he patted his friend's back, "Come then. Let us dream of this woman. Perhaps our long wait is over. Now wouldn't *that* be something? Tell me, is she comely?" Georges only laughed as he put away his gem-encased phone, and was soon ensconced in his favorite of Alec's guest bedrooms.

As he lay in the pitch blackness and soft down of his own bed, Alec mused. Gordon, his 'bonded' man, had known before his bedtime that Alec was going to hunt. When Gordon awoke soon, he would strip the deer of the back straps, tenderloins and other parts that normal men thought best. The rest was an earnest offering to those very special beings, the vultures, and perhaps the crows would partake as well. As would so many other creatures, all of which were deserving— even the beetles, flies and their larvae. His last hunt, a month before, had been a hind: an old female who'd produced many young during her fifteen years. She had gone quietly, and very nearly willingly.

His thoughts jumped. This girl, woman, would, if things were as they seemed, be a being with whom he'd have to become very close and yet, against his very instinct, must never bring into submission. That route had proven fatal by all who'd attempted it and now there was no hope, unless she was it. It would be untraveled territory in a new journey. He recognized these things now when they appeared, very well, for he'd been doing such for many centuries. But he'd never dealt this closely with a *prime channel*, if that was indeed what she was.

Tonight had shown him how compromised his powers had become due to the modern toxins. He was only capable of staying in wolf form for an hour at most. This night, he'd unwillingly reverted back to his true form as he drank, an event that had never happened before. But time had taught him it was useless to dwell upon unfortunate occurrences unless there was a lesson to be learned. So his last thought before his sleep was that just perhaps she was the antidote to what had become hopelessness and despair for all his kind. And if she was, he would move mountains to make sure she was facilitated and protected as long as he existed.

TWO

Seeds of Change

℧

I wasn't thinking about my big, bizarre secret. Instead, I was leaning over the steering wheel as I sat in my motionless truck on I-66 East, watching events unfold in front of me with a mixture of entertainment and trepidation. I was trying to get to the bridge over the Potomac River into Georgetown, but there was a verbal brawl which had erupted between two men in the cars just ahead of me. One was in a new Lexus, the other a new BMW. The left lane was merging into the right due to the usual spring/summer resurfacing. Some folks had been trying to merge with civility, but unfortunately these two were of the 'me-first-and-only' mentality and their disagreement was backing up the rest of us. Horns started blaring and I winced. 'Beamer' suddenly threw open his door and flung his Starbucks cup at the other's pristine bumper. A corner of my mouth went up in shocked amusement, until 'Lexus' got out and I saw he was a full foot taller than 'Beamer'.

"*Ohhh shit,*" I whispered, then glanced over to eye whoever was in the vehicle in the lane next to me, wondering if we should both do something. He was an older uniformed gentleman in a nice, shiny Chrysler and I raised my brows at him, but he just gave me a look indicating the wise thought, 'No way in *hell* am I getting in-between those two self-centered, self-entitled idiots.' His full-bird colonel's insignia seemed like it would hold some sway, even if his rank is a dime-a-dozen in this town.

I sighed deeply as I looked back at the two shouting men. 'Beamer' was red and screaming; 'Lexus' was about to punch him. I told myself *I* was the idiot and got out of my truck, leaving the door open in case I needed to run for it and jump back in quickly.

"Hey!" I yelled, striding slowly and purposefully toward them. They didn't hear me. "Guys!" I yelled louder. They looked at me as I came to a stop a safe distance from them. "Guys," I said, more calmly, entreating them. "Look what's going on. You're backing us all up. Look." I turned and pointed to the west, behind me. They looked past me and both faces registered shock for a moment, as they awoke to the rest of the world, which was parked and irate. Then quickly, blindly, their attention was back to each other, eyes throwing blame. And as the sound of horns got more and more impatient, they took parting shots at each other: one an "asshole", the other something worse. Unable to know when to stop, I entreated again. "*Guuuuys.*" With obvious ingratitude, they flipped me off in unison and got back in their cars, also slamming their doors in unison — like road-rage ballet.

How I adored the commuting of Metropolitan Washington, D.C.

The gentleman with whom I'd made eye contact before gave me a sincere bright smile which contrasted nicely with his dark skin, and a salute, then began inching his vehicle forward, probably on his way to the Pentagon. I let him merge in front of me, thinking I'd better practice what I silently preached. I sighed again, wondering at how much humans had changed in such a short period; *so nasty, so rude.* And I had a depressed moment as I thought of the mundanity of it. Sometimes I longed for a younger, simpler and kinder world. But had it ever really been kinder, as a whole? I only knew I'd better not go there. It led to depressing thoughts that I had no desire to entertain.

It was another thirty minutes before I made it onto O Street and found a parking space. I don't know if I was lucky, but I always managed to find parking in the notoriously difficult area. The real trick was getting out before they ticketed you a tiny fraction of a second after the two-hour time limit. DC was hurting for money and there was much wealth to be sucked from suckers who didn't know better. Not everyone who set foot in Georgetown was rich though, meaning me. So basically, I had two hours to hit all my clients, deliver and socialize. Sometimes I could find a loading zone, but they were usually taken, so I snuck my strange little vehicle in amongst the residential parking.

Hopping out of my little, green Daihatsu tricked-out cross between a micro-van and a pick-up, I opened the suicide door and pulled out the dolly. After unhooking the bungee cords, I started stacking the low crates that held my product, the scents of which mingled delightfully. Herbs, some spices and a few special fruits and vegetables; they were organic and the veggies and fruits were special orders that were kind of 'off the grid', so to speak. I had a classic, well-deserved authority problem and preferred not to deal with officials sniffing my wares or asking too many questions. I knew they were clean of any dangerous chemicals. It was just a fact. I didn't engage in practices that created any kind of contaminant, so my conscience was totally clear. And my clients loved my produce. Every one of them got rave reviews and they were among the best restaurants. I was very proud of my contribution to the fine culinary arts of Washington.

Most of my stops were basics: dill, basil, parsley, oregano, tarragon, chives, cilantro, bay, mints, etc. There was one, however, that wanted Meyer lemons and I was excited to deliver them; they were so beautiful and even better tasting this year. Not such an easy feat in the Northern Virginia climate. My growing skills were becoming sharply honed. I wouldn't dare tell a soul what I'd been doing differently this past winter. I thought it was bordering on nuts. But then, I'd discovered the startling truth that sanity is highly subjective.

For all of its pain-in-the-ass parking issues, I enjoyed being in Georgetown because so little of the human-made United States is old. I'd get something akin to homesickness for Europe, or other places. Old areas always felt more real to me—more comfortable. In America, so little is allowed to grow old and stay. Even my home of five years, a hundred and twenty-year old farmhouse about sixty miles west of DC, had been fought over to make room for a housing development. Twenty acres is a big deal in the region.

But the will specifically stated that I was the beneficiary and I had no intention of selling. It was strange to move to the farm and begin a new life away from a city — *another new life*. And it was even stranger that its previous owner, Mr. Wilson, had left the place to me. It was the first home I'd ever owned. Those trying to get the property were sure I was far too young to handle a working nursery. They knew absolutely nothing about me or how I was related to Mr. Wilson. I was mystified myself, except for the pen-pal friendship we'd developed over many years. I wasn't well-off, but I was becoming relatively content, and it hadn't always been that way.

So I smiled as I traipsed down Wisconsin Avenue, pulling the handcart behind me. I reached the right street and turned into the door, which was angled on the corner. The lunch crowd wouldn't start for another hour at least, so I entered the classic French restaurant and headed toward the back, and nearly got there before a young waiter ran at me from the stairs.

"*Madame?* May I help you?" He was new or had never worked this shift on this day.

"Yes, please. Can you let Jules know Devi is here? He's expecting me."

"Yes, Madame. One moment." And he ran off to get Jules.

'Georges', pronounced with soft Gs for the French owner's name, was a five-star (three in the Michelin) restaurant, and my favorite. I'd only met Georges once, when he'd recently asked his manager, Jules, to have me come in during the evening so he could feed me out of gratitude and regard. Apparently he only came in for the dinner shift, so I'd made an extra trek that week. It had been an exquisitely sensual experience.

Georges was an interesting person, somewhere around thirty-five, I guessed, and he'd been very white, like the table cloth, which had contrasted noticeably against my tanned gardener's skin. But he was probably the most charming person I'd ever met. I was so charmed that I'd considered him overwhelmingly attractive and found myself responding physically and mentally in a way I didn't recognize.

That was in his presence. But on my way home, I was glad I'd only had two glasses of his wonderful wine, because, with too many in me, who knows? I just couldn't understand what I'd been thinking, because there had been a rather peculiar vibe. Plus, his chin was nearly the size of his entire face and his nose was large and crooked; although his thick dark-brown hair, cut so it had a heavy fall in front, was lovely. And his blue eyes were pretty. He was attractive in a very strange way, but not my type. And not that I could definitely tell, but I had the feeling I wasn't *his* type, in spite of his incredible seductiveness.

Soon, Jules sauntered out and flashed a big smile when he saw me. "*Miss Deviii!*" he greeted warmly, opening his arms and coming at me for a kiss to either cheek. "How grows your garden, lovely lady?" It was always the same greeting.

"Fabulously, Jules, check this out." And I tossed him a lemon.

Catching it, he then brought it to his nose and inhaled deeply. "Mmm. Georges will be very pleased. You are the Mother Earth herself."

Who wouldn't love such flattery? If knowing the right amount of water, fertilizer, conditions and love made me Mother Earth, then fine. "Thank you, Jules. I have the rest in these five crates here." He actually snapped his fingers and the two young men who'd come in behind him moved forward to take the crates.

"I can wheel this into the kitchen, if you'd like."

"No, No. Come with me to the office. I have something for you."

As we walked, we chit-chatted about a recent farm bill that had been laced with goodies to benefit big biotech agriculture. It was clear Jules felt as strongly as I that those companies were evil-doers.

Jules shared, "Georges says he will shut down his restaurants before he will be forced to serve what he calls 'tasteless zombie produce'."

This was typical conversation for me and my clients. Living so close to the domed Capitol (and with some of its denizens as patrons) made the restaurateurs perhaps a little more politically knowledge-able than in other places.

The office was a single large room with three desks placed facing each other, creating a triangle in the middle. Standing inside that space was a wooden statue that looked as if it had come from some ancient European church. It was dark with age and the details were hard to make out. It resembled an angel, possibly female, with stylized wings which wrapped around her body, and eyes that were deep and penetrating. I sensed a vibe emanating from her that felt lovely and very old.

"Wow," I said, gawking at it.

Jules glanced at me. "Yes. Very much *wow*. She is quite old. Georges insists she be here. He says she is necessary to the success of the restaurant. He says she is 'Life'".

"Really?" I asked as I glanced at him and then back at the carving. "Just 'Life'? Does she have a name?"

"He calls her *Shakti*. I don't even think she's from India."

I nodded in agreement. She looked more European Middle Ages. I tried to imagine the Hindu goddess concept of primordial cosmic energy relating to this nearly androgynous image. I assumed Jules knew about whom or what *Shakti* was or he wouldn't have made the India reference. It struck me as truly odd that Georges would have an image he considered representative of divine feminine creative force as his mascot, or talisman, or whatever she was.

"Well, there's energy there, I guess. She's certainly intense."

Jules laughed. "Oh yes!"

Forcing my eyes from the statue, I turned to find him opening a safe in the corner of the room.

"Devi," he said, with his back to me, hiding the dial. "Georges asked me to give you this package. He said to wait until you are home to open it, and to be very careful while opening the smaller package inside. His private number is given in the note and you are to call him with questions." I heard the resonating click of the lock opening and he swung open the iron door and pulled out a large brown envelope. After relocking the safe, he turned and handed the packet to me.

I took it from him, turning it to see if it had writing and found it blank. "Hmm. That's interesting. Okay." I replied, perplexed.

As we walked to the door, Jules grabbed a smaller white envelope off one of the desks and handed that to me as well. I knew what this was: payment for my delivery. I felt compelled to turn and look at the carving once more. It was definitely special. It emanated something and I could understand Georges' desire to have it, even if only for its haunting beauty.

Soon, I was back on the sidewalk. The guys had unloaded the crates and had my dolly waiting for me at the front door, loaded with last week's empties. Jules had given each of my cheeks a little French peck and had said no more about the mystery packet. I completed the rest of my route in time to get back to my little truck and out of the city by noon.

Thank God. Leaving the city in rush hour traffic is no less than traveling through a circle of hell.

A young Elvis Costello played for me on my way home, so I was in a very good mood. I still enjoyed listening to albums in their entirety and hated having to leave him in the CD player, but there was work to do.

As I'd rounded the bend that led through the gate and onto the property, I saw Maria and Serena sharing the shade of the huge willow oak beside the house with our flock of chickens. It was lunchtime. The chickens were sharing tidbits on the ground and the women were seated at an old teak table with a tray of sandwich wraps on it. All heads raised and turned at the gravelly sound of my truck's engine. I waved and the two women waved back. A shape broke from the clump of birds and bolted toward me. It was the old English game rooster, 'Edward'.

"Eddie!" I called to him through the window. "Hi pretty bird!" He bounced to me as I got out of the truck, then ran a few tightening circles around me. I stopped, stooped and he let me scritch the scrawny neck under the puff of long gorgeous, golden feathers. I always found him to be a combination of hilarity and profound elegance. He then moved along in front of me, bobbing and weaving as we headed toward the group.

"Hey *chicas*. How's it going?" I greeted.

The humans smiled and Serena, the older of the two, patted the bench beside her. "*Bien*, Devi. You want tea? I put some *Melissa* in it; with honey. It's good and *frio*."

I nodded. "Yes, please." And she poured some in a glass they'd brought out, knowing I'd be home in time. Her lemon balm and green tea combination was sublime and thirst-quenching. Maria held her glass up, signaling she'd like some more too.

Without the accent of her mother, she informed, "The new batch of basil and cilantro has germinated and I think the lemon grass will be ready for next week's delivery. Oh, and 'The Glee Club' called, they're sending someone to pick up the missed order this afternoon. New management screwed up." She raised her black, arched eyebrows in silent judgment.

"Wow. All this way? They must like our stuff! I hope they stay in business. They're a great client," I responded. We'd seen so many go under in the last few years. Being a restaurateur is a hard business to make a success of, regardless of how the economy is doing.

A cicada began its ascending buzz nearby and we all stopped to listen, even the chickens. It was Nature's official sign that summer had begun.

After lunch, we got to work doing what was needed: pruning, pinching, weeding, watering, potting and mending. Mr. Wilson left three twenty-by-thirty green houses on the property. He'd grown roses in them, which I thought was crazy because most roses don't really like the Northern Virginia environment, which is just too hot and humid in the summer and has acidic clay rather than real soil.

I disliked growing anything that needed to be constantly sprayed with chemicals to stay healthy. Two of the few I'd let stay in the garden were a *Trigintipetala* damask and an old rose *Centifolia*. They produced perfume that carried me to heaven every time they were in bloom and I treasured them. But they suffered from the unpleasant temperatures and humidity through disease and insects. They were about the only plants I'd pamper with organic antifungal and insecticidal treatments. But I was willing to have, from the source, what is possibly the most beautiful scent in the world.

Maria busied herself thinning the newly sprouted basil and cilantro in Greenhouse One. She was almost a business partner in many ways. I depended on her for so much and most importantly, I'd come to trust her. Her mother, Serena, had been Mr. Wilson's housekeeper and companion. He'd brought her here after meeting her on a plant collecting trip to Belize in the '60s. It was unsaid, but Maria was their love child. Serena looked one hundred percent Maya—Maria absolutely did not. She stood nearly a foot taller than her mother at five-foot nine-inches tall. She was three inches taller than I. Mr. Wilson had been a big man and she was a lovely combination.

Why he'd not left the place to them was a mystery, but then so was my relationship to him. I'd met him at some horticultural seminars at the Smithsonian after he took an interest in a lecture I gave on rose history. He commented on how young I appeared to have so much knowledge and we began a correspondence that lasted until he died … and left me his nursery. Neither Maria nor Serena seemed put out. He'd left them plenty of money if they wanted to leave. In fact, they seemed to be happy I was there from the start, especially Serena, who tended to treat me like royalty. It was sweet, if a little unnerving.

I had arrived five years ago and we'd become almost a little family. What was great was that there was the main house and a large cottage on the property. Serena had always lived in that cottage with Maria. It was their home and always would be. Still, I wondered why Mr. Wilson hadn't married her, but it wasn't my business and they never shared about it. It seemed we all had a little mystery about us.

So we accepted what was and worked beautifully together, if perhaps a little formally. When I'd suggested we switch from roses to herbs and such, they were ecstatic and relieved. The roses were a pain in the ass and not too profitable, partly because we were too far out of town and off the beaten path.

We ended the workday around six, after sending 'The Glee Club' cook back on her way with her crates. Then we went our separate ways after putting the fowl to bed. Sometimes we'd have dinner together, but not on this night. I'd gotten up early and was pretty tired. I wanted a quick meal, a long bubble bath and to read in bed; two thirds of which I managed. After the meal and bath, I decided on a quick shower to wash my long hair. Afterward, with pajamas on and a towel wrapped around my head, I went down to the kitchen to make a cup of tea.

It was dark and I sensed the moon was rising. Looking east, it glowed above the trees, a day or two away from full. Its presence was comforting and always made me smile. I started to walk out the back door, but the *girls*, my two cats, *Theda Bara* and *Greta Garbo*, were suddenly there, winding around my legs, letting me know it was past dinner-time. I fed them, then lit a candle and thought I would take my tea out onto the porch. But I spotted Georges' package on the counter and stopped short, surprised I'd forgotten about it.

Leaning with the small of my back against the counter, I slid the envelope to me and opened it gently. I could feel various lumps. The first thing I pulled out was a note. Written on beautiful paper with a light exotic scent, the note read,

Dearest Devi,

I send these to you in tremendous hope that your otherworldly skill with living things will produce offspring. These are extremely rare and I can only tell you they come from a warm climate and do not like the sun baking them. Other than this, I know nothing. Perhaps tomorrow night (3rd) or the next (4th) would be the best time to plant them. I pray for your success. They are truly the most special specimens. Collectors would kill for them!

Bon Courage,

Georges

Hmm. That wasn't much to go on, propagation-wise. I turned and placed the letter on the copper counter top. Reaching into the envelope again, I pulled out a smaller packet. As it came into view, I was a little surprised. It was vellum.

"What?" I exclaimed aloud, startling myself. It was the real thing. Thick, old, vellum, specially folded around something, with a gold tassel tie holding it closed, like a wrapped gift. Pulling one of the ends, I held a corner of the rigid parchment so it wouldn't slide. After depositing the tie on the counter with the note and envelope, I unfolded the packet, discovering there was padding inside that felt like fur. It was nearly black and soft, like rabbit fur. But as I looked closer, I realized it was mink, maybe.

"What the—" And then I saw them. Three seeds, both black and red, or rather, so red they were nearly black. They had three points and were the size of a dime, almost a triangular star; a little bizarre, but I'd seen stranger seeds. It was the coloring that stood out.

After staring at their beauty and that of their packaging for a minute, I gently picked one up. It felt pretty solid. First, I tapped it with a fingernail, then on a tooth. *Super solid*. Then I pulled a small serrated knife from a drawer and walked over to my big oak cutting board. Placing the seed on it, I carefully tried to knick it, a technique known as 'scarifying'. *Super strong!* Putting the knife down, I wrapped the little seed in my hands and closed my eyes for a minute. Bringing my hands up to my chest, I accessed my brain's knowledge on germination. And my next thought was *start the kettle*, so I did.

After getting a cup ready for the tea, I pulled out a ramekin and placed the seeds in it. When the water was boiled, I had a moment of doubt. What if I cooked them with this approach? What if the water was wrong? I had well water that ran through a filter. Then I thought, *No. It's fine.* I don't know where the confidence came from; I just knew this had to work. It occurred to me to try one at a time, but I felt an urging, almost as if an audience was chanting, "... *go, go, go, go, go.*"

When the kettle sang its readiness, I quickly lifted it, filled my cup, and then went to the seeds. "Okay, little guys, let's go." And I carefully poured just enough of the hot water to cover them. I had a strange sensation in my belly, like when just getting seated in the car of a triple-loop roller coaster.

I noticed the moon through the window as I waited for the tea to steep and wondered at the slow rise of my adrenalin. I lifted the little bowl and placed it on the ledge so the moonlight could shine on the soaking seeds. They appeared a bit redder through the water. Looking back up at the moon, I simply said, "Thank you."

Then I remembered what it was that I'd been doing differently these past months. I'd been making what I called my 'little pagan offering' one night a month. And despite my scientific mind's doubts, I had to admit that things felt better since I'd been doing it. And anyway, that scientific mind knew that not all was as it appeared. It had first-hand knowledge that there were highly and, as far as I knew, inexplicable phenomena.

I had set up a little spot near my magnificent and healthy old American elm (see how much I had to be grateful for?), which stood on the opposite side of the house from the willow oak. Every full moon I would light some candles beside an antique *Quan Yin* statue in my living room and then take out a platter of food and a glass of wine or juice or milk. I was getting over the potential embarrassment if anyone saw me, although I suspected Serena and Maria might've glimpsed me. In the morning, there was never a drop or piece left. The wine glass was always on its side. I'm sure raccoons were emissaries for the 'Intelligence of the Universe'.

Later, in bed, I thought of this house and Maria and Serena. It had been a timely gift from that intelligence. I'd been where I was long enough. It was always the same. I could only stay in one place comfortably for around a decade: any longer and the attachment would be too great. Leaving brought on a recurring, searing pain that was lessened if I didn't get extremely close to anyone. I could only have friends for that amount of time, or at least ones that would want to see me. Hence the ease with which I'd communicated with Mr. Wilson—no visits needed.

I had moved here when he died and was able to start fresh. But the years went by fast and I only had about five or so left before I'd have to start explaining things ... things for which I had no explanation ... things which had nearly taken me in and out of sanity. I kept up a happy demeanor most of the time. The problem was, my tremendous secret kept me so very separate, no matter how much I pretended.

THREE

Gentlemen of the Night

ʊ

As usual, I woke to Eddie's call. Or it could have been any of the other myriad morning bird vocalizations, my favorite being the cardinal's. I stretched and yawned, then abruptly had a panicked thought about the seeds. They'd been soaking all night. *I had to check on them!* Once up, Theda and Greta nearly tripped me as they ran past with the excitement of the impending morning feeding. But priority one was turning on the kettle for my coffee press, *then* giving the mewling cats their breakfast.

When I finally checked on the seeds, the sun was shining in where the moon had been last night and its light was glinting off the water in the ramekin. Sneaking a peek, I saw that the seeds were noticeably larger, perhaps by a third. Now they were more the size of a nickel, and even redder. They were a perfect red, like blood.

The kettle whistled gently and once I had my coffee ready, I went back to the seeds. Grabbing a paper towel and laying it on the counter, I gently lifted one seed at a time and placed them on the towel. Noticing an odd sensation in my fingertips as I touched each seed, I wondered if I was imagining it.

Pondering what to do next, I then remembered the only real instruction in the note:

'Perhaps tomorrow night (3rd) or the next (4th) would be the best time to plant them.'

Okay, I could do that. At night; why not? I dumped the water out of the ramekin and then it hit me how strange this all was. What was I sowing, and for whom? Were these seeds a gift to me or was I about to germinate something illegal? I looked at them, deeply red against the stark white of the towel (naughty me, I'd been in a hurry and hadn't bought my usual unbleached eco-towels), and noticed something. One of them had a crack and a little white showed through. I got close and squinted, but was unsure, so I ran to my office and got a magnifying glass. Sure enough, one was germinating already!

Fussily, I decided I didn't want them on the bleached towel after all and found some unbleached napkins in a cabinet. Moistening one, I laid it over the ramekin and pushed it in a little, then very carefully moved the seeds back into the little cup, again experiencing a light pulling sensation at the tips of my fingers. I covered it with a porcelain teacup cover and set it against the copper backsplash out of the sun. I would plant them tonight, but first, some research and a phone call.

Four cups of coffee and three hours later, I discovered I'd wasted my morning finding nothing online or in my books resembling the seeds. I needed more information. What kind of planting mix should I use? Should they be moist or on the dry side; did they need to be stratified (cooled for a period to mimic winter)? Well, no, because one was already germinating, plus Georges said they came from a warm climate.

What the hell were they? Each time I lifted the little dome off the bowl and eyed them, I became more concerned over their well-being. And one was definitely putting out the tiny tip of a root. I was completely obsessed and felt an overwhelming sense of responsibility. I had never felt more connected to the outcome of a germination. I realized I was feeling a bit clingy, which was rather new for me.

Georges' phone number! Finding the note, I quickly dialed the number at the top of the page. His greeting said, in a thick, deep, French-accented voice, "*Allo.* If you have this number, then you are a friend and know I will speak with you this evening. Leave your message after the *bip. Au revoir.*"

I did, saying, "Georges, this is Devi Trevathan. Hey, I need a little more info about these seeds, and quickly. One is already germinating after I soaked them last night." I gave him my cell number and landline number, just in case. *Jeez!* It was noon and I hadn't even gotten dressed. And it was also Wednesday with plenty of work to do: paperwork from yesterday's deliveries, depositing the checks, and of course, taking care of the plants. Deciding to let go of the strange seeds for now, I got ready for my day.

Washing my hair last night made things easier, and I didn't need to primp for a regular work day. Serena and Maria certainly wouldn't be impressed if I did. So I just put it up in a ponytail and threw on some jean shorts and a tank top. And for a moment, when I caught a glimpse of myself in the full-length mirrors in my closet, I stopped. I hadn't always dressed this way, or even close. There had been a time when appearance meant everything. But not in this newer life—not anymore—which was a bit of a relief most of the time.

I went out to speak to Serena and Maria, then hit my desk for the next few hours.

Later in the afternoon, I went to the ATM to deposit checks and after a little grocery shopping, made it home as the sun was just setting. That's when my cell rang and I recognized the number as Georges'. I answered as I pulled into my parking area. "Hi, this is Devi."

"Hi, Ms. Trevathan. Devi. This is Georges Picault. How are you?"

Turning off the engine, I replied, "I'm fine Georges, and you?"

"I'm well. Quite well. In fact, I am excited. Did you say one of the seeds has already sprouted? *Germe?*" He sounded a little incredulous.

"Well, maybe by now the others have split their seed coats too. I soaked them last night, and this morning one had already started. I've been out this afternoon so I'll check them again in a minute." There was silence on the other end for some time. "Georges? Are you there?" I asked.

"Oh, yes. Yes. Yes. Yes. Plant them tonight. I'll ring you tomorrow around this same time and see what has happened."

I quickly said, "One question. Soil. What kind of soil do they need?"

"Euu ... I don't know, Devi. That is your job. But I would think something that drains well, but is very, very rich. Oh, can you take photographs and video of the progress?"

"Uh, yeah, I guess."

"*Bon, alors.* Goodbye. I'll ring you." And he hung up before I could ask what the plant was called.

Once the groceries were put away, I trotted out in the dark to Greenhouse Three, where we kept our special mixes for soil. I had a clean plastic bowl and scooped in two parts loam, a part scree and a little sand, hoping this would do the trick. Then I grabbed three six-inch, clean, clay pots and, remembering to turn off the lights, headed back in. After setting everything up on the kitchen counter, I mixed up the soil, whetted it, and lifted the top off the ramekin. What I saw caused me to gasp. All three seeds had a protruding root extending all the way to the edge of the little bowl and were starting to bend up it. They were an inch and a half long.

"Good god, you guys are fast!" I was glad I'd put the cover on to keep in the moisture. Quickly filling the pots, I took a pencil and created holes in the center of each so that there would be about an inch of soil above the seedlings. They were big seeds and I figured they'd need the cover. After very gently lifting and planting them, I tapped each pot a little and added just a bit more soil mixture and watered. Then I stared at them. I could almost hear them hum, which struck me as just truly odd ... and totally ridiculous.

Becoming aware of the moon again as its brightness hit the window, I had a sudden thought about an antique I owned: a miniature greenhouse, called a 'Wardian case', which would fit all three. I retrieved it from the living room and put them in as if laying babies in a cradle. The moon kept beckoning and I wondered what harm it could do to put them outside under the elm on my gratitude spot. But thoughts of pillaging raccoons stopped me and I placed them back in the window so the moon could still shine its silver light on them safely. Remembering to take a photo, I found my camera and did so.

The next morning brought more shock. All were an inch above the soil, preparing their baby leaves to unfurl. The speed of their growth was like a bean—even faster.

As soon as my coffee was made, I grabbed the camera, snapped a few pictures, then took a little video footage as I pulled them out of the case and talked about their rapid growth. I said a few words directly to Georges as I assumed the video was for him. After watering them a little again, I returned them to the miniature glasshouse, which I moved to the living room bay window, and then got on with the day.

That night, Georges called me as he'd promised and I reported the progress. He asked if I was free for dinner to discuss it all the next night. He explained that a car would fetch me around eight o'clock and to dress for dinner. He also wouldn't tell me the name of the plant, saying all would be revealed tomorrow and that he was more excited than he'd ever been by my success with the seeds, which seemed a little extreme. Still, his enthusiasm was contagious and when we hung up, I immediately wondered what I could wear. Except for visiting him at his restaurant that one evening, I hadn't had an opportunity to dress up in a long while.

Part of my past involved fashion and, although today I tended to dress for the comfort and practicality of my profession, I still loved fun or nice clothes. The creativity of expression that clothing and its accessorizing offered brought some simple joy to a strange and love-deprived life.

After moving in, I'd renovated Mr. Wilson's upstairs office into a dressing room/closet combination, which was attached to the master bedroom I now occupied. A lot of my clothes were what you'd call 'vintage' today. They were arranged by decade and type. The clothes lined two opposing walls and shoes took up their own entire wall along with the handbags. The fourth wall, with the door, was for the trio of antique, free-standing mirrors I'd positioned like a triptych shape for maximum visual benefit. I'd collected clothing from the '40s until now, but usually, it all just hung there.

So it would be warm. I wanted to look nice and feel cool, as in temperature. While flipping through various dresses, memories of long-ago balmy June nights drifted and flitted around my mind. Eventually I turned and went to the section from the '50s and quickly found the dress I'd thought of because its blackness showed against the more colorful items.

Pulling it out, I examined the organza and cotton for any problems and, finding it still in great shape, hung it on the middle mirror. There were some black slingbacks which would match perfectly and a snakeskin bag.

I hoped it wouldn't be too much, but I couldn't resist the opportunity. It had been eons since I'd been on a date and I had no one other than Maria and Serena with whom to go out. But they were homebodies for whom fashion was not a priority. Other than them, all of my relationships here were professional.

And again, reflected in the mirrors for a moment, and surrounded by years of memories, I allowed myself a rare, single wave of self-pity. I had been through so much, and the twists and turns seemed to go on forever, without end. So many incarnations and here I was, still separate and alone. And why should I try for closeness? My experience was that loss *always* came. It was inevitable. But, as had become my way, because there seemed no *better* way, I found a thread of gratitude and followed it. Life today held a modicum of contentment. And perhaps there was no romance, or deep personal connection with anyone (except, well … my cats), but I had purpose. I created and lived well and that had to be enough, right? That, and the 'Mystery' that I knew for a fact existed.

~

The next night, the car arrived silently. I'd only noticed when shy Greta had alerted me by growling low and slinking off to my bedroom to hide. I walked to the front door as a soft knock sounded and opened it to find a thin, fairly short, older man in a lovely dark suit standing there.

"Miss Trevathan, your transport." His accent was from Spain. He bowed ever so slightly and pointed to the vehicle.

"Hi. Let me just grab my bag." Which I did and then came out, pulling the door shut. The driver moved to my side and put his hand behind my back, but didn't actually touch me, guiding me toward the car. Soon we were at the rear door of an unbelievably shiny auto. Squinting at the front of the car for a clue to the make, I found its curves such a shimmery, glinting black, I couldn't tell. Nothing about it looked familiar. And then he opened the door.

It had a creamy-white interior and the most sumptuous leather I'd ever seen in a car. I turned as the driver tried to herd me in. "Um … and you are?"

"My name is Hervé, uh, *Mademoiselle*." He hid a glance at my ring finger and inclined his head to the side.

"Nice to meet you, Hervé. Nice car," I mumbled as I got in. Hervé leaned in and gently scooted the skirt of my dress so that it didn't get caught. "Thank you." I said, to which he inclined his head again and shut the door.

Looking around, I was just amazed at the interior. It was like those cars made so long ago that few alive today know firsthand of their luxuriance. There was black piping on the wonderfully rich-smelling leather. I guess the vehicle was a limo, but it looked like only two people could sit in the back unless special seats were pulled down; and it was not very stretched. Like a normal limousine, there was a dark glass partition and there were little tables you could maneuver as well as TV screens and other amazing details.

I smiled when I saw myself reflected in the dark glass of the partition. I was dressed to match the car! My hair looked as minimally flamboyant as it could, with the front up in a silver clip with loose, dark curls cascading far down my back and creeping around my arms.

We smoothly and silently moved forward and I realized I'd not even heard the engine start. And then I noticed, with wide eyes, that I was ensconced under a roof of smoky glass.

Hervé didn't put the barrier down, but there was music. It was just perfectly audible and I realized it was Gustav Holst's moody suite, *The Planets*. It definitely added to the ambience of the ride. And as I listened I only had brief snippets of wondering what the hell I was doing in this unbelievable car. *Georges wasn't this wealthy, was he? And why this treatment?*

And what was with the video of the seedlings, by the way?

I decided the unease I felt was a by-product of the music and tried to enjoy the journey. As the "Jupiter", and then "Uranus" movements played, I could see the stars above me in spite of the faint blue glow from the interior lights. But I couldn't shake the sense that something important was about to happen. How could it not with a ride like this involved?

Or maybe I just felt my own bizarre specialness in this beautiful, opulent carriage. The Gods forbid it should turn back into something in the *Cucurbita* genus before I returned home.

Twenty minutes later, we'd reached our destination. We were near Middleburg, a neighboring area known for its horsey, wealthy people and lovely countryside. Actually, I had a couple of clients in the town, but we were well outside that, farther in the country. We turned down a very dark, newly-paved single-lane road that had nothing but a red circular reflector to mark it. With tall, thick woods all around, and in extreme darkness, it wouldn't be easy to find a property without markings.

We drew up to a very large, very sturdy, black iron gate that had a high wall on either side which disappeared into the surrounding forest. The gate opened so smoothly at our approach that it seemed choreographed along with the beginning of the "Neptune" movement. The road turned from pavement to pea gravel.

As we drove along at about twenty miles per hour, I saw the hind end of an animal that had crossed in front of the car. Unable to see out the front, I'd missed the rest of it. But from behind, I swear it had looked like an elk, only redder. Those haven't inhabited Virginia for a long time, so I figured I was imagining the size and color.

Soon we were passing through a dark *allée* of some kind; possibly columnar Italian cedars or European poplars. I wished I could see it by day, since it wasn't a feature I'd seen much in America. As I turned from trying to ogle the *allée* through the roof, I was amazed by the view of the house—*or whatever!* It wasn't exactly a mansion, not a new one, anyway. It literally was a cross between a small ancient castle and an old-world mansion. The architecture was definitely not typical of this country. Gas torches were placed around the building, more liberally at the entrance, which had a fluted staircase. I just couldn't believe this was here, in Virginia. It had a little sinister gothic look to it; I was surprised to feel my adrenalin rise.

We pulled up to the front at the base of the stairs and I felt a surge of nervousness. *Where was I and what was I doing here?* Hervé opened the door and held out his hand for me to take. My little pointy black shoes found themselves on pea gravel, their thin, three inch heels threatening to sink. *Damn,* I thought, as I balanced on the balls of my feet. Hervé held my hand up on the top of his as he led me to the stairs.

"We part here Miss Trevathan. It was a pleasure serving you," he said, with that little head incline.

I glanced up the stairs. "Um, so I just go up … ?"

"Yes. Gordon is there to take you to your hosts." *Hosts?*

"Thank you, Hervé," I said as I turned and started up the pink granite stair case. Adjusting my little bag, I glanced up at the large, beautifully carved doors, which looked like they were hewn from English oak. Two very graceful bronze knockers in the shape of a woman's hands hung high, but I wouldn't need to use them because I could see the door opening; again, perfectly timed.

A tall, handsome, impeccably groomed and perfectly bald gentleman stepped out and stood in the doorway, just outside the threshold. "Miss Trevathan," he greeted. "We're pleased you made it. Was the ride comfortable?" He had a distinct, light Yorkshire accent and pleasant voice.

I smiled and looked back at the car, which was headed around the side of the building. "How could it not be?" I laughed a little and he joined me.

"Yeah, there are few vehicles luxurious as the Maybach. Please, enter. Mr. Gregory and his colleagues await you." *Maybach?* It seemed like I might have a distant memory of that name. I promised myself I'd 'search' it online later, then I wondered who Mr. Gregory was.

I can only say the house was as elegant as the car, with some of its extraordinary furnishings antique by hundreds of years. And the walls were actually stone blocks, like the granite outside. Some seemed to have been artfully plastered in spaces so that paintings and objects d'art could be easily mounted and displayed with a painted backdrop. It was interesting and striking, as if two worlds morphed together. It just didn't fit the Georges I'd met. This was very masculine: a little strong. And he was not 'fay', so much, as seemingly more light-hearted.

Gordon, whose presence had a slightly strange, yet pleasant vibe, led me down a wide, white marble-floored hallway to double doors and opened them with a quiet swoop, announcing, "Miss Trevathan has arrived, sirs." He moved to the side, gently urging me in with his hand behind my back as Hervé had done.

Stepping into the room, I was immediately taken by a strong sensation as the hairs on my arms and head wiggled to attention in their follicles. And I smelled the unmistakable scent of damask rose. With a bizarre feeling, I managed to smile at the disappearing Gordon as he shut the door between us. Then I turned to look at the four men: two standing and two seated. All were holding dark blue wine glasses and were staring at me. One was Georges, who hopped up from a couch, set his glass down and came at me swiftly.

"Devi! Devi, *Chérie*, you are our star!" This was definitely Georges. "How was your little journey in Alec's beautiful car? Nice, eh?" He swept a hand toward one of the men who was contemplating me; well, actually, this man was staring from the shadows as if he were trying to turn me inside out and get a good look at my machinery. There was something very intimidating about him and my skin prickled. I forced a smile and gave a little wave of the hand that was not death-gripping my bag.

The other two men stood and laughed as one said, with a German accent, "Introduce us, you rude old Frog!" That sounded downright funny coming from a German and I couldn't help a more genuine smile.

"Devi, this beast is Axel Von Reiche. He's a bit like the *secretary* of our group." I moved forward and gripped the man's hand. It was very dry … and vibrated slightly. "

And this is Piero Medici. He is like, oh, well many things. He is our *guidance counselor*." Georges laughed and gestured to a smaller man in an oddly-stylized gorgeous, black suit. He had very dark, wavy hair and a gentle way about him. I had to pin my bag under my elbow when he took both my hands in his and held them as he stared penetratingly into my eyes with his kind, huge, brown ones. He vibrated even more intensely.

"*Devi*. Such a wonderful name, and it suits you. You are lovely," he said, his Italian accent adding inflections like the gentle sway of a gondola. "A bonus to your skills. We are lucky indeed."

I smiled yet again, but felt at a complete loss. I was acutely aware that I had no clue as to what was going on; only that if germinating three measly, though cool, seeds was going to elicit such admiration, from this kind of company, what would actually growing them do? Dropping my hands, he turned to look at the last man.

Georges said, "And this is Lord Alexander Gregory, our fearless leader. Alec, please meet our miracle worker." *Lord?*

The man who came out of the shadows was tall, like Georges. His movements were languid and smooth as he placed his glass on a side table and walked toward me. He too, wore a suit, but it was light-colored and made of fine linen. His shirt was a deep blue of the finest cotton and contrasted nicely with his large, hooded green eyes. When he approached, he stopped just before he got too close and reached for my hand, which I managed not to jerk away from a voltaic touch. As he bowed slightly, light reflected off his hair making it look perfectly golden, then, as he straightened, I saw that he was actually redheaded, sort of strawberry blond: more red than blond. He looked contemplative for a moment as if appraising the strength of my steady handshake. He oozed a power like I'd never come across.

Jesus! A lord? "It's a pleasure to meet you," I said preemptively, covering my disquiet.

One corner of his lips curled up and he looked at me harder. "No, Ms. Trevathan, it is *we* who have the pleasure." He spoke with a pure, perfectly enunciated English accent. His buttery baritone resonated from my eardrums to my toes. "We are very excited to hear about your horticultural success with our small offering. Please, join us and share your story."

He turned, pulling me into the room, and added, "What can we get you to drink? Wine, perhaps?" His hand, too, was very smooth, dry and cool to the touch, and I was sure a voltmeter would register clearly if I measured him. When I attempted to pull away, he didn't let go as he awaited my answer.

I looked at their glasses and swallowed dryly. "May I have some water? Please."

He stopped and halfway turned to me, giving me a quizzical look, then asked, "Sparkling or still?"

Huffing out a little laugh, I answered, "Sparkling, please."

As the other three men took places amongst the seating, Alec Gregory still did not let go of my hand. For another moment, he just looked at me and then raised our linked hands so that my palm became flat against his. It was as if he was 'feeling' me through it. My skin was nearly buzzing now. I tentatively and gently pulled away and he just turned and went to a bar I'd not had time to notice. *Too weird. And a little creepy*, I thought.

"Devi. *Cher'*. Come sit next to me while Alec gets your drink. Did you take photos? A video? Maybe?" Georges' voice raised a few octaves at these last queries.

"Yes," I answered, coming around the huge, ridiculously long Chesterfield couch to sit beside him. I plopped down, feeling like a girl lost among strangers. They all exuded something very foreign. The Italian, Piero, felt like the second most intense one, but I forced a little bravado and continued. "Yes. I did both. I took some last night and some this morning and in the early evening. They grow fast, vigorous, like legumes. It looks like they may be some kind of vine. What are they?"

I crossed my legs, feeling small next to Georges. My lovely dress and fabulous shoes contrasted mightily with the masculinity surrounding me.

Alec came back into view with my water and placed it with care in front of me on the coffee table. Saying, "Thank you," I glanced at him, then away, suddenly feeling awkward. He just plain intimidated me—something which hadn't happened in a long time.

"Yes, Ms. Trevathan. They are a vine," Alec answered. I was forced to look him in the eye again and it felt difficult, as if I'd get sucked in if I stayed there too long.

He sat beside me, but well out of my personal space. As if he sensed my discomfort, like coaxing a fearful kitten, he asked, "May we see your photos and video?" His speech was so remarkably precise as he smoothly enunciated that it was a little hypnotizing and I had to resist the temptation to stare at his mouth.

So I looked at the other men, taking each in turn, for a moment, long enough to let them know that I understood they were not really answering my question and that I was smart enough to see how enthusiastic they were trying not to be. I ended with Piero. For some reason I thought he was the most sympathetic.

He gently nodded some kind of affirmation, telling me in that unspoken gesture it would be okay. So I quietly let out a breath and put my bag on my lap, uncrossing my legs as I did so. Clearly the images I carried in my bag trumped how good my legs looked in my get-up. I was attractive to them for my skills, not my looks, which was a good thing, really.

Pulling out the small camera, I turned it on and found the first image. Alec touched my bare arm and I jerked. "Sorry. I have a tablet, Ms. Trevathan. That would probably be easier to view."

I laughed a little and said, "Oh. Sure!"

He picked up a thin silver-framed screen from the coffee table as I pulled out the little memory card. As I noticed the high quality of the device, I smelled roses again and looked around, but found none. It didn't smell like perfume, but like the actual flower.

Alec put his hand out for the data card, which I gave him, and in quick moments we were looking at the images. Georges leaned over, pushing me slightly into Alec, who didn't even seem to notice because he'd become rigid with total interest. Their combined vibe set my body humming.

Piero and Axel moved from their seats and came behind us in order to see. The stills clearly showed a sequence from a tip peeking through the soil to all three seedlings at a stage between two and three inches, with the beginnings of some interesting-looking leaves. Alec then played the first of the three videos. You could hear my voice describing the time of day and making comments on the quickness of the growth. I'd used Georges' name, and when he heard it, he patted my back.

After we viewed it all, Alec saved the images to his computer. The men were very close to me and more still than I thought possible. They each took in an audible breath and moved away from me and back to their seats, except, Alec, who continued to stare at the screen. Then, with both hands, he rat-a-tat-tatted graceful fingers on the edges of the tablet and then placed it back on the coffee table.

He half turned to me, crossing his right leg over his left and laying his left arm along the back of the couch so it partly rested behind my head. There was something bordering on intimate about it, almost as if he'd embraced me. I glanced at Piero, who just smiled encouragingly. When I looked back at Alec, he'd been observing the exchange. I guess Georges and Axel had too, because they all looked at Piero as if he should say something.

Piero moved forward in his chair and clasped his hands. His manner and very precise movements reminded me of something, but I wasn't accessing it. "Miss Trevathan. Devi."

I waited, then after some hesitation on his part, said, "Yes?" He seemed a little unsure. "Look, just spit it out. I'm very curious and this is obviously something very important to you all. It's obviously important that I was able to get the seeds going, though I don't quite get that because it was really easy. Gentlemen. What's the story here?"

"Really easy," Piero repeated mysteriously. "First of all, It was 'really easy' *for you*. There is a long, dramatic and unbelievable story here which requires that you suspend some of what you think you know in order to believe. Do you believe in the unbelievable? Miss Trevathan?"

His accent was lovely and I gazed at him, considering his strange and loaded question. They *couldn't* know my secret, could they? But I said quietly, after a long silence, "Yes. I believe in the unbelievable. Within a certain reason."

And then Alec whispered, "*No doubt you do.*"

I jerked my eyes to him. What did *that* mean? Maybe they *did* know something. He just returned my look with nonchalance, as if he'd said nothing.

Piero continued. "What I am about to tell you may seem incredible. But first, are you interested in working with us to grow these special plants for … good cause? You will be very handsomely paid. It is also a job for life. Though of course, you can continue with what you do as well, should you choose, if time permits."

I fidgeted for a moment and crossed my arms. Then I blinked because my brain wasn't forthcoming with a response. Alec sat quiet and immobile. Georges clasped his hands in his lap. Axel began tapping his foot and Piero simply waited, unmoving as Alec.

Suddenly I scooted forward and the men lightly jerked in unison. "Well the thing is … ," I began, the 'job for life' ringing in my ears. "I don't really know anything without *knowing anything*, if you know what I mean." Alec eyed me as his brows rose. I thought he might be repressing a laugh.

Piero nodded and said, "We appreciate your forthrightness, Miss Trevathan. What we have to tell you is of a delicate matter. And your … value to us is difficult to describe. There is much to share with you—" Piero stopped when Georges raised a hand.

"*Père*, perhaps we should feed her. I *did* invite her here under the excuse of supper." *Père?* I squinted at Piero, whose dark head had turned to Alec.

Axel finally spoke up. "Yes, Alec. Feed the lady. It is critical she be happy."

Piero noticed my knitted brow and just watched me evaluate him. *Was he a priest?* The suit was certainly stylized, but I was no expert on clergy attire. He wasn't wearing a collar.

Then Alec shifted to get my attention. "Shall I have Gordon fetch something? Do you have preferences? You don't sm—*look* like a vegetarian."

I replied, "No, I'm easy; whatever everyone else is having."

Alec lifted a phone from the table beside him. After about five seconds of silence I heard Gordon answer. All Alec said was, "The tray we discussed?" He set the phone down and then continued speaking, but now to me. "Where were we? Ah. Piero was about to explain some facts which you will find astounding, starting with this one: you are the first to get the seeds of the *Vitaortus* to germinate in at least seventy-five years. Give or take."

He had the most lovely, lulling, deep voice, which had just cut to the chase. But when the meaning of his words registered, I could only drop my jaw at his revelation. Then I was able to blink at him. When he saw I wasn't ready to speak yet, he flared his nostrils a little, looked at and adjusted his cuffs and then back at me.

"You've no idea what a feat it is. It makes you very special. And if you can grow them on and repeat it, then it makes you one of the most special beings ever to have been."

I started to say something, but he'd anticipated it and cut me off. "No protestations. It may have been easy for *you*, but it is simply impossible for anyone else. And before you attempt to protest *further*, I'm sure you can look into your life and know there is *something* a wee bit different … special, about you." He'd leaned toward me and nearly whispered that last sentence.

Dear God. Did they know? Would they be able to explain? Suddenly I was scared and woozy. Alec's face was twelve inches from mine, and as adrenalin rushed through me, I watched the black disk in his green eyes expand, then contract. For the first time, I saw him smile. It came on slowly and it seemed like there could be some menace behind it. Or maybe not, as he then sat back nonchalantly.

The door opened and the lovely Gordon entered bearing a silver, covered tray. We all watched as he came around the seated area and placed it on the coffee table; this was obviously not going to be a proper 'sit-down' affair. He removed the cover and looked to Alec for approval. Alec looked to Georges, who leaned over me a little for a good scan. He nodded once and Gordon quickly and gently pushed the small platter in front of me, saying, "Miss Trevathan, there is a napkin and cutlery to the left. Salt and pepper on the right."

Unsure if I should feel like an urchin brought in from the rain, or revered royalty, I just nodded and said, "Thank you." Gordon smiled back with a gorgeous, dimpled grin, pivoted and left. It was impossible not to watch him. He was beefy perfection in his suit, vest and white shirtsleeves. (I noticed Georges look in tandem with me, confirming my suspicions about his preferences). I hadn't seen anything so attractive in a very, very long time. But then, all of the men seated with me were easily that too. Alec's appearance was way beyond it; beyond any man I'd ever personally known.

The four men observed me and I felt my face start to flush. I covered by examining the platter with its scrumptious-looking combination of foods so artfully arranged. Olives and cheeses, various antipasti and meats; *was that carpaccio?* My face must have registered something amusing because Alec laughed. That caught my attention, since he alone had not done so yet. It was pleasant and natural when I'd been expecting sinister. I felt sure he was capable of a very sinister laugh.

"Please, I insist you eat and enjoy," he encouraged warmly, as he glanced at the food and then back at me. Then I realized this was all for me.

"Aren't you eating?" I asked as I scooted forward to get near the table. In unison, they slowly shook their heads, which struck me as funny and I laughed. Choosing an olive, I looked back at Alec and picked up on his earlier revelation. "*Vitaortus?*" I asked and placed the kalamata in my mouth.

His gaze occasionally drifted to my lips as I chewed and he said, "It's known by many names, but that *is* its Latin genus name."

My eyes went back to the platter, and, using a small hors d'oeuvre fork, I lifted a piece of carpaccio and rolled it. As I took a delicate bite, I asked, "What's its species name?"

"*Magussperma.*"

I thought for a moment. That translated as 'magic seed'. Vitaortus was 'Life' something — 'source', maybe? My Latin vocabulary was reasonable, but rusty.

As I ate, the bizarreness of the situation resurfaced in my mind: the seeds, the car, the mansion, the *tingly* men. And now they were just watching me eat — intently. I suddenly felt some chutzpa and asked, "Who are you guys? I mean, Georges, I met you once, despite a great working relationship for two years. But what is going on here?" I said it with calmness I definitely didn't feel. I'd had to learn how to act, given my own oddity, and I felt somehow I had to do a bit of that now. "Are you some secret garden club or something?"

Alec and Axel just laughed. Georges scooted forward to bring his knees even with mine. "Somewhat like you, Devi, we are ... *special*. We have very special dietary needs and the plant, the *Vitaortus*, now plays a critical part." He seemed a little nervous, rolling his hands within each other. He looked at Alec and then to Piero, who picked up the thread.

"We have been searching for someone who could perform the horticultural magic to start new plants. There are a few who have some small skill in growing them, but they can only keep them barely alive now. You are the miracle we've searched for, for — "

"Seventy-five years?" I interrupted and added skeptically, "Right. None of you look that old. What is this dietary need you have? How does the plant — " And suddenly I had a strange and kooky thought. I eyed the glasses the men had been drinking from. The one nearest was Alec's. Impulsively, I reached for it and he swiftly caught my hand. It was, unquestionably, an inhuman swiftness.

It was in that defining, surreal moment that my world turned inside out.

Knowing my own hidden truth, I'd thought other strange things could exist, but this was too impossibly ridiculous to be true. Alec stared me down, not letting go of my wrist, which became uncomfortable. "Now why would you be doing that if you need me so badly?" I managed to say, still feigning coolness. He calmly let go.

As another strong whiff of rose hit my nostrils, he replied, "Please accept my apologies." But all had seen me observe the movement.

Georges said simply and quietly, "Alec."

Piero added, "She seems open and calm enough to handle this." Axel was vigorously nodding his agreement.

I frowned my lack of comprehension at them and then watched Alec move forward and grip the wineglass. My knees were pointed at an angle toward him, and they started shaking ever so slightly. He noticed, and then in an altogether too familiar move, put his fingertips on them to steady, then handed me his glass. I felt extremely self-conscious as my skin nearly undulated, until he removed his hand, and then I slowly brought the cobalt vessel to my lips.

It seemed like they all suspected I'd figured out what they were drinking. I inhaled the almost cloying odor of the dark liquid. Sure enough, it wasn't wine. In an act that rivaled my life's bravest moments, I took a small sip. Rich, thick, *Blood*.

Calmly, I handed the glass to Alec, who took it and placed it back on the coffee table, all the while watching my face as I stoically swallowed. He then picked up the napkin and brought it up, gently tapping my upper lip, then folding it so the red stain was hidden.

Knitting his brows at me, he entreated, "Please, Ms. Trevathan. Be neither afraid nor think poorly of us."

I looked from him to the others and said, "This is too hard to believe. I need a moment." But my mouth kept going. "Do you just *choose* to drink it, or do you … are you like the myths?" My eyes settled on Piero. *Could you be a priest … and a vampire?* I thought at him.

"We are myth and more. Yet we are still human in most ways," he answered in his gentle voice.

"Are you … alive?"

"We are as you see, but we did die once. Most myths have an origin."

"Are you from the last century? The Twentieth?"

"None of the four of us is."

Once I'd absorbed this information, I looked at Georges, incredulous. "I saw you eat food that night."

He smiled after a moment of incomprehension and explained, "We pretend for the benefit of mortal humans. We must pretend well. But we can also still appreciate certain tastes."

I turned to Alec, his presence seeming even more powerful now, and asked a little irrationally, "Do you have … you know … ?" It came out more quietly than I'd intended as I hesitantly touched my teeth. He only raised his brows, keeping his lips together.

Suddenly I was 'Alice through the looking-glass' with a freaky twist. I felt hemmed in, trapped as I sat between two very tall, powerful men and found myself standing with an urgent need for space. "I need to stretch," I said stupidly, looking down at Alec, whose eyes, with their extremely intelligent gaze, followed my movements. He shifted his legs to the side to let me pass since I'd not given him time to stand. He observed me closely.

Axel finally spoke up with his mild German accent. "Devi. I have no doubt this all seems ludicrous to you. *Verrückt.* Crazy! We don't exactly know how old *you* are; you appear young, but we know your life has shown you much. You seem to be taking this well, but please understand that we understand it might seem very unrealistic."

I'd moved into the center of the room and pivoted on the soles of my shoes, sending my dress' skirt into a little twirl. "Oh. No doubt! What you're telling me, what I'm to believe here, changes my whole life. It changes everything." I stopped and folded my arms over my chest. They had no idea how much it changed things for me, if certain parts of the myth were true, and unless they actually *did* know my secret. I had another thought and had to ask, "Why Washington? Why are you here? I mean, I know we're in *bumfuck* Virginia, but not really."

Piero frowned at Georges, not understanding my awful 'vernacular'. Georges whispered, *"In the country, old man, far out in the country."*

I continued, feeling a surge of chemicals reserved for life's oddest and often most dramatic moments. "If I'm to help you, what am I helping? Do you have an agenda I'd be against? You're here, in this area for a reason. Mr. Gregory here," I said, as I gestured a little wildly at him, "didn't just *buy* this place. And speaking of which, did you dismantle this and bring it across the pond or what? This is *not* local material and architecture! Shouldn't you be in New York, or New Orleans, at least? And *I* just happen to live just down the road?" I was getting a little drunk on my own adrenalin and rush of thoughts and laughed, realizing how silly I sounded. *"Oh my god this is bizarre."* And I put my face in my hands for a moment. Then, abruptly, it hit me. I looked up at them, horrified as my face drained. They stared at me, waiting. Georges and Alec had to turn in their seats to view me.

"Do you—" Alec was quickly beside me.

He put his arm around my back, took my arm in his other hand and led me back to the couch. Having anticipated my question, he answered, "Understand that we do our best; we take as little as we can and do as little harm as possible. It is our motto, our belief. It makes us, in this room, brothers. The plant helps us do that. And more. That is why it is so important—why *you* are so important." His tone was soft and gentle, like you'd use with a child or very elderly person.

And then I was on the couch. Lord Alexander Gregory had lifted me over the back and put me there with such strength that I barely felt gravity. A tiny rush of adrenalin-related butterflies hinted at my body's betraying reaction. Euphoria raced through me and I quickly squelched it. Yet another action on his part that was far too intimate for people who've just met.

He then came around and sat. "We'll answer any questions you have. Relax," he encouraged.

After a scowl at him, I turned my attention to Piero and Axel. I eyed them both for a moment and asked directly, "Do you *kill* for blood?" The two men raised their eyebrows simultaneously.

Georges just quietly laughed. When I gave him a reprimanding look, he shrugged and said, "*Mais ouais quoi? Devi, come on.* You have no fear. I find it marvelous. I laugh in admiration of you. See? You are surrounded by creatures more powerful than you can know, given a tiny demonstration of that power, yet you bravely chastise us."

"I'm not chastising, I'm trying to understand what you want to get me involved in," I insisted, hopefully with less shock than I felt. "*Do you kill for blood?*" I repeated sternly, looking back at Piero and Axel (I didn't want to look at Alec).

Axel made an odd sound in his throat and glanced at Piero, then said, "As Alec tried to tell you, our ... *group* does not believe in killing humans for sustenance. We believe in compassion." They seemed to be holding back.

"Okay, so you believe in no harm. How do you accomplish that?" I stared at Piero. I felt like I needed to hear this all from him.

Seeing my wish, he responded, "We use our 'mesmer' abilities; the myths are true in that regard. And we have other ways."

"Mesmer? Is that like mesmerize? Like to hypnotize?"

"In a sense. It is a term used specifically by our kind to denote an action that means something rather different. Anyway, generally, no one remembers we have fed from them. Some of us also have … attendants, if you will, but they are more than that. They are families, generations long, who are tied to us. Gordon is one such example."

"And he'll let you feed from him?" I asked, with horrified fascination.

"If necessary, although we try not to use our families in this way. I doubt that Gordon has given much blood in his lifetime. Besides, there are companies that provide it as a product."

Companies?

Well it was clear they *tried* to be non-lethal, if they were telling the truth. I knew there was more to this line of discussion, but I had other, more immediate questions. "Why are you in this part of the world?" I asked, turning to Alec. The other men said nothing as the silence grew.

Alec took in air and started to say something, then stopped himself. He crossed his incredibly long legs as his arms folded under his chest. His movements were so languid that they slowed time. His cream suit looked pristine despite the linen's occasional wrinkle. His shirt fit perfectly. I looked at his shoes — gorgeous Italian, or maybe Brazilian — which were a warm, dark tan in color. When my eyes went back to his, I saw he'd noticed my observation. His eyes flicked to my shoes. I sensed an acknowledgement that we were kindred spirits where shoes and clothes were concerned, which struck me as bizarrely hilarious.

49

He moved a hand to the side of his face, resting two fingertips at his temple. After a long moment of contemplating me, he said, "Ms. Trevathan. You are a seemingly wise woman. I think some things are best left for future conversations. What we need to know is how you wish to be compensated. We can offer you whatever you want."

He was shutting me down! *And succeeding.*

"Um. I don't know how to answer that just now. But I know I don't want to be a part of something I deem … bad."

He leaned toward me, but didn't change his pose a millimeter. "We are the good guys, dear. There *are* bad guys out there, but in due course, you'll discover that you're very lucky we found you first." For a moment, he stayed close and I thought he might be smelling me. Then he just moved back to his prior position. My brows knitted at his statement.

Georges said, "Here, have some *Sottocenere*. It's wonderful." And he handed me a cracker with the distinctive cheese on it. Actually, I really liked the Italian truffle cheese and hadn't had it in a while; so his distraction worked and I laughed at how easy I was.

Sloughing a little of my unease, I took a bite. The musky, earthy taste caused me to close my eyes as I savored it. As I started chewing, I opened them and found all four men gazing intently at me.

"None of you has drunk since I've been here."

Piero picked up his glass, and held it aloft. "To you, Devi. You are our savior." Axel and Georges raised theirs, but Alec hesitated. He stared coolly at Piero in a chastising way, but then raised his too. I picked up my glass of water and toasted each of them.

As I munched more of the goodies from the platter, Alec commented, "Your dress is quite lovely. It's not a current style, correct? Is that organza?" He reached over and was careful to feel the material without seeming improper, which was incongruous considering some of his other actions.

I swallowed a mouthful and took a quick sip of water, then answered, "Right. It's from the '50's. 1956 to be exact."

He eyed the dress some more, then indicated my shoes and handbag. "And no doubt, those come from the same year?"

I nodded as I put more cheese on a cracker. Peripherally I saw him cock his head, his eyes resting on me. I suddenly got the feeling he was leading me. Instead of following, I blithely ate my treat, then turned to gaze back. "Yes, Mr. Gregory. They're a set. I acquired them somewhere along the line. And that's a fine suit *you're* wearing; it could be vintage too."

He smiled, clearly realizing I'd play a game before giving up the goods on what he wanted to know, for now. I didn't trust him any more than he trusted me. And the truth was that *I'd never told a soul the truth*, not fully. What I *had* shared had landed me in the midst of a nightmare. To tell was as foreign to me as the reality of what these men were. He didn't respond, but merely stood and moved out into the room, taking his 'drink' with him.

"Well, I presume we need not be concerned about you discussing this with anyone?" Axel questioned as he reached for his drink again. I nodded deeply several times. Obviously they knew, with my own strange tale, that I was trustworthy by default. Besides, who would believe me if I did tell?

I felt now would be a good time to go and let everything settle in my mind, so I wiped my hands on the napkin and stood. "Gentlemen. This has truly been the experience of a lifetime." Alec gave a little meaningful chuckle. He was going to get my story out of me eventually. I'd bet he already knew, just not the details. It was obviously tied into my abilities with the seeds.

The other three stood as well and Georges took my hand. "Devi. You will grow to love us. We are very good friends to have and we will make you happy." He looked at me in a way that told me he meant it, profoundly. Despite the fact that a supposed *vampire* was promising those three things, they were enough to change my entire countenance, and Axel and Piero noted it, each taking on an air of humble agreement. They'd just seen me quietly acquiesce to their request, because he'd offered me the one thing I really wanted: true, long-term friendship.

Alec picked up the phone again and told Gordon that I was going home and to alert Hervé. He then asked, "Piero? Will you accompany her?"

Piero gave a single deep nod and said, "Of course. A pleasure for me." We walked as a group out of the room and to the large formal entryway where, in the foyer, Georges came forward and pulled me into a slight embrace, kissing both cheeks and then gave me a third kiss for good measure. Axel did the same.

Alec, instead, reached out his hand for a formal shake and bowed his head. With sincerity, he said, "It is truly a pleasure and honor to meet you Devica Trevathan. And we thank you. Good luck with your charges. You've done marvelously so far. Shall we discuss payment and logistics in the next several days?"

I looked at his large, cool, electric hand and thought, *Shouldn't it be colder?* But I just replied, "Sure. Whatever works for you." Which I realized was a bit of a stupid response, but of course he disarmed me, particularly when touching me.

And so Piero and I descended the stairs to the car and off we went. I felt a niggle at my neck and turned to look back. Axel and Georges were walking back inside; Alec stood, still watching our departure, with his arms crossed lightly and one hand at his elegantly bearded chin. When our eyes met, I quickly turned back and smiled at Piero, who returned it benignly.

I let my gaze linger on him. His dark hair framed his face with loose, half-moon curls here and there. We matched each other as our black clothing contrasted starkly against the white leather of the seat. He let me stare and just watched me, waiting for me to talk.

"How old are you?" I finally asked.

"Ah. You are very direct. I am close to five hundred."

I gasped and he didn't react. "Are you of *the Medicis?*"

He nodded. "I am. Although I was illegitimate. Upon my father's death, the family was asked to acknowledge me at the request of the pope, who was also a Medici." We were silent again for a moment as I absorbed his information. I glanced out the window and thought I saw another of the large deer.

Piero seemed unfazed by my questions, so I asked another. "Were you a priest?"

He nodded again, his head swaying with the movement of the car, "*Si.* I was."

I got braver. "Are you still?"

He raised his head fully and I could see he was weighing his options on how to answer. "If I tell you yes, you will have many more questions, correct?"

"Pretty likely," I said with a laugh.

"Then we will leave this line of questioning for now. In time, you will get answers to some things. I see you are extremely curious, as I would be. But for now, for safety, let us allow things to unfold in the fullness of time. Is that … okay?"

What was I going to say? No? So I just nodded. I looked out the window again, then quickly back and said, "But, hell *yes*, I have a lot of questions and that's without time to think!"

He laughed fully this time and said, "I think, Devi, you are going to be just the breath of fresh life we need."

I smiled, aware that much was underlying that statement.

I was shocked to find I'd nearly fallen asleep by the time we got to my home. Piero walked me to the door and gave me a gentle kiss-kiss on the cheeks and bade me, "*Buona notte*, Devi." And only after I'd gone in and shut the door, did Hervé pull away with him ensconced in that wonderful back seat.

I'd noticed Alec had found Piero's little telling description of me pretty annoying: *Savior.* I doubted I was that, but one thing was sure — my life had just gone much farther into the realm of the fantastical than it already was.

FOUR

Processing

†

Alec observed as the Maybach crunched away, its tires spitting out the occasional piece of buff-colored gravel. He smiled when she turned to meet his gaze and then looked hastily away, embarrassed. He felt strength in her, but he was not entirely convinced, yet. She obviously had a deeply spirited side: she'd have to, to have survived all that he imagined she might have … for as long as she had. And he had a feeling she'd have done most of it alone, in complete ignorance of what she was. After all, who would have told her? She would have needed to uproot herself multiple times to start anew, and she'd have had to make it up as she went along. It was hard enough for *his* kind, who had ancient networks and helped each other financially. What resources had she started with? He had a feeling it had been very little, and he wondered at all she may have suffered.

The world had gone into another great upheaval not long after the last suspected prime channel had disappeared and many had thought her dead before she could take up her role. It was astounding that they'd found the woman here, so serendipitously close. The mysterious ways of the universe could still illicit awe from him … if she was indeed who they thought she was.

"Alec!" Axel's voice called abruptly from just inside. "Are you just going to stand there? Or has *she* mesmered *you*?"

Georges' laugh rang from deeper inside, "Yeees. She has a certain something, *n'est-ce pas?*"

Alec silently followed them in and found them trailing Gordon back into the great room. He'd gone in to clear the tray and glasses. When he saw Alec, he asked, "Will you be wantin' more to drink sir?"

. "No. Thank you, Gordon."

"She was quite taken with *you* young man. But then aren't we all?" Georges commented as he clapped Gordon on the back. It was no secret what Georges thought about Gordon. But it was true. They'd all witnessed her ocular appreciation of him. Yet she'd been discrete and had quickly moved on.

Gordon smiled broadly and shrugged. "What's a man to do?"

Alec dropped effortlessly to the couch in a lounging position and lifted the tablet, saying, "Bloody *nothing*, is what. No one—absolutely no one touches that woman."

Gordon stopped dead and got a contrite look to him. "My lord, I meant no disrespect."

"Sorry Gordon. I didn't mean you explicitly. I mean *anyone*. Until we know more, she's off limits to all. In fact, there will be nary a declaration, regardless of what more we learn. This will be handled quite differently from the past. She will make her choices as she sees fit. We, however, will be her guard and must remember that is our fated purpose."

"And of course we need not worry about *you*, pious lord?" Axel teased. Alec ignored him again and turned on his computer to review the photos and video. As he looked, Axel and Georges sat too while Gordon left with the tray and empty glasses.

Georges exclaimed, "I knew it. I just knew it. But Alec. How is it she comes to us in such a way? What is the probability? The odds?"

Alec tore his gaze from the little screen, answering, "Georges, it is a great mystery, to be sure. And, as I have learned with such things, there is no coincidence. Somehow Providence always puts us together. But this time was a very long time, in the hardest of times. And I fear it's too late for some. We can only hope she's an actual primeval source remanifested: a *prime channel*."

Georges shook his head with wonder. "Someone who knows her must have set it in motion. A third party put me in touch with her, but I never bothered to check who it was. She claimed not to have had me on her advertising list. We assumed it was a referral. We must find out."

Axel's playful mood left him. "Shall I research her past? See if I can link her to the story of the last channel?"

"Yes, Axel. That would be helpful. Tell me, does she look as though she could have been born in India? Over one hundred years ago?" Alec posed.

Georges' expressive face took on a look of doubt, but Axel said, "Stranger things have happened. Often."

"Indeed," Alec replied.

Axel shared, "I've heard a group in New York is getting more ill by the month. They are a young splinter family and wouldn't hear Mohan's warnings. They were feeding from patients in rehabilitation centers and facilities for the insane, easy meals. Of eight, four have already perished. Mohan is trying to help them, but it is impossible without any Vitaortus."

Alec looked back at the pictures of the seedlings. "Well then the stupid are being weeded out. Any fool who drinks straight from the source in an area filled with pollutants, particularly places such as those, is committing suicide. Patients? Filled with prescribed poisons? They weren't only stupid, but mad."

He turned back to Axel, who replied, "Mad with youthful igno-rance. And bloodlust."

"Well regardless, once the seedlings have grown on, Ms. Trev-athan will have to be present and travel quite a bit as we distribute them. We'll be busy. New York will be our first recipient, but prob-ably too late for those of whom you speak."

Alec had no doubt he could entice Ms. Trevathan to help them, if she hadn't already decided. He could sense her isolation; friends such as they would likely be irresistible.

Gordon knocked and let Alec know he'd be heading off to bed once Piero returned if they needed nothing else. The smile Georges gained at Gordon's appearance was still present when the door closed. He asked jokingly, "So, my friend. Was she *comely* enough for you?"

Alec grunted a little laugh and replied, as he replayed her vid-eos. "She could look like the hind end of a hound for all I care. But it never hurts to have a pleasant visage upon which to gaze."

Axel added, "It's also pleasant to see a real, long, full head of natural locks on a natural woman for a change. This fad of forced, stick-straight hair is becoming terribly tiresome." Georges com-mented that some current styles showed a distinct lack of creativity. Alec mused that the two men's opinions were products of their orig-inal time period, when it was fashionable to have the most outra-geous coiffure of all.

While Axel's and Georges' conversation vacillated between the topic of women's hairdressing and more profound subjects, Alec became entranced by the three videos she had taken. As he watched the seedlings in their various stages, he carefully listened to her voice. He wondered a few times if he could detect a little Britishness beneath the American accent and modern vernacular.

Just maybe. Hopefully. Because if she'd been British, the possibility of a birth in India made far more sense.

Before long, Piero came through the door looking very light-hearted indeed. They observed him as he joined them with a clap of his hands. "She is very amusing. Very charming."

Alec narrowed his brows. "I beg your pardon?"

Piero indicated Alec should move his legs so that he might sit on the couch as well. "She is, as the Americans say, *feisty.*" And he gracefully sat, the smile still on his face. "I believe she is our man — woman. The one we seek. Her energy is magnificent. I was able to feel because she dozed a little after I mesmered her. I have only felt one almost as amazing and that was centuries ago."

"*Really.* Why do you say magnificent?" Alec felt a slight annoyance because Piero had mesmered her without discussion. Piero's 'position' as a double-secret *Cardinale in Pectore* didn't make him any less a potential threat than any other male. He'd had lovers throughout the time Alec had known him, except this past century (much like Alec, himself, who'd gone an unheard of two centuries), and the girl had seemed to trust those luminous doe's eyes Piero used so well to his advantage.

Piero answered, "Magnificent because the frequency is so high, so strong and so steady. I did not even have to actually touch her to feel it." Alec nodded. He'd felt it when he'd held her hand, before she'd pulled it away. "I think you will need to bring in special protection. Where is your skillful progeny? The black-haired one?"

Alec leaned to put his computer back on the coffee table and answered, "He's on a *quest* just at the moment. He'll soon return. I should think we have a few weeks at least until anyone ties us to her. I believe I shall pay her a discrete visit tomorrow night and have a look at the seedlings myself. And her property. See if I can't get her to share a little."

"That is a good plan. Alec, we must celebrate," Piero said.

Axel added, "*Ach* yes. A hunt would be just the thing, no?"

Georges looked at the other three excitedly, then his face slouched. "I don't think Alec will join us, I expect."

"No. Georges is correct. I expended what I have for a while a few nights ago … before we knew of her. Or I would have saved my energies. But please. Please. The three of you go. There is an older, very dark stag that smells distinctively of the raspberry briar leaves of which he seems fond. He is still quite virile. But be cautious. It's been a good calving spring. Nearly all the hinds are nursing."

The other men tried hard not to look on him with concern, but it was impossible not to hide it. The four of them had been together, more or less, over two hundred years. "Go! Enjoy! Careful of the hinds and calves." Alec waved them away, then said, "Besides. I'm still full from my own hunt."

The three stood and made their way out, bending to kiss his cheek as they went. Alec had known Piero the longest, nearly five hundred years. But it was the French Revolution that changed their views on hunting and feeding upon humans. What had happened during that dark time had been a combination of horror and wonder.

Alec had saved Georges and Axel from the guillotine. Georges had been a chef to the king. Axel was there to salvage and catalogue art, documents and books eventually taken from Versailles, but had become caught up in the chaos and was arrested. Alec had come for information from Axel about a specific artifact, but had to free him to get it. Something about Georges compelled Alec to free him as well, since the two shared a cell. It was either bring him or mercifully kill him. Georges turned out to be a remarkable asset because he had known the palace and guided them well.

The artifact had been Alec's sword from his days as a knight of the *Ordre du Temple*, and it was the first chance he'd had to retrieve it since it had been stolen centuries before. It took the deposition of Louis XVI for its whereabouts to become known, having shown up in a list of the secret collection at Versailles. And though it had no gilt-work or ornamentation, it was a priceless relic of the crusades. More importantly, it had the deepest personal meaning for Alec.

Both men had been just as afraid of him as of the guillotine because they had witnessed the use of his powers to manipulate the lock on their cell door—supernatural skill more astounding than any violence. He'd mesmered them, and managed to slip them past every guard to his waiting carriage.

Almost all of his progeny had been killed a few decades before in a vicious attack by a rival, so he was on his own and decided to start fresh, with these two. He'd deemed them worthy and turned them that night. Within a week, they were on a ship headed for Scotland, where no one knew them and they could be eased into their new life.

And he'd retrieved his sword. Now it went with him wherever he moved, although he knew it should be inside a safe in the *Banque Suisse*. But given what he'd seen of history, nothing was a sure bet. After all, the Templars had been the first real western bankers and had seemed well on their way to centuries of success, alas. Alec himself was one of the only things he knew that reliably persisted through time. The sword was the only possession he treasured. There had once been a woman's kerchief, but it, and his reason for keeping it, had disintegrated fully by the time he'd reacquired his blade. Everything else was replaceable.

He thought about the strength and magic he'd had for so many hundreds of years. And then, five years ago, he succumbed to the modern toxins. He'd learned in the beginning from his mentor, the renowned medieval scholar and cleric, *Michael Scotus*, that certain alkaloids and other substances could affect the likes of Alec if ingested with the blood of others. He'd always been careful to observe his prey for several weeks. But it had become much harder since petrochemicals, processed foods, pharmaceuticals and other synthesized elements had come into being. Too many humans didn't understand or know what they were consuming and exposed to. But in this instance, he'd been deliberately poisoned, although the culprit was never detected. Alec had begun to age again and it showed a little.

So for now, he had perhaps one good change in him every few weeks. He could no longer manipulate gravity or separate his molecules into a mist or fog, but he could morph for brief periods. And he could mesmer, which was the most important skill anyway. He thought it funny that the word 'mesmer' still tripped him up occasionally. His kind had taken to using it as a popular substitute for the more ancient Latin word *induco* almost two centuries ago.

He'd seen the use of different words come and go in many languages. He was over eight-hundred years old. He'd learned plenty about how to survive and adapt well, and most of it was simple intelligence anyway. He had become a very intelligent being.

The two men he'd saved had proven to be invaluable in helping him adapt to the new world order. The 1800's were the final century that nobility would have any real power in the western world, little as it was.

He had been born into the ruling class and still held lands and even a title—a feat in and of itself, as he never should have had the lands come to him in the first place. He had taken the vows of the Order, but his younger brothers had died. And of course, the

Order was destroyed, but he'd been turned almost a century before that calamity.

As for the longevity of his holdings, being in Scotland helped some. Although a small and seemingly unimportant country, he noticed it tended to produce important ideas and people. It was a good place to hide the truth for seven or more centuries, in spite of violent changes history wrought. It was not impossible to use those changes, disappear or create ruses. He'd had to rebuild now and then, or mesmer, manipulate and even kill to get his properties back after various battles or power shifts. But his birth home still stood, its old walls nestled within several incarnations of newer walls. It was now even a tourist destination.

And so the Age of Enlightenment came and went, but left its profound mark on the four men, even as it had on the rest of the Hesperian world. Alec, Georges and Axel, with some input from Piero, developed their theories on how to redeem their existence after the horrors of the revolution and the many succeeding wars. Using a little of Alec's past and much of Georges and Axel's desire for redemption, they found a way to move into the modern age—to evolve from the monsters they were. They'd had to reconnect with their human consciences, for they were sure their continued existence depended upon it.

Alec imagined the three men, hunting together in wolf form. It was an easy morph and a favored hunting guise. He had populated the grounds of this new American home with deer he'd bred by mixing the Scottish red deer with the Carpathian and Caspian varieties. They were big and beautiful, though not fond of the extremely hot and humid Virginia summers. It shortened their lives just a little, and he had to inoculate them against several New World diseases, but they seemed happy here. He was even considering crossing them with the American Wapiti next.

As he again picked up his computer tablet to view her images, he thought that perhaps Devica Trevathan could bring a measure of hope for his own happiness. He hadn't depended on another being for that in a long while, but the loss of his powers had dampened his existence significantly. He fully expected to die again in the not too distant future because of his poisoning. And he was hardly alone. The percentage of his kind with some level of sickness was in the high majority. They were, in reality, dying out. Tonight, she'd brought the first rays of hope that there was a future for them.

ʊ

I was awake before Eddie's morning crow. A cat lay on either side of me and I absentmindedly stroked them while they purred. As I lay there, gazing at the dawn through a slit in the blinds, I wondered if I was sane … again. *Vampires. Really?* Maybe what I'd been afraid of succumbing to all these years had finally come true. I was completely insane. I had to be. I rolled over and shoved a pillow over my head.

Small 'keeps' in the Virginia country side? A night-walking priest? Vitaortus magussperma? What a ridiculously dramatic name. After another five minutes of tossing and turning, Theda finally meowed at me hungrily and I realized I was not only torturing myself, so I reluctantly crawled out of bed and headed downstairs.

The cats made it to the kitchen before I did, as usual, and I rewarded them just for *being*. After making my coffee, I went to the living room window and leaned forward, sipping from my cup and staring at the seedlings. I was stunned yet again by their appearance. At least five inches tall now, their first set of true leaves were unfurling, and boy, were they interesting.

They had red veining and a slight reddish hue just barely tinting the grey-green. I wondered if that would fade as they grew older. I gently touched one and it almost seemed to move under my finger, as if trying to lean into me. I tilted it a little and was enthralled by the shape, which could only be described as 'bat-winged'. I'd seen plants that looked similar to this in the passion flower genus, but the Vitaortus leaves grew from the stem in an opposite pattern of twos rather than alternating one at each node. And it appeared that the next node was going to produce tendrils. They looked like two miniature grey-green bats hovering around a rope. It was both cute and utterly ridiculous.

"You guys are ridiculous," I said aloud to them. And suddenly I got the notion that they were going to get hot in direct light so I lowered the shade a little, but only after taking a macro shot of the leaves.

It was official. I was talking to them and taking baby pictures—I *had* to be nuts.

Deciding to move into the day ahead, which was Saturday, I had breakfast, then showered and dressed for a morning of labor. Maria and I wanted to clear a small space for another compost pile, but we had to remove three Red Mulberry trees, which meant getting out the chainsaws and dealing with the usual fussiness. It seemed like the machines rarely operated perfectly. Luckily, the three young trees were only around twelve inches thick, so not such a trial to bring down. I hated killing them, and quietly begged their forgiveness before we got started. Within two hours, we'd cut down and sized the wood, setting it aside to dry for our winter fires. By the time we had cleared the area, it was noon and Serena had lunch on the table under the willow oak.

Halfway through my sandwich, I suddenly thought again of last night. As we ate, and gently-clucking hens wound around our legs searching for crumbs, my head whirled, doubting my experience. I'd just spent three hours blissfully forgetful.

After wolfing down a brownie, I told the ladies I was going for a siesta so I could get away and not have to pretend I wasn't *loco*. After another shower and hair washing, I sat and woke up the computer. When I typed 'Piero Medici' into the search engine, only ancient relatives of his came up and current folks who, while obviously Italian, were definitely *not* him. There were several mentions of bastard sons from the general time-period, also none of which were him. I wasn't sure who his father had been.

Axel's name came up with several hits, but I couldn't tell if he was any of those listed because I didn't know anything about him and there were no photos. Georges' name was the first real hit. He was there as the owner of the Georgetown restaurant, several others in Europe and had a long list of other achievements and associations. Interestingly, Paris was listed as his place of birth, but no date was given.

Then I typed Alec's name, put a 'Lord' in front of it for specificity, and clicked 'I'm feeling lucky'. And *lo*, there he was. Several images of him came up, dressed like a model for a *Made-to-Measure* collection. So much for some myths; they were certainly photographable—photogenic in his case! In one image, he was wearing a tuxedo and standing with a senator I recognized as being from New York. But interestingly, there was virtually zero personal detail. All I could find out was that he was a wealthy British (Scottish origin) businessman with interests in various fields. Information on sources of income was nebulous. His family was of ancient aristocratic lineage and he currently resided much of the year in Virginia,

USA (which I found just really weird). There was some information on charities related to historic preservation, conservation and environmental efforts in which he'd been involved, but nothing more than that.

I leaned back in my chair and stared at his picture for a moment, then shut down the page. The photos had been taken with a flash and were definitely not outside. So no hint there, although I couldn't say what I was really looking for. I'd nearly made up my mind that they'd been feeding me a line of BS. After cleaning up the house a little, I took my siesta.

I dreamt of a place I'd banished to the dark recesses and rarely thought of now … a place that had haunted me for years after I'd been there … a place for people whose minds weren't working properly. I'd been sent there and ripped from everything and anyone I'd ever known and loved … never to see them again.

When I awoke an hour and a half later, I found I'd been crying in my sleep. Theda and Greta were on the bed, cuddled against me, and I found joy and comfort in their presence: a small thing, but it helped, and soon I shook off the darkness.

FIVE

In Business and a Game of Truth or Consequences

ʊ

That night was absolutely beautiful. I treasured my vista of the stars and faint swath of the Milky Way. If my little nursery was situated a bit farther west, in the hills of the Shenandoah, it would be even more brilliant. As it was, it was plenty. I enjoyed sitting outside on my back porch, rarely feeling alone, because I wasn't. My cats always joined me and then there were the myriad creatures of the night, like the katydids, tree frogs, crickets, toads, the few night birds, bats and so much more that made the summer darkness as busy as any urban street.

I always found it strange that so many people were unaware and not even curious about all that goes on around them in what I thought of as the *real* world: *Nature*. Entire lives are lived out right next to us, unseen, unrecognized, or feared and hated, as if they were bogeymen. But I was always aware of these presences and thought of them as friends and neighbors. Unfortunately, they're unavailable for proper conversation.

I sat on the swinging bench, hands yet again petting a cat on either side of me, gently pushing with my foot. Rather than continue to obsess over my previous night's experience, I simply 'disappeared', becoming completely aware of the living space around me, forgetting I existed. I listened for every sound, every separate voice.

The feel of the slightly moist air and the smells of the surrounding plants enveloped me.

I had learned to do this so I *could* forget and its benefit was astounding. But suddenly I sensed a communal shift and the cats' heads jerked up as their ears flicked toward the corner of the house. When they growled low, tingles sped down my spine and I quickly stood. The portly, mostly indoor cats hissed, leapt from the bench and raced to the house, ducking through the door that was slightly ajar. I moved slowly at first, trying to hear and see in the moonless dark. I heard nothing, but decided to move faster. That feeling of nearly being grabbed came upon me and I felt a strong urge to hurry as a surge of adrenalin brought me to almost frightened attention.

It was only when I got to the door, opened it enough to slide in and turned, that I saw him. My skin suddenly produced copious goose bumps.

And then he was right there, towering over me.

He moved forward, herding me backwards into the house. As he shut the door behind him, I wondered if I'd pass out from an unfamiliar surge of genuine fear and darted my eyes for a moment.

"Look at me," he said, in a gentle tone that was at odds with what I was experiencing. I did and figured I was going to be his aperitif inside of a minute, if last night's assurances of no-kill feeding were true. *Yes, any moment now.* We just stared at each other.

Finally I inhaled deeply, having realized I'd been holding my breath—he smelled … *really good?* I recognized the scent from last night, but it wasn't cologne. My mouth moved from surprise before I could stop it. "You smell of attar of roses?"

He frowned slightly and forced a sigh, his attempt at frightening me foiled. "Ah. *That.*"

His breath smelled of nothing; maybe more rose. My brain questioned my own scent. I doubted I came close to smelling so nice and became self-conscious all of a sudden, despite my recent shower. How ridiculous was it that I was in awe of his scent when he was apparently trying to scare me? So I talked to cover my embarrassment. "I know you can't be here to feed from me, Mr. Gregory. What are you doing?"

"Well of course not. I just wish to see first-hand the germinated Vitaortus, if you don't mind." He stepped out of my space and in a single swoop, removed his linen jacket. The suit was not the one he'd had on last night because it was a more creamy color; his tie was a darker green than his shirt. "May we sit ... and chat?"

I had a momentary whoosh of anger at his presumption, but when he raised his brow at me, I decided to smile and said, with mock cheer, "Sure! Come in and have a seat!" My fear factor probably should have been registering higher, but my cats seemed to have loaned me their curiosity. And besides, I was pretty sure I was safe with Lord Alexander Gregory. My intuition about these things was well-honed. Well, *I was fairly sure*. He needed me, right?

As I guided him into the living room, I asked, "Why do you smell of rose? You don't seem like an attar of roses kind of guy."

He turned back to me as he decided where to sit and answered, "Mm. Let's just say someone played a terrible joke on me a very long time ago, which, unfortunately, stuck. I'll share the tale when we get to know each other better. Let it suffice to say, he was a sort of sorcerer, amongst other things."

Sorcerer?! I had no idea of what to think or how to respond to such an astounding explanation, so I just stared.

He was going to take my favorite chair; I could see he'd eyed it, taking in its small hand-carved dragons and velvet upholstery. I was proud of that chair. He glanced at me and then around at my living room. "You have interesting tastes. Not entirely typical of a woman of your time and place."

"I'm not sure how to take that. Thanks?" I replied, narrowing my eyes at him.

He raised his brows in innocence. "It's a compliment." His deeply hooded eyes moved to gently touch on the *Quan Yin* statuette I had placed on a small table with candles. He stared at it for a moment, carefully touched the dragon beneath her feet and then turned to me. "Are you a Goddess worshiper or a *Buddhist?*" he asked.

"Neither. Maybe both. I don't know. I light those candles and I imagine she and her dragon are witnesses to my thanks to the universe."

"Very succinct and lovely." After a moments silence, he added, "Now, you want some tea so that we may conduct our business."

My mouth dropped open at the gentle command and he regarded my surprise. I wasn't keen on the authoritarian manner, but tea *was* what I was going to suggest anyway. "Um, if you'll excuse me a moment?"

He gave a single nod in response and I went to the kitchen, inhaling slowly as I walked. My adrenalin was still up. I decided it was too late for anything caffeinated and opted for lemon balm tea.

As I worked at the counter, I again knew he was there, behind me, not only because I smelled him, but I simply felt his energy, like outside when he'd first shown up. After turning on the gas and placing the kettle on the blue flame, I pivoted and smiled to hide my disquiet, saying, "I would ask if you'd like some, but I assumed you'd say no?"

He shook his head in response. "I wanted to get a better look at your kitchen." I watched him glance around. Spotting a seven inch sprig of passionflower on the counter, he then picked it up and ran his hand up the vine gently, smoothing back the leaves. It was a very familiar action and I wondered what his interest in and knowledge of plants was, apart from the Vitaortus. It suggested familiarity and fondness. "Is this for you?" he asked. *So he did know about plants and their uses.*

"Yes. Once in a while I have a little difficulty falling asleep; thought I might need it tonight," I admitted.

"Ah." He nodded once as he said it.

"Why did you feel the need to scare me before?"

In response, he smiled slightly and squinted at me in a playful way. "It's more fun that way sometimes, don't you agree?"

"Since I don't know you—not really," I replied. My hair was down and in my way, so I twisted it nervously, then tied it into a knot at the back of my head as I moved across the kitchen to get a cup. His manner was unnerving. He had the potential to be infinitely more charming than the others. He was extremely handsome, with deep-green eyes and a nearly perfect patrician nose as well as a neat and trim, red-gold beard and moustache. Wide shoulders and the outlines of a nicely muscled body spelled *trouble, trouble, trouble*. He gained some sex-appeal but retained his sinister intimidation quotient. That superior countenance made him very lofty, inaccessible and a little scary, so I guess it balanced out.

He added, "Besides, I wanted to see how you handled yourself. Would you scream like a child, or feign fortitude? I'd say you are quite skilled at the latter."

Remembering he needed me, I swaggered back to him with my cup, placed it on the copper counter and put my hand on my hip. "Well how did I do?" I asked, a little brassily.

"Fabulously," he answered, then cupped my chin and added, "And isn't a little adrenalin rush just letting you know how alive you really are?"

Startled by his familiarity, I frowned, thinking *maybe*, but I'd had those from time to time in my past, and really, I'd been enjoying my serenity. I pulled away, saved by the kettle's whistle, and answered, testily, "No. I have no problem knowing I'm alive. I've very aware of it. Promise me that you won't do that to me again." Then I turned back to him and added, "Seriously."

He came over, took the kettle from me and then poured its steaming contents into my cup, saying, "I apologize, Devi. I understand. Actually I'm going to protect you at all costs, so let that be a comfort. Also, in a way that may seem strange to you, it's a compliment. No one has inspired that sort of silly behavior in me in a very long while. Anyway, you don't need to feign anything. You have, no doubt, earned your courage." He handed over the cup and looked at me with a trace of nothing on his lovely face.

I stared back for a moment. "Well thank you, I guess. Um, do you want to see your babies?"

He looked at me quizzically, and then understood. "Oh, *yes*, please."

I motioned for him to follow and we went back through the living room to the bay window where I'd placed the wardian case. The seedlings were six inches tall and I'd stuck a chopstick in each pot for them to grab hold of with the new tendrils. I figured they'd be fairly robust since their stems were a quarter inch in diameter. I stood to the left of them. Greta had settled herself on the pillows beside the plants and was purring. She showed no fear now and looked up at him, meowing in a way I'd never heard. He reached and stroked her luxuriously. She licked his hand, then rolled over and offered him her belly.

"Goodness, Alec. What are you doing to my cat?"

He smiled a little forlornly. "They tend to be one of the only creatures that are genuinely fond of us as beings. Most are frightened." I watched him for a moment as he enjoyed the furry intimacy. Then his eyes went to the plants. "My, my, Mistress Magician. What a way you have. They are much bigger than I'd anticipated. Hurrah for you. And us."

"Yes, they're like Jack's beanstalk!" I agreed, with a smile.

He turned to me and suddenly took me into his arms and gave me a hug I can only describe as 'total', then let go and said, with no trace of his usual stoicism, "We've been searching for you for quite some time. You've no idea. It is a very, very big world. A needle in a haystack. And here you are, so close. And look what you've done." Motioning at the seedlings, he continued. "Like Jack's beans, so too are these magic. And you."

Not entirely listening, I was stuck on thinking that he didn't really feel different from a normal man except for the energy emanating from him. It was almost a light buzz, or hum, like you feel from electronic equipment. He didn't feel cold and hard like a pig or steer carcass might, but rather cool, and soft like a regular person. With curiosity getting the better of me, I said, "*Sooo*, may I ask you something?"

"Certainly." He eyed the seedlings once more, then turned his attention to me.

"How are you possible?" His gaze turned to a blank stare, which told me he wasn't sure of my question. "Seriously. How do you exist? How are your cells not aging? What's the science here?"

Alec kept his eyes on mine as he tried to formulate an answer. He shifted slightly and clasped his hands behind his back. "Well, actually, you'd be surprised at the scientific laws that do apply versus those that don't. Whatever it is that changes us, that we pass on if we make another, seems to create a situation more like stasis rather than any other real scientific norms. We are no longer subject to oxidation and certain other chemical and biologic processes that affect the normal world of *Animalia*. We're like gold in that regard. And some processes are … enhanced.

"Gravity affects our overall mass, but not its individual components, which is a thing we can tap into, by the way. And we can regenerate injured cells. But it's not all logical by normal laws and knowledge. It is metaphysical, supernatural. And yet some quantum theory goes a long way to explaining it, which is rather exciting."

"Okay." I replied, not really getting the 'how' from his answer. He reached out, surprised me by cupping my elbow and guided me to the seats in the room. I sat on the chaise because it was obvious he was going to take the special chair. "But you get my point," I continued. "This is massively, tremendously unbelievable."

He'd rested his elbows on the chair's arms and had his fingers laced together under his chin. He seemed to be expecting me to say more and when I didn't, he glanced at me to see if I was done, then commented, "Well, Devi, you didn't appear to have too much trouble believing. But then, there *are* extenuating circumstances where you're concerned, eh?" He smiled at me.

Suddenly I was annoyed and I spoke my doubts, *yet again* before I thought. "Just because you had blood in your glasses last night doesn't prove you're *Nosferatu!*"

His smile faded and he gave me a look that I could only interpret as him wondering if I was an idiot. "Is that *really* what you meant to say? Why on earth would we tell you such if it were not fact?"

Okay, so I *was* an idiot. After all, you couldn't mistake his 'vibe' once you knew what he was. I back-peddled. "Well, I just … you know. You have a day to mull things over and you start to doubt."

He leaned forward and took my hand. "Here. Have a feel." And he grabbed my index finger and put it in his mouth, actually on one of his canines. With his other hand, he reached out and placed two fingers on my neck, feeling the blood pulse through the artery. And very slowly, I felt the tooth change. I could *see* the others growing behind his lips.

With wide eyes, I withdrew my hand and took him in with his fangs partially extended. And my first thought, sick as it was, was: *God, he looks good.* My next was: *those are sharper than I'd have thought.* They were thinner too. They began to retract and stopped at normal tooth level but remained much sharper than a normal person's canines; they were sharper than a dog's. I wondered how he didn't gouge himself.

I gave him a weak smile and said, "Okay. Dumb thinking on my part. Sorry."

His lips curled at the corners. "No apology necessary. It *is* hard to believe, to be sure. But I repeat, your own circumstances make it more conceivable, *n'est-ce pas?*" After a moment's thought, I took a long, leisurely drink of my tea and said nothing. His gaze turned to a glare. Finally, he said firmly, "*Devi.*"

I looked up and replied, "Alec. I'm not comfortable discussing this yet."

He eyed me a moment longer, then softened. "All right. I've got a guess anyway. It seems you didn't entirely disappear off the map."

I stood. His prying was pissing me off now. "Look, is there any other reason you're here? Anything *else* I can help you with?"

He regarded me and then asked, "Do you think it appropriate to get in a huff when I come bearing gifts?"

The man was good. I calmed immediately. "Gifts?" I asked, unable to help myself and hoping I was just curious rather than greedy.

"Gifts," he confirmed, languidly reaching into his shirt pocket and pulling out a small black envelope. He handed it to me and added, "I also need to share a little cultural information regarding the Vitaortus."

I looked up from eyeing the little packet and sat back down as I placed it on the coffee table. "What? Share. Please."

He'd been watching my movements and asked, "Aren't you going to see what I've brought you?"

I glanced at the envelope. "Oh. Well, sure. But don't you want to tell me about the plant first?"

He laughed at me, saying, "That's admirable. Plants before perks. Duty before due." Then he shook his head at me.

"Okay. Fine. I'll look." I lifted the black envelope and opened it. Inside was a black *American Express* card. Looking closer, I saw my name and Alec's to the left below the centurion's head. "Um … why do I need this?" I'd heard of these cards but certainly didn't move in those circles.

"It's yours. Use it to *pay* for things." He had that tone one might use for the very feebleminded.

"I get that, *Alec*. But I stay away from credit," I haughtily replied.

"Devi. It's a charge card. I pay it off every month. It's just easier this way. And, I'll also be giving you this." He leaned and pulled another envelope from inside his jacket, which was draped on the other chair. It was a thick packet. "It's cash. Not everywhere takes the card. When you're out, just tell me and we'll replenish your bank." I still had the card in my left hand and he put the fat envelope in my right.

I sat there, hands full, and had flashbacks to times I'd not had a pot to piss in, as they used to say. "What the hell is this card made of? It feels like metal."

"Titanium."

While I shook my head in amazement, Alec seemed content with letting me get it wrapped around this new development. "*Sooo.* What are you saying about this card? You're paying it and I just use it as I want?"

"Yes, both for you and for anything you need to grow a crop of the vines. We need around maybe, oh, fifty of them to start so we can take them various places and then we need a continuous supply on hand. They get fairly large; about twenty-five feet long, I recall. So we need pots and trellises and, of course, a state of the art conservatory with back-up generators. You know. All that sort of thing."

I got wide-eyed and dropped the card and envelope on the table. "Oh my God. What am I going to tell Maria and Serena?!"

He observed me with his left brow raised. "Why, you'll tell them the truth. A wealthy client has contracted you to grow a special herb and is paying for the required items to do so. There's no problem here." I looked at him doubtfully and he raised both brows and gave me a little shake of his head. "*No problem here,*" he repeated with exasperation and the tone again. "Good lord, I'm not used to anyone questioning me. And you appear to do it often. This isn't going to be as simple as I'd hoped." He fell back into the chair.

I shrugged, picked up the fat packet and said, as I was opening it, "Whatever." I smiled a little at him and his eyes closed in mock frustration.

"HOLY SHIT!" I yelped loudly when I saw how much was in the envelope. He didn't react. "Alec. I don't need this much," I pleaded.

"Yes you do," he quietly stated, eyes still closed.

"Why? Why do I? I'm not really very motivated by cash, riches."

He opened his eyes, boring his gaze into me. "Because I need to fulfill any desire you have that might be used by others to *woo* you away. For God's sake, Devi. Spend it on charity if that's what turns you on. I couldn't be minded to care. But," he sat up and leaned toward me, "I need you to commit to me. *To us.*"

Yet again, I stared into his sea-eyes, or maybe leafy eyes, they were so green. "Well here's a question for you then: what's your group's mission statement."

He took me seriously and answered simply, "Not to take innocent human life. And to help our kind, who are in peril."

It seemed noble enough. "And I'm to understand that the Vitaortus will help in this endeavor?"

He raised his brows and nodded. "Immeasurably. It is also a massive bargaining tool … to bring the darker amongst us into more civilized habits. There are possibly only a very few sickly plants left in cultivation. In the entire world, for that matter." I turned my eyes to the three suddenly crucial seedlings.

We were silent for a few moments and then I remembered his other purpose. "So what did you want to tell me about growing the plants?" I decided we were getting comfortable enough with each other that I could pull my legs up and sit cross-legged; after all, he'd hijacked me just before bedtime. I was glad my pajamas were fairly substantial and covered a lot. Many I wore were on the skimpy side.

"Ah yes; one more little present." He reached again for his jacket and searched the pockets, eventually pulling out a small black leather case. He moved closer to me and I leaned forward.

"This is yours now. It's very special, very old. It belonged to some-one who was apparently very much like you. Contrary." I tsked and scowled. He opened it and inside, nestled in velvet, was a silver and gold thimble-looking thing with an oval sharpening stone beside it.

I looked closer. "What is it?"

Alec removed the thimble and that's when the needle attached to it became visible. It was perhaps only half an inch long and sprang from the center of the top of the thimble. With it perched on his index finger (it would only properly fit his pinky), he showed it to me and explained, "It's a prick."

I leaned back quickly. "A prick? *What?*"

He continued turning it this way and that, then grabbed my right index finger. "A blood-letter. You put it on and then prick a finger to draw a drop of blood." He mimed the move.

I looked at him with shock. "Why on Earth would I want to do that?"

After placing the 'prick' on my finger he leaned back and answered, "Because in order for the Vitaortus to continue to grow and thrive past use of what they had stored in the seed, you must feed them. The crucial component is your blood. The Vitaortus is somewhat photoautotrophic but mostly sanguinaheterotrophic. And *only* your blood will work, 'though any blood helps as long as a little of yours is present. And I'd say they'll slow growth once into their third leaves if they don't get a dose."

I was simply awe-stricken by this. "So I have to give them my blood? Like ... like they're *vampire* plants?!"

He appeared to observe me for signs of potential hysteria and carefully answered, "Yes."

I eyed the prick and then my fingers, wondering how in hell the plant had evolved such bizarre needs. But then I realized if Alec could exist, why not the Vitaortus?

"How much?"

"I think just a drop per plant once a week initially, then less as they get older." He watched as I got used the idea by play-acting at stabbing a finger.

"This is the most insane … no, second … maybe third most insane thing I've ever heard." I stopped my movement and looked back at him.

"Albeit, it's critical or they die," he replied.

I got up and asked, "So what, do I just drop a drop in each pot?"

He stood too, then walked to the kitchen. As I followed, he explained that I should put the blood in water. After we'd filled a measuring cup, he took both of my hands and before I could think, he'd stuck my right index finger with the thimble still on my left one.

"*Ow*," I said for effect only. I barely felt it.

He smiled at me, massaged several drops into the water and then turned my finger upright and looked at it. Then, gazing into my eyes, he asked, "May I lick the bowl, Mum?"

I jerked my hand back, whispering, "*Very funny.*"

He laughed and spotted a container of wooden spoons. Pulling one out, he then stirred the water and directed, "Now, just water as usual. I wouldn't mix the regular fertilizer with this. I'm assuming this amount will last through the next five days or so. You're going to have to do this by intuition because the information I have is … sketchy."

I picked up the jug and went out to the bay window. Lifting the lid of the case, I carefully poured some of the blood water onto the soil of each plant. As I did, there was a very slight, odd movement of each and I swear I heard a sigh. I looked to see if Alec was behind me, but he was leaning in the doorway to the kitchen.

"They love you for it," he said.

I looked back at the little plants, seriously doubting the sound or movement I'd imagined. I gently touched each one, then closed the lid. "Is it okay if I put this in the fridge overnight?" I asked as I walked back to the kitchen.

"I should think so," Alec answered, moving out of the way. I smiled up at him as I passed. "Devi? Is saving lives what will motivate you? Because that's what this all means."

It stopped me dead in my tracks and I turned back to gape at him. Something about all of this strangeness suddenly felt familiar. Was I having a déjà vu moment or was it more? The plants felt familiar. The blood felt familiar. *He* felt familiar—like something long-lost.

"Alec, *yes*. But can we just take it a day at a time?"

"Might you accept a night at a time?" And he was gone shortly thereafter.

~

Exactly a week later, I was wearing a little stretchy cotton shift I wore only when expecting ABSOLUTELY no one. It was a Betsey Johnson confection and perfect for feeling good while pottering around the house in summer. But, for one thing, it was bright fuchsia pink, and being a little short for another, it just wasn't appropriate attire for anything other than intimacy or alone-time. Maybe okay in Miami or L.A., but not in conservative Virginia. So, due to Murphy's Law, there was a knock at the door. And not just any knock: it was Alec again.

My lights were on outside, so I could see him through the frosted glass. *Shit*. I stood hesitantly for a moment, unsure of what to do. We had spoken via telephone each evening since his visit and he had *not* mentioned that he'd be coming over again.

His muffled voice said, "Devi. Not only do I feel your presence, but I *see* you. Let me in, these blasted beetles are buzzing 'round and have absolutely no agility. They are pelting me."

June bugs. *Oops!* I opened the door a fraction; enough that I thought he couldn't see my nighty. "Um, Alec, I'm not really dressed for company—"

"Hush, woman, let me in. Honestly, some creatures are without sense at all." He was irritated by the insects, but still managing to be supremely cool (clearly his kind didn't like bugs on them anymore than the rest of us did). While brushing at his jacket, he simply pushed the door open, and me with it. I started to fall back and he grabbed my hand, righting me. "Oopsy-daisy," he said as he walked in, the screen shutting with a hiss behind him. As he moved past me into the room, I noticed one of the fat, reddish-brown beetles had hurled itself to the floor.

I knelt, careful not to let any extra flesh be seen and gently picked the little creature up. It buzzed lightly between my thumb and forefinger. I squinted at its tiny eyes and told it, "Little guy, this is not a safe place." I then opened the screen and gently threw it into flight and into the night.

I turned to find the tall, elegant man considering me. Then he commented, "You are an interesting being, for a modern human. You have immense compassion and recognition." I opened my mouth and took a breath to respond but he then exclaimed, with affected drama, "*And by Jehovah,* such interesting bedclothes."

I looked down at myself then back at him, scowling. "Not to be rude, but what are you doing here?" My voice was low. He raised a perfect red-gold eyebrow, continuing to examine me. Self-consciously, I added, "Um, I'm getting a robe. Come on in, for crying out loud. Don't you call? Make an appointment, or something?"

He suddenly had my hand again. "No, no dear. Be as you are. Think of me as a girlfriend. Eh?" That, and his jesting smile, made me laugh.

"*Oohoho no!*" I said while shaking my head. "I don't think so. I'm sure the girlfriends line right up for you." I turned to head for the stairs, pulling from his warm grip. *Warm grip?* I realized something odd at that moment, but it made perfect sense. I assumed they didn't regulate their temperatures. He was coming into a seventy-five degree house from an eighty-two degree outside. I took his hand and felt it between my palms. Looking up at him, I commented, "That's interesting. You're warmer than inside just now. How long will it take you to cool to the ambient temperature?"

He twisted his hand to grasp my smaller one. Curling our fingers as he brought them to his lips, he answered, uninformatively, "As long as I wish." And he kissed my hand right in the fleshy spot between the thumb and forefinger. A shiver ran through me, stirring hibernating parts and I jerked away to hurry up the stairs before he could see my blush.

Trying hard to be cool when I came back down, robed, I announced, "I'm getting tea. May I get you something?"

Alec surprised me by saying he'd have some tea too. I told him it was chamomile and he simply nodded, comfortable again in the dragon chair. He didn't follow me this time. At the counter, I let out a tense breath and took in a calming one as I made our tea. I yelled out, "Would you like honey?" as I would so a normal person could hear.

His response was just audible to me. "A teaspoon. And you needn't yell."

I put the cups on a tray and added some ginger cookies, in case I needed an activity to cover my nervousness. I took the tray out into the living room, my bare feet silent on the wooden floor and rugs. He looked up from a *Vanity Fair* magazine he'd found by the chair as I carefully placed the tray on the coffee table and then handed him his cup. I stood silently, watching as he put it to his lips to blow on it and wondered if extreme heat bothered them as it did regular people. I was surprised he'd wanted the tea.

"Are you really going to drink that?" I questioned, a little doubtfully.

"Please sit *down*, Devi. Why would I have you make it if I wasn't going to consume it?" *Again with the tone.*

"Excuse me, but you all said you consume for show. It's not a leap for me to wonder." I responded, a tad harshly.

Setting the cup down and lacing his fingers, he scooted forward in the chair and casually turned his face up to me, cocking his head. "*Sometimes*," he said gently and liltingly, "I just want to do what a *normal* human does." And he stared at me meaningfully from those emerald eyes.

I felt chagrinned and quietly said, "Okay," and then backed up and sat on the chaise lounge. I brought my legs up, pulling my robe to strategically cover me, then added an accent pillow to cover my lap. He was silent as I leaned forward and got my tea. I was quite self-conscious as he observed my movements, eyes slowly tracking the various poses I took as I tried to get comfortable. Somehow, that little revelation of his made me less haughty, but I certainly wasn't ready to be 'girlfriends' yet.

He was still sitting forward as he reached for his cup, focused on it and blew, then took a sip. He swallowed and went, "*Ahhh*," as if he'd enjoyed it. I watched his Adam's apple rise and fall.

"Can you taste it?" I ventured.

His eyes opened and shifted to me. "Yes," he said, then took another sip. And a moment later, added, "Not only can I taste the flowers, I can tell that you harvested them recently. They were not yet fully dry. I know that not a single man-made chemical touched them or the earth in which they grew. I know that the honey is local, mostly from what the bees collected from clover. Also from lavender and catmint."

I felt my lips part. He took another sip, then set the cup down and leaned back into the chair. I was speechless for a few moments. Finally, I looked at the cookies and reached for one. Was he kidding? I was afraid to insult him further by asking.

"I picked them two days ago," I offered, flicking my eyes to him.

"Yes, Devi. I know. I can taste you in it," he said quietly. I raised a brow in response. I found that hard to believe. He read it and explained, "Our senses are so acute, we can smell and taste with the same acuity as a shark, or a vulture. Our hearing is not quite that of a cat's, but nearly. Our eyesight is better than a normal human's and we see much better in the dark." He then leaned toward me a little, turning himself in the chair and crossing a leg over the other toward me. He looked very dramatic in the dragon chair, as if it were made for him. "Tell me. Do you find your senses seem more acute than the average person? I'll wager you do."

He held my gaze and I figured *what the hell, why not share?* "Yes. I do. I find the decibels many people speak at a little too much. Loud sounds, strong smells, certain textiles all annoy me. I've always called it my 'Usher syndrome', you know, from—"

He finished my sentence. "The Fall of the House of Usher." Then he laughed and gave me an appreciative smile and nod. "But you're able to appreciate fine flavors, rather than succumb to a bland diet."

"Yes, probably a little too much!"

"And clearly, you are a connoisseur of the richly visual." He swept a hand to indicate the décor of my home.

"Thank you ... why are we talking about this? What are you saying?"

"I want you to know that *I* know some of your secrets. Some you know, some you don't. And I know the *whys* of it all."

I sighed. Part of me couldn't believe I was sitting here sipping chamomile with this amazing being. A deeper, hidden part of me having known something big was eventually going to happen. I'd known it for a long time, because the truth of my secret made it inevitable. I couldn't be the only one. And yet long ago I had accepted that I'd be travelling life's roads essentially *alone*.

And then he reached over and laid the back of his open hand on the pillow over my lap, signaling that I should put my hand in it. I hesitantly did so and he gently folded his fingers around mine. He sure could be a *touchy* guy, as in actual physical contact. I didn't take it as a come-on, merely a form of communication.

Those eyes looked into mine, demanding truth. "Devica Trevathan. What is the *actual* year of your birth?"

Shocked that he'd asked so openly, I jerked and spilled the tea on my pillow and my lap, but he didn't let go; didn't react. I tried to pull my hand from his but he held firm. I felt my heart race and slight nausea swirl like smoke inside my core. Swallowing it and setting the teacup on the coffee table, I then leaned back stiffly.

"Why?"

"Quit stalling. Just answer me. I hear tell you claim to be all of thirty years. But we both know that can't be true. Can it? Why, I was a mere thirty-five when I was transmuted. You'd never know to look at me that I'm over eight-hundred years old. I know the date, Devi. I want *you* to share the secret with me."

"Why?" I asked in a little voice.

"Because . . ." Bringing his other hand to mine, he began massaging my palm and fingers, hitting the pressure points perfectly. It felt really good. Farmers and gardeners know *all* about this. "We're going to be a team, my dear. You will have to confide in me; trust me. We have much to do and there will be things you'll be seeing, things you'll be experiencing, places we'll be going and you'll need to know I'm the one to trust."

He looked at me in a way that set off every alarm I had. *What was he talking about?* I wrenched my hand from his and started to quickly scoot to the other side of the chaise, but in an instant he was on top of me, the length of his body against mine with his right leg bent and his knee on the floor! At the speed of light, he'd grabbed my legs and stretched me out. I had the simultaneous reactions of shock and exhilaration. I could just barely see his canines moving and I shivered.

The truth he was trying to get at by taking this drastic action was the very reason my fear factor levels were way below that of normal people. Especially fear of physical harm—I just didn't have it anymore, or very rarely, anyway. And for a reason I couldn't fully fathom, his behavior seemed more desperate for truth than any desire to harm me.

"*What is the year of your birth?*" he asked in a commanding whisper. His expanding pupils told me he'd climb inside my brain for the answer if he had to. Eventually, when he cocked his head, waiting, I figured I was outmaneuvered. My surprise subsided and my arousal was stuffed *waaay* in the back somewhere, as was the brief thought that I was possibly a little twisted.

"Get off me and maybe I'll tell you," I dead-panned. Then he just kissed the tip of my nose and was in his seat before I could take a breath.

"*Jesus!*" I breathed. And, as he drolly said, "*Hardly,*" I sat up and glared at him.

"I was born in 1880."

"Aha!" He exclaimed. Then he eyed me. "You're still a baby, though."

I gasped. "Alec! I'm god-damned over a hundred and thirty years old. I had to move how many times because I wasn't aging? I've lost everyone who ever mattered to me. I had to abandon them." Suddenly I felt tears brimming. "I've changed who I was so many times … it was so difficult." *Oh my god, I wasn't going to cry in front of him.* "You fucking promised me you wouldn't try to scare me again." I didn't whine exactly, but the complaint came unexpectedly.

"Really, Devi. Your language is atrocious. And I promised no such thing." Though his words admonished, his tone was surprisingly compassionate. It broke my will to hold the tears back.

"That's no way to gain my trust. If you don't promise, you won't have it."

"Then I swear. Solemnly. I truly shall endeavor not to frighten you again."

I believed him because he clearly needed me. The tears fell harder and I was glad he didn't try touching me in a comforting gesture. He just hung his head as he fished for the fabric in the breast pocket of his jacket. Producing a handkerchief, he handed it to me, saying, "I can only imagine how life has been for you these past decades." I stopped dabbing at my face and stared at him over the soft cotton. And for a long moment, we just held the gaze. Whatever I might think, I could see he meant it, the compassion and empathy.

"Alec?" He ticked his head gently and raised a brow ever so slightly, never breaking eye contact. I tried to continue, but breathed in three rapid breaths like a toddler who's just had a crying fit. It made him smile reassuringly. "Alec. You are the first person to really know outright. Ever. In my entire life."

Theda had appeared and approached him for a pet, then meowed at me with concern. He glanced at her and reached so his fingers could caress her chin and cheeks. "It's alright, love," he said, and I had no idea if he was saying so to me or her. But it didn't feel all right.

"It's been a long, strange journey. There's been good and not so good; but living with the secret has kept me ultimately apart from others. And before that, my husband ... *he ... he* ...."

Alec's head jerked up and he focused on me again. "You were in Bedlam."

I nodded. I didn't care how he knew. Bedlam—Bethlam—Bethlahem Royal Hospital; whatever one called it, it had not been a happy place. "I was there for four years. I didn't do so well at first, after I was released; I'd only ever lived in India before that. I didn't know how to survive like this. Never aging or dying or even becoming ill."

He nodded and I could tell he was completely in agreement, perhaps remembering some of his own early experiences. He said, "I must say, your countenance does not reveal despair. Do you wear a mask or have you found some measure of peace?"

Wiping my eyes and with a sniff, I answered, "I've found *some* peace, though I'm still in the dark. What am I? It took many decades; in fact, it's only been the last twenty years that I've felt relatively okay. Well, and the first thirty. But honestly, before you and Georges, I figured I was destined to live a life with lots and lots of loss. I mean, I've no clue of my longevity. But, I might actually be able to have friends … even if they are, um …." I searched for a word that wasn't a synonym for living-dead, or whatever they were.

But then Alec stood and gestured for my hands. Lifting me from the couch, he gave me a peck on the forehead and then let go and picked up our teacups. "You have new friends and you will acquire many more around the world. And you'll learn about the mysterious you, and how to live as an immortal *prime channel*—for you *are* like us." He then took the cups to the kitchen, adding as he walked, "Well, as immortal as anyone *can* be."

That last comment struck me as funny. I sat back down, laughing silently, thinking how bizarre this would all be if I hadn't just lived over a century, most of it in a body that never aged past the late-twenties.

Theda jumped onto the chaise and got on my lap. Just as she settled, Alec returned and decided to sit again, but next to me. "I promise you, all will be revealed. You'll have friends, answers and an even fuller life than the lovely one you've created. You're not alone. And honestly, you'll probably become a bit of a celebrity, at least in certain circles. But I would be remiss if I didn't tell you there are potential enemies." I searched his eyes, not yet afraid. "They'll want you. Some may even want to harm you."

Okay. Now I felt some trepidation. "You could have told me this before."

"I could have. Would it keep you from helping us?"

"How much danger are we talking about here?" His look told me he was gauging how to respond. I started to get agitated.

"There are, as with humans, good and bad elements in our community. I think of *us*, our little fraternity, as good guys. We truly try to cause no harm and in fact advance the well-being of humans. But there are many others. Some are … of a different mindset. And then there are the other species—"

"Other species?!"

"Yes. There are different species. *I* am a sort of hybrid of North American and European human species."

"Hybrid?"

"Yes. It's a long story not for telling just now; perhaps when I share about the acquiring of my *scent*. My point being that there is an entire matrix of relationships and issues. Some of the beings are quite primitive and impossible to even reason with. And some of the more civilized will absolutely want to drink from you. Because of what makes you able to grow the Vitaortus. They will want it from the source."

"What am I getting into? Will I be looking over my shoulder all the time? Christ. You've high-jacked me!"

His eyes showed some regret. "I suppose there is truth in that statement. But with us, you'll be treated like a treasure. Many of the others would simply force you. That's probably the main reason your predecessors have perished. I cannot, in good conscience, lead you a merry dance. It is only right to inform you of the dangers."

Life had been one long lesson in acceptance versus control. Here was the final exam. Or so it seemed.

Alec appeared to take my silence as acquiescence and said, "I think I shall bring in someone to teach you a few things, so you may feel more self-reliant, despite our protections. The one I have in mind is quite good. And you seem very fit, so really, it's just some maneuvers you need to learn. And perhaps he can act as a bodyguard for a little while, until we have a better picture of the general reaction."

I had never had an occasion that made me feel the need to learn self-defense. Had I been lucky or was the universe looking out for me, as I'd so often wondered before? Since my twenty-seventh year, there hadn't been a single incident which had turned into anything physically dangerous, as if I had a protective shield. It was a major thing I took for granted now, but which made my life more bearable. Now Alec was telling me that was all about to change.

But I knew nothing came without its price. Would the chance of sharing truth, depth and 'immortal' life be worth the potential danger?

†

As he drove away in his smaller Maybach coupe, Alec did not congratulate himself on pulling the information out of Devi. He'd impatiently resorted to a little of that forceful behavior he now tended to dislike, at least with innocent persons. But she hadn't been entirely unwilling. He suspected that there would be relief for her, especially given that she'd carried alone the secret of her agelessness for so long.

How tragically lonely, he thought. Yet he marveled at her resilience. She still managed to retain some of that amazing quality that teen-aged girls, young women and some older ones carried. A life force and enthusiasm that was intensely charming, deeply contagious and healingly inspiring. It had been eons since he'd been around it and he hadn't realized how much it had been missed.

His life of late had been very 'men without women', at least since the death of one of his progeny, Leonora, nearly fifteen years ago. He didn't socialize regularly with any of his kind that lived here, other than his progeny, which he considered Gordon to be as well. Axel lived in Paris and had plenty of female companionship, but he did not bring them here. They tended to be of a rather dark demeanor and jaded. Georges had many interesting friends, a few of whom were female, but generally Georges' tastes ran rather gay. Alec found that they were as bad as, or worse even, than women around him, competing for his attention and affection. So he usually avoided them as well. Such things were as they were; he could not change his appeal and the attention he unintentionally garnered was mostly irritating.

Gordon never brought women around either, which was probably best. He would occasionally go out with Alec's most recent progeny, Jack, and together they would meet girls. Gordon didn't live a life that made having a girlfriend very simple, although Alec assumed he had a few 'acquaintances with benefits'. It was only right, too. He was an extremely handsome and virile man. Jack and Gordon together were probably an unbeatable team.

As for Alec himself, he could barely remember when he'd last felt *desire*. He found it interesting that, so long ago, his living human adulthood had been spent mostly as a celibate. But through the centuries as an immortal he'd come to view such vows as missing the point. Yet it didn't matter. Now, he found the endless cycle of loss more noticeable than the enjoyment he'd received or love he'd felt. No one had managed to pique his interest in so long it was astounding. Most of his kind were too dark in their demeanor to attract him, and humans were simply too short-lived.

What he found interesting about Devi was that she did not seem to find him overly attractive or intimidating. Or if she did, it didn't show. She appeared relatively comfortable with him and stayed herself, neither attempting to preen for him, behave shyly or pretend.

Yes, when he *tried* to intimidate her, she ceded power ever so slightly, but not as most beings did. And there was a little spice thrown in: her genial combativeness. It surprised him that he enjoyed it.

It was apparent that she followed her own rules and bowed to no authority, *not even money*. He suspected it was not simply mindless rebellion, but rather her code of ethics. It was a welcome change and he found he respected her, even with her somewhat girlish demeanor. His role in her life put him right back as whom and what he'd been before he'd been turned nearly eight hundred years ago: protector and facilitator.

Happiness poked its way through the frozen crust of his stoicism. This new development was like hitting the refresh button; new meaning, new motivations, new experience. His desire to continue his long existence required such from time to time. It felt good. In fact, it felt good just to *feel*. His stoicism was no act and had grown over time to take over most of his being. He did feel a form of compassion, though never when acute stupidity was involved. And when he hunted as a wolf or other creature, he felt the thrill, but beyond that, only affection for those close to him or irritation at the world. That was it. His range of emotions had grown very narrow. Even the bloodlust had died. So yes, the warmth of joy felt good, indeed. Perhaps these last days of his 'life' could be spent pleasantly and meaningfully.

ʊ

In the deepest part of the night, long after Alec had gone, my subconscious decided to go rummaging around inside the dusty trunks of my past. Deep beneath the pile of memories, one in particular was pulled out, dusted off and replayed.

My husband stood there, red in the face from shouting at me.

"That bloody witchdoctor will not leave! I told you to pack him off. And now I see the truth of it. You're the bloody witch he's doctoring! Now I know what your parents and their bloody Theosophist friends cooked up all those years ago with their devil worship: it was YOU!"

I shook my head vehemently, not entirely sure that some part of what he was saying wasn't true, but deathly frightened of what he might do. Tears began to fall and I begged, *"Please just listen to me. There are things I need to tell you, but I don't—"*

He interrupted harshly, *"You will shut your mouth! I cannot live with this evil. You are a demon. There is no other explanation. You are a demon!"* He then forced me into my dressing room and locked me in. Several hours later, he opened the door and two men were with him along with the doctor who had known me from my birth. The man was old, but not so old that he couldn't administer a hefty dose of laudanum as I tried to resist.

The doctor said, *"I'm so sorry Devica, but it's for the best. Something's just not right here."*

The last thing my husband said to me before the men carried me off was, *"Do not ever, ever try to contact us. I will absolutely have you killed, do you understand? You are dead now. You committed suicide. Do you understand? Never, ever contact us."*

Shock and despair ripped me apart just before I went mercifully unconscious.

When the laudanum wore off, I sobbed until I was unable to anymore, or until the next onslaught. An ocean sent its waves to rise and fall around me, and my tears were lost in it. And I had no idea where the ship I'd awoken on was taking me.

SIX

Roomie

ʊ

A week passed, and one hour after the sun had vanished behind the Shenandoah Mountains, I saw the lights of a car illuminating my drive. It was a smaller Maybach, looking chic and understated. Another came in soon behind it and was ridiculously cool. Metallic black and sleek, it was also definitely not of U.S. origins.

Peeking out the window, I glanced at my hideous truck, which I loved, and the compact Korean make I used for regular getting around. *Whatever,* I wasn't here to win the suave and fashionable contest, which I'd lose, hands down, to these creatures.

This thought was confirmed as I watched the two men get out of their handsome autos. Alec was simply elegant as he casually eased his linen-suited body out of the large, dark silver coupe. His comrade was wonderfully contrasting: black sports car, black clothes, black hair. He was out of his vehicle in a quick motion, adjusting his jacket and cuffs as he walked over to Alec. After pulling classic Ray Bans down a little as he stared over them, right at me, a line of that '80s song about wearing sunglasses at night played in my head.

I jumped back a little from the window, then decided to delete my embarrassment by just opening the door. By the time I was out on the porch, they were coming up the steps. When they reached the top, they stood together, exactly the same height.

"Hi," I said, with a smile.

"Good evening, Devi," Alec greeted (I'd left off the light until they'd gotten there so the insects would be scarce). "I bring you a new friend. This is Jack Garrity. Jack, meet Devica Trevathan."

Jack removed his dark glasses in a clean move with his left hand and came forward with his right extended. I gripped it firmly and said, "Nice to meet you, Jack. Won't you both come in?" I stepped to the side and gestured toward the door.

Jack gestured in return. "After you, ma'am." He was American.

After a shaking of heads when I asked if they wanted anything, we sat around the coffee table, Alec choosing the dragon chair, naturally. Jack put his glasses in his inside jacket pocket like any normal man would do. He seemed more *human* than Alec, but still an imposing presence. I really liked the way he was dressed: black suit, black shirt, black tie. With his black, swept back hair and very white skin, he was just super cool-looking; far more 'vampiric' in the classic sense than Apollo-like Alec. I found myself smiling at Jack and he cracked a small half-smile back at me.

Realizing I couldn't just keep staring at him, I clasped my hands in my lap and looked at Alec, who had an amused expression on his face.

"So Devi. We came to a unanimous conclusion: you are a precious, unique commodity." At my frown he quickly added, "That's how others will view you as well. We need to protect you. Jack is the absolute best at it. And he'll stay here for a while and train you in some special arts." Jack nodded his agreement. "He is the only one we have brought into our little club in the past century."

I looked at Jack with renewed interest. No wonder he seemed different. He was modern. "When were you born?" I asked.

He raised his dark, arched brows at me. "Do you want my live birth date, or my turned birth date?" he asked, seemingly amused and impressed at my forwardness.

"Well, both, out of curiosity."

"Okay. I was born in 1954 and was reborn in '84." His deep-brown eyes searched mine for a motive in my asking.

Instead of providing one, I turned to Alec and asked, "How is this supposed to work?"

Alec observed me as if I were mentally challenged, and then answered unhelpfully, "He's going to stay here with you for a bit." Glancing at Jack, who'd leaned back with his hands laced over his midsection and was watching me, I scowled. Alec insisted, with a little exasperation, "You have a four-bedroom home, Devi. There's sufficient space."

"That's not the problem, Alec. I live as a single woman with two others on the property who are pretty strict Catholics. They matter. I need them. They know I don't have a boyfriend. How do I explain this?" I gestured at Jack, who actually laughed, but didn't move or add anything.

"Devi, darling. Look at him. They'll believe you if you say he's your new suitor. If he's down in the day, they'll not think of him."

I countered, "What about his car?" Cute as he was, Maria and Serena had only known me as a 'good' girl. They were man-less women and Maria, though only forty-five, seemed content to stay that way. I think she thought I was a kindred spirit. She'd definitely wonder what that gorgeous car was doing here all the time.

A saving grace was that they rarely came into the house and would never enter a room with a closed door if they did. I let out some breath and looked at Jack. He was just gazing at me; an inno-cent face on a lethal creature. I had no doubt he'd been a hit man or something. He was too quiet. He seemed quieter and able to sort of blend into the air in a way none of the others I'd met could. He'd had to have brought the skill over with him to be better than Alec; not that a room full of searching ladies wouldn't spot him immediately.

My hair was down and I pulled it back and held it for a moment on top of my head as I thought. How the hell was I going to have him in the house and explain it? Both men watched my movements. "You can just be an old friend here for an extended visit; maybe a writer? So I wouldn't have to explain your being inside during the day."

Jack's eyes moved from my hair to my eyes. "I'm writing during the day."

"Yes, but eventually they'll get suspicious. They aren't stupid."

Alec spoke up. "Perhaps we can have the car moved to the estate from time to time so they don't suspect your constant presence."

Jack looked at him, nodding in agreement, then said, "Yeah, well, Devi's got her interesting little vehicles." His brows bounced up a little critically.

I *had* to respond. "Hey! Some of us have to make do. I don't know anyone who could afford those crazy things you two drove here. Honestly. Anyway, I need practical, not sexy."

He laughed and Alec said, "Devi, Perhaps. But you *deserve* sexy." Jack's left eyebrow rose again and he nodded lightly. I flushed, not really knowing what Alec meant. "Besides, you could afford one now."

I just shook my head and said, "Who needs one? You all seem to have plenty. I can just borrow one of yours."

Alec shook his head at me in return. "Buy a decent automobile for Christ's sake." I felt sure he knew I would completely disregard that command. Then he abruptly presented me with a *fait accompli*. "So which room will be Jack's? I've got to get Gordon over here with his sleep paraphernalia."

I figured I'd find out soon enough what 'sleep paraphernalia' was, so I got up and stood in front of Jack, having surrendered. "Come on. I'll give you a tour. I sure hope you're easy to live with."

I looked back at Alec, who nodded approvingly and said, "I've got business waiting. Do you mind my leaving you in Jack's extremely safe hands?"

"I'm seriously doubting I have a real choice."

"Good girl," he said, and before I knew it, he was planting a cool kiss on my cheek. "My thanks, Jack." And he was out the door.

After watching Alec leave, I looked at my new roommate, who asked, as he watched the Maybach coupe disappear around the bend, "So, do you have continuous fencing around the property? We came through a gate."

"Yes. It's really to keep our birds in ... and the deer out."

"That's good, but I really need to check it. I think we may have to replace it with something stronger." He'd turned to me and was looking at the stairs to the second floor.

"You know?" I said. "I'm gonna have to come up with some stories ... because this is all too much. My property-mates are seriously going to wonder what's going on. A lot of changes so soon."

"Yeah," he agreed. "Because we'll also be installing some serious security, including cameras. Those can be really tiny now. Very unobtrusive. But the fence will be noticeable."

As I led the way up the stairs, I stopped and he caught himself before bumping into me. "Okay, Jack," I said, turning halfway to find that I was two steps up and only just a little higher than him. "Alec hasn't told me the real deal. Are you? Going to share, I mean. After all, it's my life here. Security cameras?"

He smiled and searched my face, tilting his head back a little as if focusing. "Sure, Devi. You won't like it, but yes, if one has possible enemies, then one should definitely know about them. And you, well, *we*, will definitely have enemies, once they find out about you. And they will. But it's no one specific yet. There are a lot of clans."

"Clan?" Turning to continue to the landing, I asked, "Is that the term? Like a pod, or a herd, or a pack?"

He laughed. "Yeah. Or something like that. Just like the idea of a Scottish family clan, or better yet, a tribe. Most in it are related by who turned them. But really, within reason, any can join. I just use 'clan'. The term *family* is probably used more often. It crosses the language barriers."

At the top of the stairs was a long, wide hall. There was a master bedroom at each end and two smaller ones in between as well as an extra bathroom. Each master had its own bathroom. Jack had figured out the plan immediately and went to the extra master bedroom.

"I'll take this one," he announced from its threshold. After taking in the décor, he commented, "You have an interesting house. It's kind of museum-like." He turned to me and saw the look on my face and hurriedly added, "In a very comfortable and cool way. Sort of Bohemian. I like it. You have a lot of books." He looked at the rows of thin shelves along the walls of the hall which stored some of my library.

I decided to just be open about it. "I've acquired things through the years. I've always loved books. I've had a long time to collect."

Eyes back on me, he admitted, "I've never met an immortal that wasn't one of us."

He startled me with that. "Jack. I don't know that I'm immortal." The thought was very nearly frightening. But then what was I?

"Alec says you're like us. That you have incredible longevity; there have been others like you but they have wound up dying, partly because they were … mistreated. They haven't told me about it all yet. Hey, I didn't even know about the vine until last year."

He came out into the hall. A book on a lower shelf caught his eye and he squatted to see it. He was lithe and limber for such a tall man. Pulling the book from between its mates, he then opened it for a quick look at the copyright date. "This is a first edition," he announced, gazing up at me.

"Yes. I bought that in London, when it came out."

"Very cool." He raised himself in a swift move that almost looked unreal and walked back to the room and carefully placed the book on the bed. When he turned to me, he realized something and asked, "Is it okay if I read it? I promise I'll be careful."

I laughed. "Of course. They're dying to be read again. I haven't read that since I bought it. As a first edition! But I have to say, I wouldn't have guessed you'd be a fan of Waugh."

"Well. Things change. Interests change when you're looking at a future full of *time*. I've been into exploring the 1920s lately. And you shouldn't judge a book by its cover. Waugh's interesting." He came back out and gazed at me with those lively dark eyes.

"I'm gonna run down and get my bags from the car."

"Okay. I'll get you some towels," I replied, with a smile and amused shake of my head. He seemed just like a normal person, but I could unquestionably feel the supernatural vibrations emanating from him.

As I opened the linen closet and pulled out a set of towels, I marveled at how much had happened; how much the world had changed in such a short span of time. When I had read the book lying on Jack's new bed, telephones and phonographs were the high tech home gizmos. Movies were still mostly silent. Stockings were made of silk, so you could pull them on with a sensual smoothness, or unroll them up your leg. And I had turned forty-nine years old. I was also not yet living in America and hadn't been out of Bethlem long.

I was downstairs again when Jack came back in. He carried a suit bag, a medium-sized case, and a black metal container about three feet by two feet and a foot deep. I had a feeling I didn't want to know what was in *that* one. By the time he'd taken them upstairs, it was ten-thirty. Half an hour later, we were sitting again in the living room when he moved his head as if listening. He said, "Gordon's here."

I got up and opened the front door, but no one was there. I stared into the dark and a few moments later, I saw headlights as a Land Rover Defender came around the bend. I turned my head to Jack, who was lounging on the chaise.

"Okay. *Now* he's here," he corrected.

I smiled and turned back, turning on the light and opening the storm door. I was looking forward to seeing Gordon again.

Jack was beside me in a flash and then hopped down the stairs. As Gordon emerged, Jack said, "Hey Gordo, thanks."

Gordon smiled a genuine wide smile and it was obvious they were friends. Gordon's smile was breathtaking. Looking past Jack at me, he waved, continuing to flash beautiful teeth. "Hello Miss Trevathan."

I stayed at the door to hold it open, but I couldn't help giving a wide grin back, "Hi Gordon."

He opened the back of the Rover and pulled a long, sleek, black pod from it. When it was at the edge of the vehicle Jack grabbed a handle at the other end and together they deftly maneuvered it up the front steps. I opened the door and they carried it through the house and upstairs. It seemed like it might be light enough for one person to carry, but its size made it unwieldy. I noticed the rear of the Rover was still open and went down to shut it. A large black bag occupied the space next to where the pod had been, looking like maybe it too was for Jack, so I waited.

When they emerged, I asked, "Do you need this bag too?" But neither man answered, because, in unison, their gazes were diverted behind me to my left. I turned and saw Serena, in her robe.

"Oh my goodness!" I rushed over to her, concerned. "Did we wake you up?!" I asked, putting my arm around her.

"No. No. But I heard the truck and saw lights. Is everything Okay?" she asked, squinting at the men as they came down the stairs of the porch.

"Oh yes. This is Gordon and Jack. They work for Mr. Gregory. They're helping with the greenhouses and … stuff. Jack's going to stay here in the house. To …." I searched for the story, but Jack finished it.

"To coordinate things, Señora Rivera. There are things we need on the property and I'll be making sure that happens correctly." He gave her a smooth smile, which didn't seem to reassure her. I wondered how he knew her last name and it occurred to me that he probably knew a lot about me too.

But when Gordon came forward and stuck out his hand with that dimpled smile and those deep blue eyes of his, she melted. "I'm Gordon, Señora. If I can help you with anythin', just tell Miss Trevathan and I'll be here in a jiffy. I know you ladies are self-sufficient, but a man's help couldn't hurt, eh?" Serena was putty. His sing-songy accent helped. He could work it with old ladies too and he knew it.

She tutted, put her hand over his, then peeked around him at Jack. She was tiny compared to them. She then gave me a weird look, causing Gordon to glance at me worriedly. Finally Serena smiled up at him and said, "So nice to meet you both. Thank you,

Gordon. I'll go back to bed. 'Night, Devi." And she turned and ambled back to the cottage.

Once I knew she was out of earshot, I let out a huge sigh. "Thank God she didn't come when you had the—what was that, a coffin?"

Gordon laughed and Jack smiled, saying, "Kinda. But you'd never bury anyone in it. It's a sleeper. If it's too bright in a bedroom."

"Well, it was pretty snazzy looking. Do you need this bag?"

Gordon looked in the Rover. "Oh yeah, it's the bed canopy. I assumed you'd want both."

"Definitely. Thanks." Gordon hauled it out and handed it to Jack, who immediately went to take it in.

I watched as Gordon shut the back door of the SUV, then he turned to me, the porch-light glinting off of his smooth, shiny head. His eyes took in me, then the house and then all of the property. "You've a lovely home here, Miss Trevathan."

"Thanks, Gordon. You can call me Devi." Seeming to disregard what I'd just said, he looked through the dark to where the cottage was. He nodded once at it and said, "I think your missuz might know a thing or two about the world of secrets."

I frowned at him and asked, "Meaning?" I moved to sit on the steps and he joined me.

"Her response to Jack was noticeable. I'm only sayin' there's somethin' there. She recognized him, or what he is."

"*No way*," was all I could say.

"Well, I could be wrong. But I've been with both humans and vampires all my life. She knows somethin'. I'm goin' to let Mr. Gregory know about it." At the look on my face, he quickly added, "But don't worry, it'll all be fine. It's probably nothin'." I looked hard at him, knowing he was just placating me. His pretty blue eyes squinted as he smiled. "Really, Miss Trevathan." And he pulled out the dimples again. Though maybe not supernatural, he certainly had powers.

I watched as his arms, shoulders and chest muscles moved under his dark blue t-shirt when he folded his arms. Then I looked back at his eyes and he grinned even broader. *Oh Jesus*. "Um. Can I get you a glass of water or something? A beer? I have *Newcastle Brown Ale*."

"Well, that's temptin', Newkie Brown, but I'm expected." He got up and walked tentatively down the stairs. "I did mean that about the help when you need it. They're down durin' the day so it's on me when you need somethin'. And I'm not just sayin' that because it's orders." He gave me a sincere look.

"Well, I don't know how to contact you directly," I replied.

Reaching into his back jeans pocket, he pulled out his phone. After tapping the screen, he put it to his ear. I heard mine ring in the house, but didn't move. When it stopped ringing he said, "Hello Miss Trevathan. Gordon here. Handy man extraordinaire." He hung up. "Now you do." Then he flashed the grin and added, "Tell Jack I said 'bye. I'll see you soon, when the glasshouse stuff gets here."

I stood and walked up the stairs to the porch, my eyes on him the whole way as he climbed into the Land Rover. "Bye, Gordon", I said in a high voice, knowing he couldn't hear me, and waved. He started the vehicle's engine, backed up and drove off.

Ugh. It was almost painful. *Too cute*, I thought. Then, as I entered my house, I saw Jack coming down the stairs. I wondered if I was going to get through a week without sleeping with someone!

Luckily, the only reason I got in Jack's bed was to try out his canopy. It was an odd contraption that fit over the bed like a tall pup tent, or more like a dome tent. He'd let me get in to see how light-tight it was and it was pretty amazing. He held a flashlight right up against the material and I'd not seen even the slightest glow. The material was so light and so opaque that I was surprised it was breathable, which he actually commented on and I wondered why he cared, if he didn't really *breathe*. Still, we shut up the blinds and curtains on the windows as tightly as possible.

We said goodnight to each other after I formally welcomed him, and was surprised I fell asleep so quickly with someone in my house who was, essentially, a blood-sucking stranger.

~

The next day, Maria, Serena and I were inside Greenhouse Three, potting-up herbs we'd sown several weeks prior. We'd only just gotten set up, and before I could begin some explanations of last night, Serena commented, "That Mr. Gordon seems like a very nice young man … do you like the other … Mr. Jack?"

I knew Serena well enough to understand that was a loaded question. I was confused by her potential aversion to him. They'd met Alec two nights before he'd brought Jack, and both had been riveted by him. I felt fairly sure that they were impressed and I'd felt no bad vibes then. Perhaps he'd mesmered them without my realizing.

I chose my words carefully. "Well, I don't know him too well yet, but he seems very nice. Mr. Gregory thinks very highly of him and wants him to supervise some the changes we'll be having on the property, especially the security."

Maria's head shot up. "Security? What?"

I maintained my nonchalance. "Those vines sitting in my house are worth a fortune. They're incredibly rare. The people who use the herb pay big bucks for it. So, Mr. Gregory asked if he could put security in. Are you guys okay with that? I guess I should have run it by you first. I'm sorry. It's such a great opportunity and everything has happened so fast."

Serena put her hand on my arm. "You don't need to say sorry. It's *your* place."

Maria squinted at me, not quite as easily placated. "Who are we keeping out? Are those Vitaortus … illegal?"

"No. No," I rushed to say. "Like I said, they're so rare and apparently it's hard to germinate the seeds. And grow them. Maybe most people just don't know about it."

"What do they use it for?" Maria asked.

"I don't know much yet, but I think it helps people with compromised immune systems, or something. I need to find out more."

"So what's this security going to be? And which greenhouse will the plants go in?

"That's the other thing. We're putting in three more greenhouses." Both women stopped what they were doing and gaped at me. "Yeah, really fancy ones! Pretty, fifteen by fifty glass structures. You'll love them. Gordon's going to supervise." That set Serena's mind right at ease and she told Maria to hush when she tried to grill me some more.

I hoped they'd accepted my explanations, because it was all going to happen whether they agreed or not. I felt some guilt over the small lies of omission. But did it matter what the men really were or what the vine was really helping to do? I only knew that *I* was now on a mission to bring the Vitaortus back from the brink of extinction.

~

It was past early evening, the sun having just dipped below the highest visible ridge. Fireflies were gently hovering about a foot or so off the ground as they began their nightly journey to adorn the crowns of oaks and maples and poplars—the original fairy lights. Jack and I were sitting on my back porch, about to have our respective dinners—or maybe breakfast, for him. He had been here a week now and we were meshing well as we got to know each other's ways as 'roommates'. He was easy-going, thoughtful and I even forgot he was there several times. He claimed to be working on something in my basement that would be revealed soon.

As I took my first bite of salad, I eyed him in his black jeans, Dr. Martin's brogues and black t-shirt. "Do you have clothes in any other color?" I queried, half-joking.

He grinned. It was really charming, but there was something dangerous about him too. Alec and he looked only a few years apart in age, but their mannerisms and movements were *worlds* apart, making Alec seem older, or perhaps more leader-like.

Jack had a wineglass and two small vials of dark liquid in his hands that he was gently clinking together. Finally he pulled a plastic cork off one and poured it into the glass, then repeated with the other. There were probably six ounces of blood. I watched as he took a small sip. He clearly enjoyed it, because he closed his eyes for a long moment.

"Bon appétit," I said.

"Thanks," he replied, raising his glass. "You too." And he took another sip, savoring it.

After chewing another mouthful, I asked, "Where are you keeping those? Surely they need to be refrigerated."

"In your 'fridge." He toasted me again. "I put them in the cheese and meat drawer; hope that's okay."

I had been in that drawer since he'd arrived and not noticed. I had a feeling he was keeping them hidden under my lunch meat and cheeses, maybe in case Maria or Serena came in, which they wouldn't. "Absolutely. Whatever you need. Within reason, of course." He smiled and I ventured, "So how many and how often do you need those?"

Putting his hand to the base of the glass, he eyed it as he twisted it. "I need about three in a twenty-hour period. It's become much less. At first, I'd wake up each evening just starving. I'd be ravenous. It was like an addiction too—I couldn't really control myself. It's a good thing Alec and others were around and keeping me fed. I can't imagine what I'd have done in that first decade. Not good. Not pretty." I took bite of avocado as he continued. "They never once let me out of sight. For ten years, the only time I was alone was when I slept, and even then there was monitoring. Or I'd be locked in."

"Whoa," I said around another mouthful. "Did it bother you?"

He stopped staring at the glass and turned to focus on me. "Only when I wanted . . ." He decided not to continue and I didn't press.

"Were you scared?" I asked, wondering if it was too familiar a question.

But he answered, "Hell yeah. But I was also ecstatic. Gregory and company had hired me beforehand, but I didn't realize what they were. I'd done several jobs for them before I actually met Alec. And he had a woman with him. She and I took one look at each other and it was love at first sight. *Leonora.* God, she was the most beautiful, amazing thing I've ever seen." He'd gone back to twisting the wineglass from its base.

Then he took another sip and I asked, "What did Alec think?"

"Well he was happy for her. He was her *genitor* so he helped her explain to me who and what they were, after we'd dated for a while. Funny, I just thought she had crappy circulation because she usually felt a little chilly. It was pretty freaky at first; they had to show me some moves before I believed them. But she wanted him to turn me. She loved me. I loved her. And I had no one, no family."

Crazy as it was, he made it sound remarkably normal. But I suddenly got the feeling this story was going to have a tragic end. Leonora was nowhere in sight and no one else had mentioned her. "What happened?" I hoped they'd just fallen out of love.

His expression grew sad and he narrowed his eyes a little as he looked into the flame of the candle, "She was murdered. Killed by assassins . . ." He glanced at me. "Fifteen years into my new eternal life with the love of my life and she gets her head chopped off. Right in front of me."

I gasped and put my hand to my mouth. "Oh my God! Jack!"

"I got both the mother-fuckers though, which ended their ability to kill us for a while. It seems those were the only supposedly knowledgeable agents, because there hasn't been an incident since."

The last statement baffled me. "What? Why would vampires not know how to kill vampires?"

Jack replied, "Oh, they weren't vampires. They were humans." After seeing the confusion on my face, he added, "There are very small groups that know about us. I have a hunch that they were sent by a group we've been looking into; one that's based here. Well, in DC."

My heart hurt for Jack in that moment. The horror of facing eternity without the one you became eternal for was not too hard for me to understand. I had lost loves too. Very important loves. Love and loss had become synonymous. The hope brought by these immortals who'd come into my life had just been smashed to smithereens. Even an 'immortal' love could vanish.

I leaned back and felt my throat go tight.

Then he put his hand back on the glass, gripped it, and downed the rest. "Don't worry, I'll find them and that'll be all she wrote.

"You'll kill them?!"

"Not unless it's absolutely necessary, although I'll have to fight the urge. They can easily be destroyed though. They're so clandestine and hypocritical, it doesn't take much to catch them or set them up. Arrogant hypocrisy makes for an easy target. As far as killing, Alec tries to steer clear of it, but he didn't hire me and then turn me for nothing. Certainly not only for Leonora's sake; his mind works in a bigger way than that.

"This particular group was started many decades ago and even had deep sympathies with the Nazi's. They have no clue of anything but their own ideals, which are to create a global, Americanized, fundamentalist plutocracy. So, once they discovered the money and global influence flowing through the hands of Alec and company, they wanted involvement. I guess they poked around and found out more than they'd bargained for."

"Do they actually know the truth?" I asked, surprised.

"Maybe. But not really. I think they're still researching. I doubt they've found actual proof of what we are. But obviously they're assuming it. The two men who killed Leonora actually had crucifixes. When that didn't work, they threw holy water. After *that* failed, one shot me in the head and I went down for a moment. They shot Leonora, and then got to her before I could, and with a special blade, it was done."

I must've changed color or something, because he asked, "Should I have told you any of this? Why *did* I tell you this?" He scratched his head.

"Probably not." I answered with a thin smile. "Alec hasn't mentioned any of it, but he's fairly *mysterioso* anyway. It's a lot to take in … I haven't had much violence in my life." We were silent for a moment, then I asked, "When will you start teaching me things?"

He immediately said, "Tomorrow. Tonight, there's just enough time to watch a movie I found in your collection. Are you interested? Before you go to bed? It'll be nice to watch it with someone who was at least born in the industrial age!"

"Which one?"

He grinned and said in a stage whisper, "*Metropolis*."

~

The next night I discovered that Jack had turned my basement into a studio, of sorts. He'd placed spot lights in each of the corners so that the big room was well-lit. The black and white linoleum floor was bright and shiny and I wondered if he'd actually scrubbed and polished it himself after I went to bed last night. I never used the room because I disliked basements, especially in the humid environment of the mid-Atlantic part of North America. But he'd obviously worked hard to clean it and we needed the large, hidden space.

"Voila!" he said, raising his hands.

"Wow. Excellent job! It looks like a dance floor."

"And that's just what it is. Here ... ." He walked over to a small cabinet, opened it, and pulled out a pair of my shoes.

"What the—?" I said as I reached out and took them. They were three-inch Mary Janes I'd worn in the '40s, specifically for dancing. He must have recognized them for what they were. Suddenly I scowled as I looked up at him and accused, "You went in my closet!"

He made a gesture and face suggesting, '*Duh*', and then turned and went back to the cabinet, saying, "Put them on. Great closet you got, by the way."

I watched him squat to retrieve something and slid my slippers off, demanding, "Ask me next time!" I set the shoes down and stuck my foot into the first one and bent to fasten the strap. I repeated the moves and stood straight just as Jack walked back to me. He was carrying a long flat box. Eyeing my feet over it, he nodded and then held the black leather case out for me to open. There was a brass fastener and I lifted it and then the lid. Inside, was a sword-like object the likes of which I hadn't seen in a very long time. "It's a *khopesh*."

Jack explained, "Yep. It will be your weapon of choice, at least for certain types: those that are unkillable by guns and such."

I was confused and scowled at him. He swiveled the box and stood next to me so we could both examine the weapon. "What do you weigh? One-twenty? One-thirty?" I just nodded, unwilling to give the actual number. He was in the ball park. "There's no way you can beat one of us using normal fighting techniques, even if you are stronger than a normal human. You have to learn special defensive moves and you need a weapon that uses little force to produce major results, i.e., the *khopesh*." He jiggled the box for emphasis.

I stared at the super-stylized sword. You couldn't call it a dagger because it was too long; about two and a half feet. But it was short for a sword. Instead of a straight steel blade, two thirds of it was curved, kind of like a sickle, and its tip had a shallow hook at the back of the outer edge.

"This is really sharp. We'll just leave it for now." As he turned to place it back in the cabinet, I nodded, trying not to imagine having to actually swing the thing at anyone.

He was wearing thin, loose, black cotton exercise pants, a fitted black t-shirt and black pull-on slippers. I looked similar except for the Lycra shorts and high-heeled Mary Janes. I'd have preferred pants like his, but *he'd* provided the clothing. *Men* … .

After shutting the cabinet, he produced a remote and pointed it at a sleek iPod station sitting on top. As he pocketed the control, he strode towards me, grabbed my right hand and then slipped his other hand around my waist. Before I could protest, he pulled me close and started moving as the song began. It was Irving Berlin's "Let's Face the Music and Dance". My eyebrows shot up as Fred Astaire's voice crooned about there being trouble ahead.

Jack closed his eyes and nodded his head to the lyrics as he swung me around. Then he waggled his eyebrows at the next overly romantic lyrics and turned me again. I started laughing and lost my step, completely ruining it.

Pulling out the remote, he admonished, "Devi. You *have* to follow me." He pointed at the machine and the music stopped.

"What on earth has this got to do with learning to defend myself?" I questioned, gesturing at my shoes and then the iPod.

"Everything. You have only two options available if you want to do me in." He held up a finger. "One: sneak attack." Unfolding a second finger, he added, "Two: you *dance* with me until you find that one moment that I leave something unguarded. Until then, it's all defensive on your part. So your training starts now. Believe it or not, knowing how to follow in dancing is a big head-start. So, first we dance, then yoga, then a little t'ai chi."

I suddenly stopped laughing and understood. But I must have shown doubt, because he put his arm around me again and said, "Don't worry, I'm a very good instructor. And I can already tell you'll be good. Besides, any woman who owns chainsaws is no little pussycat."

I looked up at him after resting my hand on the back of his shoulder and said, "I can't believe you picked that song."

"I told you, I'm a sucker for the classics. Wait 'til you hear what else I chose." Then he started up the song again and we danced for the next hour. It was the most fun I'd had in a long time. He was easy to follow and then he began to throw in some moves I was sure he'd picked up from Astaire and Kelly movies. His skill surprised me and the more complex he made things, the harder I concentrated. Which was obviously his intention, because I became so focused that I lost our 'connection' and faltered. He paused the player.

"That's what I was waiting for. You were beginning to try to lead *me.* That's where you see the difference in mindfulness and con-centration versus control. In defensive fighting, you have to relax and go with the flow; bend with the attack and the blows have noth-ing to land on. You get the idea?"

"I think so. I mean, it makes sense. But I can see it being harder in reality."

Suddenly he slapped me; not hard, but enough to anger me, and I slapped back, except that *my* blow didn't land. And, as I watched him arch back just beyond my hand, my anger faded and his words made perfect sense. He came at me again, slower, and I copied what he'd done, arching away. He missed me and got a big smile. "Perfect! First try and you nailed it."

"It wasn't the first try, it was the second."

"No, it was your first conscious try. Don't argue. I don't tell you how to grow the vine, do I?" I laughed and shook my head. "Okay. Yoga time," he announced.

After taking off our shoes and unrolling a large mat, we spent the next hour positioning and breathing. After that he taught me the rudimentaries of t'ai chi. It was midnight by the time we were done and I was exhausted, thirsty and hungry. But I felt tremendous.

"We're going to do that every night that we are here. The t'ai chi will be the biggest learning curve, but you have natural ability." He picked up my dance shoes, which looked kind of small in his hand, and put them in the cabinet. "These make your legs look great. You could've been a pinup girl." I was shocked and before I could respond, he said, as he headed for the stairs, "Alec will teach you about the various substances that work against us as well. Ways of killing us. There are different things that work on different kinds of vampires too."

I followed him up, compliment forgotten and curiosity stirred. "Like what?"

"For starters, salt works on the bad ones—the ones with really evil intent. But it doesn't work on the nasties that are just animalistic. They aren't bad, just super predatory, if you know what I mean. But really, you need to let Alec tell you. He's way more knowledgeable."

"Okay," I replied as we reached the kitchen.

I went to the fridge and got a yogurt, which I wolfed down. Yawning as I rinsed the cup for recycling, I noticed Jack was just watching me as he leaned against the counter. "How come you don't have a boyfriend?"

His question surprised me, not because he'd had the gumption to ask, but because he hadn't figured out the reason. I hesitated. "Well, I've had men in my life. The last one would be about fifty-five now. Can you imagine what he would think if he saw me, looking exactly as I had thirty years ago? If I'd stayed with him and never changed?"

After gazing at me for a moment, he looked down at his slippers and said, "Right. I knew that. I just haven't had it happen yet."

After a silent moment, I turned on the kettle for some bedtime tea. Sighing, I continued, "The truth is, it's put me off normal men . . .

mortal men. I can appreciate them, but I just can't go there anymore. It became torture, knowing I'd have to disappear eventually. Or if some bizarre accident happened and I healed too quickly. It was too hard living with the secret. Pretending. I was constantly worrying I'd be found out. And it's the same with friends."

Crossing his arms, he said, "Except for Maria and Serena, you've been alone for the last thirty years?"

As I moved to get the tea and cup, I nodded, saying, "Well I had friends here and there, but pretty much. And at some point, I have to figure out how to deal with *them*."

He smiled a little and walked over to the drawer with the silverware and pulled out a spoon for my honey. Handing it to me, he said, "No you don't. Now you've got us." I gave him a quizzical look and he replied with a sly smile, "A little mesmering goes a long way."

I hadn't felt such relief in all my life. I wouldn't have to move again. Maria and Serena would never have to know about me.

~

The night was dark, with the moon showing just the slightest outer edge of a silver sickle. Grey tree frogs called to each other as bats swooped above us and fireflies drifted, suspended by their wings like mini lanterns.

Jack had convinced me to come with him to say happy anniversary to his father and mother. Both were interred at the National Cemetery in Arlington and he had a plan for sneaking in. Well, it was barely sneaking: just hopping down over the low stone wall across from the bell tower. We had parked on a street coming in from the west and simply walked right in. With both of us dressed in black, I didn't want to have to explain ourselves to any guards that might be on patrol, but Jack had assured me he did this regularly.

As we strode across the hill, angling between its neat rows of white headstones, we were careful to stay off the graves. I kept glancing at the city across the river.

"You know, DC really is a pretty city. Sometimes I'm astounded."

"What? That such crap can come out of it?" he replied with a snort.

"Well that's not exactly what I was going to say, but that too."

"I'm sorry. Honestly, I have been stuck on the stupidity of the Freedom Fries and Freedom Toast incident since 2003. It's gone mostly downhill ever since."

I scrunched my face in response. That had, admittedly, been as ridiculous as it gets. "How did Georges react to that?"

Jack stopped and made a deep, scary faux laugh. "Well he got one in for the Frenchies, I can tell you that. One of the blowhard congressmen that was bragging about it at the time was a regular at Georges' restaurant. The guy came in with his wife and a few other reps one night. After they'd been seated, Georges came out and had a chat with him. Told him he should thank a Frenchman for his damn Freedom Fries—that without the French, he'd be celebrating *Guy Fawkes* Day fireworks instead of Independence Day.

"Apparently he suggested that American politicians should have to pass some basic American history in order to be elected: starting with knowing about the *1783 Treaty of Paris, L'Enfant, Lafayette, Rochambeau, Degrasse,* the thousands of French soldiers—oh, and all the money France spent and going bankrupt helping the United States be born.

"Then Georges told him to stick his *pommes frites* up his ass since all that was not even two and a half centuries ago and where was the gratitude? I heard that the guy thought it was some publicity stunt by the French embassy and actually kept coming back to the restaurant. Once Georges had his say, I don't think he gave a shit anymore. It upped his business."

As I laughed, Jack pointed. "They're down there."

We walked a little farther, then Jack pulled out a small blanket from the shoulder bag he'd brought and laid it on the path beside the grave. A bottle had been wrapped up in the blanket and I stooped to see what it was: *Dom Perignon*. He'd also brought four plastic cups.

Gesturing to the blanket, he said, "Please, have a seat." As I sat, he leaned down, picked up the bottle and began unwrapping the foil around the cork. Looking somewhat resentfully back at the city, he untwisted the metal holding the cork in and suddenly the thing whooshed out with the familiar pop. As I handed him a cup to fill because the champagne was foaming out, he said, "Crazy Town," as he toasted the bottle at the city.

Jack then filled the cups and motioned for me to place two over the grave. Then he took one and raised it. "Happy anniversary Mom and Dad." He sat down next to me on the blanket, put his cup up against mine and said, "Chink."

"To your parents. They have a loving son." I raised my cup and asked about them and him.

"Dad had been in Korea. He died in '69 of a heart attack. Very bizarrely, mom died the next year, which I can only say *sucked*. I really loved her. I was an only child and was in my last year of high school. I'd been a little too young to get drafted, but I wound up enlisting anyway and served with the toughest outfit I could find, thinking I'd get killed in a Vietnamese jungle.

"Turned out I was really good. I came out without a scratch and lots of medals and high marks. No trauma; nothing. It was like reverse therapy. I was so angry and somehow the experience calmed me down. I went to college on the GI bill and boy did they come looking for me. SOG, a part of the CIA, recruited me and I wound up doing lots of stealth action after that and then went private in 1983. I seriously couldn't deal with the whole Nicaraguan Contra thing. Reagan started some serious shit that's only gotten worse.

"But all the administrations do some form of that, some worse than others. American imperialism. I quit because most of it was so bogus—innocents dying because rich people want to get richer or arrogant assholes think we're the greatest."

I nodded my head in commiseration and took a sip of the champagne as I processed his tale.

He added, "And don't think I'm a sociopath because of what I do. I've always made sure there was no collateral damage to innocents. Another thing that made me good. Another reason Alec wanted me on his payroll."

He leaned forward to pour a little of each extra cup into the grass over the grave and I assured, "You are clearly no sociopath ... although I have to say, I'm not sure such work would appeal to me. Still, I understand the need for it. Even the Dalai Lama has to be protected."

With a laugh, he said, "And *you*." We touched cups again and I thought about what he was teaching me back in my basement.

"Well thank you for having the skills. Thank you for teaching me. Here's to hoping the day never comes when I'm going to need it."

We stayed for an hour, sipping from our cups as he measured sips into the ground for the ghosts of his parents. As we told tales of our escapades from the'60s, '70s and '80s, we'd occasionally comment on something wacky that had happened during that time in the city spread out before us, with its low, white, somewhat Grecian features—a city of such wrongly-wielded power now. I wondered if we'd see its demise in our far future. Heck, it had only been around for a quarter of Alec's existence. Still, it was lovely all lit up on a summer's deep, dark night; a wonderful view from this special gravesite.

SEVEN

Glasshouses and Dinner Dates

ᶹ

T he greenhouses arrived on the morning of what would prove to be the first truly sweltering day of the summer; or rather, their various parts arrived. Gordon showed up almost immediately after and set to work supervising and helping the men I'd hired to construct them. As soon as the first pieces were unwrapped, I was ecstatic. They would become classic, white Victorian-style structures created from the finest materials.

I kept glancing at the three old galvanized greenhouses and felt a little sad for them, having to live in the proverbial shadow of these fabulous, high-end enclosures. Still, the old ones were just as important since they protected our herbs in the winter. I wouldn't be mixing the exotic Vitaortus with the more common plants; mostly because the herbs needed lots of direct sunlight and the Vitaortus preferred much shadier realms.

Serena kept the men hydrated with her iced-tea and their calorie count up with various goodies she occasionally brought out to them. She fussed over Gordon in particular, making sure he kept his hat on. He treated her to his affection and dimpled smiles. Two men worked furiously laying brick in a sand base for the flooring while three others erected the frames. I was amazed that they'd finished the first one by late afternoon.

That night, Alec came by with a velvet-lined, highly-polished, silver box that held several hundred Vitaortus seeds. After giving fifty a hot soaking, I sowed them. Once the greenhouses were completed and furnished, the seedlings would be moved in. The original three plants were now two feet long and I'd had to pot them up into twelve-inch pots and wind them onto little trellises. It was time to get them out of my house.

By the end of the third day, I had three new 'glasshouses' that were ready to be wired, plumbed and furnished with narrow benches which would leave room for the plants once they were in their largest pots. Certified electricians would come the next day for the wiring and then Gordon would set up the copper piping (I had a feeling he could build a house from the ground up on his own). The custom-made glass was very thick, double-paned and had special blinds in-between the panes. Apparently I wouldn't have to use shade cloth and that astounded me—as did the final price of it all! Alec had further amazed me by saying he thought that was a bargain when I'd shyly shared what I'd put on the Black Card. I wondered if I'd ever get used to the amounts of money he dealt with, desperately hoping not.

A few days later, Alec and Georges picked me up and took me out to celebrate since the next day I'd move the plants into their new home. Jack stayed back to help Gordon with some of the plumbing for the greenhouses. Hervé drove us in the large Maybach and I twittered on about the last six days until I realized what I was doing and suddenly shut up, assuming they weren't interested in all the details. Alec, with eyes closed, had been resting his head on the plush leather headrest.

He turned to me and insisted, "Don't stop. We're as excited as you, my dear. I'm pleased to see you so chuffed."

Georges added, "In fact, if you think *you* are happy, imagine how we feel, since it means we shall not go extinct anytime too soon!"

That sobered me and I fully intended to get answers about how the Vitaortus worked once we were ensconced at the restaurant.

We took the picturesque *George Washington Parkway* to town, and once over the Key Bridge, Hervé made a right toward the river, instead of the usual left off of M Street. When we emerged from the car, I noticed how busy the place was, being a Saturday night.

I wore a creamy cotton halter dress and low sandals so I'd be cool in this summer night's humid heat. Georges looked great in an outfit that might have come straight out of a Ralph Lauren catalogue, with a Fred Perry twist. Khaki, mod-style pants, leather boat shoes and a lavender polo shirt, fit him to a T. His shoes, however, were a much darker shade of his shirt. I'd never seen purple boat shoes. His long front 'fall' was prominent under a straw 'pork pie' with a purple band.

Alec was a contrasting study in bespoke elegance. His trousers were fine, supple dark tan linen, and moved beautifully with his graceful gait. His short-sleeved, button-up shirt, which was a light bronze, made me wish I had bed sheets of the same material. I noticed that his arms, covered in a finer version of the hair on his head, were pretty darned shapely. He wore brown, woven leather loafers so soft-looking that I wanted to feel them. It was the first time I'd seen the two men in anything other than suits.

When he caught me eyeing his shoes, I started to move away, but he reached for my elbow and cupped it. "May I escort you?" he inquired, with a little jesting tone. After giving him a half-cocked smile, he moved into place beside me and, still cupping my arm, gave Hervé a little 'at ease' look, and off we sauntered, down the stairs to the entrance.

A few people looked at me and Georges, but most were checking out Alec, who I had a feeling tended to get noticed wherever he went. Seemed like it would be hard for him to hide and I figured he'd developed some sort of hunting technique to get around that problem. It's a gift to look striking, but even that has its downside—particularly if you want to be unnoticed.

Naturally, Georges knew the manager of the Sequoia restaurant on the waterfront, so we were ushered to a great table on the terrace overlooking the Potomac. It was a good thing I didn't mind much, being an object of attention; or just *with* an object of attention, so I tried to relax. Alec and Georges certainly seemed unfazed. I wondered how the people around us would react if they knew what these men really were.

Once we'd ordered drinks, Alec looked up at the terrace door. "Ah. Here's Axel. He's back for a brief visit and eager to see you again." I twisted around, feeling my ponytail bounce around on my back. Axel was easily floating past tables as he made his way to us. Even he made a pronounced statement.

He wore white cotton trousers that showed off his 'physique' and a black fitted silk t-shirt. Black leather thong sandals finished him off. His dirty blond hair was unruly and just a little punkish. I wondered what the wig-wearing Axel of long ago would have thought of what he looked like today, which was kind of like a rock star. Definitely not a typical Washingtonian look, unless maybe you were gay, which for some reason I didn't peg Axel as being. He was just European and therefore not constrained by typical American concepts of what was masculine.

We all stood as he approached. He smiled at Alec and greeted in a whisper as he hugged him, "*My Lord.*" Georges got three kisses and a, "*Mein bruder.*" Then he turned to me, bowed, took my hand for a kiss and said, "Mistress, it is wonderful to see you again." Finally, he sat beside Georges.

Mistress?! I was shocked and nearly froze, until Alec said, "Devi, darling. Sit." I looked around and noticed a number of people were watching us. I sat quickly and felt Alec pull his chair a little closer to mine, which didn't actually add to my comfort level. I liked these men a lot, but I still didn't know them very well and they were awfully flashy. *Mistress?*

The waiter came back with my wine and a special bottle of cognac with three glasses. Alec asked, "May I order some fresh oysters for you? Georges says they have a fine supplier."

Georges nodded. I felt slightly embarrassed and flushed as I too nodded. *Oysters.* It wasn't like they had to seduce me — they already had me. I wondered briefly what others would think seeing only me eating, but clearly my companions didn't care.

Once the waiter had departed, Axel fixed his playful blue eyes on me. "Alec says you have sown the first crop and they will be in their new homes shortly. I commend you. You are happy, no?"

I smiled. "Yes. Today there were fifty little grey-green tips poking through their soil. I'm kind of amazed that every one of them germinated and is on exactly the same schedule. I'm not sure I've ever seen such a perfect success rate if the seed is old or somehow compromised."

"Well, hence the species name meaning 'magic seed'. They will perform perfectly for she who has the necessary magic," Alec explained.

"She?" I questioned, half-jokingly.

"Yes. Always *she*." He looked serious.

Not knowing what to say, I just cocked my head at him. As Alec gave me a level gaze in return, Axel explained, "The Mistress, the *Prime Channel*, is always female. There are men who can grow the plant well, but none have had the magic to germinate the seeds. This is right, Alec?"

"So far as I know."

"Can you explain what it does? How do you use it?"

As the waiter returned with a dozen oysters and took the order for my main course, Alec kept his eyes on me, hands laced, motionless, in his lap. I realized I must be getting used to his intensity, because I wasn't too nervous under his gaze and held it. It was like looking into the uninhibited stare of a cat—a very big cat.

As soon as the waiter departed, he answered, "It works in a way that is detoxifying. As we are no longer able to properly filter and evacuate our systems, the herb facilitates this, much like charcoal, or activated carbon. But it also goes a step further and purges."

He stopped for a moment and watched as I squirted a little lemon on an oyster and sucked it down after a few little chews. He gave me a small, approving smile and continued. "If we drink an infusion of the leaves, we are then able to feed from any source. But regardless, the wise stay away from the most toxic humans."

"So if you take lots of prescription drugs and eat processed, pesticide, antibiotic and hormone laden foods, then you're safe from the creatures of the night?" I joked. Axel and Georges laughed.

Alec smiled and said, "Generally, but at considerable risk to your life in other ways. There is a reason we react to such things. We're like the canary in the coal mine. And while some medicines may help heal humans, they're deadly for us."

"Well, do you only take it as a tea or can you make a pill or something?"

He shook his head. "Many have tried to separate out what it is that works. For hundreds of years there have been attempts. But when the components are separated, the properties are rendered inert, useless. No alkaloids, flavonoids or other chemical compounds have thus far been separated out that work alone. What is frustrating is that stockpiling becomes a bit of an issue.

"Dried plants have a shelf life, and if we freeze it, it again goes inert. As a tincture or extract, it has a very limited therapeutic use; it loses considerable potency. And one can only keep the infusion for so long, unfrozen. So you see, our discovery of you could not have come at a more critical time. There are, so far as I now know, no plants left. There were rumors, but it appears they are untrue."

Georges said, "The last one I saw was in Marrakesh. That was thirty years ago. It and its keeper were very old. Its trunk was as thick as my thigh, yet it had very few leaves left." Axel and Alec nodded as if they knew about it.

After enjoying a few more oysters, I asked, "Well, what happens when you become poisoned? How are you affected?"

I noticed Georges and Axel glance at Alec and then look at their laps. I wasn't clairvoyant, but I instantly knew from the unguarded moment that Alec was compromised. He'd been poisoned, which came as a shock because he was the last one I'd have thought would be. When my eyes flew to his, I could also see that he'd read my understanding. I lowered my brows in concern and he nonchalantly looked over at a woman at a table on the tier below us who'd been trying hard to get his attention.

In a lowered voice, he said, "The biggest problem is that it reengages the aging process. I was thirty-five at my turning. I have accrued another five years, approximately. I am one of the lucky ones because my aging is fairly close to natural time frames and I'm not yet ill. Some age far more rapidly, depending on how much they are polluted. It also affects many of our special skills."

I turned to watch the very obviously surgically altered woman as she gave him every sultry look in the book. He merely turned to me, picked up my hand from the arm of the chair, and brought it to his lips. Ms. Nip/Tuck pouted her injected lips at him, but he kept his eyes on me. *Was I his protection from her unwanted advances?* I forced myself not to laugh. I'd half-smiled and then realized what he'd said. "Skills?"

Axel joined in by explaining, "With our special condition come many supernatural gifts. Much like the myths you've heard, I'm sure."

"What? Like turning into a bat or wolf?" I kidded.

"Exactly. But one would really not choose to become a bat now, don't you think? Logically speaking?" Axel gave me another playful look.

I had no idea what to say and just thought about the logic of turning into a bat. I guess there were better options in these faster-paced days; poor bats. I'd always had a soft spot and great regard for them. *Wait, was he saying they could turn into wolves?*

"We have other abilities as well," said Georges. "But the toxins compromise all."

"Except mesmering. Whatever the reason, that remains," Alec added.

"That seems like a pretty important skill," I commented.

"It is. Perhaps the most important." Alec replied. Georges and Axel nodded in agreement. "Regardless, the toxification is eventually fatal."

I knew this from earlier conversations, but having him sitting beside me, knowing he was a victim, stunned me. "So how do you know there aren't any more plants for sure?"

"The box of seeds I gave to you came from a group we call *The Boule*. It is the closest thing we have to a governing body. It is they who have scoured the world for any trace of the plant. They were unable to turn up even one. Those that sprout and grow under your roof are it. Any that once grew wild have long since vanished."

I hadn't heard the Greek word, sounding like 'boo-lay', in many decades. I was almost stunned from all these surprising pieces of information and a wave of anxiety ran through me as I felt the magnitude of my role. Alec touched my hand lightly. The anxiety subsided and curiosity filled the space.

"Can you tell me about *The Boule?*"

Suddenly the waiter arrived with my grilled scallops and then handed Georges a note. Georges read it quickly and leaned over to Alec. "It's Basil. He is aboard his yacht just there and requests that you permit him to join us."

"Absolutely not. Go tell him we aren't ready yet. Let him know I'm deadly serious and will tolerate no intrusions." Georges stood and headed down to the water where several large and expensive boats were tied up to the walk along the river.

Deciding not to be nosy, I tucked into my scallops and enjoyed them silently as I looked between Georges making his way to his destination and Alec. The lady below us had still not given up and avoided my gaze at all costs. I noticed one of her girlfriends was eyeing Axel, who was not discouraging her.

As if Alec heard my thought, he admonished, "I don't want *any* intrusions, Axel. If you must dally, go to *her.*"

Axel stopped his flirty behavior and gave me a waggish roll of his eyes. Clearly this *no intrusions* business was all about *me.* I glanced curiously at Alec as I squirted more lemon and he shifted his eyes from the yacht to me.

"Firstly, Basil is one of us who resides in the city and is completely untrustworthy. He would attempt to seduce you the moment I turn my back. I've no doubt one day you'll meet him, as he's very ambitious. He's not the only one requesting to meet you, both locally and abroad. Secondly, *The Boule* is made up of thirteen beings. Three of them are the oldest of our kind who are willing to take on the job, which is thankless. The rest are elected from the ten regions. There's really not much more to it. They do occasionally take on the role of a court, but generally we keep each other in line."

Axel added, "There is a clear understanding of why rules must be followed and we tend to do what our genitors teach. We respect our elders because it keeps us … alive."

"*Tend* being the operative word." Alec didn't seem to be joking.

"Alec is very well-respected everywhere, so Basil will obey him." Axel had noted my wide eyes at Alec's first revelation and kindly tried to assuage my concern. Not that I was *all* that worried. Alec seemed to me like he was probably feared as much as respected. Plus, I just didn't feel that much fear—yet.

Eventually, as commanded, no one but Georges returned to join us and we spent the rest of the evening talking about goings-on in Europe and the rest of the world. Axel spoke briefly about the fundamentalist, plutocratic group Jack suspected had killed Leonora. He filled Alec and Georges in on a few connections to them he had discovered in Europe and Africa—how they were funneling laundered money to dictators and recruiting corporate executives of bio-tech agriculture.

His final comment was, "I fear they are a more dangerous threat than ever. Something seems . . . *afoot*. And they may be ever closer to a true discovery of us. I have found evidence of their attempts at cyber-spying on several of our friends. And you."

"This age of connected technology has begun to illuminate our dark, safe world." We were silent as we absorbed Alec's response.

Eventually, after a sharp intake of air, he added, "I shall consider what to do next. They continue to court me. I've received my *tenth* invitation: this one to a charitable event they are quietly sponsoring. Perhaps I'll go and finally meet the man who heads them." Then he looked at me with a contemplative eye.

Georges grunted and commented, "Yes, it wouldn't hurt you to get out more. You'll get too far behind the culture if you stay cooped in." He winked at me.

I gave Alec a half-smile and he said, with a forced sigh, "Yes, Old Mother Hen, I'm sure you're quite right. Perhaps now I have someone appropriate who'll join me—although what culture they have would be beyond my ability to comprehend."

As the three men laughed, I only half understood what he meant, because I assumed he meant that 'someone' was *me*. A fundamentalist, plutocratic group who hired assassins, funneled laundered money to dictators and did *whatever* with biotech executives would *not* be one I'd be remotely interested in 'meeting'—with or without Alec!

~

The Olde Ebbit Grill was just as dark and masculine as I'd remembered. It hadn't changed much in a few decades, and why should it? It was supposed to be a living museum and people liked it that way. The food was quite good and the ambience amiable. But the walrus head mounted on the wall behind the bar always seemed like a bit of an appetite suppressant, if you asked me.

We stood in line to wait and clearly caught the maître d's eye. He tried to move toward us without drawing too much attention. Addressing Alec, he quietly asked, "Are you here for the private function?" After a nod from Alec, he said, "This way, please."

Alec had asked if I would accompany him to the event, which he claimed to be *loath* to attend, but needed to in order to make a connection with the man who was the leader of the secretive religio-political group. Why I was needed, I'd yet to understand. But he'd insisted it was so. Regardless, he said the food would be good and it was a chance to dress up, so I'd agreed.

We followed, squeezing through the small crowd … well, *I* squeezed here and there, trying to stay in Alec's wake. They seemed to just part for him. He glanced back a few times to be sure I was still with him, and then decided to just grab my hand. It was another summer Saturday night and the place was packed. He pulled me gently when I was slowed by a human obstruction as we trailed after the maître d', who led us up to the rooftop. At some point he'd asked Alec his name, because when we'd reached the roof, he said, "James is your man up here, Mr. Gregory." Alec thanked him with a silent nod and a handing off of a little cash, which got a little bow in return.

James led us to a table set for six near the edge of the building, overlooking the street and the city. We could see *the* monument and White House lit up amongst other landmarks. Then I noticed the couple we'd be joining. James held out the seat at the end of the table for me and I sat as I thanked him. Alec sat beside me at a right angle, facing the man, so that he was to my left and the man to my right. Happily, we had the view, which was behind the couple.

They were a relatively handsome duo, but not particularly special looking, which is typical of DC. You rarely see real beauty. That's for the west coast, or Miami and points beyond. Beautiful people are too distracting in a town like Washington, which meant that Alec seriously stood out. He didn't even have the look of 'The Hair Politician'. He was a little too unusual with his swept back coif and short, elegant beard and moustache.

Both members of the couple stared at him for a moment, and then he took the reins. "Hello. I'm Alec Gregory. This is Devica Trevathan." He pulled his arm from the back of my chair and extended his hand to the man, who reached over the candles for it.

"Hey there. I'm John Mason; this is my wife, Mary."

"A pleasure," Alec retorted, as he smiled at Mary, who shook his hand as well. When it was my turn, I opted to shake their hands and just smile also.

First John, then Mary shifted their gazes to look me over more thoroughly than they had Alec. It was a little shocking to be so obviously sized-up. I realized they probably were finding my figure-hugging attire and long, partially unbound hair a little too sexy for their liking. The strapless, light green dress was from the '60s section of my closet. But it was the modern, dark green, very high heels that actually pumped up the sex appeal. Mary, who was not dressed to make an impression, and had hair as controlled and unisex as mine was wild and feminine, seemed to be working hard to swallow her judgment.

While John took in my footwear, Mary attempted a smile and asked, in a native Virginian accent, "How do you come to be at this fundraiser? Are you with the Brotherhood?" John nudged her and barely shook his head.

I glanced at Alec, who smiled slightly and answered smoothly, "I was invited by someone who wishes to see me part with much money for this good cause." It took them a moment to laugh, unsurely.

At that moment, another couple came to the table, eyeing the placeholders. "Ah, here we are." It was said in a well-spoken French accent by a nicely-dressed gentleman. I was glad to see the woman with him was attired not too dissimilarly to me. Introductions were made and I felt relief to have people joining our table who seemed more like Alec and I, if that was even possible. They were diplomats and seemed like fun, intelligent people.

As we went through introductions again, I noticed Mary had a cross pendant and her husband wore one as a lapel pin. It dawned on me that this 'Brotherhood' they'd mentioned must be the extreme religious group. Alec had dodged the question of his membership.

Guy (pronounced 'Gee', which seemed to confuse the Masons) and Thérèse were a wonderful couple and I instantly liked them. The Masons were out of sync, but we tried cordially to include them. A waiter brought wine and I was glad to see Alec drink it. I was dying to ask him what it did inside him, but would have to wait until the ride home. After a bit of chit-chat, the Masons decided to go mingle with some of their friends who'd just showed up. It bordered on rude, but I think we were all relieved.

Alec was the first to get real after a moment of silence as we watched them walk off. As he removed his linen jacket, showing a soft pistachio colored shirt and matching tie beneath, he asked, "So Guy, surely you aren't a member of the group hosting this affair?"

Guy's forehead creased as his eyebrows hiked up. "Me? *Mon Dieu, non!*"

"I shall forgive the pun," Alec responded, with a small laugh.

Thérèse put her arm around her husband's shoulder and added, "Really. It is a rather odd group. But so powerful in Washington. One occasionally must deal with them here and there. One nation under *their* God!" She raised her glass in mock salute. I nodded and she winked at me.

"I need a *Ricard, mon cher*. Alec? You'll join me?" Guy stood and gestured to the bar on the far side of the roof, then pulled out two cigars suggestively from his inside jacket pocket.

Alec turned to me and leaned in for a whisper. *"You don't mind?"*

"Not at all. I'm sure you'll really enjoy that fine smoke." I tried hard to say it without laughing and his eyes sparkled in response.

As Alec stood and rose to his full height, I noticed the attention of the ladies around us focus on him. Thérèse opened her mouth a little as her head tilted upward to take him in. A sixth sense told her that her husband was about to turn to her and she snapped her jaw shut just in time. Then she said, "Enjoy your *pastis*, darling." She received a little kiss, and the two men sauntered off.

I smiled to myself as I observed all the eyes following Alec. It was amusing and even though I hadn't known him very long, I knew none of it mattered to him. For all his strange beauty and sex appeal, he really seemed kind of nonsexual to me … most of the time. Anyway, I was glad I was somewhat immune. I could appreciate his friendship and our connection, I told myself.

I looked back at Thérèse as her sudden movement startled me. She'd practically jumped into the chair just vacated by Alec.

"My goodness. What a handsome man you have, Devica!" she whispered loudly.

"Devi," I huffed out with a little laugh. "Call me Devi, Thérèse. Please. And yes, he is a very attractive man. But he's just a friend. He doesn't really belong to me."

She made that pouty-lipped face that the French do best and said, "Oh, but I think that is not true. His body language says otherwise. He is very familiar with you."

I had no idea how to respond. I had a feeling it was the supernatural possessiveness in him rather than any human familiarity we might share. I was spared from having to reply when an elegant, older woman came to the table.

"Thérèse," she greeted and they kiss-kissed. "I'm sorry, but I just had to come meet the woman with Lord Gregory. First time I've seen it!"

Thérèse sucked in some breath. "*Lord* Gregory? Oh my goodness. You know Alec, Miranda?"

The lady smiled warmly at me and sat beside Thérèse. Both women had their arms resting on the table and were leaning toward me. "Actually, he's a noble of an old line. I went on a tour of his ancestral home last time I was in Scotland. I've met him exactly three times and remember every detail. He certainly keeps his looks. The first time was fifteen years ago! Anyway, who are you dear? Lucky girl." She grabbed my hand and patted it.

Thérèse spoke up. "This is Devica. She likes to be called Devi. Devi, may I introduce Mrs. Fairlington. She likes to be called Madge."

I felt a grin come to my face and I put my other hand over Madge's. "It's wonderful to meet you!"

I knew who this was! She was a well-known socialite who'd been married to two 'lifer' senators. The first had been a Republican, the second a Democrat. Each had died of natural causes … naturally, because both had been way older than she. This lady was one of the colorful crowd, which was getting smaller these days. I felt honored to meet her.

"So tell us! What's he like? There'll be chatter for ages over this little outing. He doesn't come out often, and never with a date. I mean, I'm sure he travels a lot; dividing his time between here and the U.K., no doubt. Anyway, do tell." Her exuberance was infectious, but I knew to be very careful with the info. There'd have to be a white lie here and there. Plus, it wasn't like I knew much.

"Devi was trying to tell me they are just friends," Thérèse interjected.

"Yes. And, well, partners in a little joint venture. I have a small nursery out near Paris, Virginia, and we're producing plants for select clients."

"Ahh. So you're in business with him," Madge stated doubtfully, as she eyed my appearance. I was looking more like arm candy than an associate.

"Um. You could say that."

"Has he ever been married?"

I squinted to hide my surprise at her forwardness. "You know, I can't say that he's mentioned that." Glancing to the bar to check his whereabouts, I was shocked when I spotted him and he turned his head to briefly glance at me. He raised a knowing brow. *Good lord.* He could *hear* us. I looked back at Madge and Thérèse, with an impulse to be naughty.

"He has idiosyncrasies I'm sure most women would find hard to live with." I smiled, unable to resist. "All the handsomeness in the world can't atone for an annoying nature." But when I saw both women's jaws drop and disappointment set in, I hurriedly reversed tack. "I'm kidding. Just kidding. He's a perfect gentleman. I've no clue about his romantic life; I'm sorry. But he's been an … interesting friend. And you're right. He travels a lot." That seemed safe.

"But dear. You're the only woman in all this time he's been seen with. I'm sure of it. Believe you me! I've checked."

I started laughing in earnest. "Well, I'm sure it's just that he didn't want to come to this *particular* shindig alone. He probably brought me as an excuse in case he wants to make a quick get-away." I suddenly had an inkling that I was being used *again* as his protection from ardent admirers, which struck me as pretty hilarious.

Thérèse had been taking a sip of wine and sputtered. "*Oui*," she laughed. "We drew the short sticks at the embassy."

Madge added, "Well you wouldn't catch me at one of their usual dos, but this one has a cause dear to me. So what the hell? And now I'm rewarded with seeing the lovely Lord Gregory." We laughed and raised our glasses.

As I took a drink, I suddenly felt that feeling: I was the object of someone's intense scrutiny. Slowly turning my head without seeming obvious, I scanned the crowd. And there he was. At the opposite end of the bar from Alec and Guy. He was half standing, half sitting on a bar stool. Slightly overweight, with a shock of dark blond hair that whooshed back from his forehead and face, almost in a clean mullet-type style. He could be considered attractive, but my immediate reaction was total aversion. In fact, I was repulsed. It was a strong, visceral feeling that intensified when our eyes met. His were an icy blue, which held me before I could look away. Coolly, he picked up his beer and raised it to me. I had no intention of encouraging him and was very happy when Thérèse shook my arm.

"Devi? '*Allo*? Did you hear? Look. The head of the Brother-hood just came and is chatting with Guy and Alec." She gestured at them with her head.

"Oh! So who is he?" I asked, eyeing the older gentleman who was shaking Alec's hand.

"*That* ... ," Madge meaningfully stressed, "is a man who has more power than he should."

I raised my brows at her. Truth was, I'd not been paying as much attention to politics and current affairs the last decade because it had been heading in so bizarre a direction. It was depressing and too much of the rhetoric was a little frightening. I'd lived through

World War II and its beginnings, and some things sounded frighteningly familiar.

"So let me understand. Is he a religious leader?"

Madge nodded and leaned in to explain in a quiet voice, "Donald Carr is the head of the organization, which is global, although mostly their power is stateside. It's greed and elitism masquerading as a bible club. They have middle class members, but those are just their foot soldiers. They don't belong to any denomination or church as a whole. And they are very secretive."

"Good lord," I responded.

"Yes. They've been around for a long while. Many decades. They are the enemy of the poor, working class, middle class and the liberated woman! They claim not to be political but they have considerable tentacles in government now. It's all about ministering to people in power. But there's a deeper agenda."

"Isn't that a little scary?" I whispered as I eyed the men, who were deep in conversation.

"It is a LOT scary," Thérèse answered. The three of us turned to watch them again, but I stole a glance at the man at the other end of the bar; he too, was watching them.

Soon, there was hand shaking again and Mr. Carr slapped Alec on the shoulder. Alec controlled himself expertly and smiled, nodding his head. It seemed to me that Mr. Carr didn't have a tiniest fraction of the class of Alec.

After he moved on, the two men headed back to us. I glanced at Madge and smiled. She was ecstatic. As they neared, Alec put on a face of delight and went to her as Thérèse moved back to her chair at the other end of the table.

"Mrs. Fairlington! What a delightful surprise. I wouldn't have thought to see you here."

They kiss-kissed and she didn't even try to hide her blush. "Nor you Lord Gregory. You look wonderful as ever. How on earth do you do it?" His eyes flicked to me and back at her. "Anyway . . . ," she continued, holding his hand as they sat, ". . . was that your first meeting with the infamous Mr. Carr?"

He raised a conspiratorial brow. "Yes, Miranda. And, you'll be glad to know, I've secured a dinner invitation for Devi and myself for tomorrow evening at his home." He leaned back with a naughty little smile.

Madge frowned deeply and asked, "Why on earth would you want to do that?"

His smile got slightly bigger. "Why, for a lark. Why else would a sane and rational individual want to go into the lair of such a creature? So. You've met Devi, I see."

Madge was obviously easily manipulated by him and she said enthusiastically, "Oh yes. We're already friends, aren't we dear?"

They looked at me and I agreed, "Absolutely. But I need to go back a step. You want me to come with you tomorrow night? I've got—" I stopped, sensing his mood alter abruptly. He eyed me and I would have sworn he was asking me telepathically not to decline.

"I'll make it worth your while, Devi," he said with a hint of meaning I knew was a very real plea. I didn't respond and we stared at each other for a minute.

How the hell would he make it worth my while? *Fuck*, I thought crassly. I really, really didn't want to go. It was one thing to hold my tongue with someone I liked. But this was another matter entirely. He was asking me to go into a situation I was likely to blow for him. Obviously we'd discuss it later. He was possibly the only man I'd met in seventy years who could get me to demurely lower my eyes in acquiescence, but only because I didn't want to cause a scene. When I did, he took my hand and kissed my knuckles.

I wanted to say, "Oh. This isn't over *mister*," but when I looked at Madge, I saw she was having an emotional moment watching us. Completely misinterpreting our quiet negotiation, she had become a little gooey-eyed. I didn't want to spoil it for her.

Soon after, the Masons returned and Madge went back to her table as dinner was being brought out. Unfortunately, the mood toned down a little. As we were being served, Guy asked John and Mary what they did. John ran a chain of hardware stores and Mary raised their five kids and ran the home.

While they talked and we began to eat, Alec leaned and whispered in my ear, "*You have acquired, amongst others, a rather disturbing admirer, haven't you?*"

I stopped my forkful of filet mignon that was almost to my opening mouth. "*What?*" I whispered, without looking at him.

"*Surely you noticed him. He was willing your attention rather strongly.*"

I glanced at the bar but he was gone. "*You mean … ?*"

"*Yes. Danger, my dear. Bad man.*"

I inserted the fork, chewed and then leaned toward Alec. "*Yes, I wasn't born yesterday. His energy is nasty. It's fairly clear. But what's up with him? He doesn't seem normal.*"

"*He's not.*" I could feel Alec's cool breath on my ear and neck as he created air flow with his speech. "*He's an incubus.*"

I dropped my fork with a clatter.

"Oops! I've only had one glass! Really," I joked nervously when all eyes at the table turned to me. "Sorry." Unconcerned, they went back to their conversation and I gave Alec a wide-eyed look. "*Tell me you are kidding. You're joking, right?*"

He put a piece of meat in his mouth and seemed to savor it, then answered. *"No. He's as I told you. I'll wager he attempts to speak to you before we leave. He's hunting you."* He added, *"Fear not. Number one, he doesn't really know what he is and number two, you won't fall for him. Because, I'm here."*

I set my utensils down and half-turned to Alec. Grabbing his arm firmly, I whispered assertively, *"Of course I won't fall for him, whether you're here or not. What the hell is that supposed to mean?"* He gently pried my hand from his arm and placed it in my lap. I promptly picked up my knife and fork.

"It means that he has powers he doesn't even realize he possesses, and a great many women would be susceptible. He has some mesmer capabilities. It's part of his hunting technique. You are lucky to feel aversion—those who don't risk life-altering mental and physical trauma. You've yet to speak to him. It's then that you will feel any real power he has. Just try to avoid him. He will have seen you with me and that will trigger an even stronger impulse—his competitive drive.

"Mind you, it's all subconscious. And he's honed in on your special energy. Of course it would be you, out of all the women here. I doubt this will be the first time we encounter this either. As I told you, others will want you."

"So you've said, Mr. Gregory. May we change the subject? In fact, I'm going to the restroom." I was irritated now and wanted to escape for a moment. Plus, a large glass each of water and wine had gone into me. I smiled at him to let him know I wasn't trying to be rude, and grabbed my napkin from my lap as I stood. "I'll be right back."

He stood as well so it would be easier for me to move from my chair, I thought, but then realized it was probably old-fashioned high manners. The others looked up and John asked Alec something which drew him into their conversation.

I remembered that the restroom was in the basement, so I had a distance to walk and think about Alec's warnings in spite of my desire not to. As much as I wanted friends, and people in my life with whom I could be honest, with whom I could be me, I wasn't too thrilled about this so far 'theoretical' danger. To be relatively immortal and in constant danger seemed a little nerve-racking, to put it mildly. Jack was teaching me self-defense, but still, I'd created a serene world for myself and had gotten very used to it. No fear. No worries.

Well actually, there was the worry of who I really was and the "Twilight Zone" truth of my non-aging. But then, now I could get some answers. Perhaps that was worth a little danger. I'd learn what I needed, and have faith. After all, I was now into my thirteenth decade without a scar since the first twenty-seven years. The universe obviously wanted me alive and well.

I made it to the restroom, went in and found all the stalls empty. After peeing, I came out and scrutinized myself in the mirror while washing my hands. My hair was behaving relatively well, considering its tendencies. I looked pretty good and decided gratitude was in order. I was as fortunate as could be. Drying my hands, I resolved to *try* to be less obstinate about Alec's warnings. I came out of the lavatory and looked up as I ascended the stairs, and of course, there was the 'incubus', lying in wait for me.

For a second, I had no idea what to do. I stopped, then decided to just keep moving and hopefully go past him. But he moved to block me. "Ms. Trevathan? I'm Mac Winston. Just *dyin'* to make your acquaintance." He stuck out his hand in a smooth move and grabbed mine before I could refuse.

"H-how do you know my name?" I asked, surprised. I could feel the strong energy emanating from him and found it curious. And foreign. He kind of sounded like I imagined a cowboy would. I was also very, very sure this man used up women like garbage bags.

"I have my ways. You are so gorgeous and I just had to know your name."

I doubted the gorgeous part; cute, maybe, or even pretty, but not gorgeous. Unless you added in my energy, as Alec seemed to think. My gorgeous, potentially fatal (for me), energy.

"Um. Well thank you Mr. Winston," I said, gingerly pulling my hand from his grasp. "Nice to meet you. I hope you enjoy your evening." I attempted to go around him and his bulk shifted so that I moved into him. I realized he wasn't all fat, but also muscular. This was repulsive, frightening and intriguing, and I felt a strong sense of confusion; clearly those powers Alec had warned against were at play. Thank God my mouth was still on the aversion course. "Mr. Winston. I have someone waiting for me." I looked him in the eye, which seemed to encourage rather than deter him.

He smiled broadly and reached for my hand again. "And he'll keep waitin'." I watched with growing disgust as he slowly brought my hand up to his mouth. Then a shadow fell over us.

"You will unhand my companion." Alec had appeared on the steps above us.

I had never been so glad to be followed or hear a cliché. I pulled my hand from Winston's and started up the stairs—but again, Winston blocked me. My sharp intake of breath surprised him, and me. *What do you think you are doing?*" I hissed at him.

"I'm gonna get to know you Ms. Trevathan," he answered almost threateningly.

I looked up at Alec, who furrowed his brow at me as if I were choosing this course of action. I shook my head and Alec shifted his formidable attention back to the man. Raising his right hand slightly, in a strange manner, Alec said to Mac Winston, "You don't know the name Devica Trevathan." When my eyes turned to Winston, I watched his arrogant expression turn to confusion.

He took a step back and looked at me, then asked, "What's your name beautiful lady?"

From the corner of my eye, I saw Alec move his hand slightly in another odd gesture. "You see no lady here. You will let her pass. You are going to the lavatory." And with that, Mac Winston turned and walked down the stairs into the men's bathroom.

"*Oh. My. God,*" I whispered, astounded and disturbed by what I'd just witnessed. Then I started briskly walking up the stairs, moving right past Alec. He immediately caught up with me and grabbed my elbow to slow me down.

"You keep saying that and I keep telling you, I'm not."

"Ha ha, *Obi-Wan.* That was some trick. I assume that's mesmering?"

"Yes."

For a moment, I felt disoriented because I came up higher on him than usual, then I remembered my outrageous shoes. Glancing down at them, I said, "That was unbelievable from many perspectives. I need to sort it out. Let me know when it's time to go."

He dropped his hand from my arm and gently admonished, "*Devi.*"

"*Whatever.* You were right. That had a slightly frightening element to it. It was weird and I've never had an encounter like that. I've never had a man not 'listen' when I said no. I need to figure out how I'd have gotten out of that if you hadn't come along. I need to know how to handle these situations." He started up the stairs, beside me.

"You will. And you'll have protection."

"Not always, Alec. Not always." I couldn't believe how vulnerable I felt. I was frightened and the so-called incubus wasn't even that dangerous to someone like me. What would the others be like? I was so used to being alone and self-sufficient that I didn't know *how* to trust another with my well-being.

We made our way back up to the roof and rejoined the table to finish our dinner. For another hour and a half, we chatted and interacted with a combination of non-Brotherhood and Brotherhood people. The former were fairly interesting, the latter, I found mostly bizarre. It's odd, when you've spent little time among fundamentalists, to suddenly be in their midst. It was as culturally foreign as being with the Mbuti tribes of the Congo. I'd unquestionably feel more at home with the Mbuti.

There was an other-world quality to the people, and I felt it strongly: a deep divide in consciousness levels made conversation quite difficult. And I certainly felt constrained when it came to subject matter. I thanked goodness for the other people and was particularly relieved when Alec came over and leaned in to ask if I was ready to go home.

After saying our goodbyes, we swiftly made it down and out of the front door onto 15th Street where Hervé was waiting with the car. Alec suavely helped me in and I found I was in a mood. I couldn't care less about the luxurious trappings or gentlemanliness of my 'date'. He got in on the other side and I just glared out the window. Hervé shut the door and Alec observed me dourly for a moment. After making what I assumed was a totally illegal U-turn in the middle of 15th Street so that we were headed toward Constitution Avenue, Hervé instinctively raised the barrier.

Once we'd made the right turn to get us to I-66, Alec spoke up. First he leaned toward me, then said, "Remind me to ask you to refrain from more than two glasses of wine. You appear to be a cross drunkard." He leaned back and flared his nostrils, then faux sighed, never changing the I'm-too-bored-with-it-all expression.

"I'm not drunk. I'm irritated. Those Brotherhood people were really … irritating; and I have to go even deeper tomorrow. I really dislike them. I feel like *they* are energy suckers. Life-force suckers. It's just awful. And really! I don't like being the object of *their* derision; glowering at me as if I were some strumpet."

I glared out the window at the American Pharmacists Association building, suddenly thinking it a little ironic that it had such a prominent location, given what pharmaceuticals were doing to my new friends. I'd rather have been looking out the other window, at the Lincoln memorial.

Alec chuckled. "You know, Devi. You *are* quite lovely tonight."

I glanced back at him, softening a little. "Well thanks. You look great yourself," I replied, only a little grudgingly. *Jesus, I was easy.*

"And it's the life force you channel to which those people are reacting. It's a highly positive, powerful and organic thing and quite threatening to them. *They* sense it through the sexual aspect, which naturally upsets their *supposedly* Christian sensibilities." I harrumphed in response and he continued. "You know, I was actually surprised at your willingness to accompany me. You are quite the chameleon, really, aren't you? So many roles. From farmer to seductive escort."

I breathed in loudly, alarmed. "Seductive escort? What?"

A slight smile touched his lips. "No? Bad description? How about 'desirable, intelligent companion'? You certainly turned some heads and interested a few minds."

"Good lord, Alec. You're killing me. Look, you know how it is. You've got to adapt." Shifting my accent, I went back many decades to the voice I had before 'America'. "If I sound like this, and use the language of eighty years ago, I'd look quite the pratt after so long as an American, now wouldn't I?"

Alec registered genuine surprise and just stared for a moment, then admitted, "Yes. I see what you mean. I simply wish to remark on your skill in fitting comfortably into so many roles. There are those I know who are hundreds of years old and can't manage change very well. They are miserable. You on the other hand, have found the knack of it. So, allow me to compliment you. And to say that you look good doing it. *You* can say, 'Thank you, lord and master'."

I snorted. "Thank you, Alec, and kiss my ass."

He arched a brow at my sass. "Devi. You should take care what you invite a man to do."

Completely ignoring him, I changed the subject. "That was a truly bizarre party. Faux Jesus freaks."

He began pulling at his jacket to remove it and responded, "They don't think they are faux, most of them anyway."

I watched him as he hardly struggled before the garment was removed and I continued. "Then there were your groupies. Those women would be *more* than willing to call you lord and master. I'm going to need some stories from you, Alec. I get asked a lot of questions and I'm just not that good at brushing them off."

"I shouldn't worry. I'd worry more about your own fanatic—that he was deterred enough to leave you be. I really wouldn't want to have to *do him in*."

"Alec!" I protested, his jesting attempt at using slang not seeming funny at all.

"I told you. He's an incubus. He'll go on through many incarnations, destroying other lives, never growing nor attaining a consciousness of what he is. I guarantee he has harmed and even ruined multiple women in this life. Probably some even fatally."

I dropped my jaw and stared, finally saying, "But you used 'the force' on him."

"I may have played 'Obi-wan', but on him it might not stick, entirely. He's not fully vampire, but nor is he like a full human. I've only once before mesmered an incubus and it only partially took."

I scowled, then said, "Fabulous. Just fabulous. That leaves me feeling *so* secure."

Alec leaned again and put his cool hand on my knee, which cause me to jerk slightly. "You are perfectly secure." He bored his green gaze, which looked turquoise in the bluish light of the car, into mine to emphasize his point. After I tapped the back of his hand with my fingertips, signaling him to remove it, he leaned back, adding, "Besides. Where's your sense of adventure? You could be on the cusp of saving the world as we know it."

"What do you mean?"

"Donald Carr and his cronies have a basic economic philosophy that is destroying the planet. It is destroying human health. Ultimately, that is the aim. Rampant, unchecked capitalism that is like a parasite destroying its host. They wish to destroy the world as we know it."

He'd been strange and different, but he'd never sounded crazy before. "Um. Are you serious?"

"Devi, this group is trying to bring about the apocalypse. Make no mistake."

For a moment, I said nothing, then turned in my seat to fully face him. "As in 'The Apocalypse' apocalypse?"

"The very same."

"Let me get this straight. They take the Book of Revelation *literally* and are taking steps to manifest it?" He nodded and watched my face. "You know, as crazy as it sounds, it certainly explains why things have gotten so bizarre, and just plain—" Then I had a thought and squinted at Alec. He'd observed the changes on my face and raised his brows questioningly. I hoped he'd give me an answer to my next question with which I could live.

"Do *you* buy into what the last book of New Testament says?"

He snorted gently and said, "Please. Devi. Out of God knows how many writings, they chose but a few, which combined told a specific tale. I've read nearly every so-called Christian document in existence leading up to those chosen. I've read everything written since. *I* believe the contrivance is outrageous. That particular book has been controversial from the start. Even in the fourth century there were those who warned that the so-called *John's Revelations* could be misused. Well-known Christian leaders through the ages have criticized it for many reasons. And here we are, well on our way into the 21st century, and you have fools who actually believe it to be prophetic of the future. Absolute insanity. The problem is that these are people with immense power and sway. And they've been working on this for three quarters of a century. The first fruits of their labor are ripe."

I put my fingers over my mouth as I mumbled, "*Oh my god.*"

"Quite." Alec agreed, sardonically.

"Did you always think that way about the New Testament?"

"No. I was once an extremely devoted follower. I studied it daily. But that was in my life as a human … an extremely long and less knowledgeable time ago. And to be fair, there is much in it that has merit. Those who seek it will find some comfort there, if the esoteric meaning is the focus. I myself was no longer able to reconcile the discrepancies. Nor separate the chaff from the wheat, so to speak. Besides, there is the rather obvious history of the thing, which is simply impossible to ignore if truth is your aim."

We rode along silently for a while as my brain did twirls and burls. Then I remembered something Alec had said earlier in the evening. "You said you would make going tomorrow worth my while."

He turned his golden, red head to me as it lay against the white leather. "Indeed. I did." Then he placed his hand over mine, which lay on the console between us, and added, "We need to take a special trip with the Vitaortus in several weeks. How would you like to go to The Yucatan peninsula? Go see some Mayan ruins? Swim in warm, clear Caribbean waters, Eh?" And then he wiggled his eyebrows, completely ruining his cool factor.

~

The next night, I didn't want a debate with Alec about my chosen attire, so when I heard the barely-there sound of the car's engine, I whisked out of the door, hoping to hop in before he could even notice. I stopped for a moment when I realized he'd brought the smaller vehicle, so no Hervé. He did manage to get out before I made it to the door of the gorgeous thing, though. I skidded to a halt when he was suddenly between me and the passenger door.

"In a rush, are we?" he asked, looking down his nose and surveying my appearance. It was only just dark and the sun's last, slightest rays peeking over the horizon were reflected in his eyes.

"Yes. Can we get this over with?"

Tossing his head back just a little with an equivalent laugh, he offered, "Immediately." As he opened the door for me, he added, "You look perfect, by the way."

Easing into the front passenger seat of the sportier Maybach, I checked his eyes for truth, but he gave away nothing. He just cocked his head and shut the door. I watched him walk around the front, very nonchalantly, and then, as he slid into the seat, look at me as he pursed his lips, seemingly trying to hide his amusement.

As the engine silently started, he said, "If I didn't know better, I'd think you could read my mind." He shifted into first and we were off.

I was thinking the small Maybach was cooler in a lot of ways than its larger counterpart, starting with not having a hood ornament. Then what he'd said registered with me. "I beg your pardon?"

"I believe you are clairvoyant, Devica."

"And you've come to this conclusion because?"

"Your look. It's perfect. You'll secretly thrill the men, and the women will be completely cowed by that suit. Chanel trumps all. Your hair is divine for the occasion. While *I* may prefer it in its natural wild state, the types we're seeing like control—particularly hair. It's symbolic for them."

I grasped a loose strand and ran my fingers down it to feel the silkiness. It had taken me over an hour to straighten and put up; a despised pastime. But I'd already known what Alec was saying was true: *wild hair, wild woman.*

"Yes. I figured as much. This suit seemed appropriate. I've only worn it three times in forty-five years! I was almost afraid it would be too ... too . . ."

"Much?" he finished, and I nodded sheepishly, having actually meant to say sexy. "Well it is, only slightly. But you can't hide what you are. You have a fit, trim body. What's to be done? Although I must say, aqua and pink *are* a statement. One I'm sure they'll appreciate."

I couldn't believe I was having this conversation with him. He glanced at me when I didn't respond; I was staring at him. Finally I asked, after admiring another of his fabulous suits, "Are you gay? Seriously."

He just laughed. "You like my attire?"

Was he joking or avoiding? I replied, "I do. You always look smashing."

"Thank you. Well, this strange lot's extremely impressed with power and influence. Combined, you and I certainly pull that off." I thought he didn't really need me to 'pull that off'.

And then he tapped the screen on an inboard mp3 player. I was totally shocked to hear Tame Impala's "Elephant" burst forth from what had to be the best speakers I'd ever heard. I stared at him with my mouth open and barely heard him say above the neo-psyche-delic guitars, "*Ah music. It has charms to sooth a savage breast.*"

Hilarious. We bopped along to a dizzying selection of music that seemed put together just for the fun of the incongruity of the genres. Next came a 1938 recording of Louis Armstrong singing "Jeepers Creepers", followed by Souxie and the Banshees' "Peek-a-Boo". Alec's taste in music was highly eclectic and not what I'd expected. By the time we reached our exit off of I-66, we'd travelled audibly through the entire twentieth and first years or the twenty-first century. Once we hit the neighborhoods of Arlington, he hit the off key.

"I find these habitats in United States so different from any-where else. Same ingredients to some degree, like bricks and glass and wood. But the feel is so much different. Perhaps it is the large trees that live right next to the homes on such small properties."

"Right. In other places, the trees are usually smaller, or the homes proportional to the old oaks and such."

"Yes, that must be it. Proportion. We are close. The home we are visiting is actually rather old, for here." Alec pointed at a prop-erty ahead of us that was much larger and older than those around it. It was grand, very white and up on a hill. There was a guard at the entrance who admitted us cheerfully when Alec gave our names, but I noted the extreme weapon he was toting.

As we meandered in the dark along a winding drive up the hill, I commented, "Jesus, Alec. Where are we that the guards have automatic weapons?"

"Interesting, eh? I'd have reconnoitered last night, but my skills are too untrustworthy now. Besides, Jack has been here several times and says there are only ever guards when dignitaries are present. One is in the house at a security observation station. Usually the others aren't visible."

After eyeing him for a moment as I thought about his deteriorating condition, he glanced at me and then did a double take at the concerned look on my face. As we pulled up to the walkway, he patted my hand. "Pay it no mind. I'm simply looking forward to this. Aren't you?!"

"Uh . . ." His idea of fun wasn't quite squaring with mine.

"If you begin to feel uncomfortable with what is said, either hold my hand or go to the powder room for an escape."

"Hold your hand?"

"Certainly. It will signal me and I'll be able to calm you a little. Plus, it will help put forth the impression we're a couple, as these are conservative types who expect such things."

"How will you calm me?"

"With touch. It's something I can do similar to mesmering, but it is more like a general state of *well*-being." I sighed deeply, realizing he'd done this to me already; twice at least. *Who needs Valium or Xanax with Alec around?* He added, "And will you just go along with whatever I might say? I intend to use a little dramatic intimidation, which I've discovered impresses Carr. He shall fall in love with me. Think of it as a *charade*." He pronounced the last word as the French would.

I rolled my eyes. "This Mexico trip better be fantastic, is all I can say."

He put my hand to his lips and replied, "Don't you dare open that door; allow me." And he was out and opening mine when I saw the front door of the mansion open. As Alec helped me out, Donald Carr came hurrying down the path.

"Lord Gregory! Alec. You made it. I'm so happy you came."

"Donald. May I introduce Devica Trevathan? Devica, this is Donald Carr." I gave Carr my strongest handshake, which he didn't appear to appreciate.

"It's a pleasure to meet you Miss Trevathan. Won't you please come in?" He led the way to the doorway where his wife was standing. Mrs. Carr seemed like a sweet woman, but gave the clear impression she believed in the antiquated notion that the men wore the pants. We walked in together behind 'our men'. *Whatever*. I had no idea of what she and I would talk about, until I thought of the gardens we'd passed on the grounds and remembered I always had a built-in safe-topic: Gardening!

The Carrs led us to a special room in the grand house, which seemed to serve as an old-fashioned parlor. A young man approached with a tray of beverages and nervously asked if I'd like a gin and tonic. He was obviously not a professional. I got the distinct impression he was living a repressed life, because, after I took a drink, his reaction was to stare over the tray at various parts of me.

Alec, who was taller than the young man by a lot, leaned down to take a glass too and caught the boy's eyes with his own. Mechanically, Alec raised a brow and when the unspoken meaning was understood, the boy turned beet red and made a hasty retreat. I felt bad for him, because really, the suit just wasn't *that* sexy.

There were six other people in the room: two couples and two unaccompanied men. They'd all been seated but stood once we'd fully entered the space. I noticed the furnishings were all faux Early-American; I felt no energy emanating from them, like I would if they'd been real antiques.

The Carrs introduced us all and then the women separated from the men, moving to a seating area by the window. I was shocked by this and threw Alec a glance, which he returned with something verging on empathy. I gulped the drink and was highly disappointed to find that it was really just tonic with the tiniest hint of gin.

I was glad to see that I wasn't overdressed. I fit in well enough and only stood out as the one with the highest quality outfit, next to Alec, who wore a handsome, tailored, English three-piece. The ladies were nice enough and when I mentioned the gardens and they discovered my profession, it was off to the races. Mrs. Carr had questions about the azaleas and the lace bugs that love them, the hydrangeas and why they wouldn't stay pink, and the camellias and why they didn't bloom every year.

It turned out that the young men they pressed into service were clueless. Privileged sons of their cronies, these kids (who lived in an 'education' house down the street) worked the grounds and mansion and were responsible for inappropriate pruning. I told her how to solve the problems and suggested a care-sheet for the boys.

One of the other women kept stealing glances at the men and I realized she was riveted by Alec; no shock there. I'd look over occasionally too and noticed Carr and his cohorts were working hard to convince Alec of something. Surprisingly, he had the appearance of a man who was thoroughly enjoying a game.

A couple of times he glanced over and winked at me. After one such event, I turned back to the gaze of the woman who'd found him so interesting. Her eyes widened, her face became a little pinker and she clearly was dying to ask something. I smiled. She took that as encouragement and leaned toward me.

"Is he really a lord?" I nodded. "Well, aren't you American?" I nodded again. "Can he marry you? If you aren't aristocracy?"

After a moment of surprise, I raised my brows and laughed. "He's allowed to marry who he wants. He's not a royal."

She looked back at him and sighed. "It's so romantic. He has a castle, doesn't he?" I used every skill I had to keep from snorting out another laugh. I smiled at her, Mrs. Carr and the other and then glanced over at Alec. I was fairly sure he could hear us and I felt a strong urge to smack him for bringing me into this.

I could only say, "Yes. Actually, I think he has a few of them … here and there." But before there could be any more questions, we saw the men shake hands and then move in our direction.

"Honey, shall we see our friends out?" Carr asked of his wife. She nodded and the other two women rose, both trying hard not to stare at Alec as he came over and put his hand on my shoulder. I wanted more than ever to smack him. And I was confused as to why the others were leaving. Apparently it was just going to be the Carrs and us for dinner and they were here simply to meet and greet Alec.

When they'd left the room, I sat back down and moved my glass around. I complained, "There's no gin in here. I feel like we've gone back in time sixty years. And what was all *that* about?"

As he too sat, he answered, "They were pressing me to join their little group and when I demurred, they got straight to asking me to intercede in affairs with several small pacific islands where I have some sway. There are sugar plantations on a few of them, which I began long ago. The islanders own them now, but climate change is causing major critical problems.

"I've been helping them with some solutions, but this lot wants to jump in and convert the population by bribing them with desalination equipment and sea walls. And though the offer is extremely irresistible, the islanders are balking. It's pathetic colonialism, though for what true gain I've no guess. Their aim can only be to bleed and devour the desperate islanders, who are wisely distrustful."

"Perhaps Carr's group wants a bunch of little private islands."

Alec squinted at me as if I'd said something extremely important that he hadn't considered. "Hmm. Possibly. Very possibly."

Soon, the Carrs returned and we all headed into the dining room. The very traditional table was looking about as perfect as it could and I realized Mrs. Carr was a nervous wreck under her sweet scrim. She kept watching us, seemingly to gauge our impressions. I had a feeling Alec's 'title' might not be all that big of a deal to her husband, but *she* was downright aflutter. I suspected she and the other two women really loved their romance novels.

After we sat and were served by two young women who'd appeared from the kitchen, Carr asked Alec if he'd like to say Grace. As he reached for my and Mrs. Carr's hands, Alec answered, in a surprisingly chipper fashion, "Certainly!"

Once Carr had completed the circle, Alec spoke in a reverent and slightly dramatic, loud whisper. It sounded lovely—and was in Latin. Two words stood out from the rest and I had to struggle mightily not to react. I knew one thing: the ancient Roman goddess 'Bona Dea', was *not* 'Jesus'. But from the look on their faces, I'd say our hosts didn't catch any of what Alec had said.

As we let go of each other's fingers, Carr commented, "That was nice, but I didn't understand."

"Well never mind. We have given our reverent thanks to the good deity," Alec replied as he gave his napkin an unfolding flick and then laid it on his lap. He then crooned to Mrs. Carr, "It all looks lovely my dear." She smiled and developed a rosy tint to her cheeks.

I, however, was unsure. My plate looked like something out of a 1950's advertisement—well-done roast beef, carrots and green beans, mashed potatoes and a little bowl of iceberg lettuce salad with what looked like green goddess dressing. Alec gave me a little nudge with his knee under the table and I realized I was just staring at my plate. So I looked up at Mrs. Carr, smiled sweetly, and picked up my fork and knife. It was edible.

Carr soon began attempting to take the measure of Alec and I think it was far beyond his capacity, which was actually pretty great. Carr wasn't stupid. I quickly realized that behind his amiable, simplistic front was a shrewd and conniving mastermind who had Alec in his sights. It was actually a little sinister.

But at every question or comment, Alec confounded and confused him, or just downright shocked him. Alec's ancient *Noblesse Oblige* philosophy didn't square with Carr's plutocratic social Darwinism. The nobleman vampire actually seemed concerned about the rest of humanity; the secretive pastor couldn't have cared less for them, except as voting consumers to manipulate and souls to herd under the guise of a benevolent shepherd. He was anything but, with his psychologically, politically and economically vampire-like beliefs.

I couldn't reconcile what I knew about Jesus' teachings with what this man was saying. I'd have been shocked at the juxtaposition if I hadn't been around so long and already lost my faith in most leaders. I was even reserving some judgment where Alec was concerned because trust takes time, but I approved of his comments.

Another difference between the two men was their treatment of me and Mrs. Carr. Alec attempted to include us in the conversation. Carr kept speaking only to him, so Alec would make his retort to one us ladies. Carr was pretty masterful at it and it was the only area he seemed to succeed in.

Alec surprised me by engaging in a little 'divide and conquer'. If he wasn't actually mesmering Mrs. Carr, he was certainly being playfully seductive with her. I'd not seen that side of him and it was pretty irresistible. She was obviously highly ambivalent, and I'd bet her body and mind were saying 'yes, oh yes', but her morals and beliefs were saying '*oh no*, you bad girl'!

Finally Carr touched on a topic that seemed to stump Alec, temporarily—*sports*. "How do you like our American football?" I forced down some roast beef and eyed my companion.

Alec considered the question for a long moment, then said, as inoffensively as possible, "Honestly Donald, I have a preference for sport which is not too severely tainted by external influences. In other words, I tend toward non-American or less popular types. I enjoy a little football, known to you as soccer, as well as cricket; after all, I am from the U.K. But even those are terribly commercialized. I find I do truly enjoy polo. As for American sports, baseball once had merit, but only rodeo has managed to hold my interest for any length of time."

In a weird way, that made sense, given his years as a knight and succeeding centuries of close relationships with those of the equine persuasion.

"Well what about the holiest of holies, golf? Aren't you Scottish? You *must* like that. I was really hoping we could play a round."

It seemed as if a chill suddenly permeated the room. Alec deftly laid his knife and fork across his plate at the perfect 'finished' angle. He lifted his napkin to pat his lips, replaced it, and leaned his elbows on the table. After a glance at me, he brought his gaze fully to Donald. "Mr. Carr. Pray, tell me why you say *golf* is holy? The centuries-old edicts against it as an *unprofitable sport* never should have been lifted. I'm quite sure your Jesus wouldn't have been caught half-arisen on a links. He had other fish to fry, don't you agree?" Alec smiled innocently.

Donald Carr opened his mouth—but nothing came forth.

Alec thrust again. "He'd never have played a game only the wealthy can truly afford, nor would he go in for something so meaningless. I like to think his time on earth was put to more responsible use. Somehow, I expect he felt no need for childish *escapism*. I am quite sure that such a useless drain on resources, especially time, would have been unpalatable to *The Messiah*. Your lovely and patient wife knows exactly what I mean." Alec turned his gaze to her and she flushed crimson. "Sorry if I offend, but I find golf to be a game for idle, and perhaps just a little grandiose, men."

Carr was no longer amused. But his wife had a little of the 'YESSS!' look to her, along with a little worry, I think.

"I don't know what to say, Alec. It's an important thing to me. I find it does have meaning. There's a lot of bonding among men who play. I wouldn't call it idle; we even get some business done; solve the world's problems." It seemed to me that the unflappable Carr looked just a wee bit dejected.

Alec replied, in a conciliatory tone, "Donald. You *do* realize that you and I are as different as chalk and cheese? Night and day?" Carr responded by silently placing his own implements and napkin over his plate and then feigning an innocent look at Alec, who continued. "We operate completely differently and have a different value set. For instance, as you bring up business, many of my businesses have been around longer than your country. Certainly longer than your *movement* and its ideologies, which you say is *God's work*, if I'm not mistaken. It is a mistaken assumption that your way is the only way. Or even the best way. The centuries have seen such thinking come and go … again … and again … and again. Always with the same end result.

"May I share how *my* businesses are operated, since what you really want from me is my influence in that area?" Alec subtly moved his head in that 'boss' way he had that spoke volumes. I found it intimidating and oddly attractive. I swerved my eyes to see how Mrs. Carr was taking this. She was mesmerized. Naturally.

"Please, Mr. Gregory. I'm all ears," Carr encouraged, attempting to match Alec's cool.

Alec suddenly reached over and stroked the back of my hand with the back of his fingers, saying, "It's all about taking *care*. It's not about *the money*, or even the business itself. It's about sustainability so that man has meaning. *Karma*, for lack of a better word in English."

Donald screwed up his face in disgust and laughed. "*Karma*? You don't look like some fag-hippy to me, Lord Alexander Gregory."

Alec's gaze grew cold. He stared at Donald for a moment then said, in his iciest tone, "Why, *Mr. Carr*. For a man of your reach and influence, you make the most astounding comments. Shall I simplify even further? It's otherwise known as *cause and effect*." He overly enunciated the last three words. Before Carr could respond, Alec continued. "A business lasts centuries because it makes good choices and has the humility to know where and when to stop, turn, go forward, downsize, reward it's employees, and above all, how quickly to grow and, unheard of in your circles, *whether to grow*. It stays continually aware of where it lies in the grand scheme."

Donald Carr stared, his eyes having gone blank. "Well you always have to have growth."

"Why? No, don't answer that, because I know your answer and it is complete fatuity, if you want sustainability. Nothing keeps growing forever. Not even the universe. And your little competitive kings, the powerful men you think shall care for the little people, shall never do anything of the sort. They'll only thirst for power and financial gain, which are not ends in themselves and ultimately produce nothing. Without mindfulness, your 'growth' leads to a great implosion."

Carr hurriedly said, "Right! And what you said about mindfulness, that's our belief. Godly men should run business. Men who have Jesus in their hearts are mindful. They're the ones who have the best interests of the people in mind—chosen men of means."

I was pretty done with the whole conversation. I started to pipe up when Alec beat me to it.

"And what does that mean? 'Jesus in their hearts'? And what authority chooses these men? And is there room for women in this corporate utopia?"

"Well sure. Mostly, though, they don't have the minds for business. Like sports."

I was now furious and disgusted. Alec took my hand and squeezed it, then just held it beneath his on the table. I stared at the red-gold hair that ran from under his cuff down in a neat pattern to about the middle of the back of his hand. It attracted me and I came close to stroking it.

"That is utterly, pathetically ridiculous. It is also a disastrously limiting belief. And nor is business a sporting event. Each business is a microcosm of lives, whether it be one or thousands. Its leader is no more important than its janitors. This winner-takes-all mentality is destroying our world. Without care and mindfulness, you *shall* fail. At the rate things are going, *all* shall fail if there is not a significant change in thinking."

"We agree on that." Carr insisted, but there was an undertone of disingenuousness.

"*Do* we?" Alec replied. "I think we are looking for something very different as an end result. In fact, I'd wager every penny I have that your true end goal looks very different from what you tell the masses you stir into your fold."

Carr became still, gaining a look of suspicion. "I beg your pardon?" Alec had clearly tapped into something.

In response, Alec swung my hand up to his lips, kissed the palm, and then looked at his wrist as though he actually cared what the watch read; all in a single, smooth motion. I had no idea why he was using my hand as a prop, but it was apparent to me that he'd just put Carr right where he wanted him.

"Oh, how's this then Donald? I'll play your game. One round of eighteen holes. As long as we play at night. I'm busy man."

You'd have thought Alec had offered to be baptized by him. "Well that's great news! I know just the place. But ... can you play?"

Alec stood and a moment later, I did too. "Expect a thorough thrashing. But don't expect to *bond* with me. I view that as something I do with women." He flashed a smile at Mrs. Carr, who flushed even worse this time. *Man*, was he laying it on thick.

It inspired me to add, "Well, and your best friends."

He quickly grabbed onto my opening. "Oh yes. And one of those is queer as a three pound note."

Donald smiled tersely, but the comment had an immediate cold-shower-effect on Mrs. Carr, who came around the table, weakly shook our hands, and claimed to have something to which she had to attend after we said our thanks. Carr looked miffed at her but walked us to the door.

As he shook Alec's hand, Carr said, "Well, it's been one to remember, Lord Gregory. We get lots of dignitaries and business-men, but no one quite like yourself."

I'd say the man was smitten. Alec's performance had achieved a bizarre 'love'. I doubted I'd ever understand the way some men's hierarchies worked.

"Indeed!" Alec was downright chipper. "We've had interesting discussions and I expect more to come."

"It was a pleasure meeting you Miss Trevathan." And that was all he deigned to say to *me*. I smiled quietly: *a good, demure little lady*. As we strolled to the Maybach, I could sense Carr watching, eyeing the vehicle as Alec opened the door for me. I knew he didn't care about style, as evidenced by the faux decor of the house, but he obviously got hot and bothered by power and influence. Alec's car said plenty about that.

I sat and watched the man watching as Alec came around to the driver's side. Then he was in and I waved at Carr, who hesitantly waved back. "Bye. You *sick fuck*," I said between my teeth.

"*Devi*! You honestly need your mouth cleaned with lye soap, I think. Really."

"*What*? That's exactly what he is. Jesus must be as furious as I am. He's not only a pirate preacher, he's a chauvinist pig!"

"Mayhap. Well. To be sure." He then resisted peeling out of the drive with the ridiculous 12-cylinder engine begging for the work-out. Once at the end of the block, he pulled over and tapped his player a few times. "Here. This will make you feel better." And he pressed the gas again. In a few moments, a familiar song began playing. Alec had turned the volume waaay up.

'*Reach out and touch faith . . .*'

(*Boom boom ba doom doom da doom doom da doom doom*)

He was right. Depeche Mode's brilliant, ironic commentary on what a "Personal Jesus" could do for me was the perfect antidote.

EIGHT

Revelations

ʊ

One evening in early August, Jack found me working on the wiring to the misting units in the second new greenhouse. Whatever the electricians had done was wrong and I copied what had been done right in the other two. I was just about to test it when he opened the door and asked, "Wanna go for a ride?"

I looked at my hands and clothing and said, "Only if I can wash up and change. Where to?"

Sauntering into the structure, he looked at my handy work and answered, "Of course, and home. I mean Alec's. He needs me to fix something."

Without warning him, I turned on the mister. As the water burst forth, he made a cat-like jump to the center of the room and only got a light dusting of droplets. Squinting at me, he gave a faux laugh.

"Oops. Sorry," I chuckled.

"Too bad," he teased. "I was gonna let you drive."

I stopped dead. I really did want to drive his car, in spite of my prejudices. "What if I said I'm terribly sorry?"

He shook his head with a slight smile. "Go change. You know Alec will think we should already be there."

A little later, with my jeans on and ponytail high, we walked down my front steps toward his waiting car. He threw the odd little box-like 'key' at me. I was grateful I caught it, because I was sure even this tiny item might cost as much as both my vehicles combined! As I fumbled with it, trying to figure out how to unlock the doors, he informed, "It's unlocked." Then he opened the driver's door for me. I stared at the black and red leather seat with its prominent 'Z' as the interior light illuminated its high-end styling. After I got in, Jack crouched beside me and showed me how to turn it on.

The soft roar of the huge V12-engine seemed more like what a space ship should sound like: a super, badass space ship. Or maybe a lion, incessantly roaring. I could feel it deeply resonating in my chest. As I rubbed my sweaty hands on my jeans, he leaned over me and made adjustments, then asked, "How does the clutch feel?" Pushing it in, I felt too far away. He observed this and used the electric levers to move me closer, then shut the door.

Glad I was wearing my leather sport shoes, I put my hands on the wheel and felt something very intense. Everything about the car was sensual. I'd never had such a reaction to a vehicle, not even Alec's fancy German cars. Jack dropped into the passenger's seat and then turned to view me. I just sat there, staring at the steering wheel as I turned it a little this way and that.

"Now remember, it's a six-speed." I felt my eyes close and shimmied into the seat a little. "Devi. We have to actually drive."

I laughed and asked, "Are you sure? You trust me?" He looked ahead at the gravel drive and said, "Of course. I've seen how capable you are and you have fast reflexes. Faster than normal humans. Plus, you've been driving for what, like, a hundred years? *Let's ride!*" He lightly slammed his hand on the dash.

I lowered the brake and eased it into first gear. As I gently tapped the gas, the Aston lurched forward. "Holy shit! This is going take a little getting used to. Definitely not the Daihatsu," I said, embarrassed.

Jack flipped-off my little truck as we passed it. Jumping to its defense, I yelled, "Hey! Ugly, but loveable. Have some respect." And I slipped the Aston into second and then third as I gunned it. Jack threw his hands up to steady himself against the dash, but said nothing.

It didn't take long to get the feel of the beast and Jack explained how the engine differed sound-wise from regular cars when it was time to shift. I was initially doing so earlier than necessary. I pushed it as fast as I dared, considering it was dark, there were animals about, and I didn't entirely know the way to Alec's yet. I had never felt so 'cool'.

"You know? I get it now, the allure of this kind of vehicle. It's just pure sensuality," I observed, as we hummed along.

Jack showed surprise. "Sensuality?"

"Yeah," I said, turning to meet his eyes as long as I dared to take mine off the dark road. Lit up by the dash lighting, I could see the scowl on his face. "What? You don't think it's incredibly sexy?"

His forehead smoothed, "Well, yeah, but it's the power under that hood. And the craftsmanship, of course. And its rarity."

"Exactly."

"Well how is that 'sensuality'?"

I pondered for a moment and could only come up with, "Maybe this is just a difference of perception, but I can tell you; sitting in this seat, with this kind of power and the way this car just hugs and caresses you, … the way it moves . . ."

Jack laughed all the way to the turn-off to Alec's drive. "Here!" he suddenly instructed, and I deftly turned the car into the opening. As we approached the gate, he pressed a button on a tiny box attached to his visor, and it opened. I wished I could go faster, but the gravel made for poor traction, so we stayed at 25 mph until we reached the mansion.

On the way, I noticed the *allée* again and kept an eye peeled for the elk I thought I'd seen before. As I slowed the car to a stop, I leaned over the steering wheel and stared at the house. My first visit hadn't afforded me a really good look.

I could feel Jack watching me and he said, "He built it in '80. He said he'd sensed changes in the wind and wanted to be near the epicenter. So he just moved here … for a while. Those stone blocks are each a meter high and thick. Plays hell with cell signals. They're from Brittany." I nodded. I'd been to Brittany and seen the rose granite along the coast. "Some are new, the ones on the outside; but he's got thinner stuff for the inside walls, which came from a ruin he owns somewhere in that area."

The lovely façade filled my vision and I now realized how simple, yet elegant it was. It had seemed so over the top initially, but now that I knew Alec better, it fit. It was very finely crafted and had almost no ornamentation, save the sconces and various moldings carved on the stone around the windows.

"Let's go," Jack said, breaking my focus.

As we climbed out, the front doors of the house opened. Both Alec and Gordon stepped out onto the landing and were lit-up warmly by the huge gas lanterns. Gordon's eyebrows were crawling clear up his forehead and Alec, smiling a little too sardonically for my tastes, stated, "You let her drive your *Zagato* Aston. It must be love."

"You're right. But it's not me—it's the car she's fallen for. She said it was like—" He looked over the roof of the gorgeous vehicle at me. "What did you say? Oh, *sex!*"

Gordon laughed, which was a lovely sight, and Alec nodded, saying, "Agreed. I concur. The thing is outrageous. And you deserve it many times over. Come in." He waved us up the stairs.

At the top, I tried to give Jack his key back, but he waved me off and said, "You can drive back too." I smiled and wiggled my eyebrows at Gordon, who just shook his head with a grin as he held the door for me.

Once inside, I completely forgot about the car and scrutinized Alec's home more closely than before. He noticed and offered, "Devi, I'm going to give Jack his instructions, then I'll give you a tour." Then they headed down the large center hallway and disappeared through a door on the left.

"Miss Trevathan, can I get you anythin'? Did you have supper?" Gordon asked as he motioned for me to follow him. He took me to a smaller living room than the great room I'd seen before.

"Perhaps just a little water. I ate already, thank you." He nodded and turned heel to go get my drink.

There were large, overstuffed linen chairs and a sofa. The room was painted a muted Dijon mustard color, and there were illuminated manuscripts open to beautiful, colorful pages on the walls. The large books were mounted inside thick glass boxes which appeared to be climate controlled. I slowly approached one and saw that it was a book on history. The text was Latin and I found it difficult to read because the calligraphy was so stylized.

The beautifully gold-enhanced image showed a battle scene looking like one of the crusades. There were many kinds of knights and their Islamic adversaries. Things didn't appear to be going well for the knights and I knew enough to assume this was an image of a later, unsuccessful crusade.

I moved to another wall and the next manuscript was also illuminated, but it was very different. And I recognized the main image—it was the Vitaortus. It was so beautifully drawn and painted, that it very nearly looked real. The illustrator had extended the tendrils so they twined into the calligraphy. I tried to read this one too, but could only make out 'Vitaortus'.

Two perfectly-rendered Death's-Head hawkmoths were hovering near a dramatic, six-petalled black flower, their yellow parts illuminated in gold. Behind them, the phases of the moon were shown in a circle, each image from the new moon getting bigger until it was full. Likewise, it became smaller as it waned. The full moon was illuminated in silver. I suddenly spotted the word 'Luna' in the text. Then I read the Latin word for blood, *sanguis*, but a glint from my periphery pulled at my attention.

There was a room off to the side with a warm glow emanating from it. I turned toward it and stopped for a moment because the doorway was quite different from others I'd seen in the house. It was a simple, carved gothic entryway, with numerous layered mouldings as design.

Making my way slowly, as I scrutinized the archway, I discovered a very, very old door hanging open on huge iron hinges. The whole thing looked like the entryway to a medieval church, just smaller. In fact, it seemed so short I imagine all the men I'd met in this house, save maybe Piero, would have to duck to walk through it. And it was an equilateral arch, so with the door shut, I imagined it appeared even shorter. As I approached, I touched the plain tawny rolls of stone and then the nearly black wooden door. Something about it was almost speaking … nearly whispering. It seemed almost alive.

I wondered what kind of tree the massive door had been hewn from. It was very thick and so dark I could barely see the grain. I assumed it was English oak or ash. There was a very complex large padlock hanging from a two inch thick bolt that fit into a space beside a D-ring which had been firmly drilled into the stone.

My interest in what lay inside was certainly piqued. Sneaking a peek beyond the doorway, I saw a floor of the same plain, light-colored stone, sandstone, with a fine Persian rug in the shape of a runner. Beyond it, at the end of the room, was a five-foot-tall glass case standing on a short pedestal carved from the sandstone. Something inside was very bright as the halogen lighting reflected off of it. I decided to slide my shoes off. It just seemed appropriate. I was wearing anklet socks to match my white tank top, and skinny, straight leg jeans. I figured if there was anything to knock over, it wouldn't be because of a loose item of clothing.

There were three steps down to the floor, upon which I carefully placed my feet, and stood at the edge of the long, thin, very fine carpet. I eyed the walls on the left and right. The room was perhaps twelve feet wide and twice as deep. The long walls were lined with carved, lancet arch-style window frames, but there were no windows—merely the carved stone and little four-inch-deep recesses where window panes would be. After all, this room was ensconced well inside the large house. A modern halogen spot gently lit up each faux window, but these lights appeared much dimmer than the one at the end of the room. It was all really very beautiful in its simplicity.

I walked toward the object for which the room had obviously been built and realized that it was a sword. The light glinted off it blindingly as I approached. The case was similar to those containing the manuscripts, but the glass was thicker, with an ultra-thin thread of wire inside each glass panel. The back had gold prongs attached to it to hold the hanging weapon. I stared at the buffed, but pitted steel for a long moment. This was ancient. And ancient things seemed to call to me, as if they were desperate to share their experience.

I knelt, not directly in front of it, but at an angle, because of the glare, to see if I could make out what was etched into it near the tip. It was a symbol, which appeared to be a later addition. It was circular with the words '*Sigilum Militum Xpisti*' around the outer edge. Inside that was an image of two knights on a single horse: the Templar sigil.

My long ponytail had fallen over my shoulder and just as I was about to move it, a hand reached into my line of vision and shifted it, laying it gently on my back. I turned to see Alec moving to squat beside me. "You've found the heart of my home."

I just furrowed my brow at him, not knowing what to say. *Had Alec been a Templar?* I quickly did the math. If he was just over eight hundred years old, that put him smack dab in the middle of Templar existence. He was Scots, rather than French, but there was certainly some kind of connection there. He was of noble birth, given the whole 'Lord' thing, which obviously hadn't been bestowed. I squinted at the sword again then back at Alec.

"Really? Is this ... was this ...."

He looked at the sword and then stood. Moving to one of the faux windows, he pressed something and a secret panel opened. Inside it, he tapped at a screen and suddenly I heard a hiss of a vacuum unsealing. I looked back at the glass chamber and saw the rear panel had come away from the rest. Alec walked over to the case, placed his right hand around the grip, and carefully pulled the blade from its place of slumber.

Not that I was used to the sight, but I had never seen someone look so natural with a sword. It was more like an appendage.

"Would you like to hold it?"

As I stood, his question struck me as funny, sophomoric as it was, and I raised my brows, giving him a half-smile. He shook his head with a smile and held the blade out to me. It lay across his open palms and I stared at it for a moment. I'd never touched anything so rare and priceless, and I was intimidated. Alec observed this and said, "Go on. If you threw it to the floor as hard as you could you wouldn't cause it harm except maybe a small scratch. It's been through far worse."

I reached out tentatively and he put the cool steel into my hands. It was heavy and I quickly compensated, but not as heavy as I'd assumed. I had the sensation that the sword's vibe was strange and mixed, almost as if its intent didn't square with what it had done. Reaching for the grip, I laid it in my right hand to scrutinize. The pommel had the classic symmetrical cross inlaid on both sides. I ran my finger partway down the fuller, or middle groove, then touched the stamp of the Templar sigil.

I looked up at Alec, who explained, "*That* was added by an idiot in whose possession it suffered. It was stolen from me and I searched several centuries for it. Thank God it was otherwise well cared for. I was extremely lucky to be reunited with it. That sword is the only possession I have from the time before. It is the only one I would have chosen. All other of the brothers' swords that still exist seem to be in a sad state. Only this one is relatively whole and handsome. I've had to replace the parts of the grip a few times, but I've always used the original material."

Continuing to examine it, I saw there were nicks and pits here and there as well as discoloring in places, but it was in marvelous condition for something so old. An image of my father popped into my head. He'd had a fascination for the Templars and had a replica of a sword similar to this one. It had not been as long or big. This sword had clearly been made specifically for Alec. Folding my fingers around the grip, I found there was a lot of room between the pommel and the crossguard. It was a great sword and way too big for me. But I wrapped my other hand around it too and then looked again at Alec.

All I could do was repeat, "*Really?*"

The halogen lighting dramatically picked up the copper and gold highlights in his hair, including his narrow beard and eyebrows. He replied, "Really what?"

"I'm sorry. I'm just a little awe-stricken by this. You were a Templar?"

He bowed his head deeply once and said, "Yes. I was in the fifth crusade, sadly. I was quite young, seventeen when I began. After returning from Egypt, I became a glorified bodyguard for important travelers of the Church. I was viewed as indestructible to have survived, but Egypt had ruined me as far as the glory and calling of the order. The battles had been … well, I didn't really want to do it anymore. I travelled all over Europe and the Middle-East. Eventually, a renowned mathematician and astrologer requested my service. He planned a long, meandering return home; he was a fellow Scot. But before I tell that tale, you should know you're the first to touch this, other than a master smith and myself, in over two centuries; since it was reunited with me."

I was astonished. I'd moved the sword to experience what it felt like to hold it aloft. Feeling foolish, I slowly lowered and then gazed at it once more before handing it back over to him. "Alec. Why on earth would you let *me* hold it and not anyone else?"

As he wrapped his long fingers around the equally long grip, he explained, "Because of the reverence you displayed."

I was confused and came around to watch as he fit the cross-guard onto the gold hangers. "What do you mean?" I asked, as I continued to observe the blade. When my eyes finally met his, he looked down at my feet.

"Why did you remove your shoes?"

It was when I viewed my own sock-covered feet, that I became aware that he was barefoot. I was sure he'd had slippers, or something, on before. I glanced back to the doorway and saw them neatly placed beside my little sport shoes. Moving my eyes back to Alec's, I answered, "Well. I don't really know. It just seemed right, somehow. Appropriate. If you went to the trouble to house something in a room like this, it must be pretty revered. This seems like a replica of a chapel to me."

He nodded that single affirmative nod and said, "It is. It's based upon the chapel where I took my vows, although the original no longer exists. But that door—" He turned and motioned at it. "I was able to salvage it. It is the original." He turned his head and moved it to signal that I should follow him out, but first he closed the glass case and secret window. "It goes with the sword, and the sword goes with me, or at least to wherever I'm spending the most time."

After we'd crossed the room and went up the three stairs, I turned and gazed once more at the weapon. I almost shuddered at the gruesome stories I was sure it could tell. But at the same time, I respected it and the ideals for which it stood; not the religious or pious stuff, and certainly not the killing, but the stuff of honor. And I respected that it was still around and looking good.

I turned to find Alec sliding his feet into his slippers. Then he surprised (and embarrassed) me by squatting, taking my foot and putting first one shoe on and then the other.

When he stood, he said, "I shared my prized possession with you for two reasons. One, you shared with me your secret, your agelessness, and I was the first. And two, because you are the only person in all this time who has shown the proper respect. I always remove my shoes. It is a miniscule gesture that speaks volumes. Thank you." I could only nod, feeling more embarrassment.

"Now, Gordon left your beverage on the coffee table. We'll get it and I'll show you the rest. You saw this small salon?" He gestured in a circle.

"Yes. Actually, I have some questions. What are the books? They're stunning! I noticed the Vitaortus, and is that a rendering of the fifth crusade?" I squinted as I moved up close and suddenly noticed a tiny figure in brown robes and with a monk's naked scalp. I pointed and uttered, "Is that … ?"

He gave a half smile at my excitement. "It *is* the ill-fated fifth crusade. And yes, that is Francis of Assisi. And yes, I did know him, slightly. We mostly found him rather irritating. After all, what he advocated was clearly against our purpose. But after the terrible battles. And then his own behavior, well, his example was the first I'd ever had that hinted at the concept of nonviolence as a solution. I keep it open to that particular page to keep me humble.

"The Vitaortus image speaks for itself. Those two are fifteenth century manuscripts. They are, in fact, illustrated by the same artist. She was very good. She was mute and lived in a cloister. She was a favorite of many scribes, for they would describe a scene and she could swiftly render it in chalk on slate as they spoke. Unfortunately for her, she was 'borrowed' for several years and forced to illustrate several dark books, this one amongst them. Being a nun, her captivity in such close proximity to *undesirables* was more than she could bear. And though she was returned to her former life, and even mesmered, the stress of it killed her soon after."

I was shocked, yet enrapt. "Who took her?"

"A powerful family of *Upyr*, living in Vienna. But the work they had her do was for various others as well, including practitioners of black magic. Some of it was foul work, but *this* manuscript is very important." He moved to the one with the image of the vine. "It is a compendium of known knowledge regarding our kind. All the species known at the time. There are numerous copies, but this is the original. The more recent editions have been updated as we travelled the globe and came across other species of sanguinivore. Unfortunately, there is very little information in this book on the Vitaortus. We have only come to be so desperately in need of the plant in the last sixty years or so. Those moths are one of the original pollinators, by the way."

As interested as I was in the moths, I was more curious about the 'Upyr'. "What's an Upyr?"

He eyed me. "We shall have to have to educate you. I forget that in spite of your mortal immortality, you are not all-knowing."

I smiled at that and commented, as I gazed at the meandering image of the plant, "Poor woman."

"Indeed."

Instead of showing me any of the other manuscripts, he took my hand and led me from the room. I protested and he stopped mid-way down the massive marble hallway, letting my hand go. "Per-haps, sometime, you can come and we'll have a look at them out from under glass. I'm more particular about removing them as they are more delicate than the sword. We have to wear sterile gloves … it's a nuisance, but necessary. *Particularly* in this moldy part of the world. Come, there are books you can see in the library which are equally interesting."

And he was right. I could have spent a year in that library. First of all, it had the same proportions as the great room and was its mirror on this side of the house. It had huge windows with lovely mahogany Venetian blinds. But even so, the books were safe behind UV protective glass. There were rows of shelving, the old, wooden archival glass door type, against every wall. It was a huge room, so there were a lot of books. It was obvious Alec was a collector. He had a room full of unique, rare … and not so rare books. He had one unit that was filled with the collected works of a number of modern vampire-genre writers. I laughed when I saw them and pointed.

He came over and asked, "And why shouldn't I have those? Some are quite good. Others are plainly ridiculous. It's amazing what people find entertaining today." But he didn't have Polidori's, Berard's or Stoker's novels there. They were in their own little case along with several letters and a beautiful little white embossed booklet of Mary Shelley's called 'The Mortal Immortal'.

There was a philosophy section, beside the religion section. Sciences stood next to the arts, but oddly, or not, between them was an entire single case dedicated to astrology. And every last book in *it* was extremely old. Naturally he had the classics, history and so much more. There were many books in languages other than English and Latin, and some that were scrolls and other forms. Nestled in the center of the room were two dark leather Chesterfield couches, like the one in the great room, and four matching arm chairs arranged to face each other. There was also a tall, narrow mahogany table with several tall stools. Attached to the back of the table were individual gooseneck lamps and magnifying lenses. Larger, standing versions of the lamps accompanied the chairs and sofas. All of the furniture sat on the biggest Persian rug I'd ever seen.

"Does this room get much use?" I queried, thinking it might be my favorite.

"You would be surprised," he answered without elaboration, and led me out. I had a feeling that his library was visited by those doing research.

We saw the huge and astounding dining room, which had elegant wood paneling and very large, old tapestries. Like the library and great room, a fireplace I could almost stand up in was the focal point. I wondered what kind of dinners he served at the massive table. There had to be room for thirty or forty people.

Then there was the kitchen, which was just *painful*, because obviously, unless he had human guests, only Gordon and Hervé got any real use out of it. It was a marvel in stainless steel and white marble. And as we continued our tour I noticed his bathrooms were all white marble too, even the sinks. I loved all the stone, but wondered if I'd freeze if I lived here, at least in the winter.

After climbing the marble staircase to the upper level, he showed me various bedrooms (not all, because there were fifteen!), each of which was uniquely designed and furnished. Then there was his. It wasn't the biggest bedroom — *that* had been a suite at the other end of the large hall — but it was large enough. There were a couple of chests and dressers, a divan, and a very old writing desk.

But what dominated the room was the bed. It was a huge four poster canopy made of extremely dark wood. In fact, it almost looked black, like the ancient door downstairs. There were things carved in the thick posts, and some were sporting what appeared to be gemstones as eyes. Grey-green, plain velvet curtains enclosed the bed, but one half of the left side had been pulled back. I could see a matching duvet over lighter, matching sheets and just two pillows. And in spite of looking sumptuous, and the carvings, it was very simple. I figured that when he pulled the cotton lined curtains, the bed was very probably light-tight inside.

"Wow," I said, as I walked over to it and stuck my head in to see the ceiling of the bed, which was the same, hand-carved black wood. "Jesus, Alec. I bet *you* sleep well." I was hoping he'd say 'like the dead', but he refused to fall for that.

He replied, "As a child."

A lamp was attached to the back wall/headboard on the inside. It looked as if it had once been a candle holder and then gas. Now it was electric. I turned back to Alec. "All joking aside, this is pretty much the nicest bed I've ever seen, except for those Chinese marriage beds."

He walked over and placed his hand high on one of the posts. "The difference being that this . . ." He gave the bed a serious shake, which it resisted mightily. ". . . could withstand a typhoon." I laughed and then touched one of the carved figures; it was a gorgeously etched dragon with citrine eyes. Alec added, "I've had this for four hundred years. It was made specifically for me. The regular beds at the time were simply too short, so it was popular for tall men of means to have such. I'm fond of it and, as you see, it pays to take care of things."

I nodded, thinking it was a pretty sexy antique that gave off a lovely, comforting vibe. Suddenly feeling a little embarrassed, I quickly turned to view the rest of the room.

There were animal skin rugs placed randomly around. And the other dominating feature was another huge fire place; being summer, it was clean and empty. Above it hung a tapestry depicting a scene of a female figure with long dark flowing hair and multiple arms holding various things; including a miniature, fully grown man (whom she held by the penis), a sheaf of grain, a sheep, a sword, an unknown plant, and what appeared to be a ball. She stood on skulls, but above her a perfect pomegranate tree bloomed and fruited simultaneously. From a cut in her ribs ran a small trail of blood which seemed to give sustenance to the tree. There were also various animals and plants in attendance. It was remarkable and I'd never seen anything quite like it.

"Alec? What is this? I've never seen such an image before."

He moved to stand beside me. "She is an old friend's imagined personification of The Goddess. Or perhaps multiple goddesses who control the life force. She is the Source of Life. This particular image has bits and pieces taken from various known religions at the time and he threw in a few of his own interpretations. He was never famous, 'though the best at his craft."

"She definitely seems like an amalgamation."

"Yes. Do you know, there have always been those who cannot reconcile a paternal deity as the source of all life? Even within the Roman church?"

"Well, yes. I know there have always been Goddess worshipers. And I understand about Mary and Sophia."

"Well it goes much deeper than that. And of course, even in my beginnings, they were still fighting to destroy the old pagan gods. But even many of the pagans had replaced *Her* with male versions. The Feminine created life and gave it sustenance. The Masculine was her consort, protector and hunter."

I frowned, "Surely he gave sustenance too."

"Minimally. He killed, later he farmed, but it is she who truly creates. And before you ask about creative males, well they are taught and nurtured. Generally. And anyway, all have masculine and feminine within."

I nodded then, and after a brief silence asked, "Why do you think that is? That Man couldn't stand the concept of a feminine image of god? Why did they feel they had to destroy her?"

He turned to me fully, cocking his head in a surprised look at my ignorance. "Why, competition, of course. Human males are deeply competitive. It's not that they couldn't be lorded over, it's that it couldn't be feminine. Because ultimately, the human male cannot win victory over the control the feminine has over him, so he subdues her with force, either physically or through laws and rules. And even then, he fails to behave as he should. Her mystery is profoundly frightening to him on the deepest of levels. Man is competitive, yet can never ultimately beat woman because *she* is the life source, of which he is a product. So, he must control her that her mystery stays in the dark. The churches of the paternal God-concept make very sure she is viewed as weak or evil because the truth is too frightening. Man comes from woman. Man's deepest nature is uncontrollable in the presence of woman. Philosophically speaking, of course."

I laughed at that last comment and nodded again, privately very glad that he had that tapestry. We stared at it for a moment, then I eyed his bathroom and asked if he minded if I used it, having drunk that full glass of water.

"Of course, Devi. Be at home in my home." And he turned to walk out of his bedroom to give me privacy.

So I found my way into the spacious, marble room. And when I say marble, everything but the fixtures and glass door of the shower was marble; even the toilet; even the amazing and wonderful over-sized bathtub.

I was astounded, yet again. As I sat there, on what I assumed was the priciest toilet I'd ever touched, I thought about how long I'd been near to poverty. But I'd not been born that way. My parents had been fairly well-off and I'd been well-educated and taught refined habits and tastes. I looked at the jeans around my ankles. How far I'd come. And now, I was sharing life with an eight hundred-year-old Templar vampire who had a marble toilet in his private bathroom. I tried to come up with a joke about a throne, but nothing was forthcoming. I finished, washed my hands in his wonderful sink, dried them on a lovely, fluffy, grey-green towel and then set off to find him.

I didn't have far to go; he was conferring with Jack on the main level. From the top of the stairs, I observed them for a moment and then they looked up at me.

Alec said, "Ah. Devi. Jack needs a little more time. Are you content to stay just a bit longer?"

Jack added, "Maybe an hour, max."

Both men watched as I sashayed down the stairs. "Sure," I replied. "It's not too late yet, is it?"

Jack shook his head and said, "See you in a little while." And he was off.

"How about a stroll?" Alec motioned with an open hand toward the front door. Once outside in the warm, summer air, we crunched down the gravel drive away from the road.

I turned and walked backward as I looked up at the house. "Alec. I must say, your boudoir powder room is pretty fabulous. I think *I* want a marble toilet!"

He let out quite a laugh and stopped. "So the little garden sprite is going to pass the bourgeoisie and go straight to the useless top. I thought you were a little *red*, somewhere in there." It sounded like he meant it admiringly.

"Well I am, sort of. Actually a little pink. I mean I'm really not into conspicuous consumption. But I can certainly appreciate *certain* fine things. I didn't come from poverty, not at all. But honestly, what you see going on today—"

Alec interrupted me as he swung me back around, putting his arm through mine, "Agreed. I completely agree. So many human lives, lured into mindless spending. Where is the meaning in that? Where is honor, or pride in what one does with the gift of life? "

We strolled along until the drive ended at a path. I stopped and looked up at him. "May I ask a … strange question?" He looked down at me and let go of my arm, listening. "Have you ever had times when you thought you were going a little crazy? Mad?" I then rushed, embarrassed, to explain my question. "It's just that—"

"Shhh. I understand what you want to know perfectly. And the answer is yes. Particularly in my first two centuries, in the beginning, when I understood so little about what I was. Time is a strange thing. The longer you are around, the less it matters. One's relationship with it changes. But initially, especially once you're twice or thrice the age that you should be, but don't look it, as friends and family die away, old fears and dreams die away, you are *sure* you're going mad. 'Who am I?' you wonder, as the identifying markers fall away.

"As the world goes through its political, theological, geographical and behavioral changes; and now environmental and even climate changes, and you remain the only constant, well, it's enough to drive anyone mad. Loneliness can also do it. And for *you*, not knowing what you were … with no one to tell you. In my case, I was very, and painfully, aware of what I was but did not want to be. For me, melancholia was the bigger problem, during the many decades when I was alone. Madness might have been a respite. " He then fell silent for a bit and my mind chewed on what he'd shared.

We reached a gate to a garden and went through. Alec explained, "This is Gordon's kitchen garden. He grows his own food as much as possible."

"That's wonderful!" I exclaimed, thinking that was extremely wise; although it was fairly difficult for me to see the plants in the dark as we passed through, I could smell them, particularly the pungent scent of the tomato plants, onions and herbs.

On the other side of the garden was a patio with chairs and benches. Beyond, the starlit landscape sloped downward under a long meadow and presented a beautiful vista of the forest and the low mountains beyond.

Alec asked if I wanted to sit on a cool stone bench, then he gracefully planted himself about a foot from me. We listened to the naturally musical night for a few minutes, and then he said, "The actual truth of my kind is rather sad. The rate of survival for the human vampyr is perhaps half at any given time. Most of those deaths are suicide … so your question is quite valid. Many do so because they cannot adjust to the constant cultural changes.

"Others are so dolorous, either from what they have lost, or their never-ending witness to the expanding atrocities of mankind, that they *will* no longer go on. Still others become mad with either bloodlust, or power, and commit acts of outrageous stupidity, which then ends in their demise one way or another. I have had to help dispatch more than one who would expose us with his insanity.

"So you see, there are many ways to feel unhinged in this unceasing life. You astound me because you have done so well—alone."

After an attempt at a sad smile, I confessed, "Those years in the asylum were easy in some ways, once I stopped fighting it. I spoke to only two doctors about my condition, and naturally neither believed me. But the second one did try an odd experiment. He cut me, just here." I traced a line on my right arm across where the deltoid, triceps and biceps come together. "It was fairly deep, perhaps a quarter of an inch. The next morning, when he saw it was more than halfway healed, he just stopped talking to me. I would sometimes catch him observing me. It was about six months after that that I was discharged." I gazed at Alec and he searched my eyes for a moment.

"And you suspect that it was he who arranged your release?"

"Yes. Surely it was."

Alec nodded and said, "I'd say it was likely. Although doubtful he knew anything or understood what he was seeing. Were you given anything to live on? I know your family couldn't have been of help."

I was silent for a moment and turned my head away when I felt my eyes begin to well and sting. I was surprised I still had tears left for the subject. Recovering with a deep breath, I turned back to him, knowing my eyes were probably a little shinier.

"My parents were dead and I no longer knew my relatives in England. My husband told me never to contact him. It all started when he saw that I had been befriended by a *baba-ji*."

Alec raised his brows and said, "A holy man."

"Yes. This one was a *sadhu*, or ascetic monk of the *Shakta* denomination, a *Hindu* sect that worships the Divine Feminine as the highest god form. He had been trying to tell me about who I was. He was concerned that I had no one to teach me and that's why he'd shown up at our door. I remember he seemed very old, pretty wild-looking and a bit barmy. But I was of half a mind to believe him because of all the strange things occurring. Including that I was young-looking for forty-five and I'd been hurt multiple times over the previous eighteen years but healed far too quickly, and never with a scar. Nor had I been ill in all those years!

"The baba-ji spoke of the same energy you've talked about. He said I was a 'sacred vessel of Shakti' and that I was excused from *Samsara* as long as I stayed that way. No death, no rebirth, nothing.

And that is all I have ever known about myself. I really thought he was speaking in riddles at the time."

Looking from me to the mountains, Alec asked, "And what happened to him? I have heard there are psychically proficient humans who can sense a channel. Why was he unable to teach you?"

A moth fluttered by and bumped against my cheek. Alec turned, and as he nonchalantly observed it, I replied, "Well, he was teaching me to meditate properly ... but my husband did an awful thing. He honestly thought I was a *witch*. And genuinely crazy. Freaked-out and unable to get the sadhu to leave after about six months, he arranged to have me put away. My doctor willingly helped him, having known me since birth and aware something was amiss. The doctor, and two men I'd never seen, showed up in the middle of the night. They drugged me deeply and the two men brought me all the way to London, via steamer. I never saw my husband, or—"

Alec took my hand from the bench, bent my knuckles to his mouth, and gently kissed them. Letting go, he said, "I am truly sorry. For so long, you've known nothing. But I marvel at you. You have survived more sanely than many others I know who've had support. How *did* you survive?"

Looking at my knuckles, I answered, "Well there was some money. It was in an envelope with my things and lasted me for some time, 'though I managed to earn money too. I left Britain ten years to the day after leaving Bethlem, in the year of the Blitz. I had to, of course. A decade is too long in human years not to change an iota ... at least it was then. I was sixty, but looked as I do now. And to answer your question, I don't really know how I survived mentally, emotionally. I tried my best to stay in each day, as the sadhu had taught me. And to find any gratitude I could." When I stopped,

Alec seemed to wait for me to continue and turned his eyes to me when I didn't.

I shook my head. "It's your turn now."

He quietly laughed and said, "Ah. Well-played."

I watched as he shifted himself so that one knee rested on the bench with his ankle on the other. He'd twisted his body so he was facing me. Viewing him, with the mansion as backdrop, I thought he looked like he could be in one of those Evelyn Waugh novels Jack was reading. Except for the beard; it had been fashionable to be clean shaven or fully bearded, not this elegant short boxed coif he had going on.

"As you've ascertained, I was a knight of the Order of the Temple. The crusade in which I'd participated had been difficult physically, emotionally, and mentally. I returned to Europe in 1222, rather disillusioned with the church, the Pope, the Emperor and the whole bloody mess. They'd simply let us down as they played at their politics. Some things have certainly not changed. Well, I'd taken vows and was committed. What else would I do even if I *could* get out? I was eldest, but had given up my rights as heir. I was absolutely the best at what I did; had the height and strength necessary. Having red hair helped as well. It was associated with viciousness and supernatural things in some places and more than one man turned tail at the sight of me.

"I spent the next few years gaining a reputation as the ultimate body guard. The roads were very dangerous and the order was well-served by my services. Usually it was for papal delegates or other such officials. But in time, I was requested by a man of renown. And he was from my own country. His name was Michael Scot."

I sucked in my breath at that, knowing that Michael Scot had been a legendary scholar, mathematician and astrologer to the Holy Roman Emperor, Frederick II.

Alec eyed me. "Aye. You should be impressed. As should the modern world—which has nearly forgotten who the man was." I was amazed and just shook my head. "Well, he had been close to the Emperor and valuable to him, but for some reason wanted escort to leave. So I made my way to Palermo and, upon seeing me, he swooned."

I stopped dead, then knitted my brows. "I beg your pardon?"

"Yes. My visage produced a swoon from the old man. And I would discover that he was certainly, shall we say, *Socratic* in his approach to love."

I threw my hand to my mouth.

Alec's eyes widened at my reaction, then he just chuckled. "Never fear. I was already very sure that what attracted me was feminine in nature, but I didn't entirely understand what was happening. This was a very famous, much respected man. He was simply a superstar for the time period. And there were rumors that he had supernatural knowledge.

"So, I just naively went along. At the time, you must remember, I was a young man and basically a soldier. Yes, a knight, but I wouldn't say I was a great intellect. And he was a priest. He remarked that my appearance was in many ways the Greek archetype. I accepted the compliments. And once we'd gotten underway, he spent some time each day tutoring me on mathematics, philosophy, science as we knew it then, and much more. I learned more from him than at any other time since.

"We left the court of Frederick and took our time heading north. We stopped in many of the cities of what is now Italy. We crossed the Alps at the place known as Saint Bernard's pass so that we could make our way to Geneva, and then on to other cities he wished to visit in what is now Germany. I had twenty coistrels to aid in safe-guarding the Mathematician's passage.

"We made perfect time, and got through the pass without incident. In Geneva, we hired lodging to house us through the winter. He had work to do there and also wished to finish something he was working on for Frederick the Emperor. It was there, with little to do but learn and keep fit, that I met the daughter of a local baron. Her name was Elene Di Candia and I had no business even speaking to her. But her pursuit was relentless. And I found her beauty and countenance irresistible."

I shifted so that I sat cross-legged opposite him. "But why? If you and she were of noble blood—"

"Have you forgotten what I was? A Templar's vows were quite serious."

"Well, didn't she understand? Why was she going after you?"

"I think maidens thought of us in the way modern girls look at rock stars. I was the recipient of much attention. But I never actually conversed with any of them. It wasn't allowed. Yet, I honestly believe any one of them would have given herself to me, consequences be damned. And my chastity probably sweetened the desire they felt. It was more about the 'Holy Knight' than me."

I gave him a slightly derisive look and said, "*Whatever*. I'm sure your looks didn't hurt."

He just smiled a little and continued. "For many months she brought little gifts. Chickens, cakes, flowers. Eventually Scot noticed. And he noticed I wasn't discouraging her and admonished me. I simply ignored him, and fell in love with her. And as the winter drew to a close, something happened that changed everything. A letter arrived from the Grand Master of the order himself. My mother had petitioned him. You see, my father and both brothers were dead. There were no other heirs."

"What happened to them?"

"Killed by highway men. And though I mourned, I'm ashamed to say I reveled as well."

"Because you could marry Elene."

"Exactly. I announced my plans to Scot and this time, he just laughed. He truly found the concept of love between man and woman quaint and silly. He told me he would not give me up until I had taken him through Europe back home to Scotland. And even then, never. I told him I was going to ask for Elene's hand in a week, and that she would accompany us directly there, without stops. He ceased laughing, and I still remember the look on his face when I left his rooms.

"And so, a week passed, I asked for her hand, was granted it, and we stood together in her father's garden, she, crying with joy and I gently wiping her tears. We had kissed only once before and it was just a chaste little thing. But, when, I finally really kissed her, we were in ecstasy for some long moments, until, she suddenly pulled back and looked at me, in horror. Then she retched and asked what was happening. I had no idea what to answer or what the problem was. She came near, retched again, then let out a wail and ran from me. She would not see me and had me sent from the home. No one understood her, for she claimed I suddenly smelled of rotting corpses." He stopped when, for a third time, I threw my hand to my mouth; this time less dramatically, because it was such a weird thing to say.

"Rotting corpses?" I leaned toward him, sniffed and smelled the lovely rose scent.

"Yes. But only she smelled it. Two days later, I attempted to see her again, with disastrous results. I still smelled vile and foul to her and she actually was sick, right in front of me. It was the most humiliating and painful experience of my life at the time. And when I returned to our lodgings, Scot was there, smug and ready. He'd had our things packed and our men mustered. He hadn't finished his work; it was early spring with unpredictable weather, but he wanted me out of Geneva."

"Are you kidding me? Are you saying—?" Alec touched my hand in a 'wait-a-minute' gesture.

"I realized he really did know sorcery. He had enchanted Elene so that she would be repulsed by me."

"So *he could have you,*" I whispered.

Alec nodded. "He thought that the only true love was between that of the mentor and mentored. An older man and his beloved 'student'. In a ridiculous effort to make amends, more of a joke, he gifted me with a scent that most women, and some men, would smell when near me. It is that lasting enchantment that you smell now."

I inhaled deeply through my nostrils and told him, "I hope you don't hate it. Because it's really very wonderful."

He shrugged, saying, "I am unaware of it." Then he continued his tale. "We moved on to Germany and were there for several years. I barely ever spoke to him, except during lessons. He would do what *she* had done, leave me presents. A cockerel, clothing, weaponry, bathing soaps and such. I gave it all to the local order. There was a priest of the order there who spoke with me finally, after watching my despair and anger. He explained that the Mathematician loved me and I did not have to return that love, but that he was important, and I must get him safely to Britain as my final quest for the order. I told him of Elene and the enchantment, but he refused to speak of it, saying only that I must forgive and repeating that I be of service to Scot, then go home. That I would love again. It didn't make me feel better, but it gave me renewed purpose.

"A year and some later, we reached the abbey in Scotland where he would live out his days. I had spent five or so years in his company. I detested him for what he had done. Yet a part of me *did* love him. How could I not? To spend so much time with one who is so remarkable … well, it would be impossible not to form an attachment of some kind. When we parted ways, I assumed I would never see him again.

"I returned home in time to spend a few months with my mother before she died. Life was hard then, even for nobles, and we were not the wealthiest. She was a very good woman and worked too hard to make sure there was enough food for all the people who lived on our lands. She was not so old, but the deaths of my father and brothers were too much. She'd grown very thin waiting to hear from me. The night after the funeral, he arrived."

I suddenly sat up straight. "What?"

"Michael Scot came to my home, and he did not come alone. Two men accompanied him, and they were men such as I had never seen. One was even taller than I, and broader. His hair was extremely red. More orange, really, not like mine. The other was an ancient, a Pict. He was small and dark-haired, but both were very white skinned. None of the servants were there, so I bade the men enter and got them tankards and what was left of the funeral feast. We sat in the main hall, in front of the huge fireplace which had a bearskin rug in front of it. Scot stood upon that skin and spoke, saying that he had been working on an elixir—one that would prolong life. He had a theory, based upon what he'd done so far, but needed my help to test it. He also felt that *I* needed to be preserved for posterity."

I grimaced and grunted, unable to stop myself. Alec laughed. "You *are* funny. But the situation was not. I was confused. He wasn't making sense. He said he'd been using the blood of these men, combined, but realized he needed a truer source." I scowled, realizing where the tale was heading. "Before I could move, the two were on me, tearing away my clothing. They lowered me to the rug and each bit: the big one here—" He indicated his neck "—and the Pict here." He touched his femoral artery midway down his thigh.

"I fought, harder than ever I had, but I could not move their stony weight. Scot said incantations, and threw things into the fire. I remember thinking over and over, before the last breath, 'I am dying'. Just before I breathed my last, Scot came and held open my mouth as both men cut themselves and let their blood flow into me."

Alec stopped talking and assessed me. "Do you wish me to continue?" I could only nod, wide-eyed. "I awoke in my bed, many nights later, ravenous, like a starved dog. I rose, naked and attempted to dress in the dark. It seemed odd that I could see so well, but my hunger kept me moving. I wasn't right. My movements didn't feel aligned. My body ... wasn't proper. It was *light*.

"I must have made noise, for they came to me. The two men had a girl with them whose terror was so great that she fainted. That was good, because I didn't hesitate. I instinctively grabbed her, bit with strange teeth, and took a very long, very messy time to drain her. I had yet to be trained in the finesse and skill required to puncture an artery properly. When the blood settled, and my demeanor settled, I realized what I had done and became inconsolable. Apparently this was a normal reaction, because they spent the rest of the night calming and cajoling me as I raged and wept. A month passed before I could think. Each person I drank and killed brought new waves of hatred and loathing. I had been a protector

199

of innocent life. I wanted to know what Michael Scot had arranged for these men to do to me.

"Eventually, he returned, looking a little better than the last time. I wanted to kill him—drink him—but the men, who were called Drest and Magnus, held me back. They brought me another girl. Finally I was calm enough to hear him. The two men were *vampires*. Drest, the Pict, was of an ancient lineage similar to the *Siths* of legend. Magnus, once a Viking, was not a vampire of Scandinavia, as you might think; he was of Native American origin. You see, he had travelled to the western land two hundred years earlier. It was *there* that he was reborn."

I sat up very straight again and asked, "What? What did you say? Indian vampires?!"

Alec frowned at me and replied, "And why not? I told you there are many, many species. They exist on all lands."

I shook my head in disbelief. "So why did Scot have two of them turn you?"

"He wanted to attempt to create a … hybrid, for lack of a better term, that carried the strengths of the two species. And he succeeded. I have never been able to find a Native American such as Magnus claimed turned him, so I don't know all they would have been capable of. I fear they were eradicated. I've learned as the traits reveal themselves."

I scootched a little because my bottom had started to go numb from sitting, then asked, "Well why would he do such a thing? And why didn't Drest and Magnus feed from him? Or turn him?"

"Because he was aiding them. Most of the civilized species need living human help if they want to mix in society. Otherwise they are forced to live like wild animals, and those who choose that way tend not to survive long. But Scot wasn't doing it out of the goodness of his heart. He needed their blood for his physical alchemy—for his elixir of life. It wasn't strong enough, and he reasoned that a being made of both would be stronger. And he was right—my blood kept him alive for another eighty years."

A whip-poor-will suddenly announced its presence over the meadow and we both turned to watch its starlit silhouette dip and weave as it flew after some small winged prey.

I turned back and Alec mirrored me. We stared at each other, and finally I asked quietly, "Why eighty? What happened to him?"

Alec continued to just look at me for another moment and then reluctantly answered, "I'd had enough of his ruinous meddling and *dispatched* him."

I eyed him back, forcing stoicism. "Was a woman involved?"

"Of course." He smiled a little sadly and added, "But we *did* have some interesting adventures before he died and I continued to learn a great deal from him until then."

"Do *you* know the recipe for his elixir?"

"No. I'd no need of it, nor do I find sorcery an appropriate use of one's time. I was against it then and am still today. It is rarely used to good end and Mother Nature will usually exact her price from those who would control or distort her ways. Cause does not always *only* achieve the desired effect. However, Scot had an apprentice. He disappeared and I've no idea what happened to him. If he lived, I never heard word of him. Who knows? Perhaps it survived through him."

A bat flitted and chirped rapidly above us. We raised our heads to again look in tandem at another creature of the night. When its jerky flight took it in search around the building, Alec turned his head to gaze at the mountains. I watched his face, wondering what he was thinking. How many memories could you pull from when you had eight hundred years full of them? His profile seemed very elegant to me and I simply enjoyed looking at it. But I figured he could see me doing so in his periphery so I just looked up at the stars.

"Hey!" Jack called from the garden gate. We both turned to him but only I waved. He came through the garden and stopped at the second gate.

As we stood, Alec asked, "How did it go?" Then he gestured that I should move toward the gate first.

"Great. Everything's back in order." Jack's dark figure moved to open the gate for me. I looked up at him as I passed and smiled.

I heard the gate closing behind me, and Alec said, "Excellent. Was it too difficult?"

"Initially," answered Jack "but their hacker is only so good, or else lazy; he didn't get in. He leaves too many pieces of evidence. I traced him. He'll be out of business as soon as . . ."

Alec interrupted with a single word. "Forthwith."

His intense tone made me turn around and I saw he and Jack had stopped, and Jack was looking at him with raised brows. "Okay. *Forthwith*," Jack said quietly. Then he looked at me.

Alec followed his gaze, then solved the problem of what to do with me. "Either let her take your car or we'll get her home. Fret not."

The two men flanked me, and we walked down the gravel path together. Without heels, I felt my height keenly. I looked up at Jack, who gave me a brief odd scowl and then I turned to Alec. When he didn't immediately look at me, I tried to stare harder, willing him to explain.

Keeping his eyes on the stairway ahead of us, he finally said, "Mind you don't trip, Devi. And it's none of your concern." *So much for our intimate sharing.* I gave up hoping to be clued in and put my eyes on the path ahead. But when I no longer heard the crunch of his slippers, I turned and saw he'd come to a halt. With head tilted, he moved his eyes to Jack's and postulated, "Unless it's a ruse."

Jack ran his fingers through his thick, black hair, raised his brows and cocked his head to signal 'maybe.'

Suddenly, Alec was in motion again and heading swiftly up the stairs. "Belay the *forthwith*," he commanded. "Fill Gordon in. I presume it was a local address?"

"Yeah, Arlington. Actually the same street as your buddy," replied Jack, who moved in behind him. I stood at the bottom of the stairs, wondering what the hell was going on, then jerked when Alec's voice deeply boomed, calling, "Gordon!"

Unsure of what I was supposed to do, I slowly climbed the steps and entered the door left ajar for me by the two hurrying men. I could hear them talking, but figured if they'd wanted my presence, they'd have requested it.

So I found my way back to the smaller living room and stood gazing at the manuscript with the painting of the Vitaortus. I could feel my heart beat a little faster. It was obvious I had a *thing* for the plant. I could just hear Gordon answering Alec's call, and the three men sounded like they went in the direction of what I assumed was Alec's office. He'd not included it in our tour. I wondered what was causing the mild consternation, but I was obviously not going to be enlightened; at least not tonight.

I found my little purse, which I'd left on the coffee table, and pulled its leather strap over my shoulder. Deciding to get one more glimpse of Alec's extraordinary sword, I went and sat on the top step leading into the faux chapel. Resting my elbows on my knees with my face cupped by my hands, I simply stared at the relic, and waited. Before long, I heard Alec's voice, now gentle, coming from above me.

"Devi." I looked up and saw that he stood near, observing my posture and position. His imperial demeanor seemed to have softened considerably. "Come. Jack will go with you." He held out his hand to help me up.

I asked, "All sorted out?"

He raised a corner of his mouth at my minor pry and confirmed, "All sorted out. Gordon will stop by and check that the generator equipment has arrived at some point tomorrow. *After* he attends to this business." We left the room and joined the other two men in the foyer. Once outside, Alec leaned close, "Thank you for the chat. And your revelations."

I leaned closer and replied, "Likewise."

Jack clapped his hands together and asked, "Ready?" I nodded, and attempted to hand him his key again. He shook his head and I grinned, yet again, at Gordon, who also shook his head, but for a completely different reason.

NINE

First Bestowing

ʊ

Serena had prepared the little plant and packed it snugly in the special wooden travel case Alec had given me to store it in. She was strangely subdued and asked me to be careful. When I'd assured her I would be, she said, "You still do not know these … people. You must always take care for yourself, Devi. You are special. I know that Mister Gregory and his *servidor* Gordon are good to you, but …" She looked a little embarrassed that she might have overstepped boundaries.

"I promise I'll be careful. Jack, and Georges—you know, who owns the restaurant—will be with me too. I'm sure they wouldn't take me into a dangerous situation. Besides, it's just a plant, right?"

Her responding look was *not* reassured. I wondered if Gordon's assessment of her wasn't true. Did she know something? Before I could ask about her concern, she wished me a good flight and ambled off to feed the chickens and put them to bed.

Later, I'd been surprised that Alec had travelled to fetch me and Jack in the early evening, with the sun just peeking above the horizon. But the windows of the big Maybach were deeply tinted and had shades, so maybe it hadn't hit them too hard.

Alec had presented me with a Diane Von Furstenberg dress and a pair of heeled Prada sandals. Having led me to my bedroom after scrutinizing my original attire, he'd said, "Nice as that is, may I offer these?" He'd not waited for an answer and just walked out, closing the door behind him.

While I changed, and struggled with rising anger (not too difficult when fastening perfect-fitting Prada to your ankle), I'd wondered again if he might be gay, much as I doubted it. He'd claimed he preferred those of the feminine persuasion. And I was fairly sure a gay man would know better—I wasn't his minion to dress as he pleased. If this outfit was about control, he'd be in for a rude awakening.

Still, I'd admired the shoes, but with the ambivalence of a cat presented with an open door. So far, I had no reason not to go with the flow, and was actually enjoying my time with the 'men' immensely. Who wouldn't? The perks I was getting in return for what I was giving seemed pretty congruent.

The silk, red dress was a perfect fit: clean, natural and only just a little sexy without revealing too much. Jack had given me a compliment by whistling when I'd come out and joined them in the big car.

The flight to New York was quick and easy. I was blown away to discover that Alec not only had his own transcontinental plane, but that it's interior was nearly as lovely as the Maybachs'. I'd chosen to sit by the west facing window in order to watch the tail end of the setting sun. It was lovely, but not for those accompanying me. Alec and Georges sat starboard while Jack sat opposite me with his window shade down and his sunglasses on.

Once it was fully dark, he'd put the Ray Bans in his jacket pocket and pulled out one of his mini bottles. After a quick tug on it and a smile at me, he'd turned to Georges. They began discussing a car Georges was thinking of buying and did so most of the way.

I'd occasionally glance at Alec, who seemed to be in a trance. He never once returned my looks. All three were dressed beautifully in what had to be multi-thousand dollar suits. Jack's was a shimmery black, of course. Georges' was charcoal with hints of purple in the threads and double breasted. Alec's was a deep dark blue that almost glowed.

Less than an hour later, as we descended for landing, I gripped the little plant in its case like it was an infant. The Vitaortus seemed to sigh against me. It was then that I felt a stare. Alec's stern gaze went from my face to the case in my arms then back to my eyes — and that was it for eye-contact the entire flight.

We landed and taxied for a bit before coming to an out-building at La Guardia, where a black Cadillac limo sat waiting for us.

"Showtime, lady and gentlemen," said a clearly unenthusiastic Alec.

We had to wait a few moments as Hervé dealt with the woman who'd dock the plane and then jumped in to take over the car. As we pulled onto Grand Central Parkway, Jack, who was beside me facing the back, said, "Be prepared: Mohan is not exactly conventional."

"What do you mean?" I asked.

"Well . . ." He looked at Georges and Alec.

After a long silence, Alec grunted elegantly and said, "You tell her, Georges." Then he stared out the window.

"Euu . . ." Georges actually gulped and that's when I widened my eyes. Alec closed his and Jack's were averted.

"*What?* What the hell?" My voice had gone up two octaves.

Georges pumped his hands up and down and said, "Now, now. I will tell you. He will have children around."

"Children?"

"Children. Yes."

I looked at Alec again, but his eyes were still closed and he'd leaned his head back on the seat. "What do you mean? Like, his kids? What?" Then I had a sudden sickening jolt to my gut.

"No, Devi. Not his, exactly."

I found myself smacking Jack on the arm and gripping it, as a release. "Is he a pedophile? Because I'm not doing this with a pedophile." I insisted, again with the octaves. Jack had jerked a little and looked at me with surprise.

Alec's eyes opened and he stared at me and Jack with a frown, then explained, "He feeds from them. I find I barely have the tolerance to deal with him. But deal I must. His penchant was grandfathered in by *The Boule*, as long as he takes only orphaned street urchins and keeps them alive, healthy and well-cared for. He is of Indonesian origin and quite old—much older than I. He was one of the thirteen when they made the few laws we have governing feeding practices."

So *that* explained Alec's dark mood.

We were all silent as Hervé eased the car onto the Brooklyn-Queens Expressway.

I looked at the little plant and suddenly couldn't imagine leaving it with such a creature. "I don't want to leave it with him," I pleaded.

Alec turned his eyes back to me and his demeanor softened. "If it will make you feel better, he does attempt to give them a life afterward." Then he motioned that Georges should tell me the rest.

Georges scooted forward a little and clasped his hands in a way that showed he too was repulsed. "He finds them in the worst places: the streets of Rio, Bangkok, Mumbai. They are all orphans in the ten to twelve range, I think. Girls and boys—mostly boys because they follow easier than girls. He brings them here for a few years, then returns them with money or sets them up somehow. They usually wind up much better than they would have been. Many of their kind die young or go into the sex trades. So he is not entirely without conscience."

Alec made his special snort again, and then added, "Except they are likely twisted from all the mesmering." I could see that Alec was seriously disturbed and I felt very grateful that it was he and Georges who found me.

"But he doesn't have sex with them," I stated, needing a reaffirmation.

Georges shrugged but then shook his head and said, "He claims not. He always seems to have an adult lover."

Jack, who'd been quiet the whole time, let out a series of noises mimicking shivering sounds, then shook his head and shoulders to indicate he was sloughing the whole thing off. He patted my hand and asked, "Are you going to be able to handle it?"

I looked back at him as he observed my eyes and waited. "I'll do my best—but *holy shit*. It's like—like *veal*; only worse in some ways, and better in others, I guess, since they get a better life." I saw Alec's head bob twice in agreement. Georges followed suit.

My feelings about this were suddenly all over the place. But one thread put it in a bizarre perspective: the beings I'd be meeting through Alec were all vampires. What did I expect? I doubted they'd all have the seeming civility of my 'facilitator and protector' and I'd need to be prepared for that. But if the explanation of Mohan's penchants had been darker, I'd have had us headed back to La Guardia.

Once on the Long Island Expressway, it wasn't long before we were at our destination. We'd heard Hervé make a phone call to announce our imminent arrival. He soon pulled up in front of the building—and *what* a building it was. Like thousands of separate steel framed windows oddly connected to make up the façade and sides. Hervé opened the door and let us out, making sure to take my hand in assistance. I was glad because of the heels and case.

Alec cupped my elbow and gestured that Jack and Georges should get behind us. Then he gave Hervé one of his special looks, which got a nod in response. I deduced that it meant Hervé was to stay put.

The evening was warm and a breeze coming off the Hudson shifted my long pony tail so that it landed on Alec's arm and shoulder. He didn't move it as we walked through the doors being held open by a pair of doormen. We were welcomed and then guided to the elevator. One of the doormen followed us and once we were all in, he used a keycard and pushed a penthouse button and up we went.

As we neared the top, Alec squeezed my elbow gently. Somehow, I understood he wanted to be in charge and I had absolutely no intention of butting in. I was still amazed that I felt trusting of him and his 'family'.

The doors abruptly opened and we were assaulted with sensory stimuli. First was the Japanese pop music; not loud, but loud enough. Then there was the jasmine incense, which I thought actually smelled good and was the only thing I'd liked about the entire, unnatural building so far. Finally, there was the décor: a fusion of Asian and naïve Central/South American which was jarringly colorful. It was a very strange combination.

I noticed a painting on the wall at the far end and was sure it was a *Diego Rivera*. A classic, ironic cliché: a communist's painting in a multi-million-dollar penthouse. Another of life's absurdities; which made two things I liked. It was a stark reminder of that forced marriage of the principled artist to the wealthy class.

And then there was a whoosh of color and a small, pretty man appeared in front of us. He was my height or even shorter and wearing a fine, raw silk, fuchsia sarong around his waist combined with a silk Asian-style light yellow shirt. I raised my eyebrows and looked up at Alec, who allowed himself a small smile.

"Mohan. So good to see you."

"And you, handsome Alec!"

Alec withdrew his hand from my elbow and pressed it to his other to create the 'Namaste' mudra. Mohan did the same and I felt sure Alec was pleased not to have to touch him.

"May I introduce Devica Trevathan, our treasure?"

Alec motioned to me and Mohan came forward with an intake of his breath. Dropping down dramatically on one knee, he again put his hands together in front of his forehead and after a momentary bow of his head proclaimed, "Little goddess. We are deeply grateful." He stood, came closer and added, "Can I have a hug? Please?" He looked at Alec with a delighted and expectant smile.

Alec and I glanced at each other, then I handed him the case. Mohan stepped into me and we hugged, full body, for a long couple of seconds. He giggled and said, "Oh wow! You can feel the *Ch'i*. Have you hugged her? Have you felt it?"

He bounced up and down, clapping twice and I realized he was barefoot. I could not *believe* he was an ancient vampire! Alec, Georges and Jack towered over him, but his own energy was phenomenal. He certainly commanded the room, in a weird sort of way, and I had no doubt he had lethal skills. A forbidding vibe, which was totally incongruous with his appearance, emanated from him. "Come in! Come in! Welcome. How was your journey? Good, I hope."

Alec answered, "It was swift enough."

"Georges! Jack! So good to see you. Is anyone thirsty? Hungry?" He was a quick talker.

As if choreographed, a lovely boy appeared carrying a tray of glasses and a plate. Four of the glasses had about an inch of thick, deep-red liquid. One had purple-hued wine. The plate was obviously for me and had an array of goodies from cheese to cookies. We followed the beautiful boy into the living area of the large, high-ceilinged room.

"Please. Imbibe. I think you guys will love the 'drink' and for Devi, A wonderful Pinot Noir." We all took a glass and Mohan raised his. "Let us toast."

After I drank, I had to admit, it was a very fine wine. I looked at the 'guys' and Jack and Georges were in mid swig. Alec was delicately sniffing his. I observed that as Mohan was draining his glass, he watched Alec. Alec continued to sniff, and then put the blood drink down on the tray, untasted.

"*Aleeec*," Mohan chastised. "Surely you don't think I would offer what you don't want. She's a virgin. A nineteen year-old virgin … from Guadalupe. I swear."

"She smells younger, Mohan," Alec responded quietly. The resonance of his voice contrasted mightily with Mohan's higher pitch.

"No. She is full native. That accounts for it smelling younger. And the wonderful taste!"

Alec grudgingly picked up the wine glass, noted the satisfaction on Georges and Jack and swigged. He didn't react, which brought a laugh from Mohan.

"You English. So *stiff*. Now, let's see what we have here." He motioned to the case Alec still carried.

Alec turned to me and presented the case so that all I had to do was open it and remove the plant, which I did. "This is a ten week old seedling. As you can see, it already has its first flower bud," I explained, holding it out to Mohan so that he could examine it.

With an exaggerated intake of breath, he brought his hands up to cup it, but stopped short of touching. He developed a look of awe for a moment. "Oh my God!" he said with flourish, then dropped his hands and cocked his dark head. "But it looks different. It hardly resembles the one I saw in Sao Paulo several years ago." He seemed unwilling to take it from me.

Alec stepped forward and stood close to me, moved the case under an arm, then fondled the lower leaves. "That's because we haven't had a Prime Channel for a very long time. This one is at the height of health. Do you have the space prepared?"

Still staring at the Vitaortus, Mohan absentmindedly nodded, then clapped his hands. A boy and girl clad in gold sarongs entered the room with another tray, this one much larger. It had a trowel, three candles, a pitcher of water, and two demi carafes: one with blood, the other wine. He motioned them to a room off the main living room and we all followed. I noticed the music had been turned off.

"Alec. I don't know why you wouldn't let me have a few guests for this. It's such an important occasion." Mohan whined as he elongated the last syllable. His voice was high and a little campy.

"Oh really? You can't think why." Alec's sarcasm was harsh. His protectiveness of me was clearly the reason. I guessed he wanted to ease me into this role without too many gawkers. When Mohan turned and scrunched his face at Alec, I couldn't help emitting a little snort of a surprised giggle.

Georges finally spoke up, "Mohan. Don't hurt Jack's feelings. He's a beautiful guest, as am I."

Then Mohan ruined it by saying snidely, "Yes, well, I'm sure you were both lovely boys. Jack reached for his neck. Unseen by Mohan, even Alec smiled as Jack's hands merely squeezed air.

We entered a special room that acted as a large, enclosed balcony, or patio. It made a perfect sunroom and the full moon was shining brightly a quarter of the way above the horizon, illuminating a shiny, tiled floor.

Mohan turned with a spin, his arms splayed out to indicate the appropriateness of the space. "Well? Good. Huh?" I scrutinized the specially made dais with the gorgeous five gallon pot, obviously a Chinese antique. I touched it and its vibe felt positive, which was a relief to me. My young plant would have a cozy space in which to grow.

"What about during the day? You can't have the sun beating down on it. That's west-facing and I'm sure it gets pretty bright."

Mohan raised a finger and said, "Not to worry!" He walked to the wall and pressed a button. A filtering shade immediately began to lower. "I also have humidity control—and misting!" He pressed another button and bursts of vapor shot from various spots in the ceiling.

I then noticed the orchids on the wall behind us. "Well this should do nicely. Can you get fresh air in here? Is that a skylight?" I pointed to a special window in the glass ceiling. Another button was pressed and the skylight slid back, revealing a large open section. I felt much, much better about the fate of my charge.

Mohan motioned for the kids to put the tray on a café table in a corner of the room. "Juan, you leave. Are you ready Seema?" The girl, who looked about ten or eleven, came over to me and bowed, putting her hands together. I smiled and we assessed each other. Mohan explained, "Seema is going to be the primary caretaker. She is very good with plants; these orchids are all hers."

I smiled at her again, then frowned at Mohan. Alec moved toward me and placed his hand flat on the middle of my back as he bent to get closer to Seema's height. "Well, plant mistress, has *Monsieur* Mohan explained your duties? Are you ready to take over care of this very special, very rare thing?"

214

Her beautifully huge and luminous dark eyes beheld him and I wondered what she was thinking, because she was certainly taking him in. Her child's naiveté was quite diminished, judging by her reaction to Alec. But she'd been taught well. She replied in perfect British-English. "Yes, Lord Gregory."

I noticed the tiniest jerk of Alec's red-gold head. "Excellent," he said, as he unbent to stand straight. He removed his hand from my back and clasped the other behind his own. I was pretty sure he was unnerved by the young girl, her subtle, budding sensuality being quite disturbing to normal types; even normal vampire types. I decided to take the reins.

"Okay. Let's get to it. Seema?" I nodded toward the unplanted pot. She smiled, but went to the tray instead and picked up a box of matches. She eyed me, looking for approval and I nodded and gave the plant to Alec again. Joining her, we lit the candles and placed them in an arc on the floor about three feet from the pot. That gave us space to both fit as we planted. The lights were already very dim so it made for that special ambient light that only real fire creates.

Alec came forward with the plant and the others moved around the outside of the candles. Georges', Jack's and Alec's suits seemed to glow in the candlelight. Seema and I knelt on either side of the pot. I looked at Jack and pointed to the trowel. He was able to reach it and hand it to me without moving his feet in a swift, smooth move. I then handed it to Seema. Next, I reached for the plant sitting in its open case, which was cradled in Alec's arms. He moved it forward to help close the distance and we locked eyes for a moment.

This was the first of the babies to leave our nursery. Would it survive?

As I pulled the plant in its special sleeve from the case, Seema raised the trowel. "Okay, you see how deep the root ball is?" She nodded in response as she eyeballed the root-filled bag of soil. "Make the hole dead-center, exactly the same volume." And she did just that, with a skill and confidence greater than her years merited.

"Excellent," I said, mimicking Alec. Seema smiled and glanced at him shyly. I lifted the plant, removed the bag and she refocused. "Now. You hold that side and we'll lower it in." I hurriedly added, "And do it with love!" She looked up at me with a little frown, then seemed to get it and her face became angelic. We both gazed at the plant as we lowered the little root ball into place. Gently, I began shifting the existing soil to erase any sign that it had just been planted. Seema imitated me on her side, and it was done.

After dusting off my hands, I touched the Vitaortus and said, "Grow well." Seema had been watching every move and stood with me. We turned to the men who'd been watching with rapt attention. "All done," I announced, as Seema came around and took my hand. I squeezed hers gently. "It grows very, very quickly; nothing like your orchids. But if you can grow those, you should do just fine. It's going to need a bigger trellis though. And at some point we'll have to repot it, but I'll help you with that when it's time."

She nodded, then asked, "How much should I water it Mistress Devi?"

Before I could answer, Mohan moved forward and said, "That's right, there's more to this." He smiled at me and then went to turn the lights up. It was then that I remembered what this child was to him and looked over at Georges and Jack. They were both watching Seema with a kind of resigned sadness.

Alec came to life then and swiftly blew out the candles. He unbuttoned his jacket, revealing a beautiful silk embroidered vest beneath. We all stared at it and, with graceful moves, he stuck his hand in an inside pocket and withdrew a two by four inch black leather case. Mohan moved to his side as they came over to me and Seema. This time Alec knelt in front of her. "Do you use fertilizer on your orchids, dear?" Alec asked her.

She nodded. "Yes, Lord Gregory."

He opened the tiny case and held it forward for her to see the vial safely tucked in velvet. "You can use the same fertilizer for the Vitaortus. Correct Mistress Devi?" I nodded and he continued. "But once each week, you shall put one single drop of this in your watering can and give it to the plant with a liter of water. This is absolutely crucial. Do you understand?"

She nodded, repeating, "One single drop in a liter of water once per week. Yes, Lord Gregory. But … ?"

He cocked his head in encouragement. "But?"

"But what is it?"

Without skipping a beat, he answered, "It's a special fertilizer only Mistress Devi can make. And the plant needs it or it will wither and die."

Seema's eyes grew impossibly larger as she turned to me. "I won't forget. But what if I need to ask you something after you leave?"

I glanced at Mohan. He shrugged and said, "Just give her your number. Where's your phone?"

Seema pulled her hand from mine and ran out of the room to retrieve her cell phone.

"This obviously must be refrigerated Mohan," Alec observed, as he snapped the case shut and rose from the floor.

Mohan moved forward and took the case from him, eyeballing it and then tilting his head to me. "Do you know what this is worth? Moneywise, I mean?"

I knitted my brows and replied, "I have no idea."

He turned to head toward his kitchen, saying, "You don't want to know!" He laughed on his way out. Alec went quietly after him, threat permeating his being. He hadn't been amused by Mohan's quip.

Jack and Georges joined me as I turned to gaze down on 11th Avenue and the Hudson River. *"How long are we going to stay here?"* I whispered.

Jack put his arm around me and said, "Oh. We won't be hanging around, don't worry. He's not Alec's favorite person."

I started to say, 'That poor girl', but she came rushing in, saying, "I got it! Shall we trade numbers?"

Jack removed his arm and I sat down on the floor with her as I pulled my phone from my bag, which was still diagonal across my torso. As we tapped in the numbers, I hesitated, then said, "Call me for anything. If you have any questions, just call. But I'll usually be asleep between midnight and seven or eight."

She smiled. "Me too. I usually go to bed by ten. At least on weekdays. I have school." As she bent her head and continued typing, and her long, black, shiny tresses fell forward around the phone in her hands, I dropped my jaw.

Well of course you do, I thought, feeling both horror and relief.

Alec and Mohan were still missing so I pulled the cultural sheet out of my bag and handed it to her. "There's a bunch of information on here that you'll need. But you can call, text or email me if you have any trouble understanding any of it. Don't be surprised at how fast it grows. It's like Jack's beanstalk." She giggled and looked at Jack. I figured she must know his name, and the story. I took her hands and we stood together. Once more, I went over to the Vitaortus and touched it. Then we headed for the front room.

The place was pretty big and initially we didn't see Alec and Mohan. Then there they were, in front of a massive built-in refrigerator in the kitchen. Alec had a death grip on Mohan's left arm and the two were deep into a quiet debate. Without looking at us, they stepped apart and Alec dropped the arm. I thought he looked icy and Mohan looked chagrinned, but it was subtle. Mohan had obviously made a big mistake mentioning the monetary value of my blood.

Turning toward the entrance, Alec said, "It's always a joy to see you, Mohan."

"And you, Lord Gregory." Their insincerity burned like dry ice. I'd have laughed if the child hadn't been with us.

Alec joined us without so much as a glance and Mohan pressed the elevator button. I found it strange that an elevator would open straight into your home, secure or not. Then I felt a pat on my arm. Seema stood beside me and held out her hand for a shake. I took it firmly to show her what that felt like from a woman. "I really enjoyed meeting you Seema—a fellow horticulturist. Your orchids are beautiful, by the way."

She smiled again and said, "And I you Mistress Devi. I will take good care of the Vita ... ortus."

The elevator arrived and Jack and Georges stepped in. Mohan grabbed my hand and kissed it. "Thank you. You are a savior." And when he dropped it, I was suddenly ushered onto the elevator by a firm, cool, strong hand at my elbow.

Alec and I turned. Just as the doors began to close and Mohan put his arm around her, Seema hurriedly said, "Goodbye Lord Gregory! Jack! Georges!" and she waved. With his unoccupied hand, Alec waved back, joined by Jack and Georges.

We were silent all the way back to the plane. It was nearly midnight and I was tired. I'd not adjusted my sleep patterns and wasn't planning on it. When we got on the plane, Alec sat across from me. Once we were in the air, I shivered and he removed his jacket and then placed it over my torso and shoulders. I smiled sleepily and said, "Thanks."

As he sat back down he said, "No. Thank *you*."

"Do I get to keep the outfit? These shoes rock," I joked, before closing my eyes.

"Good lord, what a question," he whispered, and crossing his legs toward the fuselage, looked out the window without answering.

TEN

Mexico

ʊ

Our next flight was to Cancun and we arrived late; far past when other flights had stopped coming in. I was very tired and just wanted to get into the car and sleep for the trip south since it was too dark to see anything. We whisked past customs and out into the warm, late September night. I could feel the drier air and basked in it. Outside in front of the small airport, I put my face up to the night sky, closed my eyes, and breathed in deeply.

Alec had insinuated that this trip was mostly vacation, but I understood the main reason we were here was to deliver the Vitaortus to a mysterious group who were particularly vulnerable. Another of his progeny, *Ch'en*, was somehow associated with them and had apparently impressed upon him the importance of immediacy. But aligning everyone's schedules had delayed us. I was very glad that I could leave for almost a week, knowing Maria and Serena could hold down the fort and make the week's deliveries.

That familiar, melodic voice interrupted me. "Devi. In the car please, if you're finished playing with the oxygen." Alec had his open hand pointed. Hervé was stowing the bags in the back of a giant, black SUV.

"Jesus! Is that monstrosity big enough?" I whispered loudly. Jack laughed and Georges harrumphed as he climbed in the front passenger's seat. I shuffled over tiredly and Alec swiftly lifted me by the waist and plunked me in the seat beside Jack.

Once seated beside me, he said, sarcastically, "You're in Mexico. It's like Texas, only bigger and much, much wilder. Perhaps you're getting spoiled by the Maybach experience." After a scowl, I turned as much as I could to present my back to him in response and then laid my hands on Jack's shoulder to use as a pillow. Not doubting that the Maybach's carbon footprint was just as shitty as the Suburban's, I closed my eyes again and slept all the way south to Tulum.

Awakened by a large, soft bump which lifted me slightly into the air, I gasped and sat up quickly. Everyone else seemed to ignore it. I looked at Jack, who said, "Good morning."

After a smile, I turned to Alec, who informed, "We're nearly there."

"What time is it?" I asked through a yawn. I knew I needed a few more hours of sleep at least.

"Four." It had been less than two hours. We'd *better* be there soon, I mused. The guys needed to bed down for the day, although I'd noticed Alec seemed to be dangerously pushing things lately, at least in the evenings.

"Ah, here we are. The hacienda is just ahead. You can't see it yet, but the archeological site of Tulum is just down that road there on the left. I find it one of the most exquisite things man has ever built." I figured coming from Alec, that was quite an endorsement and I suddenly looked forward to seeing the ruins by day.

We reached a break in the low, jungle-forest and took a left, which I assumed led to the beach. A grand gate, hidden from the road, was open, inviting us in. Hervé gently gunned the big vehicle and we slowly made our way down a beautifully tiled drive. In front of us, I could make out a gorgeous classical fountain and then the two story mansion itself, looming slightly above us. It was lovely and appeared as though it might be partially covered with a vine. I could feel a little rush of joy run through me and I glanced at Alec, knowing I had smiled. He just gave me his usual stoic gaze, but his eyes glinted for a moment. "How absolutely lovely," I commented.

And as Hervé pulled up in front of the fluted stair case, a body emerged from the house and hurriedly descended the steps. "Ch'en," Alec said quietly, pronouncing the Maya name with a little burst of air in the middle.

I squinted to see better in the dark, then motion lights came on so that she and the steps were illuminated. Alec opened his door and quickly exited to greet her after I motioned for him to go and not worry about me. Georges was getting out while Jack opened his side and held out a gentlemanly hand to me.

The woman was so petit, perhaps not even five feet. Alec knelt down on one knee to give her a kiss, on the mouth I noticed, and when he stood again, her head came only to his sternum. Her long, thick, black hair was pulled back into a loose braid, bangs left hanging in a part on her forehead and hugging the side of her rounded, heart-shaped face. Her eyes were wide and luminous, her lips full and plump and her nose could not be more different than his: it was small, sweet and seemed to hold none of the arrogance. She put her arms around him and gave a brief hug.

"It has been so long, Lord". When she let go, she looked up into his eyes, lovingly.

Gently gripping her chin, he replied, "I am so happy to see you. Ch'en." He kissed her again and she then turned to us with a huge, gleaming smile. I found myself smiling in response to her infectious joy. She was even more beautiful with her teeth showing.

"Welcome! *Benvenidos en Casa Hermosa Ha.*" She held her arms wide for a moment then scanned us. Her eyes falling on Georges, she said to him, "You must, of course, be *Monsieur* Picault?"

Georges moved to her with a hand outstretched and answered, "*Oui*. It is a true honor to finally meet you Sister Ch'en." They greeted with the same mouth kiss Alec had given.

"The same is true for me. So many years to know of you and never to meet, my brother."

"And now that wrong is righted, finally," interrupted Alec. He gestured to Jack, "And this is your newest brother, Jack Garrity." Jack knelt, embraced her, and they kissed; another full on mouth kiss, which struck me as just really odd for two people to do who've never met.

Once Jack moved away, I stepped closer and Alec took my hand, then hers.

"And this is she?" Ch'en looked from me to him then back at me, with a smile.

"Yes. This is Devica Trevathan. Devi, may I present my oldest existing progeny, Ch'en."

She moved closer and bowed her head. "You honor this house with your presence. You save us with your power. Welcome, and may it please you."

"Thank you, Ch'en," I replied, hoping I was making the right sounds of her name. I added, "You are so kind. Please tell me, what does *Hermosa Ha* mean?"

She smiled up at me, answering, "Hermosa is Spanish, for 'beautiful' and Ha is Mayan, for 'water'. In the day, you will understand the naming. The sun will rise soon. We should all rest, so I'll show you to your room. Lord?" She turned to Alec. "I will show Devi hers. Will you take Georges and Jack to theirs?"

"Happily. Come lads," he said, and started up the stairs with the other two men after him." I looked back at Hervé who started pulling bags from the vehicle.

"Hervé?" I called.

"Yes, Mistress Devi?"

"I can take my bag. Seriously. It's not heavy."

He came forward with the case of plants. "Here. You take this and your luggage will be at your door momentarily." I nodded and took the handle of the little travel case.

As we walked up the stairs and into the house, Ch'en placed her hand lightly on the case. "Are the vines in here?"

"Yes. I'm eager to see how they fared. It was a fairly long flight, but I doubt they're suffering." Removing her small hand and continuing down a long tiled hall, she led me to the back of the house.

"You will be getting the best room of all. Normally Lord Gregory would sleep here, but you are the honored guest. He insisted." And with that, she opened a set of beautifully carved doors and inside was a suite to beat all. I could hear the ocean from the open windows. Gauzy curtains billowed lightly and the huge bed was covered with even lighter gauze acting unnecessarily as mosquito netting. Still, it looked very elegant.

I walked in and set the case down on a lovely carved table and turned. I gasped when I saw the half-indoor, half-outdoor swimming pool.

With a laugh, Ch'en said, "Yes. Only this room has access to that pool. There is another for the whole house between here and the beach. If you rest now, when you wake, the housekeeper will be here. And Hervé. He will take you to the archeological site if you wish." She came over and surprised me by taking my hands in hers. Then she completely took me aback by kneeling in front of me. "We are grateful to you. My charges are dying." She then hugged my waist, and before I could say anything, she stood and hurried from the room.

I followed to the door, but she'd disappeared and instead I found Hervé bringing my bag.

"Here you are Mistress Devi." He entered the room and placed the suitcase on a trunk, as if he'd done just this action before.

"Hervé?" He turned his salt and pepper head toward me as he headed for the door. "Does Alec come here often? Ch'en said he usually sleeps in this room."

As he gripped the handles of the doors in preparation to close them, he answered, "Yes. Well, he hasn't been for some time, but it *is* his hacienda. By the way, there is a bar at the far end with beverages and snacks if you should become hungry before breakfast." His eyes motioned in the direction of the part of the room hidden behind a corner.

"Thanks Hervé. Sleep well."

"And you, Mistress," he replied, shutting the doors. It still felt really odd for him to be calling me that—for *anyone* to be calling me that.

Turning to view the room, I was suddenly aware again of how tired I was. The bed looked so inviting that I felt like goldilocks about to get into Baby Bear's bed. Only, it was really Papa Bear's. *Whatever.* I stripped down to my underwear, found an opening in the netting, pulled back the covers and got in, not caring that I hadn't brushed my teeth or washed my face. After reaching to turn off the bedside lamp, I was asleep in no time, lulled there by the sound of waves gently crashing to their journeys end on the sand.

~

The sound of a distant rooster call woke me and it wasn't Eddie. The Caribbean Sea sang softly and a light breeze wafted through several sets of gauze. The air felt so perfect. I sighed deeply, yawned and snuggled into the bed. But it seemed as if the waves called more insistently and the rooster crowed again. I could smell food cooking and that brought me fully awake.

Slipping out from under the covers and through the net, I padded across the cool tile floor to the windows, looking for a clock as I went. I couldn't find one and tried to deduce the time from the sun's angle. I guessed it was around nine-thirty, but was unsure at this latitude. In Virginia, no matter the time of year, I could tell the hour within five minutes. It's what comes from so many years of observation and just 'being'. I'd noticed my new friends didn't really care about time unless they had appointments to keep.

I inhaled sharply as I took in the view from the windows. There was a veranda around the other half of the pool and beyond that, the ocean. An absolutely, stunningly perfect white sand beach lay about a hundred yards from the house, which sat above on a twenty-five-foot-high limestone cliff. Various species of palm, including coconut and fan, were in view on the property. I could see splashes of bright color and couldn't wait to check out the garden, but first, a quick shower and clothing.

Needless to say, the bathroom was no less than amazing. It was done in mosaic tiles but rather than typical colorful Mexican, they were in a Mayan motif and looked like jadeite, obsidian and polished limestone. It was dramatic and I wondered at the expense. I caressed the beautiful green stone. The carvings were odd, and some a little frightening. I noticed many looked bat-like, which made me laugh. When I looked closer, the detail was so fine, I could see genitalia had even been carved. Well, I'd seen bats, and to be sure, you didn't have to look too hard to see what sex they were.

After the shower, I felt even better and stuck my wet hair up in a bun. Then, once I'd donned a sarong, I spotted the travel case and rushed to it, having forgotten about it last night. I quickly opened it and was relieved to find the young plants none the worse for wear. Their soil was even moist still, so I left them on a credenza near a window but out of sunlight.

Refreshed and worry-free, I ventured out to find the food. My nose led me, and as I followed it, I scrutinized the house. To start with, all of the furnishings were hand carved, whether from wood or stone, and they looked relatively old, but I was fairly sure they were recent enough because they were more for someone the size of Alec. The style seemed like it could be of Maya origins, but with a little Spanish attribution. There were pre-Columbian artifacts all over, mosaics and limestone carvings behind glass on the warm ochre walls as well as free standing pieces on the furniture. I imagined the worth of the stuff in the main living room reached into the millions. Alec wouldn't have re-productions. There was an archway leading to a dining room and I could hear voices coming from beyond it.

Once through the dining room (the table was a large limestone slab of carved glyphs covered in thick glass), I entered the bright and cheerful kitchen.

"Ah, *buenos dias*, Mistress Devi! Come have breakfast," Hervé called from a dark wooden table half in and half out of the kitchen. There was another veranda behind him and apparently a disappearing wall like the one which separated the indoor and outdoor halves of the master bedroom pool. The entire sea-facing wall was missing from the kitchen! It was wonderful, but I wondered what they did when hurricanes threatened.

"*Buenos dias*, Hervé," I said, then noticed a smiling woman behind a counter, cooking. She was definitely not Maya. She was of Spanish decent and looked older and pleasantly plump.

"Hi, Miss Devi. You want *huevos*?"

"*Si, gracias!*" I answered, as I sat down with Hervé.

"This is Juanita. Her food is the best," he praised, making sure she could hear him.

"*Buenos dias*, Juanita. It's good to meet you."

She nodded as she cooked, saying, "You too, Miss Devi."

Hervé asked, "Are you refreshed? Did you sleep well?"

"Oh my god, yes. This place is amazing. The sea lulls you. The air is so wonderful!" I enthused.

Juanita brought my plate and a large platter full of various things, including the eggs. She handed a serving spoon to me and went back to the cooking area to get coffee and juice.

There were tortillas, and after spooning eggs and chorizo onto one, I added potatoes to my plate and scanned the other items. There were slices of guava and watermelon and pico de gallo, which I ladled onto my eggs. My first bite was wonderful and I tucked in heartily. I tasted habaneros in the pico de gallo: fruitier, despite being way hotter than jalapenos. Juanita had put just the right amount in to keep from ruining the dish with too many Scoville units.

Returning with the coffee and juice, she asked, "*Buena?*"

"Wonderful!" I replied with a mouthful. Her smile was indulgent; she knew she was a good cook.

Hervé was silently enjoying his own plateful, and after five minutes of eating and drinking, he asked, "Do you wish to go to any of the ruins today? We have nearly a week. Perhaps today you would like to just get acquainted with the possibilities and go to the beach?"

I swallowed a bite of watermelon. "Yes. I think that's a good idea. Is there anything I can read about the sights?"

"I looked earlier and they are outdated. I shall go get some new information in town shortly. Do you need anything else?"

Glancing at Juanita, who had her back to us as she washed up, I leaned toward him and whispered, "I have some questions. You know Alec. He rarely gives me time to ask. Can we talk a little when you get back?"

"Certainly Mistress. *Absolutamente.* I shall find you at the beach?" I nodded and we went back to our food.

When we finished, Juanita fussed at us as we tried to help her with the dishes. I was so glad this morning had been informal. If I had to spend the week eating in the dining room alone, yet with a house full of people, I'd find it a little depressing. She showed me a plate in the fridge of things she'd made for a light lunch and said she'd be back in the late afternoon to prepare dinner for the *Patrón* and his guests. I doubted she knew who, or rather *what*, the 'Patrón' and his buddies were.

Hervé and she left together and he offered to drive her home. I watched from the front door as he took her ancient bicycle with the front basket and carefully placed it in the back of the huge SUV. She twittered at him in Spanish and I heard a lot of *graciases*.

After they drove off, I went back to the kitchen, poured another cup of coffee and did a quick tour of the garden. It wrapped around the entire house and, instead of being formal, followed a meandering path of close-in passages peppered with big open sandy beds. Every space had something wonderful. The 'bones' were the different palms which varied in height and shape. Some were spectacular and had orchids and bromeliads growing in baskets fastened to them.

Instead of the temperate perennials and annuals to which I was accustomed, multitudes of tropicals and succulents filled the spaces in between the palms. The colors outside the house made up for the muted shades of the interior décor. The vine I'd seen last night proved to be bougainvillea and it was a stunning hot-pink.

When I came around the south side of the house, I realized I was near the bedroom in which I'd slept. The view of the *hermosa ha* before me beckoned and I had to cut my tour short, don my bikini and get into that clear, warm water.

Back in the room, I dumped the contents of my suitcase on the bed and grabbed the suit. It was astounding to think how far women's freedoms had come since I'd been born. I had loved the invention of the bikini. But I didn't wear my first one until 1955, nearly a decade later. I was just too chicken. In the late '40s and early '50s I'd modeled several times in shorts with a bikini top, but never the bottoms! And though I'd grown progressively more daring through the ensuing decades, I still carried a vestige of the young Victorian woman.

Someone left a stack of towels by the pool, so I took two and headed down the natural steps leading to the beach—and then I was in heaven.

As *above, so below,* I thought, savoring all that was in my vision. The nearly white sand beach and the clear waters going from light blue to darker as the depth only slightly increased were mirrored by a few stray clouds against a deep clear blue sky. On either side of me, I could see coconut palms arching out and up, creating a tree-line along the beach.

As I laid one of the towels on the warm sand, I noticed a movement peripherally. I looked and was surprised to see a very large iguana regarding me from its limestone boulder perch. It seemed to be waiting to see what I was going to do. When I slowly sat, it relaxed and splayed its robust self out on the rock, doing exactly as I. Soon after, I was warmed enough and went to the water, walking straight in until it came up to my waist. I hadn't had this intense feeling of contentment in a very, very long time.

After swimming and floating for a while, I saw a figure coming down the steps. It was Hervé. He stopped midway, searching for me and I waved from the water, He waved back and continued down. He had a towel and had changed into swimwear. We matched—his bikini-style brief was black too.

As I walked up the beach from my swim, he was laying his towel beside mine. There were beautiful, canopied, double hammock beds at the base of the small cliff, but if you wanted rays, our choice was best.

When I reached the towels, he was sitting and handed me the extra one I'd brought. "And? How is the water?"

"It's absolutely perfect." I replied, as I dried off. "This place is wonderful so far."

He smiled a full smile, which was the first I'd seen on him and he looked great with it. "Si. Indeed it is. I always enjoy coming here. But it has been some years."

"Yes. You mentioned that before. May I ask how many?"

"It has been about thirty," he answered nonchalantly. I pulled in air as I sat down, surprised.

"H—how long have you been with Alec?"

"Fifty years."

I stared at him. "May I ask how old you are?"

"Sixty. Mister Gregory saved my life. I was ten and my stepfather was beating me. He had locked my mother in the cellar and she could not help." Hervé adjusted so he could lie flat and closed his eyes. "I broke free and ran out of our small house in the mountains not far from San Sebastian. Just as he caught me, and began to very seriously try to kill me, Mister Gregory was there and knocked him unconscious, then took me back to my home."

I had lain down too, but was upright again, emitting a little sound. I was surprised he was sharing this so nonchalantly.

He opened one eye and looked at me with it. "Yes. It was very horrible. I thanked God every day for many years that Mister Gregory appeared that night. My stepfather was very big; the strongest for many towns around. Only a vampire could beat him. Mister Gregory was a gentleman and did not feed from him in front of me. But I know he did later because the corpse was very white. My mother explained it to me. He made a deal with her: that he would educate me, and pay us both if she allowed me to work for him. She knew what he was, but she believed he would be good to me. And he has been. He even offered to let me leave many times, should I choose. But why? I'm a very contented man."

He closed the eye, clearly keeping the soaking in of sunrays a priority as he lay still.

"Is your mother still alive? Why was Alec there?"

"Yes. She is still in the same house in the small village in the mountains. But she no longer remembers that I work for a vampire. She thinks he is just a Scottish aristocrat. He mesmered her after she agreed, which kept us all safe. He was wise in knowing she might not be able to keep it to herself. Mr. Gregory was staying at the villa of a friend between there and Biarritz. I believe perhaps he was … hunting."

We were quiet for a while, then I asked, "Did you never want a family?"

"No. Oh, maybe when I was in my late thirties. But it was very brief. I truly had no desire to leave. It has been a very good life. And I would have to leave to have a family, which I feel I have, in a way. Gordon was only twenty when he came to live with us. He visited often as a child." He raised his head and shaded his eyes as he looked at me for understanding. I smiled and nodded. I could most certainly understand. I hadn't been with them long, but I felt a strong connection already. And something about Alec *made* you want to be of service.

Before he looked away, I asked, "What's the story with Ch'en? Were … or are she and Alec together?"

He scrutinized me, as if trying to decide if my motives for asking were worthy of an answer. Apparently they were. "I think she *was* his lover, once, very long ago. But can you imagine? She must live here and he lives in other places. Eventually, they became merely good friends. She has a duty and fulfills it. Her position here is very important and she is proud of it."

"How? What's her position?"

"She is a guardian." He said the last word with emphasis. I just searched his eyes until he continued. "She is guardian of those we've come to help. There will be another trip for the regular Central American group. This is a special trip."

"Well—," I started.

He waved his hand gently at me. "No. I don't know more. I've never met nor seen these people. They are secretive. Perhaps they are ancient Maya, like Ch'en, who wish not to be with the others, who are of Spanish descent. I don't know." He was clearly done discussing. "Time to swim." He jumped up with a grace that belied his years and offered his hand. I took it, he pulled me up and we jogged to the water.

After a few hours, we'd had enough sun and went back into the house. I'd noticed the iguana had gone for a siesta somewhere. After a little late lunch, I had my own siesta.

I awoke to the scent of pork being cooked. It was an amazing odor and I wondered if the clarity of the air here made things smell better to me.

After another shower, I put on a long, thin-strapped dress and went out to the kitchen. "Hi," I said from the doorway, as Juanita worked and Hervé sat at the table, reading.

"Juanita is preparing a wonderful dinner for tonight. It is called 'Cochinita Pibil'. It has been cooking in the ground for many hours. Mouthwatering!" He kissed his fingers in an Italian gesture to make his point.

I smiled at her and said, "I can smell it. Wonderful!" She smiled her smile, but continued focusing on what she was doing.

I said quietly to Hervé, "She doesn't know, right?"

"Correct. Mistress, very few know."

"How do you explain—"

"She would not ask. She doesn't assume. And if she does, or shows signs of suspecting, she'll be—"

"Mesmered."

"Yes. Anyway, she prepares the meal, I shall serve it. She'll leave just as they are beginning to arise."

"Oh."

"Look what I brought you. Information on the sights." He said, changing the subject and pushing a pile of brochures toward me. "There are torches you can light. It will be another hour before dinner. You can read on the beach if you wish." He handed me a box of matches and pointed to a bin holding a bunch of copper torches.

After picking two torches with full canisters, I lit them and headed past the main pool and down the stairway. It was cooler now, and just right. Approaching the first hammock, I plunged a torch in the sand near it and went round the other side and did the same with the other torch.

I had tucked the brochures under my arm and now laid them on the hammock. Gingerly testing and finding it was very sturdy, I hopped up and into the bed-like structure. My mustard-colored dress was long, stretchy cotton and not the easiest in which to do these kinds of maneuvers. So I hiked it up to my thighs in order to get comfortable.

Someone had placed clean, scented pillows on the hammocks and I stacked them. Leaning back, I stopped all movement for a moment and looked out at the sea. The waves were very gentle and the ambient sound could not have been more soothing, with myriad night creatures in the jungle starting up a soft cadence of song. Taking a deep breath, I then exhaled slowly and picked up the first of the brochures. The light wasn't great, but I could see it well enough.

I must have gone into a trance because suddenly there was a cool presence beside me, with an arm and leg thrown over my body. The last vestiges of light had faded.

"Mmm. You smell like sea and sun. You're really, really warm," said a soft, American voice. It was Jack and his face was buried in my neck.

I jerked, exclaiming, "Hey! What do you think you're doing?" I was both outraged and delighted. And this made me feel doubly ambivalent.

"Isn't this place sexy?" he asked, as he pulled away a little and removed his arm and leg. Turning onto his back, he scooted up against me and put his arms behind his head.

"*Maybe.* Jesus, Jack—you scared the crap out of me."

He just laughed. "How the hell am I going to last a week here without a little *joi de vivre?*"

"I don't know, *Jack*, but you won't be getting it from Devi," Alec answered, just stepping off the last step onto the sand. He was bare-footed and chested and I was a little awe-stricken. A sarong was wrapped around him, tucked in at his waist, and I was amazed at how good he looked. His freckling made him appear tanned, at least in the torchlight. He also had scars; *a lot of them.* Jack looked nearly as good in his swim trunks, but he was much whiter. Both were lean, chiseled specimens (due to a pure protein diet, no doubt), something I hadn't seen before because of clothing.

"Thanks, Alec … I think."

He let out a little sound of acknowledgement and said, "Supper is on the table, we're missing only you. Stop harassing her Jack and we'll escort her up." He came around the other side of the hammock, pulled the torch from the sand, then came over to me. Using the light to view me, he leaned over and pulled my dress hem down off my thighs. I scowled at him and he responded, "My dear. Jack has just informed you of his randy state—*that* certainly won't help."

And with that, Jack leapt off the hammock and Alec held out his hand to assist me, after steadying it.

"Oh my god. You're both incorrigible," I complained, ignoring his hand, then struggling off the hammock by myself. He laughed and we followed Jack up the path of stairs. I saw the other torches had been placed around the garden and pool.

It could not have been a more perfect evening. No clouds in the sky and, in spite of the light from the house and torches, the Milky Way was clearly visible. The sounds of night creatures and the gentle waves were our music. The kitchen table had been brought out further and laid with a feast of various fruits and cookies for later. I assumed we'd be eating dinner in the formal dining room, despite being dressed as informally as we were.

Juanita was gone and Hervé was placing the last serving spoon on the table. "Dinner is served, Mister Gregory."

"Thank you, Hervé. Please. Everyone come sit."

Ch'en gestured to one of the table ends. "Please, Devi. You sit here. You are guest of honor." She looked lovely in a simple cream colored long cotton gown not too dissimilar to my own gold-hued one. Her hair hung in a rich velvet sheet and had just a hint of wave to it.

Alec, standing behind his chair at the other end of the table, reached for the wine glass in front of him and raised it. "A toast to Devi's power, the power of the Vitaortus and to the success of our endeavors this week."

Every one picked up a glass and raised it, with Georges loudly voicing, "Here, here!" The wine was simple and good and I wondered what was in everyone else's glass, except Hervé's.

Alec pulled out his chair to sit and we all followed suit. I was amused at the formality, considering his bare chest, perfect even with scars, was screaming to be ogled.

Georges was wearing a sarong too, but he'd put on a black tank top. I was surprised that he was very well-muscled. I'd just assumed he was doughy beneath his designer exterior.

"In case you're wondering, Devi, we eat with you because we wish to honor you. I hope very much that you enjoy the Mayan food. I picked items Alec said you might like." Ch'en had placed her hand on my arm. She smiled and I could see a hint of her pointed canines. "May I serve you?"

She gestured to my plate, and feeling a little embarrassed, I answered, "Yes, please." She had to stand to be able to reach the dishes to fill my plate, but she did so elegantly. I snuck a glance at

Alec who was stoically observing. I then looked at the others, all of whom were watching raptly. It would be weird to eat with them. So far, I'd only really spent any food time with Alec, who seemed to eat normally enough. But I noticed he'd excused himself afterward and I'd come to suspect he threw it all up. I'd seen Georges eat once, but not what he did after.

Once my plate was full, the others passed the dishes. Hervé filled his plate with gusto and Alec smiled warmly at him. It was obvious they didn't sit together like this very often.

Jack leaned forward and inhaled the warm, scented molecules. "What a wonderful smell. It certainly makes you want to eat!"

Georges leaned forward too, closed his eyes and flared his nostrils. The ingredients were so different from what was in the kitchen of his restaurant that he too seemed to enjoy the newness of the scents. He could contain himself no longer and dug in. Then we all did and there was 'mmming' and 'ahhing'. Ch'en showed us how to prepare the tortilla with the pork and condiments and we ate heartily, chatting lightly about the food for the next half hour or so. Ch'en explained that originally it would be cooked in the ground.

"How old would you say this recipe is, Ch'en?" Georges asked.

She scrunched her face in thought, then guessed, "Maybe thousands of years, but it would have been with other flesh. Peccary or tapir."

"It makes me wish my newest restaurant was not only European cuisine! Perhaps in one of my others."

Once we'd had our fill, all but Hervé and I made their way to various facilities. Within moments they were back and joined us on the patio. Georges had returned with two special bottles. One I immediately recognized. It was Dom Perignon. The other was cobalt blue and had no label. After deftly removing the cork, he poured the champagne into two flutes, which he then handed to me and Hervé. The rubber and porcelain stopper in the blue bottle had a lever and he simply lifted, pulled it out and then poured. By the viscosity, I could tell it was certainly not wine.

"And what vintage is *that*?" I asked before thinking. Georges, Ch'en and Jack laughed, Alec did not.

"Never, ever ask that, as you may not like the answer." Alec gave me a look which just wasn't as severe as he was trying to make it. Then he raised his glass, first to me, then to Ch'en. "To our ladies. Beautiful, powerful, life-giving." All the men smiled and raised their glasses.

I looked at Ch'en who put her arm around my waist and I lay mine around her cool shoulders. We clinked our glasses and there was a brief camaraderie. Then I wondered at Alec's toast. *Why would Ch'en be life-giving? Seriously.* Maybe it had something to do with her job.

Only Hervé and I availed ourselves of the dessert table, then afterward, he began putting together a large plate of everything as he cleaned up. I tried to help him, but he steadfastly refused and so I sat in a lounge chair, just watching and chatting with the others. They had a dip in the pool and I had a chance to really scrutinize them. All were super fit, even Georges. He'd only appeared doughy because of his bulk.

Jack was ridiculously playful and flirtatious, and I wondered if the place had brought it on. I'd never quite seen him so charming, except before one of his 'tasks'. And suddenly he just leapt out of the water, straight up, and landed in front of me, bringing a lot of moisture raining down with him. From a normal human, the act would have been beyond possible. Jack only laughed as I gasped and tried to avoid the wetness.

He had an interesting look in his eye I'd never seen before, and although I was feeling sleepy, I had a momentary surge of adrenalin, which felt a little like fear. He came toward me in a strange way, looking quite sexy and intent, but stopped short when Alec simply and firmly said, "*Jack.*"

Jack just looked at me for a moment and I heard Ch'en say, "Perhaps it's time you go. I expect Devi is quite tired anyway." While Jack and I stared at each other, I heard the others get out of the pool, then Georges came over and put his arm around him.

"She is very lovely, no? We have business to attend, yes?"

Jack seemed to shake himself out of his bizarre state and looked at Georges, then answered, "Yes. Yes, we do. Sleep well, Devi. Gotta go change." He then moved away from Georges and headed for the upstairs. After watching him go, I gave Georges a questioning glance, which he answered with an uninformative shoulder shrug.

Once he moved to follow Jack, I noticed Alec drying himself. His fitted, black, square-leg suit couldn't have been a more perfect look for him. He turned his head in my direction, obviously feeling my eyes on him. Forcing myself to stare only at his eyes, I gave him a *what-the-fuck-was-that?*-look. Initially, he didn't answer me, but instead glanced at Ch'en, who was also drying her lovely small self.

She instantly seemed to understand something and headed out too. She smiled as she passed. "I'll see you shortly. Would you like some bedtime tea?"

I smiled back, answering, "Yes, please."

I started to get up from the chaise when Alec appeared beside me, sitting where I'd need to put my legs, effectively stopping me. *Now him?* "What is going on? Where are you guys going? What the hell is wrong with Jack?" He smiled an irritatingly relaxed smile in an effort to control my agitation. It only served to irritate me more. "*Alec,*" I warned.

He stopped smiling and put out a hand and seductively smoothed the fabric of my dress on the chaise. "Well. Devi. Jack, as you are aware, is a new to this existence. We who are a little older are better able to *control* our various appetites. But, for Jack, the energy you are putting off is becoming a bit difficult for him to resist."

"Energy? What energy? It's me. Same me as before."

"Not so, my dear. Your extraordinary chemistry is reacting with the geology of this place. It is amplified. You are in a magnified state. There's no pollution on you here and the salt is very cleansing. It's intoxicating. Jack was a little drunk with it. Even I find it distracting."

"Oh, *please.*" My protest sounded weak. I realized I actually felt something energetic going on myself, but had attributed it to enjoying the place.

He shrugged a little, then stood and offered his hand. After helping me up, he said, "We'll see you tomorrow night. I hope your day tomorrow is lovely and interesting." Then he bent to kiss my cheek, where he lingered for a moment. "Jack is correct—you do smell of the sun and sea." And he turned and left me standing there.

I had no idea what to think or feel about any of this, but I was definitely uneasy. Until now, except for the odd initial incident with Alec, they'd been relatively (with a capital R) normal. They now seemed a bit more … vampish? I wondered what would have happened if Alec and the others hadn't been there. I considered that maybe I should avoid being alone with Jack while we were in Mexico. As attractive as he was, I felt the intensity of his interest and it was bizarre—almost predatory. We'd developed a real friendship and I'd hate to see that ruined because he lost control. And besides, how far might it go? A tiny part of me was intrigued, though and I quickly threw the thought in my dustbin of hidden desires.

Stepping into the kitchen, I looked for Hervé and discovered he too had gone. The kettle was heating, so I went into the living area and picked a comfy sofa to lounge on while I waited. I *was* tired. The sun and sea had done their best to bring me into a state of languid serenity and I was pretty much there, so it was easy to let go of the incident.

The sound of the front door shutting startled me awake from a drifting doze. I opened my eyes to see Ch'en sitting at the other end of the couch, filing her nails. There was a bottle of cherry red nail polish on the coffee table in front of her. She glanced at me. "They've gone out to do manly things," she said, and pumped the muscle of her right bicep.

I laughed and sat up, saying sardonically, "*Really?*"

She smiled. "Actually, there are errands to run before we meet with the others on the full moon. They are quite formal about their rituals and so we must prepare."

I watched her unscrew the top from the polish and start painting, eventually asking, "What are they like? Are they friendly? Do they speak English?"

She'd finished one hand and glanced at me before starting on the other. "A few speak English. Their leader does; she is very old. I can tell you this: they are misunderstood. Very misunderstood. I hope you will remember that."

She pointed her chin at the table in front of me. "I brought your tea. It will be cold soon if you do not drink." She started to add another coat to the first hand and said, as I reached for the cup, "He respects you very much. You are very dear to him, I think."

I harrumphed. "I think he's just high on this place and maybe whatever they're doing tonight. It seems strange that he'd wait until we were here, considering that he's been living in my house!"

She leaned forward to deftly replace the brush and screw the top on tight, then turned to me as she blew on her nails. "Not Jack. *Alec*."

"Oh. Well. I'm fond of him too. We have a good working relationship. I think we've become friends." I immediately realized I was on potentially dangerous ground here. Would she feel territorial? That I was a threat?

"Only friends?" she asked, raising her brows as high as they'd go.

"Only friends," I affirmed. She kept blowing on her nails and looking at me.

"Perhaps," she finally said. "But he holds you in the highest regard. Do you know this? You speak in a very familiar way with him. That is uncommon for him to do with women." She had to have heard our conversation—the one we were supposed to have had in private. Well, was that an admonishment? Besides, what had I said that was a problem?

I finished my tea without comment as she admired her varnished nails. "Lovely color," I eventually said.

"Thank you. He is vulnerable because of you, but others would not see it, yet. I hope. Be good to him Devica Trevathan. He is as good as our kind can be, when it suits. His power serves yours, which threatens him, because others will covet you. They do not have his intelligence or vision, nor do they have his generosity. They would enslave you, rather than revere you as he does."

I was a little dumbstruck, so we sat in silence as I thought about it. She was both happy *and* disturbed about me.

She offered to paint my toenails, which looked pretty good after getting buffed by the sand, so I agreed. It felt nice to be pampered.

I asked questions about her life, and she asked about mine. She'd only once ever met anyone like me: an immortal 'Life-Bearer', as she called us. And I, of course, was getting to know my first female of their kind—and she was ancient Maya to boot. Having been turned in the early 1600s, she was the oldest of Alec's existing progeny.

Before long, I was feeling extremely sleepy and she suggested that I go to bed. She accompanied me and chatted while I brushed my teeth and put on my little cotton short and tank set. I slid into the bed and it felt perfectly normal when she leaned over to kiss my lips lightly. Then she wished me good night.

As I started to drift off, I thought I heard the wall that separated the outside half of the pool from the inside open. But when I tried to focus on the sound, I heard nothing and fell asleep.

Some unknown amount of time later, my eyelids flew open, but I saw only darkness. It took a moment for the slight amount of ambient light from the moon to show me moving shadows. Something was in the room with me.

I strained to hear, but only the sound of the waves revealed itself. Slowly, I raised my head, working my eyes hard to focus on any unrecognized shape. And when I spotted it, a rush of fear plunged straight through me. I lunged for the bedside lamp, but whatever it was, was faster. It somehow got through the netting and shoved something in my mouth!

Then I realized there were two, because my ankles were suddenly jerked together and bound tightly. One quickly wrapped a cloth around my face while the other bound my hands snugly in front of me as I tried to lash out. I screamed, but it was so muffled by whatever was in my mouth that I doubted anyone would hear me.

Both beings dragged me from the bed and what felt like long nails dug into my arm and leg. They continued to drag me and I realized we were moving under the wall, which *had* been raised.

Once out on the veranda, I was dropped, sending a jolt to my diaphragm that ended my attempt to scream. I lay on my stomach, hands under me, panicking and experiencing a fear I'd not known since being on the steamship ninety years ago.

I had just enough lucidity to use my shoulder to dislodge the cloth from my eyes. And then I saw them — or parts of them. Strange feet stood beside my head. The clawed toes were very long and the heels super short. And they were black and leathery. As I looked up the leg, I saw hair beginning at what I could only guess was calf level. Actually, it was fur, lighter than the color of the skin. I could see bone and sinew beneath that skin and I started to scream again, but it was impotent.

A face suddenly appeared as the creature squatted and I could truly not believe my eyes. *It was a bat*! Or rather, it was a huge bat with some almost human features.

Then a thought forced its way into my nightmare: *Surely I must be dreaming*.

This brought an involuntary smile to my face, causing my eyes to crinkle up, which in turn brought on a strange reaction from the creature. It reached out with a very scary, very boney appendage, which I assumed was a finger, or thumb, and gently touched my face. It crinkled its eyes and attempted a very frightening smile, showing two strange pointed upper front teeth and a hint of fangs further back. I felt my eyes widen from fear and it turned its head to the other, who I then felt grip my legs with its feet. The one I could see raised itself and I heard quiet flapping and felt air movement. Suddenly, those bizarre feet-claws had hold of my upper arms and we became airborne. I tried to tell myself to wake up. Then I tried shouting at myself, but I appeared unwilling to listen.

We rushed headlong over the cliff, beach and then the surf, causing my heart to pound almost as loudly as the rushing air in my ears. As we gained a little altitude, we began to arc back to the land and I felt only small relief. Dream or not, I was beginning to hyperventilate and I was afraid I'd pass out or throw up.

I worked on taking deep core breaths and thanked heaven I was a nose breather. The cloth was still tight around my mouth, but it had slipped down enough from my eyes that I could see quite well, which was perhaps not such a good thing.

I tried to turn my head but could only see the wings of the two creatures as they beat in unison, obviously avoiding hitting each other because of the closeness required to hold me. My hair billowed above and behind me and I could tell it was wrapping around the first creature's legs by the little movements of its toes. I had a flash of wonder if it was tickling the thing.

My teeth had managed to bite into whatever was in my mouth and it tasted bitter. I prayed it wasn't toxic and tried not to swallow, which, of course, caused an involuntary swallow. I started coughing and both sets of feet let go of me for a split second. My quiet scream immediately ended the coughing fit. Before I could finish the thought that I was going to die, they had me again, their nails digging in a little deeper. It hurt, but I was tremendously relieved, *momentarily*.

I saw the lights of a town, probably Tulum, to the left and kept my eyes on them as long as possible, until we were past the point where I couldn't turn my head further. The creature holding my shoulders adjusted its hold and I winced, but used every ounce of will-power I had not to squirm.

My eyes were tearing-up from our speed through the air and, between squints, I'd catch glimpses of the jungle below us. Once in a while, a dirt road would cut through; stark straight lines in the jungle canopy. But I could tell we were moving well out of civilization, because soon there weren't even roads.

The soft sounds of their beating wings kept me keenly aware of my kidnappers. It occurred to me that I didn't seem to be waking up and there was no dream quality to the experience. This was too real, too visceral and seemed just a little too out of the norm for my imagination.

I have no idea how long or how far we flew; it seemed like an eternity. And I had a grogginess that could only be explained by the tea Ch'en had given me. *Was she a part of this?*

As I mulled it over, I saw that we were headed toward a hill in the jungle. It was barely noticeable, except that as we came closer to the tree tops, the horizon line made a perfect, inverted 'V'. Soon we were nearly on top of it and the creatures dipped down.

Within moments we'd reached an opening in the trees about twenty meters across and we flew straight into it, then down even farther, past the ground level. I started to panic worse when I saw a glint below me. *Water!* But suddenly, we stopped descending and moved toward the wall of earth and then into it.

We were in a cavern. It was so dark that I couldn't see where the walls were and my quiet companions began making some very odd sounds: they were high pitched squeals.

As instinctive as my fear was, something was nagging me to stay calm. Until now, they'd been very careful with me. The pain I felt from their nails was simply inevitable as that was all they had to carry me, and I could tell they were doing their best not to dig in too deeply without dropping me. I felt a change in their movements and we rounded a corner, then they gently lowered me to the ground.

I could see light ahead and shapes moving toward me, which were hunched. I was a little concerned, to put it mildly, about being on the floor of a cave, and became acutely aware of an odor that was not entirely pleasant.

Suddenly the space was illuminated! Someone, or thing, lit a small bonfire which fired up very quickly. As my eyes adjusted, images began to form. First were the shapes moving toward me; three of them, and it was the first full image I got of the creatures. They were smaller than I by about six inches, but seemed even smaller because of the way they moved, quite literally like a vampire bat, although not as close to the ground. These guys were a little more upright because of the slight human-like characteristics they had.

My two companions moved to either side of me and gently raised me to a kneeling position with their odd appendages, which were attached at the middle front of the wing. I looked at each of them and one tried the smile we'd shared and I raised my brows. But before I could attempt one myself, it turned its head and I followed suit to see its new focus. The other three had reached us.

The middle one looked at me and then made some odd chittering sounds as it came forward and pointed to my face with its appendage. My new 'friend' moved from beside me. Rather than try to untie the scarf, it simply pulled it up and off my head. I immediately spit out the thing in my mouth. I eyeballed it as it rolled several feet away and saw it was a baby coconut, its husk still green. For a split second, my sense of humor returned, until a boney finger-thing gently touched my cheek. My attention was wanted.

I was intensely scrutinized by the middle bat, which seemed to be in charge. It looked over my entire body and then somehow seemed satisfied. It rested its small eyes on mine and made a move which looked for all the world like it was both giving me the finger and making some lewd Italian gesture. When I didn't respond, it repeated the gesture and I realized it was telling me to stand. So I did, slowly and gingerly, with the aid of my 'companions', who then managed to untie my bonds.

"Gome," it said, from a strange place in its throat. I understood it to have said to 'come'. It turned and I followed as it semi-crawled ahead of me. The others followed too. This was, unquestionably, the strangest experience in this season of the bizarre.

I was able to get a good look now at the creatures, whose fur ranged in color from black to gold and varied in different places on their bodies. They looked almost like a cross between humans and bats; perhaps more bat. How could they possibly exist? I fancied myself an amateur evolutionist and this just didn't make sense. But then neither did the fact of Alec, or Jack, or Georges, or Ch'en—or me.

I became aware of the surroundings and I was astonished all over again. The limestone cavern had carvings. They looked just like any of the ancient Mayan images elsewhere. And instead of steps, there were ramps on which the creatures half-walked and half-crawled because their feet and legs were not quite strong enough to propel them and hold them upright for long. Their limbs were thin and quite boney, but you could see the strength in their chests and shoulders.

I was frightened, but I was fascinated too. They were still treating me relatively well, in spite of the kidnapping, so I felt that panicking wasn't necessarily in order. I also had a strong hunch that I was meeting Ch'en's charges a little early, instead of having a nightmare.

As we continued moving farther into the cave, another bonfire was lit so that I could see deeper. The large chamber seemed to end about fifty yards ahead. A dais had been built into the back floor and wall with a very strange set of rocks that looked like a huge, low table and an odd bed-like chair. The latter had some odd angles and was scooped out in the form of a human body. The outside had been carved with the very recognizable style of the ancient Maya.

The table was also covered in glyphs, but I couldn't make them out. I could tell it was darkly stained, and beneath it lay a huge bowl-shaped hole that had small channels running down to numerous smaller bowl-shaped cutouts farther below. Looking at the color of the dark stained carvings, it was impossible not to imagine what it was all for.

A steeper, shorter ramp led from the floor of the cavern to the dais and we made our way up it. The odor was more pungent here and wafted in on a slight cool breeze coming from the back left of the cave. Glancing there, I noticed a creature crawling along the side of the wall as it came from a hidden passageway that obviously went beyond this chamber. I met its eye and it stopped dead, cringing a little.

At the top, I was directed to have a seat in the bedlike chair. This sure didn't appeal to me, and I protested. After the lead creature pointed vigorously at the object, I shook my head and asked, "What are you going to do with me?" I felt the others crowd in behind me, herding me.

It requested, "Pleeeth? No hurrrt," in a high growl and pointed again.

I wasn't really given a choice as the five of them crowded closer still and I fell into it as I backed up. It was obviously as hard as limestone can be. And cool. I looked from face to face and could see there were distinct differences amongst them. They really looked more like bats than humans.

And if I needed more evidence that I had strange thinking, I got it, because I found them to be quite pretty, though a little scary looking with their pointy teeth: sort of cute, like a kitten, yet ugly at the same time. But it was obvious there was a dark side here and it was likely about to be revealed. After all, kittens are really just pure killing machines, despite their tiny prey and cuddle-factor for humans.

The others moved beside my lounge and the leader went to the table, picked up a small wooden cup and brought it to me. Bowing its head, it said something like, "*Ethockolotl,*" and handed it over. I took the cup, noticing the difficulty the creature had with holding it.

I scrutinized the being very closely and suddenly realized it was a female. Glancing around at the other four, I discovered they were female too. Turning to see if there were any that might look male for comparison, I quickly found them above, at the back. They were in a group, hanging from specially carved upside-down perches, their maleness hanging down nonchalantly against their fur. It was quite a sight, but I was again brought to focus.

"Drringk," she demanded. So I brought the cup to my face and instantly smelled something wonderfully familiar—chocolate. Taking a careful sip, I was amazed at the levels of sensation I was experiencing: first the cacao, then slight sweetness (honey maybe?), then something that might be corn; and finally a strong dash of chili pepper. It was an odd and delightful flavor. But then it tasted as though there was something else and before I could question, I was encouraged to down the cup's contents.

Handing it to one of the others, I laid my head back because a wave of euphoria overtook me and I felt a little light headed. So there *was* another ingredient. But it didn't seem to cause me to take on more of a high than just nicely buzzed. The furry, winged creatures crowded around me again and managed to turn me over; I had no desire to resist them.

I was lying perfectly in the space on my stomach with my legs slightly bent and my torso raised just a little. There were spots for my hands, but they seemed as though made for someone with arms that were a little shorter. I was very relaxed and simply felt no fear about what would happen next.

And what happened was that one of the bat ladies was doing something to the back of my leg. I realized I'd been bitten, but it was so clean and quick and painless that I only felt a slight tickle. Then I heard a strange noise: a high pitched whispery sound that was coming from the lead bat. And then there was silence except for the sounds of the fires crackling.

After several moments, when I'd almost drifted to sleep, I felt another presence. I tried to look, but was held down gently. Someone began lapping at a pool of liquid that had formed in the small cavity between my muscle and ligament at the back of my knee. I felt another bite at my ankle, which was then turned so that blood could flow into the natural hollow that formed between it and the heel. I thought I should protest, but whatever they'd put in the chocolate drink was acting on me like nitrous oxide. I really just didn't care and was enjoying my euphoria.

I listened to the sound of the lapping and wondered if someone would start at the ankle. Instead, whoever was at the knee finished, let out a very odd-sounding, breathy moan, then moved down and licked more vigorously at my lower extremity.

I could see only two faces, each in rapt focus on the creature who was drinking from me. I don't know exactly how long it took, but I'd guess at least fifteen minutes. I almost laughed A few times because the soft sounds were rather humorous, though I had enough sense to know my situation was not.

Finally, the lapping stopped and after a moment of communication between them, something cool was pressed to my leg. Again, I tried to raise my head and this time I was allowed. I turned as best I could and saw the main bat was finishing applying some kind of poultice to my wounds. And behind her was another creature, old and withered, being helped onto a simple, fur-lined litter.

Once on, and in a sort of prone position, she raised her head and met my eyes. She actually seemed to smile. I smiled back slightly, drugged and unsure. I was helped onto my back and felt the poultice sticking to me despite the movement.

And then she blew my mind by speaking.

"You are the holder of *Ik'*. Lord Ahlek' said it wass so. I must know for mi pueblo and haff of your blood. You see? It helps now?" She held up her wing for us both to see, and before my eyes her skin was becoming thicker and suppler.

Her voice was so odd: a combination of high pitches and throaty growls. Her tongue was pointed and had a groove running down the center, so it was hard for her to make some of the sounds of consonants, but she did quite well, considering.

As I watched her furry face slowly becoming younger-looking, she said, "I thangk you, for you bringk back mi youth. I wass near death. Mi pueblo feared, for there iss no other. Mi child, who would be queen, died. Now I can make a new child for the pueblo."

Perhaps it was the drug, or maybe the loss of blood, but I found I had no reservations about sharing my blood with her after this explanation. Her demeanor was humble, yet regal, and she seemed genuinely grateful.

I sat up in a wobbly way. "May I ask … who are you?"

She cocked her head, "They did not ssay?" I shook my head. "We are the Camaszotzsss. I am the queen, the last ruler." She then let out a very strange set of squeaks and squeals. "That iss mi name. You are not able to say it."

"No," I said, shaking my head again. "But I'm honored to meet you and help you."

She indicated to the bearers of her litter that they should move her closer to me. After they did, she entreated, "You must say this to your Lord Vampyr. Lord Ahlek'. He will be so very angry that I haff stolen you. Your blood. He refussed me. They are strongker than we and kill us eassily." Her expression told me that this had happened before and she was very sincere. They appeared really quite delicate.

What the hell, Alec, my fuzzy brain fussed.

She made a movement and one of the others shuffled forward while holding something very carefully. She gave it to the queen who maneuvered it so she could get hold of it. She motioned for me to sit up further, which I did immediately, despite my soporific state.

"I wish to gif you a gift for the gift I haff taken. It iss old. It belonged to the humanss who were here first. It belonged to a Queen who wass a king! Humanss are loco that men rule. It is why the Earth diess, for human men are killerss of all thingss."

I raised my eyebrows and glanced over at her group of males. "The Queen had this ass long ass she lived and stayed ruler. It iss said *Ik'* flowss through and iss … iss made more strong. Her priest-ess sacrificed it to us when she died. That wass hundredss of yearss ago. It iss best that a bearer of *Ik'* haff it." She stretched out her odd appendages toward me. They held a small bundle, which appeared to have been fashioned from a leaf.

Tentatively reaching out, I looked at her for reassurance, which she gave in the form of a head-bob. I took the bundle and opened it. Inside was a somewhat triangular, two-inch stone, a gem, which was translucent and a deep orangey-red. When I turned it, other colors deep within it glowed. I didn't know what it was, but it was one of the most incredible rocks I'd ever seen.

"Thank you. This is amazingly beautiful. What is it?" I questioned, as I turned it this way and that.

"It iss *quetzalitzlipyollitli*. I do not know what *you* call it."

That made me want to laugh, but I resisted. I noticed it had a hole drilled into one end, and I examined it. "Was it worn?" I asked her.

"Yes. But the band wass made of animal so it did not last thesse many yearss. You must wear it. It needss your moisture to be best."

We gazed at each other and I could only smile. Which she mirrored and said, "Mi attendants will return you now. We see us again in four nights. The *quetzalitzlipyollitli* iss not enough to repay you for mi life, but you will alwayss have mi gratefulness."

I felt like I wanted to hug her, but she just motioned and her bearers turned the litter and headed for the passageway at the back. I and the others watched her leave until there was no further sign.

Her aide, or priestess, or whatever she was, removed the poultices and gave me a special head bow. She didn't have her ruler's skill with language but she very clearly said, "Thangk' you." And soon, I was being carried back to the hacienda.

ELEVEN

Another Hunt

†

They made good time across the Yucatan peninsula with Jack driving. Despite the dark and desolate roads, his skill and reflexes, along with the extremely good night vision they all possessed, made the journey as quick as possible and road-kill free.

Jack had also been extremely useful with setting up the meeting with the cartel leader and his seconds. Being a weapons expert, he had been posing as the liaison for them as high-end, high-tech arms dealers. The criminals had chosen to meet at a home one of them owned in Merida, which was apparently never used as a place from which to conduct their normal heinous business. Merida was not a friendly town for the cartels and the villa was used more as a getaway spot for family.

It was critical they meet close enough that Alec's plan could be completed within a single night, and Merida was the closest they could get. Cancun, or closer, had not been offered as an option because Alec didn't want their whereabouts guessed at; the resort town seemed a little too close. Plus, Alec just couldn't abide Cancun.

He had been concerned that the distances they had to drive would not allow for them to accomplish the hunt, deposit their sacrifices and return to the hacienda by daybreak. Jack had insisted it was possible and, due to his extreme speeding, had them on the outskirts of Merida within two and a half hours.

They were wearing rather flashy Italian suits that Georges had joked were Cosa Nostra-approved. Underneath, each of them wore black stealth gear. A very special (and expensive) satellite link revealed to Alec that there were only two men outside the house as security. That made it so much easier, as he, Jack and Georges could deal with them last. The speed with which they would operate inside shouldn't alert the two men. Jack and Alec had been surprised at the small number of the security force, but this was a very secret meeting and Jack had expressed to the leader that he and his associates were shadow-like in their dealings and would be arriving without any security. That had apparently impressed the cartel *capo* as very ballsy.

Once at the gate of the small compound, Jack texted the number he'd been given and the two men appeared. The automatic weapons they carried were held only barely in view as they asked to look in the vehicle. They were thorough, but respectful, and soon asked Jack to park behind the villa.

The front had been fairly decent-looking, but the back had a swimming pool and children's play area which was littered with junky objects and grilling equipment. Alec eyed it all, thinking it quite a disturbing thing that these men had families, considering the mass slaughter and dismemberment they perpetrated on anyone they deemed a target. They were indiscriminant.

An understanding of the drug cartel mentality eluded him. As a business, it was bottom of the barrel—not worth the money considering the horrors perpetrated and the short life-span. And though he felt the slightest compassion for the children's impending loss of their fathers, it was superseded by his conviction that ridding the world of these parasites was a good thing. He'd chosen this particular group for their extreme viciousness and high body count.

Alec had made tea of the Vitaortus before they left the hacienda and they'd all had a ration on the way. They would do so again on the return trip as Alec was sure these men were full of illicit pharmaceutical poison in one form or another. He had total confidence that they would be out of the compound and back on the road to Tulum in an hour. After all, it takes a little time to drain several bodies, wrap them up and strap them to the top of a vehicle.

Ten men poured out of the back doors of the house to greet them, which Alec read as an attempt at intimidation. But when he, Jack and Georges coolly emerged from the Suburban, the Mexican men tried to hide their surprise. Unquestionably their trio's height and elegant clothing made for an impressive impression.

One man, who he knew was the *capo*, came forward with his hand extended and said in fairly good English, "Ju mus be Mister Gray. It's a pleasure." He was fiftyish and wore a Tommy Bahama look. He also clearly knew instinctively that Alec was the leader of the trio. There was no way he could have known who they were prior.

Alec shook his hand and replied, "Quite. And may I introduce Mr. Black and Mr. White. Mr. Black is the one with whom you've been communicating." Alec aimed his hand at Jack.

"I'm Mr. Delgado. Please, come in and meet my team."

"My, my; so many of you. I don't think we've brought enough to go around," Alec smoothly commented, alluding to the weaponry Delgado thought they'd brought.

"Oh. It's only the six of us, like I tol' you. Those four are security." He gestured at the men who hung back near the door. Alec nodded and knew Jack and Georges were listening carefully.

Jack moved forward and said, "We have a couple of cases to show you. I'm just going to get them from the truck. Can I have some help?"

Delgado rubbed his hands together and said with a grin, "Oh, jes!" And he motioned to several men to assist.

Soon, the three of them were being escorted through the overly interior-designed house, with four of Delgado's men in front and five behind. Delgado walked beside Alec, who smiled inwardly when he heard the locks being engaged on the door behind them. It was like baitfish attempting to contain sharks.

He listened and smelled for anyone else in the house and determined there were only the thirteen of them, and an animal—a carnivorous, wild animal. For a moment, Alec was surprised by that, until they entered a large, main living room where he sought the source of the scent. An extra-large, portable dog cage held a jaguar, which looked both miserable and frightened. He could tell the beast was nearly broken and on the verge of madness; and female; and very hungry.

As he quickly scanned the room, which was decorated in a bizarre mish-mash of styles and yet had nothing he deemed of actual value, the men made their way to the seating area that surrounded a large square acrylic coffee table. Delgado indicated to Jack that he could place the cases on it.

"May I get you anything to drink? Or maybe ... use?" Delgado offered.

Jack, Georges and Alec all shook their heads and Alec pointed to the seats. "Please gentlemen. Be seated." The men looked uncomfortable at his command, but they sat, hesitantly. When Delgado remained standing, Alec urged, "Mr. Black will give us all a little presentation so you know how to use our gifts properly. They are, after all, quite deadly. Please sit, Mr. Delgado."

As he did, Jack quietly moved back a few paces so that he would be able to reach the two security men who were on either side of the doorway. Alec knew Georges would take care of one who was behind the couch, while he himself would take care of the fourth.

He looked again at the jaguar. She'd raised her head from her prone position when they entered, but had turned her back and tried to curl into a tight ball. His silent call made her look over her back at him again and he held the gaze.

Delgado noticed and asked, "Ju like my cat? I'm going to take it back with me to Nuevo Laredo. Cool pet, no?"

Alec languidly shifted his gaze to him. "No. She is too magnificent to be a pet. How long have you had her?"

"It's *la hembra*? Female? How did ju know?"

As Alec moved into position, he replied, "Isn't it obvious?"

Delgado shook his head and eyed the cat. "I got it a couple of weeks ago. It won' eat though."

As Alec kept him and his minions engaged, Georges and Jack readied themselves. "What are you feeding her?"

"Dog food. Some *pollo*."

With a scowl, Alec informed, "Well There's your problem. She eats raw meat. Meat that has blood in it."

Raising his eyebrows, Delgado queried, "Ju know wild animals? Ju got any?"

"I do. A herd of Eurasian red deer. But they do not have the depth of character of this majestic creature." Alec turned back to her and said, "Be patient, dear, you'll eat in a moment." Then he smiled benignly at Delgado—who frowned.

Suddenly the two men at the door had their heads violently knocked together by a supernaturally swift Jack. As they fell to the floor, unconscious, or maybe even dead, the man behind the couch had his throat pierced by Georges' four canines as they slid in to reach his carotid artery. He'd never had a chance to go for his gun.

As the men seated on the couch struggled to take in the visual stimuli, Alec reached the fourth man, twisted his neck and bit. Their attack took three seconds. By the time Alec drained a pint of his man's blood, his audience was only just starting to stand. Delgado shouted, but the rest were silent, in shock.

Pulling his mouth away from his now limp victim, Alec held him up by the hair and stared at those seated. He knew how terrifying he looked with his bloody teeth.

"You will stay seated unless you desire to end like your friends," he whispered in his most menacing voice.

As one, the men slowly sat.

Alec glanced at the table, then saw what he wanted on the bar to his right. It was a bowl filled with corn nuts, which he dumped. He then dropped his victim to the floor, wiped the remnants of salt from the bowl and squatted to place it to the still spurting wound.

When he'd filled the bowl, he pulled the unconscious man's neck to him and drank another pint. With his mouth still at the wound, he turned to glare at the men again. He could see one had developed a wet stain on his lap. Delgado had gone white.

When his victim became a corpse, Alec withdrew his teeth. He then stood, grabbing an inert arm and twisted, creating a sound and image that caused the men to try to shrink into the couch. The arm snapped and separated at the elbow; skin, muscle and sinew tearing. Very little blood was left to seep out as he laid the forelimb beside the bowl of blood. There were whimpers from the couch.

Keenly aware of the irony his actions presented, Alec drolly chastised, "Delgado. It is simply unconscionable that you would treat living creatures the way that you do. It surprises me that you don't care that you'll burn in hell all eternity for your crimes."

He knew hell didn't exist, but he also knew these men *did* believe, and it pleased him to play with them. He looked back at the jaguar then and made a soft sound to her. She had been watching the whole time, as he knew she would. She stood and he turned, went to her cage and just opened it. He coaxed her out and slowly squatted. She tentatively stretched her neck so that her nose moved toward his face. He closed his eyes as she came so close that he could feel her hot breath and whiskers as she sniffed and greeted him, just as a housecat would. He heard several gasps as she rubbed her head first on his face, then her whole body along his. Then he stood and said, "Come. Eat."

Leading her to the bowl and dismembered arm, Alec watched the men, who were cowering as the beast came closer. She was a very big cat and she was hungry—and free. Letting out a growly roar at them, she waited for Alec's comforting presence to squat beside her as she crouched and sniffed the bowl. When he did, she began delicately lapping up the blood.

Alec noticed there was a watch on the forearm so he lifted it and removed the item, saying, "We are going to take you all on a little journey. I want you to stay quiet or we'll simply dispatch you. Do you understand, Delgado?" The man nodded, looking like he was on the edge of passing out. "Tell your friends—"

The cat interrupted him by snuffling the arm he still held. She moved her ears toward him and gave him an odd look. "Yes, I know. It's inferior to your usual, but it's all we've got for now. You'll need your strength for the hunt. Eat, beauty." He reached and gave her a long stroke starting at her cheek and ending at the base of her swishing tail. Then he handed her the meaty arm. She took it with her teeth, held it between her large paws and started gnawing.

As Alec looked up, one of the men passed out. He knew the sardonic laugh he gave was pretty evil-sounding. "What? You find yourselves squeamish after all you've perpetrated. *Really*. I'd have thought you tougher. Are you ready? Jack, Georges? Who wants the men outside?" Georges was finishing his 'meal' still; he'd always been a delicate feeder.

So Jack said, "I'll be right back." He tossed the two men he'd dispatched out of the way and went out to do more damage.

Alec finished saying to Delgado, "Tell your men we'll be taking a ride and I don't want to hear a word. Not one. She'll be coming with us, so you'll receive either her wrath, or ours. *Comprender?*" Delgado just stared at him, completely in shock. Finally Alec leaned menacingly forward. "*Comprender?*" he repeated in a growl. Delgado nodded his head hurriedly and attempted to speak to the other men. He managed to get the point across well enough.

It wasn't long before Jack came in dragging two bodies by the ankles. It looked as though he'd exsanguinated them both. He'd earned it, as he'd held off before while Alec and Georges had supped, thereby ensuring that someone was fully vigilant. Alec felt a twinge of pride and gave him a brief nod and smile.

Jack returned it, only just hiding his own pride and satisfaction at seeing Alec's approval. "I'm just gonna go get the tarps and rope," he informed, then joked at Georges, "We could've drunk the rest of them between us in the time it takes you to have one."

Georges raised his finger for a moment as he drew the last of his man's blood. Letting go with a flourish, he used his pinky to wipe the corners of his lips and retorted, "*That* is because you have no *savoir faire*. What are you waiting for? We must hurry!" Jack rolled his eyes with a smile and left again.

Georges then came around the front of the couch, giving the jaguar a wide berth so as not to disturb her. "Alec, you have such a soft heart under that stern exterior. It makes you so attractive."

Alec reached to give the cat another stroke. "Thank you, Georges. Delgado. Tell your men that Mr. White will be removing all items from them. They will cooperate. If he finds anything on you afterward, he'll have a second course for his supper. You first. And there will be no jackets and no shoes." Georges moved forward and motioned Delgado to stand as he opened one of the cases they'd brought, which were all empty, but lined with foam padding.

As he stood and eyed the case, the drug lord croaked, "Who are ju? Ju are ... Ju are *vampiro*."

"Yes. That is what we are. And you are a sociopathic drug lord. Worse than us, no?" Georges replied, as he shoved his hands into Delgado's pants pockets, then tossing what he'd found into the case. He pointed nonchalantly to his shoes, indicating the man needed to remove them.

Georges eyed the items in the case and picked up a phone. As he took it apart to remove the battery, he commanded the others, "*Rapido, rapido! Cosas en el caso; quitese los zapatos.*" The men attempted to comply, in spite of their terror-induced immobility. As the phones were tossed in, Georges disassembled each of them. He also searched the pockets of the dead men, finding each of them had one too.

Once Jack returned, he set about bundling the bodies for transport, making them look like giant, rectangular parcels. You could not tell just by looking that they were wrapped-up dead humans. He and Georges tied them to the roof of the suburban while Alec watched the men as he squatted beside the hungrily munching cat.

She seemed to enjoy his affections and he continued to stroke her. She was a dainty eater and had only finished half of the forearm by the time they were ready. When his companions returned to the large room, Alec asked Delgado, "Where are the computers for your security cameras? Or tapes or whatever you use."

"Uh. I don' have none." He was sweating profusely, despite the air conditioning.

You don't *have* none? You expect me to believe that?"

"Really. I's usually jus' my wife and kids who come here. No one knows about this place. I swear."

Jack interjected, "I've been looking and haven't seen a single camera."

Alec stared hard at Delgado, who crossed himself and again said, "I swear."

It was then that one of the men tried to make a dash for the door, but Georges was suddenly in front of it and carried him by the neck, one-handed, back to the group. The man made odd gurgling noises, though Georges was careful not to kill him.

Ignoring it all, Alec announced, "Right then. Shall we get under way? Georges in front, sociopaths in the middle and Jack behind. I'll come out with the jaguar when they've been settled."

After agreeing nods, Alec, Jack and Georges removed their suits, revealing black t-shirts and cotton exercise pants. They traded their fine footwear for black sport shoes and Jack and Georges carefully placed the suits in the other cases.

After they'd finally gone out to the SUV, Alec convinced the cat to follow him. On the way, he found the kitchen and went in to see if there was anything edible for her in the refrigerator. The arm was hardly enough. Finding an uncooked brisket cut of beef and a chicken, he took them and soon he had her ensconced on the second row bench seat, sniffing the unwrapped items. He had been able to instill in her a deep sense of well-being; a skill that was not unlike mesmering and one he was sure had come from the Native American influence. He knew of no others with so strong an ability with animals as he had.

Leaning his back against the door and window, he eyed the cowering men as he got comfortable, with only two feet between him and the wild beast. He glanced at the jaguar, who'd had begun eating the chicken, which was little more than an appetizer, bones and all. Alec hadn't been particularly thrilled by tonight's endeavor, but the opportunity to help a fellow threatened creature was an unexpected bonus.

The men sat with their hands tied behind their backs. Alec felt sure Georges had placed them because he would be concerned that they weren't in too uncomfortable a configuration. Jack would have thrown them on top of each other in the back, like firewood. Unlike Georges, Jack had never been in prison. And unlike Jack, Georges had never been in war.

The drug men's crimes were beyond heinous, but additional brutality wasn't necessary considering what they'd be doing with them. It was obvious they'd been traumatized already, and it was only the beginning.

It took almost exactly the amount of time Jack had estimated to get to their next destination, which was deep in the jungle, at least an hour from the hacienda. Upon being removed from the Suburban, Delgado had pleaded, offered vast sums of money, but eventually fell quiet after no response from Alec. Then he ran at Alec and grabbed his shirt when Jack untied him. He hit and lashed out when Alec slammed him to the ground, but his blows had no effect. Two of the others struggled also, but were no match. Jack finally hogtied the men and laid them on their stomachs.

It was explained that someone would bring food and water for them tomorrow, and not to underestimate her; that she was also *vampiro* as well as an ancient shaman. Ch'en was old enough to walk in the day and strong enough to deal with all of them on her own. Alec had no fear that the men would escape because their natural, limestone prison was impossible for a human to climb out of without rope.

Not far from there, on their way back to the hacienda, they stopped to let the Jaguar go. She didn't hesitate and simply left the comfort of the seat with a single leap into the forest along the small, white road. It was fairly far from human habitation and close to another bio preserve, like this one, so she would have a large range if no other female had staked a claim. Alec felt sure she would avoid humans after this experience. She stopped to look back once, then disappeared.

Soon after, they built a quick fire on the hidden road, using a blow torch. Jack took each tarp-wrapped package, doused it in petrol, and threw it on the fire. Once everything was cinders, they shoveled the hot debris into a metal can to be dumped into the sea when they got back.

An hour later, as they neared the property, Jack said, "That was cool. What a pretty animal. I sure hope she survives."

"Yes. Majestic. How could he not know to feed her raw meat? So stupid," opined Georges.

But before Alec could comment, he saw a sight in the sky which left him absolutely dumbfounded.

TWELVE

Bed-Mates and Dance Partners

ʊ

My buzzed condition allowed me to enjoy the trip back without the fear I'd experienced before. It was like a magic carpet ride without the carpet and if you were being uncomfortably carried by giant bats. I was surely content, but then, as we neared the hacienda, I had a brief moment of woe as I spotted the huge black SUV on the road below. Its occupants must have seen us because it suddenly burst forward with incredible acceleration. My magical journey was at an end and I could feel Alec's wrath from here.

I shouted to the creatures, "Get me back! Quick!" as I tried to point. They too accelerated and swooped down toward the house. My stomach went into my windpipe, costing me the happy buzz. I had no clue of the hour, but our timing was lousy. They got me to the patio and let go, then gave me a goodbye gesture.

It was just the time needed for Alec and Jack to appear. Startled, the creatures tried to take off, but both men, dressed from head to toe in black, leapt in tandem. Each grabbed a thin leg and the bats screamed their high-pitched noises as they flapped their wings frantically. I rushed and grabbed Alec's arm as he was about to land a blow on the frightened creature.

"*Don't!!*" I yelled and he dragged me as my weight slowed his arm, which was enough to stop him. I turned to find Jack with the other as she writhed on the ground, his knee about to go into her back. "*Jack! Stop!*" And thank God he did. He'd have broken her delicate spine instantly.

The bats and I were breathing heavily and noisily. I bent down and forced Alec's strong fingers from my new friend's spindly ankle as she struggled and her wings clawed at the patio tiles. She was scared to death, but understood that I was helping and calmed a little.

A furious Alec let go to grip my upper arm tightly and pulled me to him to hiss in my ear. "What *are* you doing?" I daringly ignored him and jerked away, then turned again to see if the other was okay. Jack was observing me and still had hold of her, but wasn't trying to hurt her. Alec bent his knees and crouched beside me, looking from the bat to me. "Devi! What are you doing? What did they do to you?"

I turned back to him, feeling woozy, and answered, "Let them go and I'll tell you. Just let them go home."

He gave me a look of total incredulity and dropped open his mouth. He let out a burst of air, saying, "How can I—"

"*Let them go Alec!*" I demanded. I caught a glimpse of Ch'en in the doorway of the bedroom, but she quickly disappeared. *Boy, was she gonna be in trouble*, I thought briefly. The bat stirred and Alec reached to grab her again. I threw myself onto his chest and grabbed his shoulders. It was very dramatic, but the situation seemed to require it—Alec's eyes held murder.

"*Please.*" I whispered as I stared as hard as I could into his green eyes. "*Please.*" This absolutely took him aback and he fell onto his rear and was forced to put his arms around me for a brief moment. I let go and then he let go, as I struggled off of him, but all the while held his stare.

Then he acquiesced. He closed his eyes and just sat there on the tiles, not exactly beaten, I figured, but regrouping. I then attended my bat friend and found she was fine. She called quietly to her companion, who was also fine, though shaken and quivering. After I briefly touched their strange thumb-appendages, they took flight.

Then I crumpled to the tiles and just stayed down. Jack walked over and squatted on the other side of me. "Devi. What the hell just happened? Are you okay?" I smiled because I felt pretty woozy, which was a combination of drug, blood loss and receding adrenalin.

"*This is hardly amusing*," Alec growled.

"I know Alec, but I'm a little drugged and I'm missing a wee bit o' blood."

"Up!" he suddenly demanded. "We speak *now!*" He was up in a flash and had grabbed my hand to pull me with him. But once there, everything went white and I started to pass out. Someone caught me and lifted me into his arms. It was Jack—no attar of roses. "Put her on the bed and go get some water. And bring some of the left-over meat from the refrigerator."

I managed not to go completely unconscious and opened my eyes once Jack plunked me down. "I'm okay," I said, as Alec began adjusting me in the bed after somehow pinning back the netting. I was surprised when he thought to pull my tangled hair from behind my back and spread it out on the pillow. He smoothed its extreme lengths and just eyed them for a moment.

"What happened?" he asked, without looking at me.

Leaving out my suspicions about Ch'en, I gave him the account as best I could. When I'd finished, I said, "The queen was kind to me, Alec. In fact, look what she gave me." I opened my left hand and the stone rolled onto the bedspread.

Alec had to reach to pick it up, and as he was doing so, Jack came back in the room with a tray and whistled, saying, "That's a hell of an opal."

I tried to sit up, but Alec absentmindedly, yet gently, pushed me back against the headboard. "The queen of the Camazotz gave this to you?" I nodded and he looked at me disbelievingly, then held it up to the light to scrutinize it. "Remarkable. This is worth a small fortune. Where did she get it?"

I took a drink of the water and stabbed at the pork. "She said it belonged to a human queen who was king. I can't remember the word she called it. *Quetzil*-something. That it amplified something she called ... Ich ... Ick ... *Ik'*." I finally got the word right. Both Alec and Jack looked from the stone to me. "What is it? It's very pretty."

Alec answered, "It's a fire opal. One of this quality is very rare indeed. It has a hole drilled in it."

"Yes. She told me to wear it, that it *needed* to be worn."

Alec gave it one more good stare, then handed it back to me. His demeanor was thawing. "Well. We shall have to get it in wearable condition."

It was then that I noticed the condition of the usually impeccably groomed man. His black T-shirt had a tear in it and was a little stretched, as if someone had grabbed him by it. His black pants had a few dark stains and there was a small patch of smeared blood on his cheek, just above his moustache. It was the first time I'd seen his hair messy.

By the looks of it, their night had been eventful too. Jack looked a bit less disheveled, but had rather stained hands—blood stained hands. I didn't want to know what they'd been doing.

"Don't touch me again with those. Did you touch my food?" I asked and pointed.

Jack looked and saw the mess that his hands were and said, "I'll be back." But as he headed for the door again, Alec stopped him. "Jack. Take a fast shower. Dawn is another two hours away and you're going to sleep in here. You need to be clean."

Jack grinned at me and left.

I pushed the pork away. "What do you mean he's sleeping in here?"

"No more risks. I was an idiot. Naturally, Ch'en feels strongly about the queen."

At that I sat up a little and poked him in the chest. "Hey! Speaking of which, you don't own me Mister *Lord Grand Wizard Vampire*. She was dying. How could you refuse her? I don't think she'd have lasted another four days."

He grabbed my finger before I could pull it back and gave me a glare. "*Never call me a grand wizard, girl*," he warned darkly.

I leaned back, trying not to show he'd scared me, and said, with feigned bravado and a raised chin, "It's my life. My blood." He was clearly pretty riled and I could understand why.

He let go of my hand and disarmingly cupped my chin. "Yes. It is. Now how would you feel if someone from every visit we make were to take as much as she did tonight?" His hand slid to my throat where he caressed the area outside my carotid artery for a moment with his thumb, then held two fingers there and finally said, "I'd say you're down nearly a pint. Imperial, that is."

I swatted his hand away. "Alec. Am I wrong or are they seriously endangered?"

"No, you are correct."

"Why didn't you ask me?"

"Because I knew you'd say yes. It takes time to replace that blood. We have to be very careful about the amounts you lose. Devi, would you like to know what would happen for me should *I* drink of you?" I just stared but felt my eyes widen a little, which he took for a 'yes'. "I would again be able to change into *any* form and flout gravity, not exactly like your new friends, but in my own way. I could *even* go out fully in the daylight for a few hours. Imagine that. We could have a *pique-nique* and see flowers blooming beneath the warming rays of the sun."

After absorbing this information, I folded my hands in my lap and looked down at them. What was I supposed to say? I completely understood his point, unsaid in a very poetic way. He needed my blood too, but was sacrificing for the good of all.

"Where did she bite you?" he asked, as he got up and went into the bathroom.

I heard him turn on the water and answered, "On my ankle and behind my knee."

He returned with a moistened wash cloth. "Turn over," he commanded, after wiping smudges of cave floor off my knees. I felt him gently examining the wounds. Jack came in quietly, wearing black boxer briefs and a fitted, black ribbed tank.

Ohhhhh, I thought.

And as if he'd heard me, Alec warned, "I'll kill you if you touch her inappropriately. Even if she forces you somehow, do you hear me?"

"*Force him*? Jesus Alec, what do you think I am?" I protested.

"Highly in need of affection," he answered, as he wiped around the wounds. "Do you hear me Jack?"

"Yes. Absolutely," Jack replied, and went to the back wall to lower it completely.

"They were tender with you. The bite is so carefully incised. There is *stuff* around the wounds."

"They put some kind of poultice on."

"To help with coagulation, no doubt. Amazing. They are surprising me. I always thought they were barely more than animals." He moved to my ankle and held my foot up for a better look.

I shared haughtily, "I thought they were quite civilized. It's a matriarchal society."

"You don't say," came Alec's droll reply.

"Yes. *Mister*. And I loved something the queen said, sad as it was." Alec laid my foot down and I turned over. "She said humans were fools to let men run the world; that human males are killers of all things."

Jack walked over and stood beside Alec, saying, "I'd say she was right."

Alec got off the bed and stood, adding, "Likely so. We'd probably not be in this mess." I was surprised, but then he went and ruined it by adding, "We'd likely be in some other human cock-up."

Deciding not to argue, I got up to go wash my face, brush my teeth again and put on fresh night clothes. But I took the wash cloth from him first. He turned to go and I requested, "Alec. Don't be cross with Ch'en."

He half turned and said, "*That*, I cannot give you." And he left, shutting the door behind him.

When I came back out of the bathroom, I saw that Jack had seriously battened down the hatches. Special shutters would keep every photon of sunlight from entering come dawn. The wall bisected the pool all the way to the bottom so that I couldn't even hear the ocean. Jack was lying on top of the covers with his arms folded behind his head, eyeing me.

"I'm kind of amazed at your reaction to this."

"Why?" I asked, as I lifted the covers and slid in.

He turned on his side to face me. "Because I'd think it would have been a pretty frightening experience. I mean, these freaky, ugly, huge bats carry you miles away, do what they did . . ."

I turned to him so that our faces were a foot and a half apart. "They weren't ugly. At least *I* don't think so. And they actually were very careful with me. I mean, yes, at first it was scary, but it turned out … okay. They're just misunderstood, as Ch'en said. And they're fighting to survive." I wondered who it was that was misunderstanding them—unless it was other species of vampire. Because obviously humans didn't know about them anymore.

He smiled at me. "Too bad Alec's being puritanical."

I squinted at him. Earlier he'd been on the verge of attacking me. Now he was in total control? "What happened tonight? You seem a little different."

He startled me by doing a quick jump that got him under the covers with me. In fact, now that I got a good look at him, he was glowing a little; kind of flushed.

"We fed tonight. *Really fed.* Do you know how long it's been since we've had fresh, pumping, arterial blood?" He turned his head to me and I could see a little fang glinting as well as his eyes. I just shook my head quickly. "Well too long for my liking. Should I turn off the light?"

I had a lot more to ask, like why Alec thought he should be in my bed, but I understood it would have to wait. "Sure." He reached toward the light and then it was pitch black. I felt a pair of lips very lightly touch mine, then he managed to flip me over so that my back was to him. And then he was up against me, with his legs curved into mine and his arms twining around me. For a moment I didn't breathe, then I let out a big sigh.

He whispered, "Sleep well, brave one." And I think he was out in seconds. My brain twirled and burled for a while longer, but soon sank into sleep as well.

~

I awoke, somehow already thinking about the Vitaortus, and panicked. They'd been unattended for too long and, since they were still in the room, in pitch darkness for too long. I started to move and realized I was still in bed with Jack, whose long, lovely body was also still wrapped around mine. I momentarily forgot about the plants and savored the feeling of being held, tepid of temperature as it was.

It had been decades since I had been properly held. I decided to try stealing a 'frontal' and turned in his arms, putting mine around him. I was pretty sure he wouldn't wake and pulled myself to him, cuddling up against him. He didn't wake, but he moved a little and pulled his arms tighter. And then I felt him start to get aroused and decided maybe it wasn't such a great idea. I'd obviously pushed it, so I slithered out of his embrace and carefully got out of the bed.

After a quick shower, I put my hair in a braid and dressed in linen shorts, a halter top and flip flops. I found the plants and my bathing suit by the light from the bathroom and then snuck out. I didn't smell fresh food and when I looked at the way light cast little to no shadow outside, I was fairly sure it was between noon and one pm. In the kitchen, I found a note from Hervé which read:

Mistress Devi,

I had to run errands for Mister Gregory. I'll return in the late afternoon. Juanita put food in the refrigerator for you. There is a Jeep which Mister Gregory hired for you in the front.

If you wish to go to the Tulum ruins, there is a map in the front seat. It is very near and easy. He asked that you not go farther than there without me.

Your servant,

Hervé

I'll bet he did, I thought. But then I could understand Alec's protectiveness. After all, giant vampire bats had kidnapped me last night.

After giving the Vitaortus the care they needed, I walked to the fridge and noticed a little movement. An anole was trying to move along the wall without catching my attention. I looked at it and said, "It's okay little guy. I don't want you." It stopped and we stared at each other for a moment. Then it tentatively unfurled its red dewlap and started bobbing its head.

With no idea how to respond, I just laughed and opened the fridge. I found the plate made up with fruits and cheese and lunch meats and headed out to the beach.

On the way, I plucked a gorgeous orange, pink and red hibiscus. Once down the stone stairs, I debated on just sitting in the sand, but I was feeling a little weak for full-on middle-of-the-day sun and thought the covered hammock bed would be better.

As I ate, I contemplated the flower. I wondered if Alec was telling the truth. Could he walk in the day? Could he shape-shift? *Could he fly?!* Or whatever the hell he meant by 'flout gravity in his own way'. I wanted to understand how *my* blood, directly, without the essence of the Vitaortus, could make all these things happen. Like bringing back the Camazotz queen's youth. Then I decided I should go see Tulum or else I'd drive myself nuts.

I was in the parking lot of the site in ten minutes. The view that hit me after walking the path to the ruins astounded me. The sky was deep blue and the white, tan and grey of the limestone buildings contrasted beautifully. I had a momentary flashback to places I'd seen in southern India: ancient temples and palaces, but they were so much larger and complex. The simplicity here was organic and fit so well into the land, as if the buildings belonged. So much so that a very large, dominant male iguana had commandeered the top of one of the highest buildings so that he could survey all that was his. Naturally, I had to take his picture—no hiding that I was a tourist here.

I took a lot of photos because everywhere I looked was a photogenic vision. My total fascination kept me there for several hours, exploring the site's flora and fauna as well as its human side. I tried hard to imagine what life was like when it was a vital, thriving city. Would Ch'en be able to fill me in? I thought suddenly of how old she actually was and how she'd started her existence.

Which got me thinking further; what did the queen mean that the priestess of the ancient Maya queen had sacrificed the 'Quetzilwhats-its' stone to them? My mind's list of inquiries was growing. I took some photos of a large flowering crinum with one of the ruins behind it, and then suddenly had a strong thought about Ch'en. What had Alec done to her?

I tried chasing off my thoughts by finding the perfect vantage point from which to get a picture of the famous 'Castillo' building which overlooks the sea. I found it down on the beach. Winds picked up and I was able to get the coconut palm leaves swaying as the sea and sky complimented the wonderfully crafted structure standing strong on the cliff above.

I figured it was around four-thirty and decided to head back, so I turned once more to survey what was left of the small city. Did those who had once lived here know and understand what the Camazotz really were?

The wind died down and I just stood there, pondering and taking in the view. A small bee landed on my arm, blown there by a last gentle gust. It was dark and somewhat smaller than a honey bee. Unlike too many people, I had no fear of bees and wasps.

It doesn't take much knowledge to realize their intent is rarely to harm. And even when it is, how many times smaller than we are they? If they sting, it's suicide for most, one way or another. The odds against them are highly stacked. Plus, as a gardener, they are simply sacred. The planet would do way better if our species disappeared—but the same cannot be said of them.

Not caring how silly it was, I said, "*Hello*, Ms. Bee." She moved around in a half circle and seemed to regard me. She decided to rest a moment and cleaned her antennae. Slowly, and one-handed, I turned on my camera, pressed the macro button, and took a couple of close-ups. It may have been my imagination, but she sure seemed to be posing. Then, with a special short dance and tail wiggle, she lifted off and was gone.

I thought of the irony considering the ever-present representations of a bee god carved on the ruins. And then I figured it probably wasn't irony at all. I fancied that she was wishing me, 'Goodbye, thanks for visiting, and good luck'.

On the drive back, I realized I was tired and depleted. Perhaps Alec had a point. I'd still give the blood to the Camazotz queen, but I knew I'd need to give this whole thing some more thought. After all, each visit would involve giving at least one vial of my blood, depending on how long it would be before I could return. And of course, there were the needs of the plants back home. How many more were in the desperate state in which *she'd* been? I'd need to become an expert on how to build my blood supply.

And Alec's revelation about what it would do for him echoed in my head. I felt the desire to give it to him, but knew I wasn't ready for that yet. While I'd seen that they drank from glasses, I wondered if it would entail biting far worse than the Camazotz; like serious penetration of teeth . . . and sucking; sooo, yeah. *Nope.* Not ready for that yet, or maybe ever. But the image of Alec with his lips on my neck lingered a while.

The gate was still open and I drove in and parked behind the huge Suburban. The thing irritated me so much that I stuck my tongue out at it as I walked past to climb the hacienda's front stairs. No one had any business still making vehicles like that. Maybe for a working ranch, but goodness, they were everywhere in America. Heck, the secret service used them. I decided I was getting too irritated and maybe a swim was a good idea. If there was one piece of magic I knew, it was that salt and water seemed to remove negativity, at least temporarily.

Hervé was nowhere in sight and didn't respond to my hello, so I donned the bikini and sarong I'd left in the bathroom outside my room, and went down to the beach. I'd noticed the clock on the stove read 5:15. It would be only a little while before the guys and Ch'en were up. So I swam and bobbed for half an hour, then decided I'd shower, whether it disturbed Jack or not.

He looked for all the world like an elegant sleeper. It dawned on me that one advantage to having their kind as a bed mate was no snoring! I wondered what I'd hear if I put my ear to his chest, but decided it wasn't worth the risk. This morning's surreptitious attempts at closeness had gotten extremely premature results.

I carefully made my way in the pitch dark to the bathroom and turned on the light only after I'd shut the door. Once in, I didn't care much about the noise I made; so I eventually forgot and sang a little in the shower as I eyed the carved tiles. Between shampooing and conditioning, I compared what I'd seen last night with what the tiles showed of the Camazotz. The biggest error was that these carvings were all male. *Wrong!*

Turning off the water, I reached over the glass door for one of the towels and found it being handed to me. I shrieked slightly and heard, "Christ, Devi. It's just me. Did you get your back?"

I stood inside the shower for a moment with the towel hugged to me, pondering what my reaction should be. Finally I said, "*Jack.* Why are you in here? Couldn't—" and then I heard the toilet seat hit the tank and the unmistakable sound of a strong, steady stream hitting water.

Again, I was quiet for a moment, then raised my voice. "*Oh my God!* You couldn't wait until I was out?"

While I grappled with the concept of vampires urinating, he answered, "Obviously not. I had a lot to drink last night."

My annoyance trumped my fascination with vampire bladder workings and I said, "That's pretty uncivilized. In fact, I'd say it's rude. Get out! Please!"

He continued relieving himself and replied, when done, "No problemo. You sure you got your back?"

"*Yeees,* Jack. Thanks just the same." And out he went, leaving the door wide open.

"Unbelievable," I said, loudly. I heard the bedroom door shut as I stepped out and grabbed the other towel for my hair. Vampire or not, he was pretty typically modern male. He'd also left the bed unmade. With towels wrapped around my body and head, I proceeded to tidy up. The first thing was to open the blinds and wall to get some air into the room. Twilight was just allowing the stars to start their twinkling. I made my way back to the bed and removed the top sheet and covers.

As I leaned over to grab the pillows, there was a knock at the bedroom door. "Who is it?" I asked sharply. No answer came but the door opened and when I swung around, I saw that it was Alec.

His eyes ran from my face and head down the length of my towel-wrapped body and back up again, and with an upturned curve of his lips, said, "We're going out. The club attire I suggested you pack would be appropriate."

He started to shut the door and I said, again with a raised voice, "Wait!" He stopped and I checked to make sure my towel was tight. "Where are we going? And can you ask Ch'en if she'll come in? I want to see what she's going to wear. I brought a couple of outfits."

Alec moved himself into the doorway, leaned against it and crossed his arms. He was clad only in his sarong, which caused my eyelids to dance around on their own. "We're going to an establishment Georges knows. It's a new dance club belonging to a friend of his. As for feminine camaraderie, you'll have to do without. Ch'en shan't be accompanying us." Then he just stood there, obviously waiting for my reaction.

There was something serious behind his words and I chose to tread lightly. "Um. Why?"

Regarding me, he seemed a little surprised at the gentleness of my query. "She will be unavailable for the remainder of our stay—except you *will* see her the night of the ceremony with the Camazotz."

He wasn't really answering me. I looked down at my toes with their cherry red nails. Wiggling them, I sighed. I just hoped she was okay. With my eyes still on my toes, I said, "She was really only doing her job."

He stood straight and dropped his arms to his sides. "Perhaps …
in a sense. But it was in direct opposition to my explicit desires. She
made an expensive choice and is now paying for it. She's lucky it
didn't cost her everything." With that, he turned and shut the door.

An hour and a half later, we were pulling up to an amazing
building in one of the high-end resorts north of Tulum, closer to
Cancun. Georges commented, "Frederico was always one for *glitz*".
We all leaned and took in the astounding façade. It was silver, with
purple-colored enamel Mayan glyphs. The neon all over matched
the color. It was actually quite beautiful and, although could be
considered gaudy, it was done with such obvious quality, that it was
more like a gigantic piece of jewelry.

Hervé parked and came around to open the doors. Those in
line on the sidewalk watched, and when we bypassed them, a few
of the more easily offended tourists commented rudely. My companions seemed oblivious. I felt the guilt of one not used to being a
VIP, or in the guys' case, *VIVs*.

Within moments, we were being led to the main room past
many smaller enclaves. The inside was a marvel. Everything was
done in silver except the floor, which was some kind of very dark
and shiny stone. Tables, chairs, steps and the long bar seemed to
meld into each other, unless they had cushions on them, or other
non-silvery objects, as demarcation. Once you became used to it,
you could see the individual pieces. Interestingly, the dance floor
was thick acrylic with a giant jaguar glyph made of purple neon
lights beneath it.

I tugged on Georges' short sleeve. He slowed and looked at me
expectantly. "What's the name of this place?" I asked in a raised
voice, so as to be heard over the world-fusion electronica music.

"*Night Jaguar.*"

Well of course, I thought, smiling. I began to notice images of jaguars here and there on the walls. The upholstery on the benches, table chairs and lounge seats was faux jaguar pelt, both light and dark forms.

We were led to an area that was obviously reserved for the most desirable guests. It was a large round alcove set back a little above the rest of the club and more luxuriously decorated. A low, silver table fit perfectly within a much larger round couch system that lined the wall. The seating was plush, with velvet cushions that alternated the light and dark jaguar skin motif.

Its wild look contrasted mightily with my companions' attire. Georges had on pink-striped, seersucker mod-style pants, a pink button-down short-sleeved shirt and a straw trilby hat with a pink band. To finish it off, he was wearing pink espadrilles. Truly, he looked fabulous.

In almost opposition, Jack wore a sort of beachy-punk look. He too had on straight legs, but they were dark gray jeans with blue stitching. He also wore a black silk button-down with the same blue threading. To finish it off, he sported a pair of black Dr. Marten's he'd called Drift Andys. I thought he looked darned good with his shiny black hair smoothed back and his widow's peak prominent.

And then there was Alec. His casual look was remarkably elegant. Natural, raw-silk pants and a matt-gold silk shirt were complimented by Italian, strappy, closed-toed sandals with a matching belt. He looked like he should be on a yacht in Monaco's Monte Carlo Harbor.

I felt only slightly more noticeable in comparison. I wore an outfit I'd never dared before. And the wild thing was that I completely matched the club. It was a mini dress of pure silver foil. The top part had a balconette-style bra built in with a slightly curve-hugging A-line dress. The straps were set wide apart so it had a flattering look. My super-high shoes and handbag matched. I felt like a bit of a pop diva, but the guys seemed to like it. Georges had been effusive. I had to admit that the attention was fun. My hair was teased up a little and I'd simply pulled it back with some silver clips. I'd reminisced about 'Barbarella' when I'd seen my finished visage in the mirror.

What the hell, I'd told myself. *How often do you get to go out clubbing?*

We were just about to sit when a gentleman came rushing to see us. He was my height (with the shoes, which meant he was still shorter than my 'dates'). His dark hair was smoothed back and he had a pencil-thin moustache. His attire was exactly what you'd think men wore in Havana in its heyday. Frederico leapt up onto Georges and wrapped himself around the big man. They kissed full on the mouth, lingering for a moment. There was love here, a different kind from Ch'en and Alec's chaste kiss. Once the embrace was over, the teary-eyed man regained his composure and turned to us. The music was not quite as loud in the alcove, so we could hear without shouting.

"Lord Gregory. It is an honor to see you again and to have you visit my new establishment." He bowed slightly and said, "Please. Welcome. I'm so happy to see you". When he laid his eyes on Jack, they glinted.

Alec said, "Your club is a work of art, Frederico. You've outdone yourself. And meet my newest progeny, Jack Garrity. Jack, meet Frederico Valezia."

They shook hands and when Frederico finally turned to me, he did a double take. He gasped and said, reverently, "Señorita! You do me such an honor." He clapped and a waiter came running. "Get a bottle of Dom and one of those blue ones from my private stock.

And get Bernard. Bring him!" The man went running. "Oh, lady. You must be she that we've heard about." He took my hand, kissed it, and then raised it to slowly spin me around to get the full view. "Spectacular. May I get a picture of us? You are so fabulous-looking. I love it. Bernard will absolutely want to copy you."

Georges stepped forward. "Frederico, please meet Devica Trevathan. I told you that dress was right, didn't I?" Georges said, and winked at me.

After Georges took a few photos with his sparkly phone, I scooted into the middle of the large C-shaped couch and Alec and Jack sat on either side of me. Then Georges and Frederico sat.

"Mistress Trevathan. Do you like seafood? My chef makes the best from local fare. May I get you shrimp? Perhaps a tapas plate? With a bit of everything?"

"That would be lovely. Thank you!"

The music was fun and interesting, with various international influences and the occasional dance mix of well-known singles spanning the last four decades. It created a cosmopolitan feel as well as a desire to dance. Frederico's waiter returned with the champagne, glasses and a familiar cobalt blue bottle. This one had been dipped in wax at the top.

While the drinks were being tended to, I looked around at the place and its patrons. Unquestionably, many of these people were well-heeled, fabulously clad, mostly gorgeous people. And many of them were eyeing us curiously, I assumed because of our VIP status.

I was feeling the music and definitely wanted to dance, eventually, after a glass of champagne or two. My body was lightly bopping to the beat when Alec leaned toward me and whispered, *"You are about to be thoroughly scrutinized. Ready, dear?"* Confused, I looked at him. He had a devilish little smile and I abruptly found out what he meant.

A high-pitched squeal made me jump and its source was a remarkable creature coming up the short set of stairs toward us. He/she was about six feet tall, the color of cinnamon and dressed as Raquel Welch in *One Million Years BC*. My eyes went wide and he dramatically clasped his hands to the furry bikini top over his heart.

"Oh, *pleeease* get up and give me an eyeful. This is the best look I've seen here in ages!" he said, in a lovely Jamaican accent. Tentatively I stood, as did Alec, who took my hand and led me to the gentleman, or rather, 'lady'. This must be Bernard.

He looked me up and down and then eyed Alec. With extreme appreciation, he looked back at me and wiggled his plucked, arched brows. "Does Apollo come with this goddess outfit? Mon girl, but he's a looker."

Frederico shot up and said sternly, "This is *Lord* Gregory, Bernard!"

Bernard bowed and took Alec's hand, but kissed it suggestively, rather than shook it.

Alec laughed and said, "The pleasure is mine. Please. Admire Devi as much as we." And he returned to his seat.

Bernard and I observed Alec's posterior together, then he put his arm around my waist and led me to a more open spot at the bottom of the stairs. Pulling a smartphone from his furry bikini bottoms (I think it was real mink), he asked, "May I?" And I nodded. He started taking photos and commented, "Your extensions are so good. Your hairdresser is an artist." Interestingly, our hair was very similar looking, except his currently was dirty blond and mine was very dark brown, and a lot longer.

"I don't have extensions. I don't even have a hairdresser."

He dropped his jaw and nearly his phone. "*Nooooo*," he responded, then came closer and grabbed a handful of my hair to inspect. "Wicked. Just wicked. You lucky minx." He flounced my hair back into place and stood back, then walked around me. He took several pictures of me from behind and asked, "May I create a character based on you and call her 'Deva'?"

I laughed hard and answered, "Of course. I haven't trademarked this look."

He squatted in front of me and grabbed my ankle. "Hand on me shoulder, dearie." I complied and he lifted my foot. "Oh, to have such little hooves!! These are some bashy shoes, girl." I think that meant he liked them. He stood and asked who made the shoes and dress. After telling him, he insisted, "Dance with me." And I said, "Okay," as he dragged me out to the dance floor. After an hour, and five very long songs, he let me go back to the table and went to get on with the business of preparing for a floor show in the upstairs theatre.

Back at the table, I saw there were several beautifully prepared dishes of various kinds of seafood. Alec was alone but comfortable-looking as he pulled the champagne from an ice bucket and filled a glass for me. I fell into the seat beside him, breathing rapidly.

"I can practically feel your heartbeat. Here." And he handed me the glass.

"Thanks. *That* was a workout!" I said breathily. He raised his glass, which was opaque blue and matched the blood bottle. "Cheers." I tapped his glass with my champagne flute and drank greedily because I was thirsty and it was quite cold and tasty.

He observed me and commented, "Devi. Honestly."

Ignoring him, I started eating. "Oh wow!" I exclaimed, mouth full of limey cilantro shrimp. "That's exquisite! You should try some." Then I realized I'd said it as if he were a normal person and glanced at him shyly.

He shrugged, looked at the platter and opened his mouth. I quickly finished peeling a shrimp and held it for him to bite, which he did, but surprised me by taking the whole thing, tail and all. I watched his face as he chewed and he raised his brows finally, saying, "Agreed. Quite well done. His chef knows his trade."

As I continued eating, I looked around for Jack and Georges. Both were on the dance floor. Georges was with Frederico and Jack had a gorgeous, large-breasted blond. In fact, Jack had his hands all over the gorgeous, large-breasted blond. I was surprised to discover that I felt a little deflated.

It must have shown on my face, because Alec asked, "What is it?"

I didn't know what to say. I wasn't jealous, *exactly*, just disappointed it wasn't me, *sort of*; mostly because I'd wanted him to dance with me … *mostly*. But no way in hell did I want Alec to know that.

"Well. I was hoping to dance some more. Jack looks like he's got his hands full of something he isn't going to put down."

Alec had his arms draped along the back of the couch and his legs crossed, looking as cool and at ease as possible. In fact, one would have thought *he* owned the place. His eyes rested on Jack, then upon me, a little too knowingly. He asked, "Will *I* not do?"

Surprised, I stammered, "W—well of course. I just thought you'd go for one of the models at the bar." We both glanced at the group of women who were very obviously part of something requiring extreme beauty and a perfect, skinny bod.

He leaned toward me. "Let me ask a question, which hopefully you won't find as condescending as your assumption was. Hmm, let's see … ah! Who was Martin Heidegger?" He stayed in his leaning position as he awaited an answer.

I reached for the champagne bottle and refilled my glass. "Uh … he wrote 'Being and time'. He was an asshole, bloody Nazi. I find his philosophy a little difficult to follow, but pretty intriguing too—how cool would it be to start over. I mean, I'm no fan of nihilism and after all, if someone so obviously brilliant accuses everyone since Plato of asking the wrong questions … . Why are you asking me that?" I squinted suspiciously and sipped from my glass.

Alec gave a satisfied smile and said, "You've made my point beautifully. You are infinitely more attractive than the lot of them combined, particularly in your *unique* little outfit. Such a tantalizing juxtaposition that I'd not find amongst them, I'm quite sure." He nodded toward the models, then leaned back and added, "Just allow me to choose the song."

"Okay," I said into my glass, wondering if his compliment was a little peek into his private tastes or if he was just teasing.

I'd finished most of the food, and was into my third glass of champagne, when I got the nerve to ask Alec about Ch'en. He dispassionately answered, "It's none of your business Devi. What do you care?"

I glared at him and replied, "That's arrogant and rude; it *is* my business. You've brought me into this. It *is* my business and I care very much." I leaned toward him in an aggressive manner, intent on getting an answer.

He stared at me with slight astonishment, then took my hands. His pupils contracted as he focused on mine and said, dead-pan, "She's at the bottom of a very deep, dark, dry cenote near the Camazotz temple. She is with six men who are heads of a drug cartel. She is guarding them, but not allowed to feed from them. Nor can she sleep, or they will try to kill her if they get untied, no doubt. She will be in pretty bad shape by the end of it, but she'll survive. She's as tough as they come. And she's a shaman, so knows a trick or two.

Stop worrying. She got off lightly." He let go of my hands, handed me my champagne and picked up his own beverage.

I watched him drink, took my own sip and stupidly asked, "What are the six men for?"

"The ceremony."

I suddenly developed a gross feeling in my gut. "Alec?"

"Yes?"

"Is that what you guys were doing last night? Kidnapping Mexican drug lords?"

He stood and took my hand. "Here's our dance." Then he pulled me to my feet and escorted me to the floor. The song was an extended remix of Roxy Music's last hit, "Take a chance with me".

Pulling me into him as he flattened his hand on my lower back, he kept a gentle hold on my right hand. And as he held me against him, he started to slowly sway with the sensual guitar and synth intro and I followed. Except for Jack's lessons, I hadn't danced like this in a very, very long time. Long ago it would have been a waltz, a ragtime hit, a Broadway tune or a slow swing song, but it was more or less the same elegant, intimate movement. He turned me and twirled me now and then and even dipped me a few times. His eyes stayed on mine and I was sure he was using a little of his mesmer skills, because I was getting kind of turned on.

It was perhaps the most sensual, romantic dance of my life and I was a little shocked at how intense he felt. Bryan Ferry's sexy crooning seemed a perfect fit for Alec's smooth and rhythmic moves. And when he ended the dance with a final, butterfly-inducing dip, there was nothing schmaltzy about it. Every woman there, and some of the men, wanted to be in my place. I rested on his arm, staring up into his eyes and smiled as the song ended.

Eventually, when the moment became very pregnant, I nervously said, "*That* was wonderful. Thank you."

Pulling me back onto both feet, he retorted, "It takes two, Devi. You're a marvelous dancer. Thank *you*." And as we headed back to the table, I decided his romancing was just part of his dance package, which was pretty much a work of art.

Georges and Frederico were cuddled and engrossed in each other on the couch when we reached it. I turned and looked for Jack who was headed on his way out, with the blond. Clearly, Jack was going to get his '*joie de vivre*'. Well, at least I'd stay chaste and have nothing to regret in the morning. I downed the last of my fifth glass and realized as I did it how many I'd had, feeling just the tiniest bit lonely.

As if reading my thoughts, Alec asked, "Are you willing to call it a night?" I forced a smile and nodded. He leaned over and spoke with our two companions. Soon, we were all on our feet. I got my cheeks kissed numerous times before just Alec and I left. Georges was definitely staying.

Yet again, Alec was leading me through a crowd, and I was glad for it because I felt a little wobbly on my five inch heels. But this crowd was easy as they parted like the Red Sea for him. A few gave us bravos and some claps for our dance. I'd wanted to see Bernard perform, but that wouldn't start until well after midnight. I had no idea of the time, but was sure I'd never make it that late. I was exhausted, and verging on drunk.

Once outside, I saw Hervé standing beside the SUV. He observed Alec's handling of me, which was to have his arm completely wrapped around to steady me. Hervé didn't betray a shadow of judgment. At the vehicle, I started to climb in a little awkwardly and Alec, yet again, lifted me into the high seat, but he did so delicately this time. He got in beside me and Hervé shut us in.

Back at the hacienda, I headed for the bedroom and turned to say goodnight only to find Alec right behind me. "What are you doing?"

"No Jack. You get me. Go wash up and get in bed, I'll be there in a moment."

"Alec. What are you talking about? I don't think we should—"

"I'm staying in your room with you for protection. No discussion. Go wash your face and brush your teeth. I'm doing the same." He turned and went up the stairs.

"Oh," I said, tipsily, to no one but myself. After following his instructions, I put on my least revealing night set: another soft tank and short combo. As I was slipping under the covers, he came in, wearing a sarong.

I'd not felt shy or embarrassed with Jack, but I did now. As I pulled the covers up over my chest, I watched him place a book on the table and then go back out for a moment. He returned with a lit candle that smelled wonderful.

He turned off the light and I commented, "That smells good."

As he lifted the covers and slipped in beside me, he replied, "Yes. I have them made in a small village in Scotland. The same family has been doing it for centuries. They use essences of my favorite herbs." Then he shocked me by reaching under the covers, removing his sarong and tossing it to the foot of the bed. I decided it would be completely provincial of me to react.

Instead, I asked, "I'm not complaining, but why do you need to be in here if the Camazotz got what they came for? Surely they don't need me until the ceremony."

He was sitting upright, with his back on pillows he'd placed against the headboard. His arms and chest looked like mottled marble, or granite; he was one of those redheads who had a lot of melanin. I wondered if he'd been in the sun a lot just before he was turned.

Lifting the book from the bedside table, he explained, as he laid it in his lap, "It's not about them alone. Yet I will allow, their abduction of you pointed out the error in my protections. I was being too lackadaisical. Probably still am, allowing Georges and Jack a night of whimsy. But they need it after last night. I'm fairly sure the enemies I worry about don't yet know we are here, and by the time they do, we'll be back in Virginia."

I was getting sleepy listening to his voice. I snuggled my face against my hands and asked, "Who are they?"

For a moment he didn't answer and opened his book. Apparently he intended to read by the candlelight, which he'd obviously done for the majority of his long existence. "That will take too long to tell and you really do need sleep. You haven't had enough the last few nights. True?" I closed my eyes and nodded.

A moment later I opened them and he was reading. The candle glinted off his swept-back, amber hair. I observed the line of his very short beard with its elegant cut. His large eyes moved lightly as he scanned the page. Feeling my gaze on him, he turned his head slightly to look at me. We stared at each other for a moment and finally I cleared my throat.

"Can I ask a personal ... and possibly stupid question?" He smiled slightly and nodded. "Jack came into the bathroom while I was showering and ... and ..."

Alec furrowed his brow. "And *what?*"

I realized he was about to jump to the wrong conclusion and I hurriedly said, "He peed. He urinated."

Alec's brow relaxed and he laughed. "How uncivilized. And your question is?"

"Well. Why? I mean, is it normal? For your type, I mean?"

"It's normal if we've drunk an extreme amount. He had over an entire human body full. What you'll find if you analyze our urine is that it's pure water, unless we've just had the Vitaortus." I hadn't heard the word 'urine' pronounced with a long 'i' in many decades. "Our organs don't function as before. They expel somewhat, but they don't really act as a proper filter. Or, rather, they create only water if there is a large quantity of fluid. So perhaps they work *too* well as a filter."

I took the information in and said, "Oh."

But he continued to look at me, "Any more questions?"

"I thought you said you don't kill for blood. Why are there six men for the ceremony? Whose blood did he drink?"

"There were bodyguards. And I told you we *try* not to kill. There are very few absolutes in reality—surely you've figured that one out by now. Besides, the six are for the Camazotz, who have no such sensibilities. Any *more* questions?"

I started to sit up and said, "Well—"

Alec turned the book over and put his hand on my head. "Deviii. *You need sleep.* We have plenty of time to talk." I laid my head back down and he stroked the hair at my temple for a moment with his fingertips. I could tell he was doing that calming 'valium' move on me. "I truly don't want you to get ill or … . I have no idea how long you can do well without appropriate sleep, but I doubt you are that superhuman. You lost a little too much blood last night, considering you'll be donating more night after tomorrow. *Sleeeep.*"

"Okay. Okay. It's just nice to have someone to talk to. Good night." I turned over and heard him say, "*Agreed.* Good night."

A memory arose of another man who'd spoken similarly to Alec, though not in quite as 'posh' a manner; a man who'd been my husband a very long time ago. He'd not had red-gold hair, or even black. Just plain brown. And a lovely moustache. He'd not been quite so handsome as either of these beings sharing the bed, but he'd been handsome enough. And he'd been such a good man. His character had been so fine, until he'd realized something was very 'off' about me; that I wasn't aging or getting sick. But tonight, nearly ten decades later, I was okay, for now. And seemingly safe, and with that thought, I drifted off.

I must have tossed and turned in spite of sleeping deeply. At some point, I awoke as my arm encountered Alec. I opened my eyes and saw that I'd thrown it over his stomach and that my head was nearly up against him. He was still reading but I could see the candle had burned many inches. Sleepily, I croaked, "Oops, I'm sorry."

I started to move away and he whispered, "*Come here.*" He opened his free right arm like a wing and scooted down a little, indicating that not only should I keep my arm on him, but that I could rest my head there too." Too sleepy to resist, I did so and fell asleep again.

When I again opened my eyes, there was the tiniest bit of light. I felt my cheek on cool skin and raised my head. My hair felt entangled and I realized it was under Alec's arm. And then I panicked. Dawn was happening right now and he was not in a light-tight place! I hesitantly shook his shoulder. "*Alec,*" I whispered. He didn't respond and I got a little more concerned. I pulled my hair from under his arm and pushed myself into a kneeling position. Leaning toward his ear, I whispered loudly, "Alec!"

His eyes flew open and he swiveled them to me. "*Devi.*"

"It's dawn!" After a moment of confusion, he comprehended my concern.

Calmly, he replied, "Just shut up the room, please. The buttons are on the pad by the bar." I crawled to the bottom of the bed and hurried to the bar. Finding the buttons, I initially sent the pool wall up, and hissed, *"Shit. Shit!"* But then I got it right, and the wall lowered and the shutters shut.

Then, of course, I had to find my way back in pitch-black darkness. I stubbed my toe at one point, but made it. I was still in pain as I crawled back into the bed, brushing against Alec in the process. I finally laid back down and was shocked when a hand gently grabbed me and pulled me back to the position I'd been in before.

I laid my head on his chest again and he said, "You make a great protectress. Thank you. I'd truly forgotten about the dawn. Imagine that." He sounded amazed at these concepts. The last thing I remember was thinking that I heard a quiet humming sound and that it was coming from his body: deep inside. It quickly lulled me back to sleep.

My dreams had been odd but lovely. And one had been X-rated, well, maybe R-rated, and had involved Alec. I awoke and thought, *good lord*, which made me want to laugh, but I remembered he was beside me and I didn't want to wake him. At some point, I'd turned over and so now had my back to him. After doing pretty much the same as the morning before, I snuck out and gently pulled the bedroom door closed.

I could hear someone in the kitchen and went to say good morning. As I entered, I saw it was Hervé, alone, and said cheerfully, *"Buenos dias."* He looked up from the counter and then turned his back silently.

Once his movement registered, I was in total shock. "Hervé?" I questioned as I came around the counter. "What's the matter?" When he continued to ignore me, I raised my voice a little. "Hervé! What the hell is going on?"

He turned on me with a furious look. "You have gotten him into your bed!"

Again, he'd totally shocked me. "What are you talking about?"

"Lord Gregory should not be in your bed!"

I stared hard for a moment and then rounded on him. "You know what? That may or may not be. But get this straight, I didn't ask him to. He's there for protection. It was supposed to be Jack, who happened to get lucky last night, along with Georges. What the hell, Hervé? What must you think of me? And for that matter, what if we did? Why on earth would you treat me poorly over it?"

Hervé glared at me for a moment and I decided to see if there was coffee. I was so hurt that I felt like I might cry. Thanking the Gods there was some, I poured a cup and turned to stare back and waited. Under my gaze, he wilted a little and said, "Since I have served him, he has never had a woman. You are particularly dangerous, for he is less powerful with you."

"*What?*" That was the second time in a few days that had been said.

"You often speak to him without respect. You are a young girl. It's improper. He is a celibate."

I had raised the cup to my lips and stopped dead. I shook my head to be sure I'd heard properly. "*He's a what?* No. No. Wait. First of all, how old do you think I am?"

He shook his own head and answered, "I don't know. Maybe Twenty-five?" Alec hadn't told him. *He didn't know what I was.*

"Hervé? Why do you think Alec is interested in working with me? Why do you think he brings me to these places?"

"Because only you understand how to grow the plant."

Looking into my cup, I debated with myself over what to say next. Alec hadn't told him for a reason. "Okay. First of all, I'm much older and more *special* than I look. Second of all, why on earth do you think Alec is celibate? Did he tell you that?"

Hervé seemed uncomfortable but answered, "No, but I have never, never seen him take a woman home. And I know he was a *Templier*. Last night is the first I think in my whole life."

"Well, if it will make you feel better, I have no designs on him and absolutely nothing happened. Also, I totally, completely respect him. But remember this, I *don't* serve him. Do you understand? And sometimes he expects things of me that I'm not too happy about. He's totally changed my life, but I'm free to do as I please and he and I will occasionally disagree. *He* doesn't seem to mind too much. Have you noticed?"

Hervé raised his nose and said defensively, "He is a true gentleman."

I had a sudden image of Alec with his teeth sunk into a Mexican drug lord's bodyguard's carotid artery, gulping as the terrified guy struggled and his life juice spurted. Did he do *that* in a gentlemanly manner? Could anyone do that in a gentlemanly manner? I'm sure my imagination didn't even do it justice, but I was sure it had happened. *Jack had drunk over a human body full.*

I asked, "Hervé. Are *you* a gentleman? You have hurt me deeply. I did not, nor will not, seduce your *Saint* Alec. *I'm* more likely in danger than he is! I thought you had become my friend. You accuse me unjustly."

"I am your friend still. But I am very loyal to him. And as I said, I never saw a person—woman, have such a relationship with him. He allows you to—"

I didn't want to hear more, so I said, "Look. I have Alec's best interests at heart. I think. And you need to believe that, not that you should even be saying any of this to me. But understand this, Alec and I are friends and we are really good with each other. That has to be good enough for you. Alec's not an idiot? Right?" Hervé considered my words for a moment then nodded his head in agreement.

I suddenly wondered if Hervé knew about my abduction. He'd not mentioned it, not that there'd been much of a chance. It seemed like Hervé should know some things—suddenly I had a thought. "What are you doing tomorrow night?"

"Oh. Well I was given the night off. Lord Alec has let me have sort of a holiday while here. I will take Juanita to dinner and the cinema."

My mind was doing some serious connecting. "How lovely. She'll love that. Is there anything to eat? I'm hungry." I looked around him at the clock on the stove. It read 9:30.

"Yes. Juanita left you some breakfast burritos and some fruit and potatoes." He turned to the fridge, pulled out a plate and stuck it in the microwave briefly as I poured myself juice and more coffee. "I must drive to Cancun. I have things to pick up and must fetch Cardinale Medici."

Another stunning revelation.

My jaw dropped and finally I asked, "What time does his flight arrive?"

"At five."

"How is that possible?"

"He is old. The old ones can walk a little in the light. Not long, maybe two hours in the morning or evening."

"Why doesn't Alec?"

"Because he drank tainted blood. The drugs and poisons that were in it diminished his powers. Cardinale Medici has been spared this because … well, I don't know why." He popped open the microwave and handed me the plate. He was gone soon after.

After breakfast I felt tired, deflated and a little hung over. I had questions and choice words for Alec, but I'd have the whole day to wait. I wasn't sure how I felt about Piero's impending presence. From last night's escapades to sharing a roof with a Roman Catholic cardinal; even if he was a vampire, it felt just a little too bi-polar.

I spent an hour fussing with the Vitaortus. They'd grown even faster down here, obviously loving the latitude and proximity to the equator. I had to use the prick to add a drop of blood to their water because I felt somehow they needed it. And *I* needed something. I was still stinging from Hervé's accusation and I felt like withdrawing from the whole group. First I get the mixed messaging from Jack, then Alec's affections, though no advances, and now accusations of seduction. Combined with Ch'en's statements and actions, I was not so sure anymore where I stood. And even more deeply, the six drug lords were weighing on me.

I stared at the lovely plants. I caressed them and felt a return of some kind. The life-force within them seemed to mingle with my own, familiar and comforting.

I decided to meditate and, instead of going to the beach, found a secluded spot in the garden, setting the Vitaortus beside me. A gorgeous passion vine was flowering and I chose to sit near it. My charges looked like they could almost be related.

It took a little time to move out of my thoughts and just *be*, but when I did, the relief was tremendous.

I had learned to meditate in India. The practice was sometimes the only thing that had gotten me through the many decades without losing my sanity. And until the latter '60s, I'd had to hide that as well, because most people found it too strange. Thank God for George Harrison.

It had been a while, so I was surprised I was able to sit for an hour, during which the universe assured me I was on the right path. I came away with my mind in a new place. I would try to be more respectful to Alec, but I had a feeling my behavior was exactly appropriate if I didn't want to become subservient—*and I didn't*. Somehow I expected it would be an easy thing to fall into with him.

After finishing what I'd not eaten for breakfast, I then went out to the beach. I felt like a slug not going to a ruin or cenote or something, but I was obviously depleted, as Alec had pointed out. I swam, laid on the beach, managed to keep my mind somewhat clear and fell asleep. When I awoke, I was fairly sure I'd fried myself to a crisp. The only saving grace was that I'd rolled over at some point and pretty much toasted both sides. I really was batting pretty poorly in general I thought. *Stupid girl.*

Then I heard the baba-ji's voice from long ago. '*Compassion. Have compassion for yourself*'. The truth was, the burn would only last for a day and would be healed by tomorrow. It was how my body worked. Just like the vampires, I suspected. I hadn't had a wound that hadn't healed with superhuman speed since I was twenty-seven. I had a feeling my blood would replenish itself more quickly than a normal person, but still, I'd never lost a lot of blood before.

I could see it was getting late as I gathered my towel and sarong. Traipsing up the steps, past the pool and into the kitchen, I came up with a little plan. After laying my things over a lounge chair, I looked in the refrigerator and found what I'd noticed earlier: a plain black box about ten inches square and four inches deep. I opened it, and as I suspected, it held vials of blood. I picked the next obvious one beside the empties (*did the vampires recycle?*). Wearing only my bikini, I quickly shut the box and 'fridge door as goose bumps broke out on my skin. Next, I found the wine glasses, but chose an aperitif one instead and placed it on a small tray.

Remembering the huge and beautiful hibiscus flowers, I went out to get one. Luckily, there was one large blossom still open and I plucked it. Setting it in an identical glass to the other, I then found my purse and pulled the finger prick from it.

They'd be rising very soon. So I poured the vial into the glass, then used the prick. Hesitating, I thought, *Oh my God. How many? Would he taste even one drop?* I chose to put in three because I felt like anymore would very likely be tasted. Maybe there was enough in the vial to mask three measly drops. I hoped so, because I was sure Alec would be more furious over this than anything so far. I didn't know when I'd get the next chance to slip him some.

I couldn't articulate why I was doing this other than I was sure both of us were going to benefit from it. I wanted Alec at his best. I was fairly sure I needed him to be for my own well-being.

Eschewing my sandy sarong, I took the tray in wearing just the bikini—not for any reason other than that I was burned and didn't want anything but Aloe vera to touch my skin. I doubted it would impact a man who was over eight hundred years old.

I'd found the stash of candles and lit and added one to the tray. The sun had yet to set, though it was imminent. Once in, as soon as I shut the door, I saw and heard him stir. I watched him as I walked around the bed to the other side and carefully climbed on while still holding the tray. I got into a cross-legged pose and just as I was scooting my bottom into a comfortable position, he opened his eyes.

I set the tray down beside me and said, "Buenas tardes, Lord Gregory."

He seemed to shake his head free of the vision before him for a moment as if he thought he was dreaming. Then he said, as he raised himself a little onto his elbows, "Do my eyes deceive me? You appear to be glowing, Devi. What did you do to yourself?"

"I fell asleep on the beach."

"Mmm," he responded. "Well, good evening to you too, foolish one. Is that a drink for me? *And a blossom?* Take care. One might think you were trying to curry favor."

I felt a scowl creep onto my face. "Hey. Fine. If you don't want it . . ." I started to pick up the tray and move off the bed, but he had his hand on my leg instantly and laughed.

"*Ohhh, no you don't.* No one has done this for me in so long it would shock you. I apologize for my cynicism. I humbly accept your offering. May I?" He pointed at the glass and I forced myself to nonchalantly pick it up and hand it to him.

He threw it back in one gulp and, before he could think about it, I said, "Piero's coming. You didn't tell me." I watched carefully to see if he'd detect something and I saw a flicker on his face. I hurried to add, "Hervé picked him up a bit over an hour ago and I imagine they'll be here soon." Alec looked at me, then at the little glass for a moment and smacked his mouth twice as if trying to taste again. "Do we need to get ready or something? Or is it just informal with him?"

My incessant jabbering seemed to do the trick. He handed the glass back to me and said, "Thank you, good lady." I jerked when I saw more than a little fang showing. Alec laughed at that and suddenly he was out of the bed in his full glory! Before I was able to avert my gaze, I got quite the fabulous eyeful.

"Alec! For Christ's sake!! Hervé read me the riot act this morning and now you go and do that. *Jesus.*" I could just see that he was putting the sarong on and I turned back to him.

305

"What do you mean?" he questioned with a half-smile.

"Hervé was very, very upset that I had 'seduced' you into my bed."

Alec went from nearly perky to suddenly very still. "*Was* he? And he accused you?"

"He did. He said some things that echoed those that Ch'en said. It's disturbing and I'd like to talk about it. It's obvious he doesn't know about me. I was careful not to spill *those* beans. But Alec. *Why* doesn't he know?"

He walked around the bed, leaned over and carefully put his cool hand flat on my singed back. "Because he cannot be trusted." Kneeling on the floor, he then put his other arm around my stomach and slid me across the blanket to the edge of the bed.

Quite shocked, I very nearly shouted, "What are you doing?!"

"Shhh," he replied and put his right cheek on my back. His coolness actually felt good against the heat and calmed it for a moment. Even his soft whiskers felt cool. But his intensity was almost frightening. Then I felt him turn his head and put his nose and mouth against me. As he inhaled, I could only assume that he was … smelling?

"*Alec*," I tentatively whispered. "*What are you doing?*" I felt his mouth open and could feel pointy things against my skin. *Oh my God*. I shivered, then went rigid. Did I just make the biggest mistake of my life by giving him my blood? But after a few cat-like rubs, he seemed to get hold of himself and stopped.

"The sun is so strong on you that it is irresistible. Please forgive me. I hope you don't feel affronted."

He stood and I twisted around to see him. "No," I said, unsure. But I fibbed and added, "It's okay. I … trust you."

"Good. As you should. And as for Hervé, his intentions are the best, but he is human and therefore easily controlled."

"So then what's the problem?"

"Should an enemy get hold of him and interrogate, he'd be a cinch. Just a simple mesmer would get your address or the layout of your property. He isn't bonded to me and therefore more susceptible. Do you see?"

I 'saw' and I didn't like, although I didn't really understand the 'bonded' comment. "I don't want to be responsible for possible harm to him."

Alec made a soft grunt at that and went over to the switch by the bar. As he pressed buttons and the wall and shutters opened, he said, "Fret not. I'll have a chat with him."

"He thinks you're celibate."

He stood at the largest window and crossed an arm over his midsection. Using it to balance his other elbow, he then cupped his short-bearded chin. "The waves are quite calm this evening."

I got up and padded over to him to look. "Yes. The water was particularly nice today. I saw a turtle!" He turned his head to look at me and I did the same to him.

"Really? I have only seen the females on the beach at night, and that was decades ago. But there was a time, *before*, when if you took to the seas to the southwest of Britain, you would see endless numbers of them. Huge leatherbacks. Amazing creatures. It was joked that one could walk across their backs to the Americas."

We stood in silence for a moment, watching the gentle waves. I'd assumed he wasn't going to respond to my celibate remark.

"Celibate, eh?" he said, proving me wrong. "Well since he's known me, I have been. But not specifically to be so. I have been in this life a very long time. I became bored of all the antics, whether with human or my kind … and the loss. I simply lost interest." I nodded, because it made sense. Because I'd gotten to the same place, more or less, in a fraction of the time.

"You understand?" he asked, raising a brow.

"Absolutely. Positively. Completely," I replied, with a single, closed-eyed nod.

He turned to me fully, dropping his arms to his sides. "I'm so very sorry."

I headed toward the bathroom and asked, "Why? It's not all there is to life. And if the universe sees fit to change the situation, hey, I'm not going anywhere? Right?"

He stared for a moment, then laughed. "Marvelous philosophy. May I join you in that thinking?"

I smiled. "I've got to shower before Piero gets here. I don't think he'd appreciate me like this."

He headed for the door, turned on the light and blew out the candle. "Well, then you don't really know Piero yet."

THIRTEEN

Priest and Priestesses

ʊ

Hervé called ahead to let Alec know he'd be arriving with Piero shortly. Alec's voice boomed as he called us all to be in attendance. I'd only heard him raise it once before and I told him I thought he might have a career on stage. This was highly amusing to Georges and Jack, who laughed even harder when Alec countered with, "And you, Devi, should keep your current occupation rather than attempt comedy." I smiled playfully at them as we went through the front entrance to wait on the steps.

The SUV arrived soon after and Piero emerged, looking like he belonged in the Alec club, wearing a natural-colored, linen suit and a fine raffia Tilley hat. Together, the four of us greeted him with kisses on the cheeks. Georges, naturally, had to give him that Parisian extra third.

When it was my turn, Piero commented, "My goodness, Miss Trevathan! You are radiating." He gently pushed me back from our embrace to scrutinize and I think I blushed.

"Yes, well … I fell asleep in the sun today. Silly me." His eyes widened and he came toward me again for a moment and bent his dark head to my shoulder. Though he didn't touch me, I could tell he was taking in my scent and energy.

"Radiant," he said, as he again stepped back. I glanced at Alec, who was eyeing him interestingly.

Georges asked, "How was the flight? Did you travel well?"

Piero turned, headed up the stairs and answered as we followed. "Yes. Very well. Uneventful. And I trust it has been so here?"

Alec answered stoically, "Not entirely."

As we entered the house, Piero turned to him and replied, "Oh?" But when he saw Alec glance at Hervé, who was climbing the stairs after us with Piero's luggage, he simply continued on into the living room. "Oh, but this is a beautiful abode. I'd forgotten how marvelous the sea is here."

He swept on through the entryway past the dining room and on through the kitchen to the patio and pool area. He didn't stop until he'd hit the top of the small cliff. I came up beside him and he smiled at me. "Is it not marvelous here? I bet there is where the sun burned your skin as you slept." He pointed down at the beach.

"Right," I laughed.

Alec asked, "Piero? Would you prefer sustenance out here or in the salon?"

"I think here would be quite nice, no? The air is good here."

Alec went into the kitchen and the rest of us sat on the cushioned pool furniture that Jack pulled out and placed in a semicircle looking out over the beach and sea. Alec brought out a tray of glasses: four with blood; one with sparkling water. The torches cast a warm glowing light on us.

"So tell me. What occurred?" Piero asked, as Alec finally sat and Hervé was out of earshot.

Nonchalantly, Alec answered, "The Camazotz kidnapped Devi the second night, with the assistance of Ch'en."

Piero nearly dropped his glass. "No! How...*weeeell*..." He pointed his glass at me. "She looks quite well. What did they do to you?"

"The quee—"

Alec cut me off, saying, "The queen wanted her blood in order to rejuvenate. Clearly she had no trust."

I rushed and explained, "She was dying! There was no choice!" Alec didn't look at me but leaned back and laced his fingers together rather than debate in front of everyone.

Piero regarded me. "You have compassion for the queen? Is that what I hear?"

"Of course. She was kind and grateful. She didn't take much." Piero looked at Alec, who indicated a measurement with a hand signal I didn't understand.

Piero leaned over and asked, "May I touch you?" He motioned with two fingers that he wanted to feel my neck. I leaned toward him and he pressed them against the artery. He wasn't as quick as Alec in determining, but he finally pulled away and said, "'Much' is a subjective measurement, especially when the blood in question is the most valuable on the Earth. Outside of us, no one must know of this. Hervé does not know?" The four of us shook our heads. "And Ch'en. What punishment did you administer?"

"She's spent a few days and nights with the offerings. And nothing upon which to feed."

"Where?"

"In the pit."

"Ahh." I was a little surprised when Piero nodded his head in approval. "That was very compassionate of you Alexander."

I piped up at that. "Compassionate?!"

Piero gave me a wide-eyed look, then chuckled. "I forget you do not know our ways yet. You fit in so comfortably. You think this was not a good choice?"

"No! I asked him *not* to punish her. I'm sure she's starving. What if the men got loose? How do you know she's okay? What if—"

Alec suddenly stood and went into the house. The act seemed so disrespectful. Especially in light of Piero claiming my blood was the most valuable on Earth; a statement which I found hard to take seriously.

Piero said, "Devi. Do you realize it is well within his rights to actually kill her for such a thing? The precedent it sets for others is extremely dangerous for *you*. She committed a heinous act. She offered you to a vampire queen who is quite well-known for her voracious appetite. And the Camazotz drink far more than our species. They would think nothing of draining a being to death if need be."

"She didn't seem voracious. She seemed … decrepit."

"She is not the queen for nothing," Alec said, as he appeared with his tablet. "And she has managed to stay queen for a very, very long time." He motioned that he wished to sit beside me on the loveseat, so I moved to give him room. Then he tapped the screen and said, "Let's check our darling, little shaman and her prisoners."

I had no idea what he was talking about. But after several moments, it became clear — or rather, sort of clear. An image came up on the screen that was in night vision.

I saw a figure jerk its head toward the camera, which was about two feet off the ground, and I realized it was Ch'en. She was wearing the same night gown she'd had on that night but really didn't look too much the worse for wear. It seemed like she might be a little dirty, and her hair was messy, but she'd tied it in a knot on top of her head. We watched as she crept toward the camera and then gave an eerie smile.

Pointing, she hissed, "*Look. Our feast awaits, Master Gregory.*" Alec used the virtual controls on the screen to make the camera pan to the left. I noticed she had something large in her hand, but couldn't tell what it was before she was out of the frame.

The camera zoomed, and there they were, on their stomachs, hogtied. The men looked awful; bloody, bruised and stained from their waste. Their gags had been removed and a metal cup lay beside them. It seemed she must be giving them water at least. Alec started to pan the camera back to Ch'en, but suddenly she was beside the men. Their eyes opened wide in horror—and so did mine.

She was holding a long-limbed spider monkey. And in a slow and deliberate move, as she held its mouth shut, she bit into its little neck, then held it aloft and opened her mouth to catch the blood spewing down. Some of it missed and hit her face and chest. The look on her, when she finally glanced at the camera, told me she was hardly miserable. She was having fun tormenting these horribly evil men—and now messing with Alec.

When no blood was left in the now limp monkey, she carefully laid it down and said something that sounded to me like she was genuinely thanking it. Then moving it as if it were a teaching aid, I think she said in Spanish that *they* would be the monkeys tomorrow night. She blew a kiss at the camera, stood and disappeared behind it.

Alec deftly tapped and the screen went to his desktop background (which, incidentally, was one of my close-ups of a Vitaortus leaf). We all leaned back and Alec sighed, which I thought was odd.

"She's so wonderfully creative," Jack said, admiringly.

Georges added, "Such attitude. Dedication. You must be proud, Alec."

Piero nodded. "You must admit, she works her magic for you still, no?"

Alec, whose hands were tight on the edges of his computer, sniffed in and then looked up at his comrades. "*Women*," he critiqued, and then turned to me. "I think you might have got your way. This was no punishment to her. Merely a challenge." He smiled and appeared to be accepting his defeat with dignity.

I eyed him back and finally said, as gently as I could, "Well surely, when you picked her to become like you, there was good reason."

He nodded. "Quite so. Quite so. She was—*is* remarkable."

The image of Ch'en's black head jerking toward the camera in an unnatural way kept creeping into my mind. It was a scary picture and it reminded me of horror films I'd not particularly enjoyed, because they were just too, well, *creepy*. But I hadn't really seen the true dark side of these beings yet, and that was my first frightful glimpse. Her simple theatrics had been astounding, but the truth was, those men were going to die tomorrow night and it was likely I'd be witness to it. Suddenly, I didn't feel so good. As the blood drained from my face, all four men looked harder at me.

Jack asked, "Are you okay? You just had a serious pressure shift."

It didn't surprise me that they could sense such things. I looked at each of them, then out at the sea, uncomfortable with the eye contact. "Those men are going to be killed tomorrow night, aren't they? That's why you chose drug lords, so it could be justified. I'll be a part of it, won't I?"

No one said a word for a moment and finally Piero took a verbal step forward. "It is necessary. The ceremony is very important. It is very, very critical for the Camazotz."

I turned and asked him, "Is that why you're here, for the ceremony?" He nodded and I said, "I don't know if I can do this."

This time Georges spoke. "The bats will die. They need what we are going to do for them. Devi, they are going extinct."

That had me for a moment and I gazed at them all in turn, then ended at Alec's deep green eyes.

The ambivalence that danced across my face inspired a zinger from him: "Do you know what these men have done? They are responsible for the brutal deaths of thousands. It is they who do the torture, dismemberment and chopping off of the heads you read about. These are truly evil men. They kill anyone—*children*, for God's sake."

I looked down at the now dark computer screen on his lap, feeling strong resistance.

He added, "We're killing the proverbial two birds with a single stone. Saving a species and ridding the world of a few psychopaths."

More quietly than I'd intended, I said, "You told me we had enemies, but not that there would be premeditated killing."

Alec got a very grim look on his face. He stood, then put his hand out in a gesture suggesting I should take it. I hesitated, but did and stood, even though it surely didn't bode well. He then headed into the house, carrying his tablet and I followed. Without turning around, Alec informed the others, "We'll return forthwith."

He led me up the stairs and through a long, tiled hallway with a row of carved doors on either side. After opening the one at the end, he pulled me in and turned on the light at the same time. After he deposited the tablet on a dresser, he shut the door. Leaning against it, he then crossed his arms and stared in silence with his brow furrowed.

I stared back and impatiently asked, "*What?!*"

He took in air and said, "You vex me. Truly you do."

"Well, what do you expect? The world I've lived in has different ways and is extremely tame compared with this. I'm bound to have opinions and feelings about some of the gorier details here. You've asked a lot of me. I doubt most humans could handle what we're about to do. I'm really not sure *I* can."

He pushed himself from the leaning position and moved into the room, which had murals of local flora and fauna. His sarong lay on the bed, seeming a little tantalizing, despite my annoyance with him.

"Tell me now. Are you committed to me?"

I frowned. "I beg your pardon?"

He understood my confusion and said, as he sat on the bed, "Are you committed to our cause? Four months ago, I asked for your commitment—that you'd be willing to see this all through. I need to know Devi. I have spent much effort and coin on a vital endeavor which hinges entirely upon you." He was deadly serious.

"What makes you think I'm not still committed?" I moved closer and then stopped because something about this was feeling so very intimate, more so even than this morning or last night. I wouldn't say he seemed vulnerable, but perhaps he was letting a little guard down to try to get through to me.

"I'm *unused* to this level of questioning and disagreement. It's vexing and disturbing. I'm unsure of where you stand and what you'll do." I realized this was, in part, what Ch'en and Hervé were talking about. I sat down beside him, with one knee on the bed and angled myself toward him.

"Look. I *am* committed. Completely, but that doesn't mean I'm going to be totally subservient and just go along with anything that comes down the pike. I'd like to be consulted if I'm expected to take part in the taking of a life. This is as serious as it gets. It's—come on, don't you remember—" I stopped. When he was a human, death was quite a bit more *in your face*. He'd been born in rough times; his work had been rougher. And of course now he was what he was, even if he claimed he didn't kill for his supper.

He surprised me when he laughed as he guessed what I was thinking. "We are what we are, Devi, and death is a part of that.

Most of our visits won't be like this one. But sacrifices are occasionally required. The Camazotz do not have the capacity to evolve as we do. Their ways are ancient and there is no way to change them. We can only preserve them. Nevertheless, I understand your grievance and we'll work it through. I'll attempt some level of awareness regarding your distastes. And you'll attempt the same awareness for my needs and requirements?"

"Well, I kind of thought I was. I can tell you this: don't get cross with me if I have a reaction tomorrow night. I will try not to freak out, but I can't promise you I won't *pass* out."

"Well then it won't matter, will it? You'll be unconscious and none the worse for it. Just do it after you've done your part. You shan't be wielding the weapon, Devi. No one anywhere would expect that of you. You are a life *giver*, not taker."

And with that last sentence, I suddenly felt better. I smiled at him and he leaned forward. I started to panic because I thought he was about to kiss me. And he did, but only on the forehead.

The rest of the evening, at least until I went to bed, was spent telling tales. Mostly by Georges, Alec and Piero. And what tales they told. To hear the history from the perspective of those who were present can turn everything you thought you knew on its head. But then, I knew that to some degree. I'd been present for the entire twentieth century and even the generation that actually experienced a certain event tried to change the story. Humans are mindboggling in their ability to be creative with truth.

At midnight, I decided to turn in. The sun had really done a number on me and I was tired in spite of the nap. Jack followed me in and shut the room up tight while I went in the bathroom, slathered on Aloe vera and brushed my teeth. When I came out, he'd turned down the bed and was sitting where Alec had been the night before. His shoes were still on so I assumed he'd rejoin the others.

I stopped at the bed and put my hands on my hips. "If you're getting in this bed with me later, tell me you've showered since last night."

He scowled for a moment then raised his expressive black brows high in understanding. "Hey. I've got needs. What am I supposed to do? I'm not Alec."

I got in the bed, shoved my feet under the covers as I pulled them up and answered, "I don't care. I just don't want some strange woman's essence in my bed. " I faked a shudder to emphasize my point.

"Point taken. But it's impossible not to have desires being so near you here. I have to slake the need or I'd succumb and Alec would have my balls hanging from his Maybach's mirror," he joked.

"Oh, come *on*, Jack. What was she, a lingerie model? I get it. I'm just a little disturbed by the fact that you'll be in bed with me the next night after—"

Jack put two fingertips to my lips to hush me. "Seriously, Devi. I mean every word. You may not be in a magazine, but you are far more desirable than that girl."

I gave him a look of absolute derision.

"Okay," he conceded. "She was incredibly hot—but superficial, and without your *energy*. I can get girls like her any night. They love me."

I'd have given him a speech on humility, but I had no doubt it was the truth; and he was being matter-of-fact rather than boastful.

"Your 'hug' yesterday morning was more than a guy should have to take without—" He stopped when he saw my jaw drop. Laughing, he took his index finger and placed it under my chin and closed my mouth. Then he winked and jumped up off the bed. He looked great in his black jeans, shirt and tie. He just looked great and I couldn't have him. Nor should I, really, considering our living situation ... and Alec's very clear commandment.

"Goodnight Jack." He blew me a kiss and left. I had never remembered being so 'frustrated' in all my life. I began to wonder if something was wrong with me.

~

The next morning was similar to the last two except it was earlier and when I got to the kitchen, Juanita was there, cooking breakfast, naturally. Hervé was at the table cleaning snorkeling equipment. I got a cup of coffee and sat.

"I thought we could go to a cenote today," he shared. This was a totally different Hervé from the morning prior. I assumed Alec had 'a word' with him. He was smiling and seemed enthusiastic.

"That would be great!" I really did want to experience the unique watery world.

We visited five of them and the day could only be described as sublime. At each, Hervé and I would enter the water together, but we'd veer off in different directions and explore alone. The day was hot, the water was cool and the visions were wonderful. It couldn't have been lovelier and I was grateful to Hervé; a little distrusting, but grateful.

It was five o'clock when we returned to Hacienda Hermosa Ha. I decided a nap would be a good idea, and bade Hervé a good evening and *muchas gracias* for the wonderful day. It would likely be his last evening with Juanita and I hoped he had a lovely time. Doffing the shorts, t-shirt and bathing suit, I put my sleep attire back on and snuck into the bed. I was so relaxed from the magical swim that I fell into a deep and dreamless sleep.

Later, I awoke in the darkness to find my stomach was being caressed. Opening my eyes quickly, I nearly panicked, but heard Jack's voice whisper, "You have a great stomach. Perfect. Soft on the outside and nice muscles underneath." I lay quietly for a moment, feeling his caresses and debating on which route to go. I had an image of a testicle-shaped black bag hanging from the rearview mirror of Alec's Maybach coupe.

"Jack. You have to stop. I can't take it. I've been alone for a long time." But instead, his hand started to head toward my right breast, and just as he reached it, I grabbed. Neither of us said a word. He gently pulled his hand away and got up. I saw the twilight as he opened the shutters, then I saw him, as nature beautifully intended (except for the boxer-briefs), silhouetted as he walked back across the room. It was a lovely sight and I mourned the imposed restriction. Why was Alec being this way? I felt whiney about it, but in my defense, if they were going to be in this kind of proximity to me, it just wasn't fair.

I *think* I wanted Jack. But I was a little nagged by the feeling that it had strengthened because of this place. How would I feel back home, with him living in my house? Cute as he was, there had been no sexual tension there. He was my friend. I'd be sure not to tell Alec about the inappropriate touch, considering his dire warning.

Jack turned on the light. "It's the big night!" he said with a grin, smacking his hands together and rubbing them. "You look great when your hair's all messed up."

I sat up and put my hand to my head. "I need a shower."

"We all do. This is a very sacred ceremony. See you in a bit." And he left.

For a moment, I'd wished he could get in the shower with me, but my thoughts drifted to the Queen of the Camazotz. Alec and Piero had refused to share details of the ceremony with me. I felt trepidation about going into this blind, but I'd have to trust. So far, no one had hurt me, really, and I was positive Alec and Jack and

Georges and Piero would be darned sure to make sure I was protected. And now that I'd experienced the creatures, I felt confident that I could fend them off if need be.

As I dried my hair, I thought I heard a knock and turned off the dryer to listen. A second knock came and I opened the door. Alec stood there holding fabric. "You'll need to put this on," he said, as he carefully handed the item to me. "You have remarkable hair Devi. Dramatic. Leave it as it is."

"Alec!"

He shifted his eyes from my long, full tresses to my eyes, with surprise.

"I'm not a Barbie doll," I stated.

He then rolled his eyes and said, exasperatedly, "For the Lord's sake. Must *everything* be an argument? These are the Camazotz. Natural is the way we are *all* going tonight. No synthetics, no manmade chemicals. Pure and natural." It was then that I noticed his hair had a little wave to it I'd not seen before—*no 'pomade' for him tonight.*

I turned my attention to the outfit and shook it out. It was a long, natural, linen shift with six wooden buttons. It was simple and really soft.

"Oh. Okay," I said, looking back up at him.

He threw a hand to his heart in mock-shock and turned to go.

"Can I at least put my hair in *something* to keep it out of my face?"

"I've got something, just get ready. And where's that stone she gave you?" I pointed to the drawer beside the bed. He reached in, grabbed it and, as he left, added, "No undergarments. They all have synthetic elastic in them." He shut the door before I could argue.

When I emerged, the men were milling about, discussing various past ceremonies they'd attended. I felt a little self-conscious in the dress. It was thin for linen and hung a little big on me. It was only just dragging on the floor and I had to hold it up. It felt like a fancy, somewhat revealing, potato sack. Jack was the first to see me.

"There she is."

The other three turned and Georges added, "Goodness. She could be a saint from the sixth century."

Piero raised his eyebrows so that they disappeared under his dark locks. As he smiled, Alec moved through them and withdrew something from the pocket of his linen trousers. He stepped behind me, and as I started to turn around, he put his hand on my chest, which was very exposed as the dress seemed cut for someone slightly larger than me and had only thin straps to hold it up. I stayed put and he smoothed my hair a little, then I felt something on my back, which he then tied. I reached and felt that it was a thin leather string.

"Thanks, I—"

"Just a moment," he said, as he moved in front of me. He bent a little at his knees as he smoothed out any stray hair, then reached in his other pocket. I noticed his shirt, which was short-sleeved, had a single wooden button and his ensemble matched mine. I could just see through the opening of the shirt that the pants were drawstring. He pulled out another thin leather thong and, as he shook it out, I saw that he'd strung it through the hole in the fire opal.

"I've no doubt the queen will appreciate you displaying this so prominently." And he put it over my head, then carefully pulled my hair through. As the stone fell against my chest, I reached for it.

"Thank you," I said to him. I admired it for a moment and then Piero came forward.

"I brought these for you to wear." And he produced a pair of espadrille-type shoes. These had no rubber, only linen and hemp. Kneeling before me, he hiked up the hem of my dress and lifted my foot. I felt really awkward and couldn't look anywhere but at his back. He then put the other shoe on and stood.

I took the cotton bag Alec had provided to carry the Vitaortus and put it over my head so it crossed over my chest. Maybe they were treating me a *little* like a Barbie doll, but they were doing so very reverently.

Piero said, "Before we go, we pray. Each in his own way, to his own understanding." We stood in a circle. Piero bent his head. His voice seemed to change a little and not necessarily in a sweet way. He spoke in Latin and I understood him to be praying that Sophia should bless us in our righteous endeavor. I stowed this away for later questioning. *Sophia, eh?* For some reason, I immediately thought of Georges' 'Shakti' figure in his office and Alec's tapestry above his bedroom fireplace.

Then Alec announced, "We go. Come, Devi." And he held out his hand to escort me to the big, ugly, gas-guzzling carriage.

Jack drove with George sitting shotgun. The old rutted road was pretty bad, and for the first time, I had an appreciation for the vehicle, especially its shocks and suspension. It suddenly struck me as funny that my special friends had to drive and take planes.

"Aren't you supposed to be able to fly?" I asked anyone I could engage. Jack just laughed as he attempted to keep the tires out of the deep ruts.

Piero smiled beside me. "Myth mostly. For our species anyway. The Camazotz fly, but they are built for it. Human bodies are not. But there are those who have some supernatural skill that defies gravity. You will eventually see. The older the vampire, the better the skill." I turned from him to see what Alec would say but he kept his eyes on the road and stayed silent.

Piero continued. "But you've seen some of our skill. Strength. Speed. Mesmer ability." I nodded and looked ahead through the front windshield. After a while he said, "The twentieth century was such a miracle century. For transportation especially."

Alec and Georges voiced their agreement simultaneously, with an 'Aye' and a '*Oui*'.

Georges added, "You never knew how long it took to get anywhere until the aero plane came about."

Alec chimed in. "Yes. The combustion engine changed everything. An invention from Britain."

"Wrong", argued Georges, "The water in the fountains of Versailles moved via such engines."

Piero entered. "No, No. It was a Florentine invention."

I added, "But wasn't it the Germans who really got the ball rolling?"

Jack laughed again and said, "An argument in which all sides are correct! But don't forget the Arabs and Chinese. They were the ones who really started it. Hey, is that the first ruin?"

We all leaned forward and saw what appeared to be an ancient lookout-tower.

Alec replied, "That's it, Jack. You'll hit the remnants of the *sacbe* soon and then it should be easier going."

"*Sacbe?*" I asked.

Alec answered, "An ancient Mayan road. This one connected to the main causeway from Coba to Muyil. The temple of the Camozotz lies somewhat between them in reclaimed jungle to the west, although, it was never entirely cleared in the vicinity around it because they didn't want the humans cultivating too close to them. The growth you'll see on the temple began perhaps five hundred years ago."

"So the Maya knew about the Camazotz?"

"Oh yes. They venerated them. Some groups more so than others, yet all had deep respect and made regular offerings. But the full truth was known only by the religious elite. Ch'en was a priestess whose position was to keep the Camazotz happy with humans. It was she who would choose sacrifices for the Queen. She helped to make her a glutton, I personally believe. Ch'en loves the queen too much."

I knitted my brows. "Well, that's obvious."

Alec leaned in to me. "Is it?"

"Yeah. She let them take me . . ." I looked him in the eye and cocked my head. He raised his eyebrows and I asked, "As in romantically? Are you joking?" He shook his head. "That's—wait, I thought you and Ch'en—"

"Briefly. When I first changed her. It's been a long time. Some become quite open-minded indeed. Although I think for *them* it's emotional rather than physical. But it explains Ch'en's willingness to risk her existence for the Queen. Their survival has been intertwined for many centuries."

Georges interrupted, "We are nearly there. Look." He pointed ahead and we all peered through the glass.

The moon was halfway to the highest point, so already quite bright. Despite the light from the headlights, I could see the silhouette of the large hill ahead. Its shape was familiar and I had a feeling we were coming at it from another direction from which the bats had brought me.

I realized we'd been rolling along much more smoothly and looked down at the ancient road in front. It was nearly white, being made of crushed limestone, and relatively smooth. The dark jungle hugged the vehicle on either side creating a tunnel and I decided whoever kept the road clear made sure it wasn't visible from above.

Within ten minutes, we were at the base of the hill, or rather the temple, which was unbelievably well hidden beneath its green shroud. It was explained to me that Alec officially owned all the property in a fifty mile radius from this point. Ch'en had a small group of her own progeny which kept the place secure.

Once we'd all gotten out of the vehicle, Alec opened the back door and pulled torches from inside which he handed to each of us. Jack motioned that we should put the wicks together and he deftly lit all in a single efficient move with a single match.

Alec turned to me. "Devi, there are snakes and they may or may not be sleeping and may or may not be of danger to you, but I'd prefer if you stayed behind me. Jack, I want you behind her. The steps are steep and numerous. If you get tired, say so and one of us will carry you. I don't want your body stressed much before we begin, so don't try to be … what's the American term? *Macho* about it."

Perhaps I should have been frightened by his warning, but snakes just weren't a source of fear for me. I threw my hand to my forehead in a salute and said, "Aye, aye, cap'n."

He eyed me for a moment, clearly forcing himself not to smile, then requested of Georges, "Would you see if there is any rope in the boot?" Georges rummaged in the back of the SUV and emerged with some twine.

"Cut one for me as well, *per favore*," Piero added.

Its purpose became clear when Georges wrapped a three-foot length around my waist loosely and tied it in a bow in front. Alec came forward, gently lifted the Vitaortus bag and pulled the dress until it flounced out from my midsection and its hem was hiked up nearly to my knees.

"Lovely," I unhappily commented, thinking *Barbie* wouldn't be caught inanimate at the bottom of a toy chest in this outfit.

"More practical," Alec retorted.

I turned and saw that Piero had done the same with his cassock, also having tucked his red sash into the twine. All of us were wearing clothing made of the same unbleached and dye-free linen, except for Piero's sash, which I assumed was silk. I had a sudden wish for my camera. Knowing it was not with me and that I'd have nothing but memory upon which to reminisce, I decided to become extremely present to the here and now. I didn't want this to be hazy in the future when I tried to remember.

Alec led the way and we began ascending the ancient pyramid. The sounds of the jungle at night started up again after the car had been silent for a while. It wasn't easy going in espadrilles and a dress, in spite of its shorter hemline. Occasionally, Jack would push my rump from behind or Alec would grab a hand or arm and pull me up. The steps were at least fifteen inches high, but apart from me, the party had no trouble with it.

Maya Nut trees, with roots spilling down the steps, blocked our path here and there, but again, someone had been keeping a trail relatively open. When we reached the top, I had to stop for a few minutes to catch my breath and let my muscles calm down.

"My God! Is this the only way in? What about the cave entrance?" I asked, breathing hard.

"Short of repelling, that way is impossible. It is one hundred and fifty meters deep. And the bats don't like it to be entered by any but them," Alec replied. The guys had taken the steps as if they were merely a landing, but waited patiently for me to recover.

As we took in the view, I noticed the moon was not far from its zenith: perhaps an hour. Suddenly the men's heads jerked in unison toward a sound I'd not heard. But I could see the movement on the other side of the platform. Ch'en stepped into view. She looked initially only at Alec. Something unspoken passed between them during a meaningful stare, and then she walked to me and fell to her knees, startling me.

"Please forgive me," she requested as she gazed up at me.

My breath had finally calmed and I whispered, "*I already did.*"

She reached out a hand and touched my knee, then stood and turned to Piero. With head bowed, she said, "Welcome Father *H'man*. It is many years."

Piero moved toward her. "I am happy to see you, Ch'en, but not that you disgraced he that begat you. You are very fortunate to have a genitor so compassionate, as well as the forgiveness of the Mistress. Do not forget that you are a human vampire, not a rare Camazotz. Need we find another?"

Her head shot up and her eyes held as much fear as they did defiance. They told me she knew he'd do away with her in one of my rapid heartbeats from a few moments ago. Then, after an awkward moment and a shake of her head, she started toward a single rectangular small building which looked like it might be an entryway.

"They await," was all she said.

Her nightgown was cotton and so I figured it must be acceptable for the ceremony, although I was surprised; she must have washed it because I saw no sign of last night's monkey blood. Granted, the lighting wasn't too good, in spite of the moon's beautiful brightness.

Curious about what she'd called Piero, I whispered to Alec, "'*Father H'man*'?"

He leaned down to whisper, "*It means shaman. 'Father Shaman'.*"

We had to really duck to get into the doorway, but as the stairs descended, it was apparent to me that Alec, Georges and Jack were going to have a rough go of it. There were some seriously tight spots. But oddly, as I watched ahead of me, Alec moved and scrunched his body like a cat through those spaces and I realized what I was seeing was supernatural. No living human could do that, except maybe people who practiced Houdini's craft.

It was a spooky, uncomfortable trek. Various creatures, particularly insects and arachnids, adorned the walls and inevitably were brushed onto me because of the tightness of the steep tunnel. I wanted to scream unabashedly, over and over, but Jack, who was again behind me, merely brushed or scooped each creature off. I silently vowed I'd give him anything he wanted when Alec was not present. It appeared that my fear-factor was alive and well after all.

There were glyphs and carvings on the wall, but my obsession with keeping creepy crawlies off of me kept me from really scrutinizing them. As we continued our descent, no one spoke, and it seemed like it was taking much longer than the climb up the temple; which made sense, since the cavern I'd been in was well below the surface. I wondered if that was our destination. As we trekked deeper, the air grew slightly cooler and, though less muggy, it became very still. Every biologic and geologic scent was cloying.

My grip on my torch was so tight that I'd not realized my hand had nearly gone to sleep. Switching hands, I shook out the pins and needles and then suddenly ran into the back of Alec, who grunted but barely moved. He turned his head as much as he could and said, "Mind yourself, Devi. We're here now. Stay beside me until Ch'en directs us." I nodded an affirmative.

We entered a limestone antechamber and I saw Piero whip off his chord, so I did the same. Then I shook out the dress, looking down inside the front of it and hoping there were no creatures crawling within.

"Devi." I jerked my head up at Alec's voice and saw he had his hand out. I walked to him and took it, then glanced over at Georges and Jack, who both smiled a little weakly for my liking. With something more like moths than butterflies in my stomach, I moved beside Alec and watched as Piero and Ch'en walked together in front of us. I noticed she'd let her hair down and had smoothed it some.

We ducked into a small, natural tunnel and finally emerged into the huge cavern I recognized, but from a place I'd not noticed on my previous visit. We were entering opposite from where I'd seen the single bat climbing through on the wall a few nights ago. It was much brighter than before because fires burned all over the floor of the giant room and there were torches along the wall. The smoke rose to the ceiling and travelled out to the cenote. I noticed a pool I'd not seen as well as a small stream that ran the length of the floor to the grand opening and the cenote beyond it.

And there were the six men, impossible to miss because, instead of hogtied from behind, they were now sitting, feet and hands tied together in front of them, completely naked, clean and gagged. I struggled to squelch the rising torrent of terror I felt for them.

A constant, unrecognizable whispery sound filled the cavern and I searched for its source. I soon realized it was coming from all around and that we were surrounded by a hundreds of Camazotz, above, as well as on the ground in front of us; the entirety of the swiftly dwindling population. The sound was simply their movements and breathing. Then the odor hit me; it was intense, but the fires were slightly masking it.

Reorienting, I found the dais and its various furnishings. I recognized the bat at the ceremonial table as the one who'd bitten me, and she was watching me now. I nodded once at her and she bobbed her head likewise.

Alec noted this and leaned down, commenting, "You seem to recognize that one."

"She's the one who … it was she who bit me so the queen could drink. I guess she's her priestess or something."

He nodded and added, "By the by, you need not be embarrassed by what will happen. I know you are originally from a time more timid about physicality, although today you seem less shy."

I had no idea what he was saying and gave him a confused look. Just as I was about to ask for clarification, a ripple went through the bodies hanging from the ceiling and then moved through those around us. From seemingly nowhere, the Queen appeared, looking significantly younger and healthier than when I'd last seen her.

Alec stiffened momentarily and I had a sudden flash of insight. This ceremony, and sharing of 'me', really was a big deal. After all, these two groups were actually competition for each other. Of course they wouldn't be *buddies*.

I began to have an inkling of why Alec might be a good thing for me. Even humans didn't have enough compassion as a single group to save endangered species. Why would his kind? Yet his newly enhanced aversion to the Queen wasn't stopping him from helping them survive. He was a creature with a cause and I was his means. I made a little promise silently to work harder to slip him a few drops of my blood here and there.

Ch'en and Piero moved forward as the colony parted for us. All the while, those on the dais watched our progress in silence. I felt as if there should be a drum beat or something, but only the sounds of the fires crackling and the moving multitude of furry bodies accompanied us. I might have even thought it funny if I didn't know the drug criminals' fates.

Upon our arrival at the platform, Ch'en said, in a strong, loud voice,

"Great Queen of the Camazotz, I and the Father H'man of the Vampyr ask that we may join you and prepare for this feast which unites us, and that we may honor her that bears the Life Force and gives freely to us both."

A series of strange sounds came from one of the creatures on the dais. She appeared to be translating for the colony what had been said. The Queen moved to the ceremonial table and her priestess stepped back.

In her odd voice, she said,

"You may gome."

She looked and sounded much stronger now and obviously had no need of her litter.

After sticking their torches in convenient holes at the front of the dais, Piero and Ch'en ascended the steps and were greeted by the priestess and then the Queen. Both got down on their knees and then put their heads to the ground before her. She crouched and gently licked their faces and then wrapped her wings around Ch'en. Piero showed nothing but respect as this played out.

Finally, all three stood and faced us. Alec, Jack, Georges and I were lined up in front of the dais.

"Lord Ahlek',"

the Queen declared, and spread her wings as she pointed to him with a thumb claw. The entire colony erupted with squeals and twitters, which I assumed was a good thing. I watched him look around the giant room for a moment. He bowed his head deeply, and I wasn't surprised when he didn't show the deference Piero and Ch'en had. It was clearly his 'remark' on her stealing me and she seemed perfectly fine with that I guess, since he was the champion who had found me.

She turned her eyes to me, ignoring Jack and Georges.

"Ik'-Bearer who iss Defffik'a."

She struggled to pronounce my name, but gave her grimace-smile as she gazed down upon me. After the translator squeaked, the room again got loud. Once it had died down, Piero came to relieve me of the torch and brought me up to the Queen. She greeted me with a nuzzle, which was frightening and awkward, but I gave my best to return it. Then Piero indicated the bag I wore, so I removed it and carefully pulled the plants from it.

The queen examined them as if they were from Mars. These creatures lived alongside and, I figured, respected plants, but had little conscious relationship with them outside of a little medicinal and 'household' use. They were not vegetarians and obviously lived more comfortably amongst rocks, than trees. I looked at Ch'en, confused about the next move.

"Come now. We plant them in the cenote. There is a good protected spot I have prepared that is high above the water level and bright enough in the day." She lifted a knife-like, shiny, black implement off the table and we moved down and out through the crowd of crouched bodies.

"I will be here regularly to care for them, but the priestess will do so as well," she explained. As we reached the spot, I felt fairly sure it would do. The soil was good and seemed deep enough; it was far enough away from the water that flooding shouldn't affect it and there were rocks and other plants for the vines to cling to. So Ch'en and I crouched down and planted as Piero said a blessing over us.

When we were done, I touched a leaf of each as a goodbye. It was as if every plant I gave away kept an emotional tendril attached to me.

"We need to water them."

Both Ch'en and Piero nodded and he said, "Before we let blood, we must purify in the waters of the cave." As we made our way to the small pool I searched for Alec, Georges and Jack, who I soon realized were all waiting on the other side of it.

The Queen announced,

"Pleasse. Cleansse away the human impurity."

And I watched Alec undo his shirt button as he casually pushed off each of his espadrilles with his toes. Georges and Jack did the same. Piero undid his sash and Ch'en simply pulled her nightgown over her head. Soon they were naked. And I was not. *No one said I had to get naked!* They all slid into the pool except Alec, who came around it in his glory and stood in front of me.

I kept my eyes on his as he said softly, clearly understanding my reticence, "We must do this. It won't take long. You're safe and beautiful. Besides, look at them." He waved at the colony. "They're all *sans* clothing."

Then he reached out toward a strap, but I stopped his hand and then bravely pulled the straps of my gown down my shoulders and the thing slid right off. Taking my hand, he pulled me so I stepped out of the piled linen and slipped into the pool, which was only slightly chilly—*and very, very dark.* Already, the others were getting out. Alec stayed close as he and I dunked several times.

I saw a hand ready to pull me up; it was Jack's. He yanked me up smoothly and I quickly went to my dress, stepped in, and pulled it right up. When I turned around, I was shocked to see that the others were not even near their clothes. They were headed toward the dais.

Not knowing what to do, I gathered up all the outfits and laid them on a rock nearby, then hurried to join them. I felt silly somehow, re-clothed, but it was sort of sticking to me and wet, so it was nearly see-thru anyway. No one seemed to care or even notice.

Once there, Ch'en addressed the Queen.

"We have purified our offerings to you and ourselves. We are ready to unite the three bloods with the blood of the Ik'-Bearer."

The Camazotz priestess made a motion and two of the retinue walk-crawled to the tied up men, then looked back, awaiting instruction. Alec moved to her and said something. It was amazing to see his naked, marble-like body so tall amidst the sea of dark furry creatures. At any other time his physique would have my complete attention, but not now—I knew the humans were about to be sacrificed.

The priestess chittered and the two bats lunged at one of them, pulling him from his position. He tried to scream, but the gag was fairly effective and I wondered if they had used a baby coconut with him too. They pulled as the man flopped from side to side in his futile attempts at resistance. But when Georges and Jack walked down the steps to take hold of him, his body went rigid and his eyes held terror … and recognition.

I concluded he must have seen them drain his cohorts, amongst other things they may have done. The vampires were easily ten inches taller and they effortlessly lifted him, each with an arm and a leg. As they ascended the steps, Piero came forward, and though he wore no vestments, or even underwear, it was clear by his movements and posture what he was.

As Jack and Georges held the man, he removed the gag, and asked in Spanish if he wanted to confess before he died. The man sobbed and began speaking very quickly. His sins were clearly numerous. After several minutes, Piero stopped him and said some things in Latin that I didn't understand, but assumed were an absolution. He then blessed him and the man started sobbing again and pleading. Piero stepped back and the man was carried to the altar like a goat.

Ch'en ceremoniously lifted another obsidian blade from the table, turned to Alec and then nodded. He stepped up on block beside the large basin that raised him three feet—a statuesque creature on a pedestal. Ch'en cut the man's bindings at his feet as Georges and Jack lifted him. Alec grabbed the ankles with one hand, easily raising the drug leader above the table, upside down.

Then Ch'en's arm moved so swiftly that I didn't immediately grasp what had happened until the blood began pouring forth from his neck into the huge bowl carved within the table.

Around me, the Camazotz became really restless. They were inching forward and jostling each other, leaving at least a two-foot perimeter around me, for which I was grateful. My stomach heaved and I was afraid I might be sick; I didn't want any of them near me if I was. No, I didn't want any of them near me at *all*.

The drug lord's body finally twitched a few last times and I felt an odd sensation, as if I could sense his life-force departing this dimension. An unrecognized voice from an unexplored place within me graciously thanked him for the sacrifice of his vessel. I was intrigued by my strange internal experiences, but had a more fully conscious thought of all his victims. Hopefully this was some sort of justice. I was no fan of capital punishment, so I didn't presume to know.

As I tried to process the experience, Alec made an amazing hop down off the block while still holding the body. The priestess pointed her boney thumb to a hidden space behind the dais and he simply tossed it in that direction, as if the exsanguinated body was nothing more than a chicken bone. I was horrified.

He turned to look into the crowd and his eyes landed on mine. My legs suddenly felt like they might give way. I knew he was trying to summon me with the look, but I felt immobile. I'd just witnessed my first killing, the first of six, and I was in a little shock. I then heard his voice gently saying, "Please, Devica. We need you."

Had his lips moved? I didn't really know; I was surprised I'd heard him over the drumming thud of my heart beat. I lurched forward and found myself suddenly in front of him, behind the table. After half turning me, he stood right up against my back and said, "We are ready, priestess."

Jack and Georges moved to our left, Piero and Ch'en to the right and the priestess and Queen stood in front of the table, their backs to the throng. Ch'en was the first to raise her left hand to her mouth and bite into the radial artery. As the other vampires followed suit, I saw (over Alec's hand, as he'd pulled me so close that he'd had to bite it over my shoulder), that the Queen and priestess had bitten into each other's wings. Their bites were smaller and not in such a prominent vein, but was enough to cause a decent flow to fall from their thumb-claws.

After several minutes of extremities bleeding into the bowl and adding to its volume, the wounds slowed and the human vampires each actually licked their own bites and Ch'en licked those of the bats. I guessed that this helped in the healing. I had a memory of Sir David Attenborough telling me from my television that proper tiny vampire bats had anticoagulant in their saliva, so perhaps that explained it.

And then all eyes were on me, sending a jolt of fear rocketing through me, which caused me to jerk against Alec. Piero, who looked more like a stripper at the end of his act than a priest, coaxed, "Mistress, yours is the magic ingredient."

Finding my voice, small as it was, I asked, "Um. Does it have to be an artery?"

"Yes. That is the fresh blood. We can make it close quickly. Are you ready? I will allow Alec to do the honor."

"No, Piero. You—" Alec demurred.

"It will be you," Piero firmly stated.

And so, from behind me, Alec wrapped his right arm around my torso, took my left hand in his and brought it to his mouth. First he kissed my shaky palm, lingered for a moment and I felt something close to a swoon. His presence against me was suddenly supremely erotic and I hoped no one else could sense the type of adrenalin rush I was inappropriately having.

I sobered when I felt brief pain as his teeth punctured, then quickly withdrew. He held my hand over the bowl and I watched, entranced, as the stream fell into the mingled blood of the others. The color of mine was different, brighter, and as it hit, the liquid around appeared to swirl toward it. It seemed as if we stood there, very still, for a long time and a slight euphoria burst inside me.

Finally, I could hear the last drops of my blood hit even as I heard my own slow breathing and heartbeat. And I could feel that vibration I'd heard deep within Alec. It was oddly comforting—like someone humming.

Then Ch'en spoke, and the spell broke.

"We take part of this life force and contain it so it may be used to feed the sacred plant—The Vitaortus. The rest will sanctify that upon which we shall feast."

As her words were translated for the Camazotz, she took a small gourd and scooped most of the blood from the bowl, then set it aside on the table. While she did this, I felt Alec raise my hand and give the still-bleeding bite a single strong lick, which stanched the flow. Then he gently placed it by my side and stepped back from me. My moist dress clung where he'd been and I modestly pulled at it.

Chen then took another gourd bowl and flicked a little of the blood mix into it with an obsidian knife. "Are you ready?" she asked of me, then turned without waiting for my answer. I followed her and we stopped at the pool where she dipped the gourd into the cool water, which mingled with the blood droplets until they were invisible.

Once outside the cavern, I gently poured the water around the three young Vitaortus, which, to my eye, seemed to shimmy with joy. Once they were watered, I noticed my body relax a little. We were soon back on the dais and I realized my part was done.

I felt a warm touch and turned to see a bat I recognized: one of my friends who'd carried me. She gestured to a raised spot at the back left of the dais where banana leaves had been placed with a fur over them. I noticed a bowl adjacent filled with cut-up dragon fruit, coconut and papaya and something dried that I couldn't quite make out. Her movements urged me and I followed her to the fur where she indicated I should sit—so I did, cross-legged. With her wings folded tightly against her, she squatted low beside me and looked out onto the proceedings.

Alec turned slightly and said, "Eat the dried flesh. It will help you replenish faster. Kindly partake of their gifts to you. It is difficult for them to prepare such things. It's an honor I've never known them to bestow."

I looked down at the bowl and realized it was a sea turtle carapace which had been slightly polished. Hesitantly, I took a piece of the dark dried meat and tasted it. Surprisingly, it was quite pliable and tasty; pretty much like jerky. I took another piece and heard the Camazotz make their unique, squealing, cheering noises. When I looked up, I realized it was for me and my appreciation of their efforts.

But before I could get embarrassed, the throng lifted the five bound and gagged men and crowd-surfed them toward the dais. All five still-naked human vampires stepped forward and took one (it was bizarre to see tiny Ch'en easily manhandle a human that was bigger than she). They dropped them at their feet and turned to the Queen. She moved toward them and carefully sniffed each human. Finally, she stopped in front of the man at Piero's feet.

"Thisss one," she sensuously growled.

Piero then questioned the five men, whose terror was absolute. Three nodded at him but I think the other two had either passed out or were simply immobile from fear. Like the first, he seemed to be giving them absolution and then a blessing.

Then suddenly he arched his head back, bared his teeth, and quickly struck his man's carotid.

I stopped dead, in mid-chew, horrified and enthralled. It was the first time I'd witnessed one of them attack and really feed. I could see the red, pulsating flow as it came too quickly for Piero to actually be able to swallow it all. Both he and his victim groaned like lovers.

With his mouth still attached, Piero lifted and put him in the chair I'd occupied four nights prior. The priestess was suddenly beside them and had a specialized bowl at the ready. Piero unlatched and she quickly placed the bowl where it would catch the spurting liquid. The man's feet were positioned so that they were above the level of his head as the queen crawled closer, flicking her tongue in anticipation. Ch'en then brought the other gourd with the blood mixture and poured a little into the special bowl as the blood still flowed.

It wasn't long before the body was drained and the man's heart stopped. Piero took the bowl from the priestess, knelt down and held it at a comfortable level for the queen. She moved to him, smiled in her grimace-like way, and then delicately tucked into the bowl. It was bizarrely sweet and gentle and she pretty much looked like a giant version of the tiny vampire bat the world knows and loves.

It seemed to me that Piero, whose lips, cheeks, nose and chin were covered in blood, had bowed his head in prayer. I found the juxtaposition of the animal vampire with the human vampire confusingly at odds. It was the human version that was so much more violent and awful in its technique, although I had no idea how the Camazotz actually hunted.

The queen must have drunk five pints, easily. Now I understood why they'd accused her of gluttony. When she'd finished, she was slow and very full, but crawled off the dais to a spot near the wall and, with her queendom watching, spent a full minute relieving herself. They erupted into squeals and squeaks as she motioned for things to continue.

Alec, Jack, Georges and Ch'en took their humans and did exactly what Piero had done, but instead of placing theirs in the chair, they let go over the huge ceremonial bowl built into the altar. As four naked vampires held four naked humans so that they bled-out through their necks, I felt the aberrance keenly. I watched as Alec stepped again onto the block and lifted his drug lord victim by the ankles so that all drained. I think the guy had gone unconscious long before.

I'd felt this aberrant absurdity before, when the human world had gone so far into atrocity that it was unfathomable: the Nazi concentration camps, the Soviet Purges, the Killing Fields. The only difference was that there was meaning in the deaths tonight. I understood that this would be the first step in helping this species survive, but my human, almost Buddhist, sensibilities could barely handle it. After tears appeared, I hurriedly wiped them away. I tried to focus on the repeating sensations of the men's energies sliding away and the strange, distant voice that was thanking them.

When finished, Jack traded his body and took Alec's to be dumped with the first, and so on until all the drug criminals were drained and the bodies disposed of. The bowl was nearly overflowing with close to five gallons of blood, which I could smell from where I sat. In a strange sense, it reminded me of very fertile soil.

When the last body was stowed away, Ch'en reached under the bowl and pulled a small, wooden stopper. She then readied the second gourd with the mixture. And now I saw how the system worked as I observed the blood flowing down little channels to the many smaller built-in recesses along the base of the dais.

Ch'en poured tiny amounts of the mix and the first of the Camazotz began drinking from the lower basins. Each got only a good mouthful, but they were not greedy and stepped aside so that their sisters and brothers could drink. Finally, there was enough room in the large bowl to add all from the gourd and what was left of the queen's unfinished blood. Ch'en was careful to make sure the mix with my blood was evenly distributed within the rest.

As the hordes moved forward to lap, I noticed Alec quietly move down the dais, grab two bodies by the ankles, and head toward the pool. He was followed by Georges, who took one, Jack, who also dragged an extra body, and Ch'en, who took the final one. The four of them entered the pool and disappeared into its lightless depths for many minutes. Clearly, the drug lords' bodies would never be seen in the light of the sun again—like so many of the ancient Maya sacrifices.

The foursome eventually returned to the dais, clean, clothed and looking very *alive*. I guessed each had drunk at least a pint, which seemed much more than their usual intake. Their eyes glinted brightly and Alec's flicked to the still full bowl beside me.

Before he could give me any kind of admonishment, I reached in and grabbed the first thing my hand touched and brought it to my mouth. I just started stuffing fruit and meat and chewed as fast as I could. I was sure I'd start retching at any moment, but I never did. I felt his gaze but refused to look at him. Instead, I watched the creatures as they moved in loose rows to and from the basins. Eventually, I felt a hand on my right arm and looked up.

"*Surely you are full now*," Alec whispered.

Piero, who'd stolen away to bathe as well, reached the dais, his cassock looking none the worse for its temporary divestment. My bat friend inched closer to me so that he could sit beside her. Her body was warm. As she moved close, against me, as seemed bat custom, I could feel her heartbeat and breathing. Looking at her face in profile, and then Piero's, I wondered how on earth these beings were related by anything other than diet.

And then, as Ch'en went to the queen and became engulfed by her stretchy, leathery wings, it hit me—*supernatural*. Living or not, the Camazotz *were* supernatural. And if not immortal, they were certainly very long-lived. This made me realize that I too, was supernatural.

It was a profound moment.

It wasn't that I hadn't known I was most certainly not a normal human, but I'd never had anyone with whom to compare myself. And look at what company I was in: human vampires and giant vampire bats. Who and what else was out there? *Who* and *what* was I, for that matter? Nearly a century of knowing I was different didn't prepare me for the moment that I realized I was not of the normal world. I suddenly felt squirmy and really wanted to go. I wanted the familiar comfort of being alone.

Turning to Alec, I barely touched his arm and he leaned near to me as he kept his eyes on the procession of creatures. Putting my lips to his ear from fear I'd be heard, I said, "*I want to go.*"

Without looking at me, he put his fingertips to his ear where my lips had just been and said, "Thirty-three more Camazotz need to drink. *Then* we may leave."

What could I do? I had no way to escape. Plus I knew I was being selfish and unthinking. The bats weren't done; the ceremony wasn't over. And with so few in existence, each individual mattered. So, accepting this, I put my arm on my furry friend, who seemed happy for me to do so, and I waited.

Finally, once the last bat had licked up the last of the blood, Piero, the Camazotz priestess, and Ch'en moved to the table and stood together. All three took each other's hands (or long boney thumb), raised their arms, and each spoke in their own language. I have no idea what they said. I doubt I'd have understood Piero's Latin, or maybe old vernacular Italian, if I'd been able to hear him properly anyway. Then the three of them kissed. In the case of the bat, she licked.

Several of the creatures appeared beside them, holding bowls filled with water. Ch'en and Piero took hold, with the priestess placing her thumb upon the bowl and tipping it into the huge basin. They did this seven times until the upper bowl and its lower counterparts were fairly clean.

Beyond them, the mass of furry bodies was busily grooming. My ears were buzzing in the near silence. Then the three turned to face our small group. At some point, the queen had joined us, although she was sitting on her litter, which had been placed at the center of the back of the dais. The priestess moved to her in a reverent manner, then crouched low before her. The queen leaned forward, nuzzled her and communicated something. She then reached down beside her and moved an object toward the priestess, who picked it up with difficulty. Ch'en, seeing the problem, moved forward to help.

The queen announced, "Father *H'man*. I haff g'ift for you. It iss very old and wass holy to thosse long agko. I haff forgotten why."

Ch'en helped the priestess offer it to him, and when he took it, I could see that it was a mask. It was a gold, jadeite and turquoise mask in the likeness of a human vampire, with upper and lower canines extended. Piero was genuinely appreciative. It was obvious he knew the worth and rarity of the gift and gave the queen not only a smile of gratitude, but went to her, got a nuzzle, and whispered into her ear. Then he came back and sat with us.

The queen called Alec next. When he stood before her, she gazed at him thoughtfully for a moment, and said, "You haff the power of a k'ingk, Lord Ahlek' and all here are yourss to c'ommand. We thangk you. Here iss an ancient k'ingk's blade."

She pushed forward an object and Ch'en and the priestess handed it off to him. As he held it aloft, I could see through the long dark obsidian blade by the firelight, which glinted off the gold handle. He too showed true appreciation for his gift. They did not touch and merely bowed deeply to one another.

Then she called me. I rose stiffly, and with an aching belly and stupefied senses, attempted to walk to her with grace and dignity. Her face grew soft at the sight of me. She just stared at me for a few long moments and then turned to Alec.

"It iss so strongk' in her. You feel it'?" He nodded and she said, "Protek't' her." As he nodded again, she turned back to me. "No g'ift can pay for what' you haff giffen us. So I giff you a thingk to remember us."

Leaning down to her furs, she scooped a gold object onto her wing and held it out to me. Carefully, I picked up the gleaming, heavy, egg-sized statue and scrutinized it. It was a tiny, stylized Camazotz and it was beautiful.

"That iss very, very old. Older than Lord Ahlek'," She told me, and gave her grimace-smile. I smiled back and she gestured me closer and took me in a bizarre leathery, boney, furry, and musky embrace. The licks to my face were not enhanced by her razor-like teeth brushing my chin, but I took it all numbly.

When she let me go, I said, "It has been an honor to serve you."

Her small eyes widened and she said, "Noo, Ik' Bearer! Honor iss mine." And she touched her thumb to her chest, keeping her wing tucked.

Not knowing what else to say, I stepped back and she rose as high as she could on her small, thin legs. Stretching her wings to a span of at least twelve feet, she twittered and whistled as the throng grew louder, until the entire humongous cavern became filled with their painfully piercing voices.

I turned, scanned them and couldn't help smiling just a little. Their adulation created a strange, deeply fulfilling feeling, which led me to the familiar question: *'Was I insane?'* Did I want the adulation of creatures that had just sacrificed six humans … ?

A voltaic hand cupped my elbow. But before I let its owner guide me out, I turned to look back at my warm companion who'd held me aloft by my shoulders a few nights prior; the one who, with her compadre, had given me the trip of my life. She crouched humbly and quietly against the cavern wall, still next to my now empty spot—just one small part of a very special whole. I had a sudden image of her face appearing before me that first time and I smiled softly at her. She raised herself up, surprised at my attention, and then gave me that freaky, vampire-bat grin.

~

The next and final day of our trip, I took a long walk along the beach, trying to savor the amazing sensorial richness of the place before our return home. I also wanted to weed through the jumbled mess of thoughts and emotions sprouted by last night's activities. I had gone maybe a mile when I noticed an osprey was keeping a slow pace above me, gliding just over the surf. I waved at it and said, "Hey, beautiful bird." It dipped a wing and sailed off inland over me and then into the trees.

Not long after that I heard my name from the line of palms, Sea Grapes and *Chechen* trees along the beach to my right. I was surprised to see Ch'en step barefoot onto the sand, wearing a short brown halter-dress. She called out, "May I walk with you, Mistress?"

Laughing at her use of the title, I stopped and said, "Of course." As she neared, I commented, "It's strange to see one of you out so early." The sun was still well above the western horizon.

She replied, "I forget that Alec can no longer tolerate the sun's light. Through the centuries, I have known him to be one who could stay in daylight many hours longer than most. Jack and Georges are too young still for the day." I assumed that meant Axel was too.

We dug our toes into the warm sand as we started walking. "How do *you* keep from being compromised? I mean, the Camazotz have been sick, right?"

"Yes. Three-quarters of them have died. They are more delicate and susceptible because they must drink so much more than we.

"I am a shaman as well as a priestess. I was a healer and have always stayed abreast of medical information. Alec shared with me very early that certain chemical compounds are dangerous. I can taste a drop of blood and know what is in it. I am wary of who I drink from and choose the traditional, rural Maya as my main source."

She then touched my arm and stopped. I did too, and faced her. "Devi. Alec says the only death you have witnessed was your mother's … perhaps a century ago. I saw that last night was difficult for you. I wish again to apologize for your abduction. Perhaps it is too much to ask, but … I hope to know that you understand why I did it."

"Of course I do, Ch'en. It would be easy to be angry, I guess. But really, I completely understand. She needed more than what I'll bet Alec was willing to let me give." Ch'en nodded and I smiled. "Well, he didn't get a say, ultimately. The Queen seems to have taken only what she needed, so no harm done … except to Alec's authority. And to you." I started to walk again and she followed.

"I'm unharmed, which is a testament to his true nobility. Any other would have killed me. Even Piero. I thought perhaps he would and was prepared. What you gave last night would not have been enough. She would not have survived." After a nod of my own, I glanced at her, then saw a quiet desperation etched in the lines between her brows.

I stopped again. "Ch'en. It's alright. I've forgiven and forgotten."

She looked out to sea. "You understand why he would expect the Queen to sacrifice herself for her population?"

"Uh … not really."

"Because he is doing so himself. He has not partaken of what you channel and will not. But he *is* sick and it will get worse. He thinks he will die a normal death. I have seen his fate and it is unlike those who go quickly through old age. He will age—and age, and age. His body will not release his consciousness until it has disintegrated and its cells dispersed like dust. His line is different than some; I think it is because of the Sith who was half of his parent. It could take hundreds of years."

"H—how can you know that?"

"It will be my fate too, eventually. As a shaman I am able to see beyond this world; it was revealed by my guides during my travels to the otherworld."

I abruptly sat in the sand. Ch'en too sat in place, as if it was the most natural move. I feebly insisted, "He says he's aging along the normal time frame."

"He will begin to age more quickly. But again, his body will stay alive as long as his consciousness inhabits it—which will not be an eternity, but until it has disintegrated molecularly."

"How do you stop it? There has to be a way to stop it." I decided not to tell her I'd slipped him a few drops.

"Dismemberment—burning—ashes scattered far and wide. It would be the only merciful thing to do. It would free him. Being the oldest of his heirs, the task would be mine." The idea brought a miserable look to her sweet features and I scrunched my brows in sympathy. We sat quietly for a moment and finally she asked, "You will stay with us? The sacrifices of last night will not cause you to—"

"No. I did think about running briefly, because of the killing. But where would I go. How can I go back to the life I had, alone, knowing you are all out there … slowly dying off. I abhor the killing, but I abhor the idea of entire species going extinct more. Even if you are …."

She laughed, knowing what I was thinking. "We are not really dead, Devi. We live in a suspended state. As if time ceased acting upon our corporeal selves. We move through time and we use it, but our bodies stay mostly as they were the moment of our turning, just as death happens and new life begins. At least, that is how it is for the species to which I belong. There are so many kinds. As you saw, the Camazotz are a living, natal species. But we must all ingest energy in one form or another. Usually through blood."

We stood and continued on our way as I absorbed her comments. Ch'en and I spent the rest of the time before the others woke talking and developing a bond apart from them. She had clearly learned the white man's languages, knowledge and ways, but underneath, she was something truly separate. She was a Maya priestess whose job had been to intercede on humans' behalf with the Camazotz (who, by the way, had refused to deal with human males.)

She had done all she could to hide and protect them from discovery when the Spanish came, but all was nearly lost until Alec showed up one night. He was like a sun god, so strange and white and tall—with red-gold hair!

He had been watching her. He had explained that he knew of the Camazotz and had seen her helping them. He offered her immortality if she would continue to do so. It took her a while to realize and accept that he was not a god.

He petitioned the Spanish and staked claims around the areas the bats lived in, professing he wished to farm native crops and introduce them to the old world. He stayed for a year and then left one of his progeny with her to teach her and help her learn to deal with the Spaniards. But Alec tended to keep things running smoothly, so she had few problems. She created a small army to help her and had managed very well through the centuries—until about the middle of the twentieth century, when DDT was born and petrochemical products started to slowly proliferate.

Things had been deteriorating ever since.

When we later hugged under the gaze of the gentlemen, in front of the Hacienda Hermosa Ha, and beside the monstrous vehicle that would carry us back to the Cancun airport, I knew I was leaving having made more than one new friend, with a few hundred of them being Camazotz.

FOURTEEN

A Dangerous Game

†

Not long after returning from the eventful trip to Mexico, Alec made good on his promise to join Donald Carr for a game of golf. It was a lovely early-autumn evening and he fetched Carr at the appointed time. They would be playing at the Army Navy Country Club in Arlington and Carr seemed to think Alec should be impressed by that. He was not. But he knew Carr would be when they walked off the last hole. He had no intention of dampening his abilities to match Carr's; about which he felt not a mote of guilt. They were playing a deeper, unspoken game—one that the superficially older man had no hopes of winning. Alec would give him just what he needed to keep him in it, which included a glimpse of something hidden.

He was pleased to see the American minister was wearing attire that was fairly understated. He'd been afraid he'd be playing with someone in the dreadful clothing some seemed to favor when playing the so-called 'sport'.

Alec knew that skill and precision were involved, yet he did not understand how the term 'sport' applied, any more so than with darts or billiards. He was well aware this was his own perspective from centuries past, but had no desire to consider otherwise. A game was a game, sport was sport and there absolutely was a difference in his mind.

Carr's dark green ensemble contrasted with Alec's usual light linen look. He'd had to order golf shoes from Edward Green's, who had his specs on file. They were really very fine and when he'd donned them with a pair of well-worn, cuffed linen trousers from the twenties and a dark Dijon mustard polo, he'd thought them quite handsome. It was unfortunate he'd be unlikely to ever use the shoes again. They would make a good donation for a charity auction.

Once seated beside him, Carr eyed the bespoke interior of the Maybach coupe and asked, "What made you choose this make of vehicle over any other?"

"I could have it any way I like it. They had a vast selection of choices. Plus, the craftsmanship is quite fine and I felt a bit of odd nostalgia for the brand. Also, I found I liked the shape of the vehicles better than others which are comparable. Not *quite* so obvious from the outside. Right then, lead on." And Carr directed him so that fifteen minutes later they stood at the entrance to the course.

Their play lasted only a little over two hours because Alec lobbed, sliced, pitched, curved and putted his way to a perfect game. His caddie had been on the brink of fainting several times because of those shots, he was sure—particularly the purposeful slice. Carr had been incredulous at first, but then bore it with an old man's wary dignity and did his best, which was pretty good considering the long shadows cast by some of the temporary lighting set up on the greens and the occasional distracting errant deer.

After giving the awe-stricken caddie a handshake and huge tip, Alec observed as Carr removed his gloves and nervously rearranged his various clubs in their bag.

"Now I know why you wouldn't take my bet, you're a man of integrity. I thought you hated golf, Gregory." Carr shook his head frustratedly as he pointed toward the club house, adding, "I don't usually drink, but I think a brandy would be good right now. Shall we?"

They found a secluded couple of chairs and sat as a waiter brought them each a snifter. Carr took a big gulp, scrunched up his face at the intensity of the beverage, and then rested his eyes on Alec's.

Eventually Alec said, as he crossed his legs, "Hate is a rather strong word. I merely have *disdain* for golf. Regardless, I'm one who is blessed with abilities for which he didn't ask. It isn't wise to wager against me."

"I can see that. Your *ability* seems almost … miraculous. It's hard to find out about you. Why is that?"

"Because I don't wish to be 'found out about.' Much like yourself, wouldn't you say? What would you like to know?"

"Tell me your story."

Alec gave him a level gaze and replied, "What's to tell, Carr? I am a fortunate man. I was born fortunate and I am still fortunate. Beyond that is just details, such as I have no wife and children."

"Well, all men have darkness somewhere. Is that why you have no family? What's your darkness look like?"

Alec chuckled because Carr's suddenly intense demeanor seemed a little contrived and it occurred to him that this was a technique used to bring hope of redemption—enticement for his quarry. Alec had discovered it was how Carr brought others into his fold, by getting them to confess some secret trauma and then offering succor and a path to redemption. It would be amusing if it hadn't worked on so many powerful persons around the planet. Regarding Alec, Carr was so absolutely clueless as to what he was dealing with that Alec felt the slightest stirring of compassion for the man's naiveté, but he also remembered Carr's own extensive darkness, and his probable role in the death of Leonora. Alec would again enjoy engaging in a game of—as Gordon would call it—*fuckery* with him.

"I was reborn, Donald."

Carr jerked slightly at this and squinted under fluffy, furrowed brows. "I beg your—did you say 'reborn'?"

"I did."

"Well that's great news! So you admit you have Jesus in your heart."

"No Donald. Once, I had The Christ in my heart, my head and my gut. I carried him in every part of me. I endeavored, as you claim to do, to live a Christ-like existence."

"I don't understand how that's different."

"It started with vows. Including a vow of poverty. You see, my understanding of Christ was—is quite different. Wealth and such an existence were incompatible. Charity and compassion are the hallmarks of Christ. Not power and control, especially financial." Carr's jaw dropped slightly and he scowled. "But, like you, I and my cohorts believed we knew what God and his Son wanted. We were holy warriors so to speak. So we had some of it right, but the most important actions were wrong."

"When was that? You seem kinda young. Plus, that sounds Catholic. You're Scottish."

"Really, Carr. There are still Scots Catholics. But it doesn't matter. Religion eventually perverts or bastardizes the teachings. Some much more so than others. I know better now and understand that all that matters is the teaching of compassion, which leads to charity. Christ is irrelevant, except as a teacher."

Carr looked at Alec as if he'd just sprouted twenty heads. In Carr's world, without his simplistic Jesus personality cult, all would fail. Life would be meaningless. The comment was too much for him, so he asked, "I don't understand how you were reborn, then."

"It was the teachings of a mentor. A man who was a great scientist *and* a priest. He changed my life so completely that there was no room in it for religion anymore, though I don't believe that was his intention.

"What else would you like to know? I am unburdened by the kind of darkness you're seeking. Perhaps something else."

Carr sipped uncomfortably at his brandy again as he thought and eyed Alec, who rested his elbows on the arms of his wing-backed chair and laced his fingers together. "There was some talk that you might be homosexual. My wife insists this is a total misreading by men."

"My, my. And which queerly observant men might these be? Why would they think that? And what of it if I am?"

"They are … associates. It came to our attention that you're really close to Georges Picault, that restaurant owner. He's a known homosexual."

Alec actually had to work a little to swallow his disgust. But he wasn't surprised they'd linked Georges to him. "You say that as if there is something wrong with it. I associate with persons of all persuasions, professions and opinions. Their penchants say nothing about who I am. We are in the twenty-first century, Donald. And after all, I have just played a game with *you*. I am sitting here, three feet away, and we're nothing alike."

"Well what about your young lady friend? Her information is lacking too. I found photos of her great grandmother. She's the spitting image. She's named after her, I guess. It's an eerie resemblance"

"Photos?"

"Yep. From the forties. They're in the Harper's Bazaar archives."

"How on earth did you come across such a thing?"

"I have a repentant young man at the little house who's a whiz and he created a program that searches really well. I don't understand all the techno-mumbo jumbo, but they were pretty pictures. You seem to like her a lot."

"I do. Very much so. I'd not have dragged her along with me to your event and home otherwise."

"My wife said no one's seen you with a date in the last fifteen years."

"Well then that should tell the inquiring minds how much I adore her. Donald, *really*. Perhaps we should delve into *your* story and its darkness. Tell me all your secrets. *Tell me of your father.*"

Carr jerked noticeably but clearly decided to ignore Alec's dark taunting. "She seems a bit younger than you. Still, couldn't even find birth information on her. Or about her parents. You're both pretty mysterious in this age of information. It's pretty interesting."

"That is true Donald. We *are* very interesting. She *is* a bit younger than me, but older than she looks. Regardless, I'm quite protective of her so I insist you cease your hunt for her details. But you are welcome to mine the world for information about *me* as you like. So tell me, what is your vision, Donald? Your end goal. Because I very much think you have one and it isn't simply about ministering to the powerful. What *are* you up to?"

Carr stared hard at him for a moment then looked around to be sure no one else was within earshot. After licking his now very dry lips, he took another sip of brandy and then replied, "Maybe no one is what they seem. *You* certainly aren't. I know that completely now, after tonight. No one could do that. I just want you to work with me a little. Here and there. I know you have influence; I know *some* things about you. And now I know you once had a relationship with Jesus. You could have that again. Redeem yourself."

Alec genuinely laughed and uncrossed his legs to lean forward. He ticked his head to Carr and said with a smile, "Oh, Donald. Unlike yourself, I am beyond redemption. At least the kind you are seeking. It is no enticement for me. But perhaps I'll think on your request. Perhaps you have a cause or two I might find worthwhile."

Apparently unable to process what Alec was saying for a moment, Carr just stared at him with a dumbfounded expression. Alec was unsure what part of what he'd said had elicited the awe and he sat back and picked up his brandy, taking a large swig. It was a Rémy Cognac.

"What do you mean, you're beyond redemption?"

"Exactly that," Alec replied after he'd swallowed. "I have rather a lot going on just at the moment, so I shan't be able to give you any answer for several months. But I definitely shall be in touch." When Carr just continued to stare at him, Alec finally added, "See here, Donald. In spite of the seemingly *one* reality, it is remarkable how many man creates for himself. I do not think like you, behave like you, nor have the problems of normal men. I do not need your redemption. Guilt and sin are not issues for me. Nor do I engage in practices which might elicit such. Does that explain a little better?"

Carr shook his head and drained his glass. After setting it on the table between them, he said, "No guilt, no sin, no need for redemption—that's supernatural, isn't it. I see you're a horse of a different color from what I usually deal with."

"Yes. *A horse with horns, scales, claws and that breaths fire.*"

That astounding comment quieted Carr, who barely spoke a word during the ride back to his compound. Alec reassured him he would contact him as soon as he'd taken care of his busy calendar. Carr would have to be patient.

FIFTEEN

A Rival's Mischief

ʊ

The crows were gathered in the top of a tall loblolly pine, making their raucous, early conference caws. Autumn mornings are almost incomplete without them, but they were disturbing the chickens. I often wondered if, inside those little dinosaur brains, the ground birds thought that their smarter, black-feathered cousins might warn them of impending doom, but if that doom got them, the crows were just as likely to come down to dine. Plus, we'd actually lost a chick or two to them, so the fowl tended to gather closer to a human if one of us was outside.

On this particular darkly-overcast morning, it was I, wending my way to the greenhouses. The birds were crowding more than usual and I tried to distract them with feed. But they followed me all the way to the first new greenhouse and I actually had to use my foot to gently shoo them from coming in. Maria had taken Serena for a check-up and they'd planned to be gone well into the evening, so I would be caring for everything myself.

Once inside, I acknowledged the two rows of Vitaortus and got the hose. Today was not a feeding day, so I wouldn't need to prepare a can. The plants were eight feet long now and most had flowers. After fondling one of the beautiful and bizarre blossoms, which were nearly black and had six spade-shaped petals of various sizes as well as 'whiskers', I attached the sprayer to the coiled hose and began. But the sudden silence outside caught my attention.

I looked through the glass door and saw the chickens suddenly squawk and briefly fly, or scurry, in all directions. A huge crow had landed in their midst.

I started to laugh at the brazenness of the bird, but my grin faded. It was far too big to be a regular crow. I had a sudden, jolting memory of where I'd seen such a bird and it had not been on this continent, even though I knew they existed farther west and in the higher elevations of the nearby mountains.

The raven shook itself to smooth the blue-black shiny feathers ruffled from its flight. As it marched to the door of the greenhouse, it cocked its head, appearing to eyeball me. And then, defying all rational expectation, it casually rapped, with its big black beak, on the glass of the door.

That was too much for me, and I dropped the hose in shock. As it landed, the trigger hit and my jeans were sprayed for a second before it turned over from its own force and sprayed the brick path between the rows. I squatted, never taking my eyes off the shaggy bird's strange sapphire-colored ones, and fumbled to turn off the water. Then, slowly, I rose to a slight crouching position.

The raven waited patiently. Yet, the point was—*that it was waiting*—for me! Then it tapped again. We stared some more and I thought, *what the hell am I supposed to do?* Because obviously, I didn't want a raven in my greenhouse, but more importantly, why was this bird here, doing this? Was it someone's pet?

When a certain amount of time went by and I was still immobile, it moved away from the door, simply stepping backward a few feet. And then I watched as it elegantly morphed from a two-foot-tall black bird into a full-sized blond man in fine black clothing.

With even more numbing shock, my jaw dropped. Suddenly fear, rushing in the form of adrenalin induced blood, pumped hard through my entire body.

For a moment I felt woozy and thought I might pass out from the flood of chemicals. Through my haze, I saw him develop a wry smile, which reminded me of Alec's early shenanigans and I suddenly found myself pissed-off.

Clarity came with the rush of anger. I scowled and the man raised a blond brow, ticking his head slightly in surprise at my reaction. He was observing me very closely. As my own head got wrapped around the idea of the whole morphing thing, my survival instincts seemed to be kicking in.

Rising to my full height, but staying where I was, I demanded, loudly, "Who are you?"

With a vestige of the surprise still registered on his face, he said, in a smooth and seductive voice, "Don't you know?"

I could hear him as plainly as if he were right in front of me. The magic or supernatural effects I was experiencing went way beyond anything up to date, apart from my own longevity and healing. Until he gave me something to go on, I wasn't going to move a muscle. Then it dawned on me that he'd knocked; maybe he couldn't just come in, like in the old myths.

Finally, he commented, "He didn't tell you of me. How *like* him." He had an accent which you'd initially think was English, but there was something underlying which indicated strongly that he came from elsewhere. I didn't need to question who 'he' was, so I waited for more as he stared at me through the transparent door.

He looked me over and I did the same to him. He wore a suit similar to what Alec favored, easy-to-move-in linen. But this man wore a more fitted black with a charcoal grey shirt, the top three buttons unfastened so a little chest showed. He was sockless in his

Italian black leather loafers. His longish, light-blond hair was cut in a single layer which whooshed back from his widow's peak and ended at his jaw in an arc. He was tall, but not so tall as Alec, Jack and Georges.

In contrast, I had on skinny jeans, old-fashioned wooden Dr. Scholl's, a simple black t-shirt and my hair was up in a ponytail. He definitely out-classed me. But I out-waited him, silently, and finally he smiled and smoothly said, "Well I know who *you* are, Devica Trevathan. And I've been dying to meet you. I'm Demetrios."

I don't know how he made his voice sound so close. And though very attractive, it was obvious to me that this was a more sinister version of Alec and friends. My hackles were up and I was very compelled to continue standing stock still. I felt exactly like a cornered cat. Maybe it was his dramatic entrance, but his energy seemed foreboding and I just didn't want him on my side of the fragile barrier.

As if reading my mind, he raised a hand to his chest and cajoled, "Upon my honor, I am not here to do you harm. It grieves me to frighten you."

I laughed a little derisively. "Mister. I have never seen anything like what you just did. It couldn't have grieved you much."

He raised both eyebrows. "Truly. I am here to honor you. To meet and honor you. I have brought a gift." Reaching into his pocket, be brought out a leather box and held it up a little to show me. He raised his blond brows even more, as if the gift should entice me. When I still didn't move, he assured, "If I were to harm you, Gregory and his minions would hound me to the ends of the earth, separate every part of me and then burn it all into far flung cinders. I prefer to stay intact." He moved so he rested on one hip and cocked the other, still holding the box out.

Every instinct in me said to stay away, but he obviously had a good argument there. I had no doubt Alec would do exactly that. I debated for a long moment, and he could see plainly that's what I was doing as my eyes shifted around.

"Fine," I finally said, and walked toward the door. He backed up again so that it could swing open. When he didn't initially walk through, I assumed I had to invite him. "Come in." And in he walked, with a slight smile, casually eyeing the plants in the two rows before him.

Politely, he stopped, and once I'd shut the door and turned to him, he held out his hand to shake mine. I stuck mine out and shook his cool one firmly, then quickly let go. He smelled of a fine, citrusy cologne. "Now. Who *are* you?"

He stood very straight, and rested his hands behind his back. "I'm Demetrios. You could say I am an old *friend* of Alec Gregory."

I eyed him suspiciously, commenting, "You don't say."

He laughed and took a good look at my face. "I imagine *you* have given him trouble. He has obviously not *had* you."

I was shocked at that and responded bitingly, "*Excuse me!?*"

Calmly, silkily, he replied, "I merely state it. I would smell him on you. You're clean, mostly.

Something bit you not so long ago, but you've not been drunk from by one of us."

"How do you know all this?" I didn't bother to deny anything.

"I'm gifted. But then so is Gregory. Hasn't he shown you?"

Ignoring his words, I huffed out a breath, and said, with attitude, "Why are you here? I'm uncomfortable and don't know what your intentions are—only that you can do things I've never seen. I prefer not to be ambushed."

His beautiful features took on a contrived, compassionate look, and he nearly whispered, "I only wished to meet you and pledge my service, should you ever be in need. Please, I offer a token of my esteem. I feel your energy as we stand here. And seeing what you've accomplished . . . ," He turned and indicated the Vitaortus. "*You* are the most powerful channel we've seen in centuries."

Then he knelt down, one knee on the ground, and took my hand. He held it between his and then brought it to his right cheek. I had a momentary flash of something which amounted to a serious betrayal by my body.

Good God, not again, I thought, frustrated.

But before I could yank my hand back, he looked up at me and said, "It is unconscionable that you should be left thus, and expected to tolerate our presence." He then kissed my hand slowly, seductively, and I let him.

When he let go, I stepped back, asking impatiently, "What are you talking about?"

"Why, the *pheromone*, you might call it. Surely Gregory told you." He stood, brushing off his knee.

He was neither quite as elegant as Alec, nor as athletic as Jack, but he did have plenty of both qualities, and a feminine, or maybe feline, smoothness to boot. I just stared at him, which was answer enough.

"We're like catmint to your kind. It goes beyond the normal attractions. In the past, those who channel the source have always taken lovers from amongst us."

Source? Lovers?

Not wanting to be led down such a path, I said, "Look. Demetrios. I have a business partnership with Mr. Gregory. And I'm very content with that. I'm willing to give you a look at the plants, but after that, if you want something from me, you must go through him."

I don't know where the courage to say that came from because he was seriously still frightening me, albeit seductively. Potential danger, or something, rolled off him in waves I could practically smell, but that ol' bravado kept coming out at times like these.

He evaluated me for a moment and replied, "You're obviously wiser than your appearance would portent. I see I cannot seduce you—*today*." He gave me a half-smile, admitting he'd been called-out.

"No. Not today."

"Pity. You would enjoy me and find great pleasure and release." I rolled my eyes and he laughed again and then turned toward the plants. "Your children are magnificent. I heard that you only birthed them in June."

I nodded and we walked between the rows. "They grow quite vigorously. I'm not sure what to expect."

"No. Well, the books on them were destroyed long ago." His slight femininity actually enhanced rather than detracted from his appeal. His presence was pretty darned dramatic. "But we are lucky you are here. That Gregory found you, because most of us are in peril." He stopped and cupped a palm-sized blossom, not looking the slightest bit like he was in peril. "You seem to know instinctively what is needed."

Then he turned to me and, while still cupping the flower, bent his head and just kissed me. He had no trouble getting me to open my lips a little and I can only say, in my defense, that the pleasure of it overrode my brain.

But before I could fully succumb, I felt a tingling, which was not due to the fabulousness of the kiss, and I opened my eyes. I watched his face become vapor as his molecules separated. And the fog that was Demetrios quickly gathered itself and created a tip, which then moved down my neck and back and into my shirt. It wound around my body, caressing, and I gasped. Then, with perfect timing, just as I was about to scream out, he vacated and moved like smoke from inside a bellows toward the door. Once there, he re-formed, blew me a kiss, opened the door and morphed back into the raven. And off he flew into the grey sky.

I stood there, completely disheveled, verging on outrage and totally gob-smacked. And my body was confused. But my brain knew exactly what Demetrios was after, or at least, it thought it did, and it wasn't 'love'; at least not in emotional form. With my physical self still aquiver, I decided shakily to finish watering Greenhouse One. I then marched back to the house to get my cell phone. I speed-dialed Alec's number and left a message after the beep.

"Who the *fuck* is Demetrios?!" I crassly and loudly demanded and then hung up, wishing phones still had Bakelite bases so that I could slam it down with a satisfying and telling gesture. I figured I'd share the love a little and stir the pot.

What angered me the most was, if it was true, the *pheromone* part: that Alec had kept something that, although personal, was *that* important from me. I also knew by now that they had skills. But seeing it live was a whole other thing. And I realized now how important it was to me for Alec's skill-set to be up to snuff.

Also, I could stop beating myself up for being so … *wanton* in my thoughts. I remembered Alec's remark in Mexico about me being 'highly in need of affection'. *No shit, Mr. Holmes. It's been nearly three decades, I'm stuck in perpetual late twenties body chemistry, and you come around throwing off 'pheromones'.* One should most certainly be apprised of such things.

I made some more coffee and had a pumpkin muffin while standing and staring at nothing out the kitchen window. Allowing my emotional state to diffuse, I thought about Jack sleeping (or whatever) away upstairs and all the good his presence had done me this morning.

My mind took a little side trip and wondered what would happen if I slipped into his canopy and lay down with him. Then, I shook the thought out of my head. I was rewarded with an image of Demetrios, and my body tingled until it came to a focus in a certain spot. Unsure if it was *his* magic or *my* imagination, I frantically wolfed down the rest of the muffin and put the coffee in a travel mug, hurriedly, so I could get back to work.

After attending the rest of the Vitaortus, I stepped into old Greenhouse One and breathed in the mingled aroma of the herbs. It wasn't super strong because it was a cloudy day, but I could still smell the basil and mints, sage, thyme, lavender and others. It was like being with old, neglected friends.

They seemed to welcome me and I picked up a four-inch pot of rosemary. I held it in my right hand and ran my left hand up the branches of the aromatic plant. With my nose close, I inhaled deeply. *Something about rosemary* ... and lavender. I did the same with each of the herbs that had strong oils in them. I felt like I was seeking something, and for the moment the scents pleased my senses, I was satisfied, but after I finished watering everything, I had a strange desire I couldn't place.

I made sure all the heaters, fans, and vents were working properly and locked each greenhouse. Back inside the house, I had two more muffins and thought they were perhaps the best I'd ever made. They were soft, scrumptious and I could taste the individual spices in them.

It was three p.m. and the sun wasn't setting until at least five-thirty. I had time to kill before I'd *better* hear from Alec.

After spending about half an hour petting Theda, whose fur felt amazingly luxurious, I decided to go for a walk in the woods.

It was around sixty degrees and it just seemed like such a beautiful, beautiful day, in spite of the morning's event. I visited all my favorite trees, including the huge old crape myrtle that was planted, oddly alone, in a small clearing. I assumed there had been a house or something here at some point. The trunks of the giant shrub were nearly a foot in diameter and looked like they should be able to just move of their own accord. Their smooth, tawny-pink, sinewy-looking surfaces invited caressing. So I did. Smooth as silk.

The clearing was covered in a thick layer of newly-fallen gold, orange and red leaves from the surrounding trees. I could smell them and found myself kicking them around and enjoying the sound and scent. Finally, I just collapsed into a large pile I'd made. Like a child, I squirmed a little into it and then watched the ominous clouds and the constantly mutating shapes within them. I watched as the light changed and shadows lengthened and I didn't want to move.

Finally, the crows began congregating again after their day's excursions. Their early evening conversation was as lively as the morning's had been, but it indicated that dark was approaching, and what was the point in just lying there when I had things to take care of? I kicked my way home through the leaves to the chirps and twitters of many other birds telling each other tales of their day.

The sun had set by the time I approached the outer edge of the cleared part of my property. As I moved past the outermost greenhouse, I heard, "Devil! Jesus Christ!" And a hand grabbed my wrist. It was Jack. "Where have you been? Are you okay?"

I answered, "Well, yeah, I just—" And he pulled me along behind him so that I had to trot to keep up. "Come on, we're going to Alec's. Now!"

"But Theda and Greta—"

He interrupted me as I waved my arm toward the house. "They already harassed me into feeding them. We gotta go." And he gently jerked me so I moved faster. Once he'd pretty much *tossed* me into the passenger's seat of the Aston, he jumped in and gunned it. We were at Alec's in fifteen minutes flat.

I had snuggled down into the leather seat and closed my eyes so I could focus on the deep vibrations of the car. My good vibe was over when the engine suddenly stopped. Opening my eyes, I saw we were there, the manse looming large in front of us. I turned to the slightly rattled sound of Jack's voice.

"Devi?"

"Yeah?"

"What the *hell* are you doing?"

"Nothing. We're here." I roused myself and got out of the car. The sound of the gravel intrigued me, so I started scootching my feet back and forth so I could listen to the warm noise. I was still wearing my Dr. Scholl's and I was surprised I wasn't getting chilled.

"Devi. Jesus. What is wrong with you?" Jack grabbed my wrist again and ushered me up the stairs. Gordon suddenly appeared, but instead of his usual handsome smile, he had a look of concern.

"Hi Gordon," I said cheerfully, keeping my eyes on him, even as I was roughly pushed through the door. I smiled but he just furrowed his brow at me, which struck me as odd. I continued to watch him, craning my head as Jack nearly dragged me.

"He's in his sittin' room," Gordon called after us. Jack suddenly took a left turn, and I stumbled after him as he continued to gently yank me.

I noticed we were passing through what must be the office. Computers and other equipment dotted the fine dark furniture. And then we entered another room, which was a small version of the great room. Alec was lounging on a leather chaise, reading *Le Monde*. As soon as we'd entered, he looked up and put the paper down. Jack pulled me to a stop and I teetered for a moment from the abrupt halt of our momentum.

I smiled and looked around Alec's study, which I'd not seen on the tour. "*Niiice,*" I commented.

"What's wrong with her?" Jack asked, frustration, and maybe a little concern, tingeing his voice.

Alec moved so one leg was cocked under him and leaned forward, eyeing me. "Hmm. I'll find out."

I kept smiling and returned my gaze to him, enjoying the gold and copper play of light on his perfect, lovely hair. He squinted at me and then said to Jack, "Take Gordon; I want the two of you to scour the property. Then check the video. She was breached, but my guess is there's not a bloody thing we could've done to prevent it." I glanced at Jack in time to see him raise his brows in surprise. Alec continued, "What's important is that she appears relatively … *unharmed.*"

I suddenly remembered I was supposed to be angry and piped up. "Hey. I'm just peachy! But I certainly have a bone to pick with *you*, mister!" After I dramatically jabbed my forefinger in Alec's direction, he rolled his eyes before giving Jack a meaningful look. Jack immediately departed.

Alec scrutinized me some more and then commented, "You're a fright. Are those maple leaves I see embedded in your hair?"

"Uh . . ." I reached up and realized that at some point my pony tail had come undone and my hair was filled with leaves. I looked at Alec with confusion on my face as I lowered my hands, each bearing an orange-tinted leaf.

"Devi, from the beginning. What happened? Come here." He patted the chaise beside him and moved back a little to give me room. "Here, I had Gordon leave some wine and water for you. Have this first." He handed me a quarter-full burgundy glass as I sat. When he reached to remove my jacket, I clumsily moved the glass from one hand to the other as he pulled the coat from my arms. Tossing it over the back of a tufted leather chair which matched the lounge, he prompted me, "Demetrios came?"

I was taking a sip and nodded my head as my eyes swiveled to meet his. But I found I didn't yet want to swallow as I held the amazing wine in the hollow of my tongue. The taste was so exquisite that I went, "*Mmm*," and dipped my nose back in the glass to get a whiff while rolling the earthy liquid inside my mouth.

Finally I swallowed and Alec, whose eyes had widened, went to take the glass from me. I moved it out of his reach and said, "Oh no, no, no. I'll tell you. Okay. So Demetrios came. *Hoh, yes he did!* He showed up—get ready for it—as a *Raven!*"

I waited for Alec's response and took another drink for dramatic pause. I had yet another moment with the wine and found Alec waiting patiently, but definitely with a peculiar look on his oh-so-handsome face.

He finally said, slowly, "Yes ... that *is* a favored form; particularly by him."

I squinted, nodded as if I knew this fact and then continued. "Well he scared the hell out of my flock, but imagine my surprise, this big bird, gently rapping, rapping at my greenhouse door." His brows jumped as he quietly huffed out a little laugh at my Poe reference. "Well, obviously I wasn't keen on letting him in; and when I didn't move after the second tapping, he turned into, well, himself, I guess. Handsome guy." I took yet another sip and continued after seeing I'd gotten a miniscule reaction from Alec. It was likely to be the most and last in *that* vein. "Anyway he convinced me that you'd pulverize him out of existence if he harmed me and he only wanted to meet and adore me. Or something."

And suddenly I remembered he'd never given me the present. I inexplicably looked around, but it obviously wouldn't be *here*. "He had a little box he said he was going to give me but he never did." I shrugged and looked at Alec for … something.

"Devi. Are you quite aware you appear intoxicated?"

I frowned at him and considered this information. "I don't really feel intoxicated. But I'll tell you, this wine is lovely. Volnay Pinot Noir? And today was so beautiful in spite of that visit. *OH!*" Alec jerked a little, obviously not expecting me to suddenly shout amidst my ADD chatter. I poked his chest with my finger and narrowed my eyes. "He told me about the *pheromone*. You are a bad man. It's true, isn't it? Isn't it?"

I noticed then that Alec's shirt was made of a raw silk and cotton blend. It was a lovely golden green color and I reached out to touch it. He only had it unbuttoned to the unsexy second button. Placing my fingertips on the fabric, I just rubbed as I took another drink. Finally, I had a tiny inkling of what I was doing and looked up to find Alec watching me intently.

He slowly reached out and removed the wine glass from my hand. As he placed it on the side table, he moved forward with his legs so that they had mine sort of pinned. Taking my chin gently with one hand and placing the other on my back, he moved my head back and forth as he scrutinized me. I decided to keep talking while he examined.

"He said you are all like catnip to me, and that he'd be my lover if I wanted. That it was *unconscionable* that you have left me in this kind of condition."

Alec let out a little surprised laugh and stopped what he was doing. He started chortling, a sound I'd never before heard come from him. He also gave me a look I'd never seen before and then said, "I do believe he enchanted you. Did he touch you?"

I scowled. "Don't change the subject! Why didn't you tell me about the pheromones?" He raised his head in an elegant gesture, obviously deciding how to respond. Finally he answered, "Well, for one thing, not every channel feels it, or at least, reacts to it." As I continued to scowl, he added, "Admittedly, I've heard most have."

I nodded and said, "That's what I'm talking about. A little honesty for a change."

He seemed to be trying not to smile and replied, "All right. I'll strike a bargain. You tell me what he did to you, exactly, and I'll answer any questions."

"*Okay*," I said profoundly, and grabbed his hand for a shake.

I put my other hand on his and began feeling the smoothness and coolness of his skin. "Demetrios came into the greenhouse only after I invited him. Would he have been able to do it if I hadn't? You're not like that."

Alec had been observing my fondling of his hand and looked back into my eyes; he shook his head only once to indicate I was correct. He didn't stop my fondling.

"He got on his knees for a moment to kiss my hand, which was quite interesting, let me tell you." A corner of Alec's mouth went up at that. "Anyway, he said I was the most powerful channel of the *source* in centuries." After a questioning look about 'source', I turned his hand over and began tracing the lines on his palm.

He softly said, "He means the life-source. Divine energy. *Ch'i. Prana.*"

"Oh. Right. So, he viewed the Vitaortus briefly and then touched a flower and then whammo, he was kissing me!" I put my hand flat on Alec's and gave him a look of 'can you believe that?' Alec furrowed his brow and contained yet another laugh. I could see it and said, "Hey. Because that's not all. He's giving me what is about to become one of the best kisses ever, and he suddenly fades into … into . . ."

Alec turned my hand over and gripped it gently, prompting, "Mist?"

"Yes! And then, in that form, he goes down my shirt and all over my body!"

"Oh *dear*," Alec responded.

I realized he wasn't taking it as seriously as I thought he would. "Alec! I can't figure out if I was violated or deeply admired."

Somewhat compassionately, he replied, "I'd say a little of the first and a lot of the second. Tell me, are you feeling desirous? Sensuous? Amorous?"

With none of the embarrassment I thought I should feel, I nodded, then reached for the wine again. He cut me off, but then acquiesced and handed it to me. As I took a sip, he asked skeptically, "And you're *sure* he didn't give you something?" I nodded again.

Letting me finish the wine, he then took the glass from me. "Come on." He rose and started to pull me with him. It was awkward because of the way we were seated and he pulled me so that my face wound up in the hollow of his neck. The strength of his rose scent was suddenly so intoxicating, that I barely felt myself fold into him. I inhaled deeply through my nose and closed my eyes, basking in the heavenly perfume. I had no idea how much time passed, but I found my body being gently guided up the stairs.

I felt suddenly disappointed and complained, "That smelled *sooo* good. Let me just go back."

Alec's arm was supporting me around my back under my arms. He said, "My dear, darling Devi, let's just get you sorted out." He had to keep me from trying to cuddle up to him, which was difficult because as soon as he succeeded, I was back at him, like a puppy.

We made our way through his bedroom to his bathroom and he gently plunked me down on the edge of the huge tub. "I want you to get undressed while I go fetch something. You have been enchanted, d'you understand me?"

I looked up at him and managed to refrain from reaching out and pulling him to me. I nodded and tried to keep my balance on the marble. "Can I have some water too? I'm so thirsty."

He nodded, then, reaching behind the door, he produced his robe. "Remove clothing, then put this on. I'll be right back. Try not to fall and break your crown. Please."

As he left, I thought that was funny for a moment, but my state was deteriorating and I wondered how I could've gotten drunk off so little wine. When I stood, I teetered, but managed to start removing things. Eventually, all was off and I pulled on the white robe, which was huge and enveloped me. When he returned, he carried a glass of water with ice cubes in it and a large wooden urn. Setting both down on the counter, he turned to check on me and tsked, saying, "You are an absolute mess. How am I going to deal with your hair? It's a rat's nest."

I reached up to touch it and said defensively, "No it's not. Just give me a comb and some conditioner. The snarls come right out. Wait, what are we doing?"

"We are clearing the spell. You have to take a bath in this." He patted the lid of the wooden jar. "Salt," he announced. "Oh, candles. Hold on a tic."

I frowned again to myself. '*What?*'

He returned quickly with a lit candelabrum. "Right. On with it then." And he walked to the tub and turned on the taps, feeling the water for temperature. He'd placed the candelabrum in a nook that looked specially built for just such a need. When he was satisfied that I wouldn't boil or freeze, he retrieved the jar, opened the lid and began pouring. He put in about two pounds of salt.

"May I have bubbles?" I asked.

He turned to me and then let his head drop over the tub in mock frustration. "You may. If they'll froth in this much salt," he answered and reached for a marble dispenser.

While we waited for the tub to fill, he got up, turned off the lights and moved the fluffy white rug closer. "You can go ahead and get in while the salt is still fairly concentrated. Here . . ." And he reached for my hand, pulled me up and undid the sash of the robe. He only briefly looked at my body, but then did a double take, his eyes resting on my belly, just below my navel.

"Devi. Do you always wear such a thing?"

I looked down and, glad that I was 'coiffed' in certain parts, spotted what he was referring to. Around my hips lay a thin gold chain. It had drupes of some kind of green stone attached at three inch intervals and was really very pretty. I shook my head slowly. He'd already guessed I hadn't known it was there and that I'd never seen it before.

He leaned over to turn off the spigot and then came back and knelt in front of me. I wanted so badly to pull him to me and smell him some more, but I understood enough in my sensual haze to know that he was going to inspect the piece of jewelry, not 'me'. He reached inside the robe, feeling where a clasp might be. A tiny piece of self-consciousness crept in, but I tried to ignore it. As his hands moved against me, I felt parts of me start to harden and I looked away, into the bathwater. Goosebumps appeared on my skin which was not because I was cold.

"*Alec*," I finally whispered.

"Hmm?" he replied, as he focused.

"*You're killing me.*" Stopping his movements, he looked up at me and I must have gazed down with intense hunger into those pretty eyes of his, because he sped up his search and had me de-chained pretty darned quickly.

"In! *Get in*," he commanded, as he rose, somehow pulling the robe off me and then starting the water back up.

I did as told and slid into the amazing marble tub, which had a backrest that came up higher than the foot end. It was custom carved for his size. Alec had turned to the counter and I sank into the bubbles. The water reached my chest and the deep tub was still filling. It was very hot and my body sang hymns, rejoicing. All was nearly right with the world.

SIXTEEN

Mischief Wisely Managed

†

D
evi was clearly not in her right mind. And it was beginning to dawn on Alec that this could end in a way she
mightn't be too happy about in the morning. He would
have to ring Gordon and Jack and tell them to stay at her home in
order to spare her some embarrassment, but that Gordon would
need to be back to make a good breakfast for her.

She was behaving awfully humorously, but that look she'd just
given him was as sultry and intense as he'd seen in two centuries.
Her earlier fondling of his hand had been somewhat distracting, but
when she'd moved her entire body into him, her face rubbing like a
cat's against his chest and neck as she inhaled his aroma, he'd been
certain that troubling choices lay ahead.

Finding the wooden hair brush, he turned to the shower for the
shampoo and conditioner. This was going to be an interesting diver-
sion. It had been two hundred years since he'd brushed a woman's
hair. But when he turned to view her in the tub, all he saw were
strands of those shiny, rich-brown tresses and a few leaves on top
of the bubbles. Walking slowly to the edge of the bath, he waited.
When she didn't rise, he went to put the bottles down so he could
pull her up. Surely it hadn't been long enough for her to drown.

Suddenly she popped up with a splash just in time to drench
his shirt. But he'd been planning to remove it anyway so he just
started unbuttoning it as she sputtered and pulled the hair out of

her eyes. When she could see what he was doing, she said, with a fading grin, "Oops. I'm sorry Alec."

He shook his head and just smiled at her as he worked the shirt loose from his linen trousers, keeping his under tank tucked in. What else was there to do? Demetrios had obviously given her an intoxicating sensuality spell. He was sure the salt would take care of it, but its effects could last hours beyond the bath and the spell had been strengthening. At least the belly chain was off, which should temper things since it had obviously been the vector of the spell. And then he realized he'd better clear the piece of jewelry.

As he pulled the damp shirt off his shoulders, he caught her eyeing him under her long lashes. Those big, almost copper-colored eyes were her most remarkable asset. But he'd never have suspected she had such a seductive potential, because, while certainly attractive, she was so down to earth and somewhat tom-boyish in her manner. She simply wasn't the type to use feminine wiles. But there she was before him, a force of femininity of a magnitude that could not be denied.

Tossing his shirt on the floor with her clothing, he then picked up the chain and knelt at the side of the tub. His feet were bare and he curled his toes forward on the rug. Devi watched every move he made with rapt attention.

As he looped the chain around his hand, she asked, "Isn't it lovely? Should I keep it? I've never had anything like that."

Raising a brow at her, he replied, "No?"

"Some women in India wore similar things. I thought they were lovely then, but improper for someone like me. At the time."

"It is yours if I can clear it," he told her, as he dipped the chain in the water and then dropped it in.

The tub was full now, so he reached and turned off the spigot. She moved and her breast showed in the bubbles as she scooted the chain so she wouldn't sit on it. Her mood was infecting him. Demetrios knew precisely what he was doing—nothing too serious, *initially*.

Wanting thoughts of his rival out of his head, he said, "Right. Let's wash your hair."

Devi replied, enthusiastically, "O.K.!", and sat up helpfully, giving him nearly full view now of her chest. He chastised himself for finding the image very appealing. He reached and began first by pulling the sodden leaves from her hair and the bubbles. His left hand lightly brushed her left breast as he reached for the last one and she shivered visibly. *Had he done it on purpose?* Perhaps this spell was a little more serious than he'd assumed.

She became demure and waited for him as he poured the shampoo into his hand. She looked at the amount and advised, "You'll probably need more."

And he shook his head at himself, saying, "Of course I will." She had a very long and very full mane. He carefully put the stuff on her crown and began working it in. Her eyes closed and she put her head back a little, obviously in ecstasy from his massaging.

It occurred to him that this was the first time in many years, probably, that she'd been really touched. It was the first time in many more years that he'd done any touching. So he decided there could be no harm in giving it his best. He was rewarded with facial expressions of total delight.

Too soon, it was time to rinse and she ducked her head back under the water. Her hair was so long that it didn't all go down below the surface. There was a hose and sprayer so he turned the water back on as she came up. After rinsing, he put on the conditioner and used the brush.

Alec was old enough and experienced enough, starting with the horses' tails he'd once groomed as a boy, to know that he must start at the ends and she gave him a look of approval. She had to sit up on her knees so he could get the full length and the picture she presented was, he thought, again with surprise, very beautiful. She was strong but not too thin, somewhat athletic, but obviously a woman. He gazed upon her as he brushed out the tangles and decided he didn't really mind if he was being pulled in by the spell. He was still *alive*, so to speak. He could still feel something. And that gift alone was worth succumbing.

As he got out the last tangle, he raised her up a little more and carefully brushed the glossy, chestnut-colored hair against her back. While wet, it came all the way past the top of her buttocks.

Finally he gently pushed her back down. "You'll need to immerse another five times, to be safe. The salt has to permeate your skin. Understand?"

She nodded, and like a naiad, slipped again beneath the frothy surface. When she reappeared, she reached for the soap and began rubbing herself clean. He stopped her. "Devi, you have to come out with the salt still on you. You'll be clean enough. You can shower on the morrow."

He then dipped his hand into the water and began rinsing off the lather. She touched his hand gently and then lightly ran her fingers up his arm. And then she dunked herself yet again. He was beginning to think she had the skill of a natural seductress—that move had just created some arousal in him. He decided to get up and get a little control back.

When she surfaced again, she asked, "Are you going to be taking me home? Didn't Jack go?"

He bent to pick up their clothing and answered, "No. You are staying here with me tonight. To be safe. Is that alright with you?"

She gave him a sly smile and ducked down yet again, silently. She rose and dunked a few more times and finally he decided it was enough. After depositing the clothing on his divan in the bedroom, he pulled two large white towels from the rack behind the bathroom door. Then, retrieving the belly chain, he pulled the lever for the plug and gestured for her to stand.

This time, he didn't hide his gaze. As she stepped from the tall tub, he could see that she removed her hair so that there was smaller, tidy inverted triangle than he was used to seeing. And it looked as if she trimmed that to keep it shorter. It was lovely, he thought.

She stood there, dripping, with her arms out and he wrapped the first towel around her, carefully tucking in the end just between her breasts. After drying what was exposed with the other towel, he then put it around her hair.

Grabbing her hand and taking the brush from the ledge, he led her into the bedroom. After ensconcing her on the fluffy mouflon rug in front of the fire place, he handed her the water he'd brought and then went to light a fire.

"Alec, I feel extraordinary," he heard her say behind him, almost in the accent he imagined she had decades ago. He turned to see the towel was slipping off her hair, but she was too busy feeling the plushness of the sheepskin to notice.

All he could think to say was, "You *are* extraordinary," because it was true.

"Well so are you," she replied.

A smile touched his lips as the fire took. Then he retrieved the candelabrum and put it back in its place. After turning off the lights, he joined her on the rug. "Here, let me dry your hair."

After rubbing it with the towel, he brushed it, then rubbed some more. And it was soon fairly dry—and quite dramatic looking. It reminded him of times long, long ago. Modern women didn't tend to wear their hair thus. He caressed it for a moment and she leaned into him.

"*You feel so good and smell so good and look so good,*" Devi whispered, as if she was thinking aloud.

She was still bespelled, and intoxicated by his magical scent. She was usually a talker but was being remarkably quiet in spite of the compliments. And then she suddenly turned and mounted his lap, wrapping her legs around him.

His arousal was immediate and obvious and caught him completely off guard, all of which was monumentally surprising. But he wasn't going to let this happen while she was in this state, much as he realized he wanted it. He wasn't sure it was really what she would want in her right mind, having never shown the slightest inclination. In fact, she seemed more interested in Jack and Gordon; hence, one of his reasons for sending them out for the night. Neither of them could, nor would, resist this.

She placed her warm hands on his shaved cheeks, then pulled him to her. Her lips were warm and lovely and he let her kiss him, eventually wrapping his arms around her and returning it until it became unbearably passionate. He realized she could force him with her kiss alone. So, reluctantly, he retracted his tongue and began giving her soft little kisses to gently stop her. Then he pushed her away ever so carefully.

"Devi." She opened her eyes, which looked as if they were the color of the fire behind her. He faltered for a moment because he wondered if there was a little magic in her that was not the spell alone. But then they shone normal and she just gazed at him, almost lovingly.

"Devi. As much as I desire you as well in this moment, I cannot take advantage of this. You are enchanted. Demetrios cast a spell upon you and he has purpose. His intent is to start a chain of events which could cause a rift between us. Then, when ripe, he will show up to pluck you for his own ends, which are doubtless not as magnanimous as mine. Do you see?" She frowned for a moment and then reached to smooth the place between his brows. It was an odd and intimate thing that he was unsure he'd ever experienced from anyone else.

"I think so," she replied. Suddenly she fell back onto the rug, her legs still around him and exclaimed quietly, "*God!* I'm so frustrated. I've been . . ." and she looked at him almost fearfully, continuing, "I feel like I'm going to explode. In a certain part of me. I'm ... I need . . ."

And then he knew exactly what she needed—what the end result of Demetrios' spell required in order to be fully broken. *Wise and wicked man, that one.*

She squirmed off of him and rolled so that she lay on her side, facing the fire, almost fetal. The towel had slipped open to reveal her left hip, which was licked by firelight, and part of the buttock as it tapered down into the shadow. Alec appreciated the view for a moment, then moved to lie behind her. He put his mouth to her ear and began brushing his lips on the outer shell. When the anticipated shiver came, he offered, "We cannot fully make love tonight, but I can offer you release, if you wish it."

She went very still and he thought perhaps she'd started to come to, but then she rolled onto her back and gazed up at him, eventually saying, "I love your eyes."

He smiled at her and she raised her head and put her face into his neck again. And, shockingly, she started to bite him. Gentle nips though they were, the effect created was like an aphrodisiac and his teeth began their growth as his body slightly jerked.

She was oblivious and he had a momentary debate with himself on whether being relatively 'good' was really worth it. One half of him lost and he pushed her back onto her side, deftly removing the towel. He might not take full advantage, but he'd enjoy what he *could* take.

He moved her hair and began kissing the back of her neck. She tasted of salt and smelled of his bath foam, with an underlying hint of various dying leaves. Caressing her arm, he ran his fingers lightly up her shoulder and slowly across her collarbone. He used his hand to create a light kissing effect and another shudder showed him the results. Kissing her neck and back, he then ran his fingers down her chest, brushing over her breasts. Continuing down her abdomen to her belly and further still, until he made just the slightest contact with the targeted area, he then slowly moved back up until he lingered over her breasts and began caressing the tips. She arched slightly and moaned and he couldn't help but smile again.

Without thought, he rolled her over, kissed her deeply, and then moved his head down to suckle each hardened tip in turn. As he did this, he slowly moved his hand back down and gently, deftly began massaging her. She pressed into him and moaned again, tossing her head first one way and then the other. Flicking his tongue brought even more ecstasy and he could feel her harden. He could tell she would not last long and moved his mouth to her neck for a moment to lengthen her process. But when she arched again he couldn't resist going back to the breast.

He was surprised at how wonderful it was to taste and feel again after so long. But he could sense the blood coursing in her neck, and with extended canines, it wasn't safe to linger *there*. So he latched on a little harder than before and flicked his tongue. He moved his hand for a moment to feel her moistness and perhaps probe a little, but the welcome was too strong and he'd never resist if he stayed, so he went back to the precision massaging and she lifted up into him and let out a stifled scream. She grabbed his hand to seemingly make sure he didn't move it or stop the swirling. Then she arched again, screamed softly and pushed even harder into him; then another arch—another breathy, low scream. She did this over and over again for a surprisingly long time, until finally she was too exhausted to continue and fell back onto the rug, pulling him with her. She panted for a few long moments as she calmed and then kissed him leisurely. Her breathing was extremely rapid and he could tell she was thirsty so he reached for and then handed her the glass.

"Thank you." She said, in a small voice, after she'd had a long, slow drink.

He responded "No. Thank *you*."

She smiled lazily, put down the glass and reached out, pulling him close so she could nuzzle him. "No. Really. Thank *you*. You are wonderful. But ... I missed you."

She reached to touch him and when she did, he stiffened more and then pulled her hand away, saying, "And I you, but that will not happen tonight. You'll be ... likely feeling otherwise tomorrow and I'll not be responsible for more than what I've done."

This spell was stubborn. His erection completely disagreed with his honor.

But, to both his chagrin and relief, she backed off and turned her head to gaze into the fire. Soon, he heard long rhythmic breathing and her heart had slowed to its softest, mellowest beat. He wondered if he dared lift her onto the bed. He didn't want to wake her, but it would be better, so he tried and found she didn't even flutter an eyelid. After smoothing the duvet over her, he carefully laid her hair out over the pillow. Somehow this action felt different than when he'd done it before, in Mexico.

He liked the look of her in his bed, so he savored it for a moment, as he figured it was unlikely to happen again, despite how well they interacted physically. Their kiss indicated all. The encounter had been passionate and elegant, no matter how abbreviated.

"*Ah well*," he whispered and moved off the bed.

Leaving the curtain open so he could see her as well as not have her confused by the blackness when she awoke, he went to tidy things. Her clothing was enmeshed with his shirt, so he untangled everything and folded it all. Her underpants gave him pause. The tiniest thing; the label read 'low-rise string-bikini', and he marveled at the changes in women's under garments during his span.

He was still shaking his head as he picked up the towel. After cleaning up the bathroom, he went to get his cell phone, which he'd removed from his pocket and put on the mantle. Slipping into his house shoes, he quietly went out into the hallway.

It was nine p.m.—too early probably for her to have fallen asleep. And he was fairly sure, unless the spell kept her sleeping, that she'd awaken pre-dawn, as she generally slept about seven hours. He could see Gordon had called. He returned it and Gordon immediately answered.

"Sir. All we found was an empty small black case on the floor of one of the glass houses. We're only just gettin' to the video footage.

Maria and Serena got back about an hour ago and they're won-derin' what's happenin'."

Without skipping a beat, Alec said, "Tell them Devi thought she had a trespasser. That I made her stay here with me. Tell them you'll stay there tonight. Hopefully that will assuage them."

"Very good, sir."

"And Gordon, be back in the morning so you can prepare breakfast. She's likely to be very hungry."

"Is she all right, sir? May I ask what happened?"

Alec pulled in air as he debated about what to tell, and then shared, "Let's just say a powerful old rival caused her some gentle mischief. She'll be right as rain in the morning."

"Oh. Well that's a relief then. Anythin' else, sir?"

"No. That'll do, Gordon. Thank you. And don't ask her too many questions. I'm sure she'll be somewhat … disturbed."

"Yes, sir. Good night."

"'Night, Gordon."

After ending the call, he made his way down to the office. Time to find out what dear, old, clever Demetrios had been up to recently. Alec usually kept tabs on everyone, but he'd let that lapse lately and here he was, caught with his trousers down, so to speak.

But first, he noticed his hunger. It had to be Devi. Or rather, what she'd induced in him. He made a detour to the kitchen to get a drink; a rare thing for this time of night. He'd noticed since Mexico that he'd felt slightly stronger and had been able to morph sooner than usual.

His desire to feed seemed to be coming back and that was very odd, because one human a year usually satisfied him. He'd had two in Mexico and he was desirous at this moment. But he was extremely mature for his kind and it was not an insatiable need as it would be for someone like Jack.

He chose a five ounce vial, which was quite a lot for him, and poured it into a burgundy glass, then headed for the office. There was a website he would access that accounted for the whereabouts and doings of most vampires who lived in human society. There were twenty levels of security codes, passwords and questions. The consensus was that the information contained within was sacred. It had never been breached nor misused since it was created twenty-five years prior, and only the oldest and most proven of them had access to it. It offered protection and assistance for all who were willing to be accounted for.

He sat in his leather desk chair and began. It took about five minutes for him to get in. There was always a site master on duty and this one welcomed him deferentially, via a pop-up chat window.

'Lord Gregory, Welcome. We are honored by your presence Please let us know if we can be of assistance to you.'

Alec typed his thanks and exited the instant messaging. Now to find out what the miscreant had been up to.

SEVENTEEN

More Revelations and a Private Offering

ʊ

My eyelids fluttered as they opened. Initially, I tried to force them to stay shut, but my eyes seemed to want to see of their own accord. So I stretched as they stared into the sheets. My body felt fantastic and I realized I was smiling a little. My sheets felt so soft and smelled so good—and then the dawning realization came. It was a different darkness to what I was accustomed.

Moving my head, I felt a duvet with a cover that was different from my own, and then I saw the heavy drapes of Alec's bed. Dying firelight was flickering against the shadows and my brain allowed me to stay in nothingness for one moment longer before depositing me square in the middle of the reality of what had happened. I gasped extremely loudly, turned over and sat up quickly. Beside me, I found no one and was momentarily relieved. I was naked, confused and clueless as to what to do.

Burying my head in my hands, I groaned aloud, *"Oh my God."* And the day's events rushed by like a video fast-forwarding, until it got to Alec. Highlights played at normal speed and even slow-motion. At each remembered moment, I gasped anew, both at my own actions *and* those of prim Mr. Gregory.

Good God, I remembered everything—his hands, his lips, his tongue. And it had been I had who caused it all. I'd seduced him. Sure, it was the spell that made me do it, but still. *I* did it. Never, in my entire life, had I done such a thing. The men I'd had had always come to *me*, never the other way around. I felt shame and I could feel the blood rush to my face. And then I felt more shame when I realized it was one of the best sexual encounters I'd ever had—in fact, *the* best, in spite of no actual coitus. Heck, he'd been nearly fully clothed!

It wasn't that it was about love, but rather Alec's skill and the fact of my being completely uninhibited due to the spell. But thank God he'd held me at bay and not actually—*well*, how would I feel if *that* had happened? And then I cocked my head at my thought. Would I feel worse? Would I be any more mortified than I was now?

It could be worse, but now I had to face him. *God*, he'd certainly given me release though. I could feel something I'd never had coursing through me and I wasn't sure what it was, but it felt absolutely amazing. No one, not a single one of my past lovers had worked my body so perfectly. And only one had even tried or been able to bring me to orgasm. Alec had made it multiple and hadn't broken a sweat! Not that he *could* sweat. But, it made sense that he would be a master. I wondered how many lovers he must have had in all those centuries. And then I stopped the rushing train of thought, because what did it matter? I had to go face him.

So, I crawled out of the wonderful huge bed and searched for my clothes. When I couldn't find them, I looked for the robe and found it hanging behind the bathroom door. It would have to do. The fire was out now and I was cold. I was darned sure I didn't want to walk on stone floors without at least socks, so I opened Alec's closet and lights miraculously turned on by themselves. Rows of gorgeous suits and shirts, pants and cardigans and sundry other items met my eyes. *Jesus*, I thought. More clothes than I had and I'd been collecting for decades. I found a pair of shearling slippers and scooted into them. They were huge on my feet but toasty.

The door to the bedroom was only open an inch and I listened hard for any sounds. Nothing. It was fairly dark in the huge central corridor, but enough ambient light from skylights made it possible for me to make my way carefully down the marble stairs. At the bottom, on the main level, I listened again. The lights in the rooms were all off except for a flickering coming from the room where it had all begun: the study. Alec seemed to prefer candlelight. He tolerated electrical lighting for the benefit of others, but I'd surmised that, when truly alone, he used candles when possible.

Staring down the wide hallway, I sighed deeply, but very quietly, plucking up the courage to go in and face him. I didn't exactly tiptoe, but walked very carefully and as softly as possible. When I reached the door, I stopped, held my breath, and listened. Typing; I could hear soft typing on a computer keyboard. So I slowly peered around the doorway, and there he was, shapely shoulders still bare in his undershirt, sitting at the big desk that was placed at an angle so he could see the doorway. But he was so engrossed in what he was doing that he didn't see me. I mused, *Shouldn't a vampire have heard me gasp all the way upstairs? Shouldn't he smell me? Feel me?*

Suddenly his eyes met mine. He hadn't even raised his head up; just moved them under those languid lids. We gazed at each other for a pregnant moment, and then I pulled my head back behind the door before I could stop myself. I leaned my back against the wall. I was deeply uncomfortable and clearly not ready to face him.

When I heard his chair move, it was obvious he was going to come out, so I turned and started to hurry back to the stairs. But he caught up with me and entreated, "Devi ... ," as he gently grabbed my arm. I stopped and turned as he bent at his knees a little so he could get a good look into my eyes. Finally he put the edge of his magic finger under my chin and raised my head.

"Devi." He tilted his head but I had no idea how to interpret that. What could I do? I just smiled bleakly at him. Apparently it was all he needed, because he put his arm around my shoulder and led me back to the study. "Are you thirsty? Hungry?"

I couldn't believe he'd just asked me that. I didn't immediately say, but when I saw the water from earlier, I answered, "I'll just have that water." I was thinking I might have some wine after that. I *really* thought that would be a good idea.

"What time is it?"

"Three. Tell me how you feel. Talk to me." He gestured toward the chaise and then pulled his plush leather office chair into the back room for himself. I sat as he did and awkwardly tried to make eye contact.

Finally I just spit it out, too quickly and emotionally. "I'm embarrassed and mortified. I'm so, so sorry. I can't believe—"

Alec put his hands up in a 'stop' gesture and scooted closer, interrupting me. "Whoa, Whoa! Do not. I repeat. Do not dare apologize for what occurred. You are absolutely innocent of wrongdoing. Why would you do that? Take on the guilt of another?" I gaped at him, not knowing what to say. "Devi. You were bespelled. Really. The fault lies with Demetrios."

"But—"

He scooted closer still, leaned forward and took my hand, holding it lightly. "He set something in motion. Do you remember what I told you?"

"I remember everything."

I was surprised at his devilish smile. "Good. Then you remember me telling you that he wanted to create a situation that could potentially cause us to dissolve our partnership. Do you want to do that?"

I scowled at him. "No! Why would I ... but still, I caused you to—"

He shook his head and I saw those highlights in his hair that I'd loved before. They were still lovely. He looked me in the eye and squinted a little. "Think of what happened as a little gift to me. How about that? And I gave you a gift. Why not? You seemed quite happy about it at the time. Are you really not still? I, myself, am feeling a bit of an afterglow."

I felt my eyebrows rise and the blood flow into my face. He could see my blush and my eyelids started fluttering. I had to look at my lap. Of course I was a grown woman, and not naïve, but I'd been raised by Victorian parents, however liberal they were for the time, and my formative years were certainly spent in less *sexy* times. It was still a shy subject for me, all these years later. Plus, Alec still had a bit of an intimidation quotient—even when sex-related. Yet I managed to say, "But you didn't—"

"No," he agreed, sparing me from having to say the words. "But you did enough for the both of us ... a few times over, if I'm not mistaken." I laughed in spite of myself. He actually sounded happy about it. I began to feel better.

He smiled at me and asked, "Do you realize that we may have hundreds of years of friendship ahead of us?" I just raised my brows again. "Demetrios and I began our rivalry over a woman. That was nearly seven hundred years ago. We despised each other initially. Well, he despised *me* because she saw me and rather abruptly abandoned him. I didn't even know about him until he challenged me, foolishly. He didn't understand what I was—that he couldn't possibly best me physically because of my dual nature. And I was probably more sapient by then as well. After all, I'd had the training from Michael Scot.

Demetrios had been a fourteenth century Macedonian prince, with Hellenistic schooling, but not on the level I'd received.

"So the lady chose me. Well, since then, we have been through several trials. Demetrios turned to magic in the sixteenth century, studying under some very good sorcerers, or very bad, depending on your view. He has occasionally been a thorn in my side, but not the worst enemy. We have a grudging respect for each other. We have survived all this time when very few others have."

"He said you were gifted, like him," I ventured.

Alec ticked his head in thought, then joked suggestively, "Surely you think so now."

I smacked his arm gently, prompting him to say, "Perhaps, in some things, but he is genuinely a brilliant sorcerer. I would not be happy to tangle if he became truly bent on my destruction. I've been very glad he didn't have magic when Constantina left him for me. Magic is what gave him any power over me, as you are now witness."

I was certainly a witness—participant, more like. Curious, I asked, "Constantina? What happened to her?"

"She still lives. We'll see her in New Orleans … in a few weeks."

I jerked at the revelation about New Orleans. Yet again he'd not shared information. And I observed him subtly steeling himself. He almost gained a look of guilt. My eyelids narrowed a tad as I viewed him. After a long moment, I accusingly queried, *"New Orleans?"*

"Yes. It's the current location of our decennial 'Immortal's Gala', which is always held during Hallowmas. We have been using New Orleans for fifty years now. In fact, we should go on a shopping outing for clothing . . ." He tried to buy me off and then seemed to realize this might not work. ". . . for the … various events."

Although he wasn't the type to wither under a gaze, he finally got a look of contrition for not informing me sooner and appealed, "I apologize. Truly. I am unused to considering the needs of another. Perhaps you'll pardon me. After all, I did bring you some measure of joy not but six hours hence."

This was true; *so, so* true. My annoyance melted away.

"Alec, Alec." I chastised, for the not-so-cunning shopping ploy, then asked tentatively, "So what about Constantina? Are you still …" I was a little surprised to find I was concerned about the answer.

"We were together for nearly a century, but for mortal immortals, it is simply impossible to sustain such relationships. Time passed and we grew apart. It's the normal way of things."

"*What!?*" I exclaimed, with a little shock.

"Sentient beings grow, they change and they develop. Bonds tend to have cycles. The parties may come together, grow apart and come together again, sometimes in a different way, or not at all. A romantic relationship often plays out and is eventually over. There is a shelf life. It's extremely rare to find one that is, in essence, eternally emotionally symbiotic."

I gaped at him again. I understood what he was saying, but it made me a little afraid. He sensed it and reassured, "You are young yet and I gather it has been a long while since you were in love?" I nodded, not feeling particularly young. "I've come to understand that romance is a thing of the here and now. You cannot try to hold onto it, for it will slip away even faster. All things come and go, even romantic feelings for another being. I have no doubt you will be inundated with opportunities for love for a very long time. And you certainly have me."

This last sentence took me aback and I wasn't sure what he meant. I didn't really think he was professing his love for me. I looked over at the tray that held my wine and water from earlier and saw the wine glass still there, though empty. A demi-carafe sat adjacent, which had several big mouthfuls still in it. I reached over and shakily filled the glass. Without looking at Alec, I explained, "For medicinal purposes." I gulped it all down and then hesitantly turned my gaze to him.

He registered no self-consciousness or embarrassment. He'd simply said what he said. I'd begun to understand that the older ones, like him, Piero and Ch'en, didn't live with the same emotional and mental traps as the rest of us. I had no idea how to respond and kept trying to say something, yet nothing kept coming out.

Finally he said, "Perhaps you view me as cold and dead, but—" I shook my head vehemently at him. "—*But*; our experience tonight has illuminated something between us. I'm growing ever fonder of you. Yet we have known each other but a mere four and a half months. In my life, that is a blip on the screen. And you and I have a higher purpose, do we not? I am your champion. Your protector and your facilitator. I will not jeopardize that at any cost, nor will I allow Demetrios or anyone else to do so. If you and I eventually come together romantically, so be it; but for now, we must be focused on that higher purpose. Nothing, absolutely nothing, can deter us." He stopped then, seemingly to let that sink in.

Finally I nodded and said, "I understand." And I did. I believed in the nobility of the cause.

He reached out and traced my jaw line. "And for honesty's sake, let me say that you felt better than anything I have known for … well, I don't know how long. I can't imagine what it would have been like to have fully made love. But I think you need to spread your wings and figure out what is best for you. I am something of a conflict of interest. For now anyway. But, know this. In your desperate moments, whatever they be, I am always, and will always, happily be your comfort."

I looked at him wide-eyed, knowing full well that he was committing himself to my well-being, no matter what I asked of him. It was really what Demetrios had offered, except on a grander scale.

I suddenly thought of Alec's sword, hanging, ever vigilant in its special place of honor. And I remembered my wish for *his* well-being. I mustered all my courage and said, "Then you need to be at your full capacity."

He ticked his head, confusion registering lightly on his face. "I'm sorry. I don't—"

"After this morning, I realize I need you at your best. Don't I?" I moved so that I sat on my legs and rested my hands on my thighs. He raised his left brow with dawning suspicion. Then I added, "Did you realize that I gave you a few drops of my blood when we were in Mexico?"

After narrowing his eyelids at me for a moment, he asked, "You mean other than during the ceremony?"

"Yes."

"Ah. Before. When you brought me the drink. Devi, I forbid it."

I sighed and said, "Now it's my turn to be the wise one. It doesn't matter if you forbid it. It's my blood and if you want me to choose you over Demetrios … , or whoever else is out there, as my *champion*, well then you'd better be the best. Same as Constantina." Alec gave me an indulgent smile and then it faded as my argument sank in.

I continued. "I have confidence in you, but he still got to me. I have not seen you walk in the day. I have not seen you morph into a raven. I have not seen you become fog. I know you're strong, super smart and rich. I know you can mesmer. I now know you can bring me to orgasm in probably seconds flat. But that won't keep me safe when the beasts come around." His gaze was penetrating and he continued to narrow his eyes at me. "I *need* you at your best."

After that, we had a brief staring contest. I won when he shook his head.

"All right," he reluctantly said. "*Well played*. So what do you suggest?"

I furrowed my brow, suddenly irritated. It wasn't exactly my area of expertise. "Well I don't know! *Here*." I pulled the robe's collar away and presented my neck.

"Oh, Devi. *Really*." He stood, exasperated protest written all over his face.

So I got up too, and defensively said, "I can't believe I have to *convince* you to drink from me. Christ, you could've had sex and you said no. What kind of vampire *are* you?"

He almost cracked up at that.

"Silly girl. If I put my teeth into your carotid artery, you'd likely die from sudden blood loss before the wound would close. It's not like in the movies or books—big arteries take a big bite. We don't know your healing capacity so I'm not willing to test it."

"*Oh*," I whispered, as I looked down at my slippered feet. "Well what are the other options?"

He could see I was serious and suggested, "We could use a prick. Your blood-letter."

"And that would produce enough for you to heal up quickly? By the time we go to New Orleans?" I could see he wanted to lie, but he shook his head. "You have to bite me, don't you? How much do you need? To make you completely better?"

He seemed to make a decision and suddenly cupped my elbow. In almost a whisper, he answered, "A pint, likely. You carry the energy in extreme quantity, but that's still a lot. Especially so soon after Mexico."

We went to the kitchen first and he took a zip-lock bag from one of the marble faced drawers and then filled it half full with crushed ice from the refrigerator dispenser. He held it up and explained, "For your wound." I nodded and smiled a little sheepishly.

In the bedroom, he relit the fire and got it blazing pretty quickly. I was sitting on the divan and he motioned for me to move to the bed. I did and turned to see him remove his trousers and drape them on a clothing rack, which I realized also held my clothes. His box-cut briefs fit him perfectly and I looked from them to his face, quizzically.

He offered, "I'll lie with you so you sleep, after. You'll need it." I nodded and, after kicking off the slippers, climbed onto the still mussed-up bed, unsure of what to do next.

He gently instructed, "Lie on your stomach. Wait—" And he pulled the sash on the robe. I held it closed and did as he bid. He climbed in after me and sat on his knees near my side. I could hear him put the ice on the edge of the bed. Then he pulled the robe from under me and slid it off my left arm. "Do you wish to wear this when you sleep?" I guessed not and shook my head shyly. "Then let us just be rid of it," he softly suggested and then removed the whole thing. I lay my head flat on the bed, and watched him. He gazed at me for a moment. "Are you absolutely sure about this? Know that I do it under duress, if only that it is unfair to all the others."

I just nodded quickly, very clear that to help the others, I needed him. Then I asked, "Where are you going to do it?" He finally gave me a smile that made him look like what I thought a vampire who was about to drink ought to. He reached for my left thigh and gently ran his hand up it to my cheek until he nearly reached the top of my buttock … and then he tapped. I laughed, feeling nervous and excited by his remarkable touch.

"Really?"

"Really," he replied. "It will go unseen. And you'll hopefully only feel it later if you sit, which you don't seem to do much of. And although the superior gluteal artery is just a little below, there's no artery just there to puncture.

"Besides, your derriere is *so* lovely."

I laughed again, and waited breathlessly as he got himself comfortable and wrapped an arm around my lower torso. His head was at my side and he moved it to lie on my bottom. Then his lips caressed me briefly and suddenly he bit. There was an excruciating moment of intense pressure and pain, but then, once the sharp teeth were in and he started drawing blood, the feeling changed to pleasure, which attacked my groin in a sensuous lunge.

I was absolutely shocked at myself when the sound I emitted was a moan of ecstasy. I opened my eyes and saw, at the edge of my vision, that he was observing my face as he drank. My lips curled into a smile and his eyes glinted back in the firelight. My shyness and embarrassment disappeared.

We had to have been like that for twenty minutes. He obviously could not pull too hard and he had to move his teeth and massage the flesh a few times to keep the blood flowing, which actually felt remarkably good. As it was, I figured there'd be a literal 'love bite'.

It felt so good that I wondered if there was something wrong with me, if maybe I was a latent pain freak. But I'd never shown signs of that. Granted, no one had done anything pain-sex related to me before. *Whatever.* It was a uniquely amazing experience and I drifted into a state of torpor, a quiet moan occasionally escaping my throat.

I felt my body being turned and lifted. It took me a moment to realize that Alec had finished and was moving me so I would lie on him as he rested his upper back and head against stacked pillows. He pulled me to him, with his arm around my waist, then he whispered into my ear, *"I'm going to place the ice on your wound, my dear."*

Drowsily, I said, "Okay."

He cocked my leg up over his lap and made sure I was tilted so the ice pack would stay and then he laid it on. I gasped at the cold and arched my head back, opening my eyes. He stared straight down into them.

Before I could complain about the cold, he bent his head and pressed his lips to mine. His hand went to my head and wove into my hair to hold me to him. We may have stayed like that for an hour. I don't know.

I could taste a little of my blood on him as it mingled with his aroma. Blood and roses. Cliché or not, his kiss was the single most remarkable thing my mouth had ever experienced. And when he ended it and pulled his head from mine, I just stared at him, dumbfounded and aching. He had kissed me earlier and it was great, but something was different about this one. He continued to stare into my eyes and finally I closed my mouth and smiled at him, unwilling to tell him he'd just knocked my socks off. Again. Only I wasn't under a spell this time, I think, and I've no doubt he knew.

"Sleep now. You're going to be a little weak come sunrise. I'm afraid I may have taken a little more than I meant. You've made me a bit impetuous. But don't worry, not too much more. And Devi. Promise me something?"

I snuggled against him and lay my head on his fabulous chest, thinking his bite had been the hottest experience of my life, by a long chalk. "What?"

"Let's not dwell upon this. We mustn't complicate matters. Just let it all be for now and we go back to things as they were. Is that all right with you? Can we do that? " I tried to think but was too tired.

I just said, "Okay. I'll try. You were truly great though." And into sleep I fell.

~

The next morning, the scents of bacon and coffee woke me. I was initially a little bemused to realize where and how I was, enmeshed in Alec's arms and naked, feeling way too comfortable. But the reality flooded back and I remembered the last thing he'd asked of me: 'don't complicate it'. I decided I'd never heard a better suggestion and didn't feel offended in the slightest.

The drapes were closed, so it was dark as pitch. I leaned over Alec, who actually felt, well, like a normal sleeping person, except not warm and breathing, and pulled the curtain just a little. The room was dark but a night light glowed with sufficient brightness to help me see my way over him. As I climbed, I stopped and stared down at his face. I had the notion that he was a ridiculously handsome corpse, or, as Ch'en had explained, a being in stasis. I touched his lips and when he didn't even twitch, I kissed him lightly and then moved off of him.

It took a few moments to remember what he'd done with my clothes, which he'd laid with care on his clothes tree. When I moved his linen pants, I saw that he'd laid the items out in order of how I'd be likely to put them on, with the panties on top. I smiled at the image in my head of him putting them there.

Before I left the room, I went back to the bed, retrieved the baggie that was now just full of water and emptied it in the sink, intending on taking it back to the kitchen in hopes it would get reused. I turned, bowed reverentially to the bathtub, and made my way out. I'd opted to carry my Dr. Scholl's because they'd make too much noise on the stone flooring, which was as chilly as I'd anticipated.

Once I was on the main level, I went to the kitchen and found Gordon frying up some bacon and eggs and what looked for all the world like *bangers*. When he glanced up and saw me, he grinned brightly and greeted with, "Good mornin' Miss Trevathan! Feelin' better today then?"

That single sentence put the last twenty four hours into its place: the past, which was where I was going to leave it.

"Yes, yes and yes! Are those bangers? I haven't had those in a million years."

"Yeah. They are. Home-made venison bangers at that. Made 'em myself."

I came around the huge marble island and saw he had the kitchen table set for the two of us. "That is highly impressive. I can't wait."

"There's coffee in the carafe, cream and sugar on the table. Mug's by your plate. Have a seat."

I did, and fixed my coffee. The thermos was the kind that had a top you press to get the coffee flowing. It was very good coffee and I told Gordon so. Privately, I realized Alec was right. My newly acquired buttock-bite, with its four, nearly equidistant tooth piercings, was announcing itself.

As he brought the food to the table, I asked, "Is everything okay at home? Were Maria and Serena okay?"

He set down a plate with meat and eggs and another with stewed tomatoes. So British I couldn't help but smile appreciatively. He smiled back, dimples prominent, and poured me a glass of orange juice. I think he was delighted to be sharing his breakfast with a companion.

"There was concern for you, but I reassured them. We found a small, black leather case in the first glasshouse."

This revelation made me realize I'd left the piece of jewelry upstairs. Well it would have to stay for now. I gave Gordon a much abbreviated version of Demetrios' visit and some of what the spell had done. I left out everything after I got here, except that Alec had made me take a salt bath. I figured Gordon was observant enough to figure out that I'd slept in Alec's bed, but hopefully he assumed it was all innocent. I mean, if *he* didn't clean the house, who did? He didn't seem to be looking at me funny. And I certainly wasn't getting what I got from Hervé, who, Gordon informed, was visiting his mother.

After stuffing ourselves, Gordon drove us back to my place in the Land Rover. After I changed and fed Greta and Theda, I accompanied him on a daylight survey of the fencing Jack had insisted he make.

"Fat lot of good it'll do when the likes of *that* creature comes 'round."

"No kidding. Short of Alec or Jack actually having been there, I don't know what would have stopped him."

"I met him once, back home. Well, in Scotland I mean. He was there with others for a meetin'. I *thought* he was a bit ... different." I could only smile. Gordon obviously felt protective of me. I could feel it in his demeanor and I appreciated it.

The morning was beautiful. The clouds had cleared overnight and the air was crisp, clear and slightly colder. As we trudged through leaves and drying grasses, we startled a whitetail doe and buck that bounded off on the other side of the fence. As we watched them, Gordon commented, "I don't fancy their taste as much as our red deer."

As a white rump disappeared into the orange yellow leaves of the brambles that were dying back for winter, I replied, "Well your bangers were fantastic."

"Yeah. But those weren't whitetail. They were from the red deer."

"Oh. You ship the meat in then."

He looked at me with a squint. "Nawww. They're Mr. Gregory's special deer. On the property. The ones he hunts when he's a wolf."

I stopped in my tracks. "I beg your pardon?"

He'd taken several steps beyond me, stopped himself and turned. The morning sun glinted off his head. "Yeah. He hunts the red deer. Satisfies the need. The urge."

"What urge?" I asked, realizing those were the deer I'd been thinking were American elk.

He scrunched his brows together and cocked his head at me. I raised mine at him and then he obviously made a choice and explained, "Miss Trevathan, all of them need to drain their prey until death. It's what they are. He just doesn't like killin' humans anymore. So usually, once a month or so, he'll bring down a deer and I get the finest bits."

I rubbed my chilled hands together and blew on them for a moment as I absorbed this new knowledge. Finally I asked, "And he does this as a wolf?" I started walking again.

"Yeah. Guess it's the only thing he can become now. Used to be he'd change it up."

"Because of the tainted blood."

"Right." We were quiet for a few minutes and then he tentatively asked, "Is it true your blood carries healin' powers for them?"

"It appears so. It's confirmed for me after what I saw in Mexico."

We came across a short, fat, pretty snake sunning itself beside a large boulder on a patch of somewhat plant-free ground. I was pleased to see Gordon knew it was a copperhead and yet respected and admired it as much as I did. I was surprised it was out on such a chilly morning, perhaps its last foray before winter hibernation. We gave it plenty of room and passed by without disturbing it.

Once we'd gone a little way, he stopped to check a spot along the fence that had come loose from its post. While he fiddled with it, he said, "It's a shame, you know. What he could do was magnificent. I once saw him become a lion. *That* was a sight to behold. I was only twenty-two and he fucked about with me, knocked me over and I thought he was goin' to off me right there. He started makin' this sound and I realized it was him, laughin' inside this massive cat." He turned his head and looked over his shoulder at my reaction.

My eyebrows were scrunched as high as they could go and I started laughing. "Oh my God!"

"Too right! Scared me half to death, he did." He went silent again, and when he managed to hook the fencing back up, he stood and nodded his head once at it. Then he turned and gave me an odd look. "Still. It's a shame."

"What?"

"He'd never ask you. You know that."

It was obvious to me that Gordon's relationship with Alec went much deeper than Hervé's. He knew too much. I wondered if he knew how old I was. I decided to test him before divulging anything. So I nodded at his comment and started walking again. He came up behind me and I asked, "Do you know how old I am, Gordon?"

"I know you're a lot older than you appear." I stopped and turned to look up at him, in the eye.

He stopped too and gazed down at me. Finally he said, "I know you're a bit over a hundred."

I nodded. "Okay. If he shared that with you then I'll share. I started sneaking him a little in Mexico. But after yesterday—well, last night I forced him to take what he'd need to get better."

After a moment's processing, he started laughing and moved his torso about in that way one does when very happily surprised. "Well I'll be a monkey's! I'd have liked to have seen that. You *forced* him? Never seen anyone force him before!"

"Yes, well it took a little convincing. He's pretty principled about some things. But after what I saw Demetrios do yesterday, I want someone on my team who can do that too."

Gordon nodded enthusiastically and said, "Aww. Good on ya. I'm impressed. He's usually not easy to convince and I know he views you as sacred ground, so . . ." He trailed off, probably going in a direction he wasn't supposed to, then asked, "How much did he need? Are you all right? Shouldn't you rest?" He put his big hand and muscled arm on my back and I liked the feel of it, but he was not next in line. That was wrong in too many ways.

"I'm fine. Really. I'm a little tiny bit weak, but nothing serious. I promise I'll rest when we get back." He nodded and backed off. I decided to ask if Jack could morph. The answer was interesting.

"He's learnin'. He'll start to get it down soon. My understandin' is it takes a very long time to get to where Mr. Gregory is. Only the oldest ones can become *any* creature."

We finally made a full circuit back at the front gate. I insisted Gordon fill his travel mug with some coffee. He came inside the house with me and said, "I'll be goin' with you to New Orleans it seems."

"Really? What about Hervé?"

"Naw. Mr. Gregory usually only brings one of us if it's a short visit. He said in the usual mornin' notes that you would be needin' a body guard durin' the day. That'll be me."

I smiled. "Good. I'm happy about that. But I'll be dragging you to some places you might not find interesting. *Shops!*" I said the last word in my English accent. I was rewarded with the gorgeous smile and laugh. After a sudden memory of a little unresolved business in New Orleans, I added, "And to eat beignets—and maybe to a *Vodou* ceremony!"

He rolled his eyes, but looked very happy.

After Gordon drove off, I felt pretty good about things, considering the very large, black bird I'd seen high in the trees, tracking us as we walked the perimeter. I somehow knew he wouldn't bother me today. I figured he would wait to see if his meddling had worked. Maybe he'd be in New Orleans, that cool, old vampiric cliché.

And as I entered my bedroom to rest, I stopped to gaze at a newly-placed piece of furniture. It was a side table I'd put beneath the south-facing windows. A silk runner protected it from scratches potentially made by the special items it displayed. So far, there were only four: a large beeswax pillar candle at each end, the fire opal (which I was storing in distilled water in a small, antique apothecary jar) and the golden Camazotz statuette.

As my eyes loved the two venerable items, I had the strongest sense that they were right where they belonged—*with me*. I also sensed that they were sacred souvenirs of a bizarre, yet crucial journey I'd only just begun, but had been waiting to take for a very long, very lonely time ... a journey I was *compelled* to take, despite the bizarre unknowns I was pretty darned sure lie in wait.

27646597R00250

Made in the USA
Columbia, SC
30 September 2018